ALSO BY DAVID G. HALLMAN

Caring for Creation

AIDS—Confronting the Challenge

A Place in Creation—
Ecological Visions in Science, Religion, and Economics

Ecotheology—Voices from South and North

Spiritual Values for Earth Community

August Farewell—
The Last Sixteen Days of a Thirty-Three-Year Romance

Searching for GILEAD

A Novel

David G. Hallman

iUniverse, Inc.
Bloomington

Searching for Gilead
A Novel

This is a work of fiction. All of the characters, names, incidents,
organizations, and dialogue in this novel are either the products
of the author's imagination or are used fictitiously.

iUniverse books may be ordered through booksellers or by contacting:

iUniverse
1663 Liberty Drive
Bloomington, IN 47403
www.iuniverse.com
1-800-Authors (1-800-288-4677)

Because of the dynamic nature of the Internet, any Web addresses or
links contained in this book may have changed since publication and
may no longer be valid. The views expressed in this work are solely those
of the author and do not necessarily reflect the views of the publisher,
and the publisher hereby disclaims any responsibility for them.

Any people depicted in stock imagery provided by Thinkstock are models,
and such images are being used for illustrative purposes only.

Certain stock imagery © Thinkstock.

ISBN: 978-1-4620-4694-2 (sc)
ISBN: 978-1-4620-4695-9 (hc)
ISBN: 978-1-4620-4696-6 (e)

Library of Congress Control Number: 2011914637

Printed in the United States of America

iUniverse rev. date: 9/15/2011

Cover author photo: The United Church of Canada

Preface

Gilead, a mountainous region east of the Jordan River, means "hill of witness." *Searching for Gilead* is my attempt to give witness to a series of issues with which I am grappling.

I stumbled onto the name Gilead.

The novel is a story of the interrelationship between two families over a period of three and a half decades—a chronicle of love, laughter, and loss.

Below the story line run difficult questions that don't have an easy resolution, for me at least. Some of these questions are personal and existential. Others are global and systemic.

Friends of mine, aware that I had begun working on a novel, asked what it was about. I didn't know how to respond. I started making a list of the problems that I was trying to address in the novel. I played with various words that would describe those issues. I was looking for an acronym, a shorthand way to capture the range of concerns that was coursing through my head and my heart, and then onto the page. What emerged was G-I-L-E-A-D:

> God—issues around spirituality and religion in our lives and in our world
>
> Injustice—global inequities in power and conflict over resources
>
> Love—a source of joy and pain for us all
>
> Environment—threats to the well-being of the Earth and its most vulnerable peoples
>
> Arts—the role they play as we seek to make sense of our lives and our world
>
> Death—our own, and those we love

I do not mean to imply that what you hold in your hands is an explicit discussion of these issues. It is not. *Searching for Gilead* is a story. I am using the story to think through these issues in my own mind.

I began writing what I would come to call *Searching for Gilead* within weeks of having finished a memoir, *August Farewell*. The memoir is, obviously, autobiographical. *Searching for Gilead* is not. What occurs in the novel, related to the main characters' lives, is a product of my imagination.

Those who know me, and those who have read *August Farewell*, may see a few parallels between my own personal history and the characters and actions in the novel. Readers might be tempted to read more into those parallels than is warranted. I caution against it. One of the joys that I am discovering about writing fiction is that I get to make things up. And I have.

David G. Hallman
Toronto, Canada
July 2011

Acknowledgments

The following people read an early draft of *Searching for Gilead* and provided me with valuable feedback and much-appreciated encouragement: Ed Bennett, Joan Burton, Michael Cobb, Gail Czukar, Armand Gagne, Tamara Glazier-Pariselli, Diane Hallman, Deborah Marshall, Alanna Mitchell, Doug O'Neill, Deborah Sinclair, Janet Stemerdink, Susan Wiseman, and Denny Young.

I consulted with the following people regarding historical events and personages, medical issues, and theological themes that form the background for the fictional characters and plotline: Michael Bourgeois, John Goodhew, Lee Holland, Marilyn Legge, Gail Lerner, David MacDonald, Heather Macdonald, David Robertson, and Janet Stemerdink. Their information was helpful, but they bear no responsibility for how I have portrayed the people, events, or issues in the novel. I alone am accountable. Further, I remind the reader that this is a work of fiction.

Reference material from the former Taskforce on the Churches and Corporate Responsibility and from KAIROS Canadian Ecumenical Justice Initiatives was useful in writing the sections regarding Marcopper Mining Corporation in the Philippines and Talisman Energy in Sudan.

The Research Centre at the Tate Museum Britain in London assisted me with information on the works of artist David Hockney in their collection and dates of exhibitions.

The discussion that takes place in Part Four between Tom and Lukas is adapted from a resource of the World Council of Churches entitled

Solidarity with Victims of Climate Change, published in Geneva in 2002.

Music critic Richard Freed and Mahler historian and conductor Gilbert Kaplan were very generous in helping me access resources for the Epilogue. A great deal of Mahler's comments in the dialogue with Tom come from actual writings by the composer. For Mahler's programs, I have drawn on "Mahler's Programmatic Commentaries," a chapter written by Gilbert Kaplan in the *New Critical Edition of Mahler's Second Symphony* (Renate Stark-Voit and Gilbert Kaplan, editors) published by Universal Edition and the Kaplan Foundation in 2010. Mr. Kaplan gave me his kind permission to utilize this source. The text of Mahler's poetry that is included in the Epilogue comes from the conclusion of his Second Symphony and appears in *A Concert Goer's Companion to Music: Programme Notes of the Toronto Symphony Orchestra* by Godfrey Ridout, published by Gordon V. Thompson Music, Toronto, in 1996.

The Art Gallery of Ontario provided information about their history of acquisitions of works by Aboriginal artist Norvel Morriseau.

One of the key inspirations that propelled me to write *Searching for Gilead* was reading Karen Armstrong's *The Case for God.*

As was the case with my recently published memoir *August Farewell,* I have been impressed with the professionalism and sensitivity of the staff of my publisher, iUniverse. I am very grateful to them.

Part One
1976

Chapter 1 ———————————

"**Would** you like to dance?" asked a hesitant voice behind me.

I was standing on the small landing, halfway up the flight of stairs between the dance floor and the balcony lounge, my preferred place to people-watch at the Arches.

Turning around, I found myself face-to-face with the current number one titleholder on my "completely-out-of-my-league" list, the category for guys too good-looking to possibly notice me. At the clubs, my friends and I would rate the hotties in a system of ascending inaccessibility as "possible if he's drunk enough," "only if you pay him," and "completely out of my league." For me, it was a game born of looking in the mirror at home and always being disappointed at the nerdish appearance of the bespeckled geek looking back.

This god who had just now spoken to me stood about two inches taller than me. His dark brown eyes perfectly matched the colour of his dense and immaculately groomed head of hair, no doubt tended by a hair stylist considerably more expensive that the corner barber who looked after my blond brush cut. His white polo top hinted at a modestly sculpted torso—attractively slender, not skinny. From my previous months of ogling him, I knew that the thin waist led down to a copious basket, buns made for grabbing, and firm thighs, all of which were on display, thanks to the stylish type of pants he usually wore.

I had on a slim-fitting pair of jeans and was relieved that he was looking me in the face. His unanticipated proximity had produced a spontaneous hard-on. He threw a quick glance at my tight white T-shirt. I subtly flexed my pecs and biceps. My addiction to working out was equal measures of health consciousness and vanity.

"Okay," I mumbled. "Let's dance." I hid my surprise at his surprise.

He headed down the steps, and I followed, hoping that my friends would see whom I was accompanying out onto the dance floor.

I was a regular at the Arches on Sunday evenings, the end of the weekend, free from the Friday and Saturday night dating pressure.

We all went there just to have fun with our friends and dance to the pulsating beat of the reigning disco divas.

The DJ had just thrown on Donna Summer's "Love to Love You Baby," the full seventeen-minute version. That meant that I had a quarter hour before I needed to fret about whether Mr. Perfect would signal that he was up for another dance or nod thanks and wander off. Though we were bouncing around within a few feet of each other, I studiously avoided eye contact, particularly with Donna's explicit lyrics pounding over our heads. I became familiar with the floor pattern between us and the shoe styles of those around us.

As the song wound down, Mr. Perfect took a hold of my shoulder, pulled me closer, and yelled over the music, "Another?" He tightened his grip. I nodded yes, far more enthusiastically than I had intended. He threw his head back and laughed.

After a few more songs, he reached over, grabbed my hand, and hauled me off the dance floor over to the bar. He pulled out his wallet and leaned in close enough so I could hear him without his having to shout. "What can I buy you?" I could feel his warm breath graze my cheek. I didn't respond. He looked at me quizzically and then came closer and repeated the question. I jerked my head toward him and closed the three inches separating our faces, pecking his lips with a quick, unabashed kiss.

He stepped back and frowned.

Shit, I blew it.

After an interminable pause, he held out his hand and said, "Hello, my name is Jonathan."

I shook his hand, in a state of panic.

"Tom," I replied soberly.

He smiled, squeezed my hand a bit tighter, and said, "I've seen you around. You're cute. Nice to meet you, Tom. Finally."

I smiled back. "I think that I've noticed you before too."

We continued to talk; my nervousness subsided enough to allow a more secure Tom to emerge.

We returned regularly to the dance floor, especially for the slow ones.

We met for lunch on Tuesday.

I treated him to a movie on Thursday.

On Friday, he invited me to his place for dinner. I stayed over.

By Saturday, we were a couple.

Chapter 2

The family Sunday dinner at 4 May Crescent was a jacket affair. If Walter Compton could have enforced his druthers, it would have included a tie as well. Women were expected to wear dresses. Not that there were often women, other than Margaret, doyenne of the household, in attendance. Since Jonathan's unequivocal declaration of his gayness on his sixteenth birthday, and with his twin brother's seemingly voracious appetite for female company that never extended to morning breakfast, Margaret had little chance of trading neighbourhood gossip with potential daughters-in-law over Sunday pot roasts.

As we walked from the parked car, I scanned the heritage homes and storied mansions of Rosedale, nestled amongst jack pines and monstrous oaks, each with impeccably manicured lawns and gardens. I had rarely ventured before into Toronto's preeminent enclave of traditional wealth and privilege.

Jonathan casually let it drop that I was the first boyfriend that he had brought to Sunday dinner since he had come out seven years earlier. I stopped dead in my tracks and glowered at his back. He travelled a step or two ahead before he realized that I wasn't by his side. He turned and, with the flicker of a smile, asked, "What's wrong, dear?"

"It didn't occur to you before now that this titbit might be rather a big deal to me?"

Reaching back and grasping my hand, he said, "Don't worry. It isn't a big deal. They're going to love you. Trust me. Anyway, it's about time they saw some concrete evidence of my fagolaness."

"Can we have a conversation about this before I enter the lion's den?"

The tremor in my voice brought him up short. He reached down and took my other hand in his. "Listen. I didn't mention it before because I figured it would freak you a bit."

"You think?"

"I've never brought anyone home for Sunday dinner because I've never had anyone to bring home for Sunday dinner."

"This is supposed to be your reassuring speech to me?"

"I want to share you with Jeremy and my folks."

"Well, okay," I said. "Just promise me you won't leave me hung out to dry."

"I promise."

"One more request. Give me a kiss right here in the middle of prissy Rosedale. That's the one thing that will stiffen my spine. It *is* my spine that I mean."

Jonathan looked around. There was no one in sight. He leaned in and kissed me full on the lips. He stepped back and smiled. "There. Now let's get going. I don't want to keep my family waiting for the grand unveiling."

Jonathan let go of my hand as we passed through the wrought iron gate and walked up the semi-circular drive. A massive limestone portico extended from the front door. He rang the doorbell. *Who rings the doorbell and waits to be let in to their parents' home?* I wondered. It was an important clue. The door opened, and Mrs. Compton, martini in hand, smiled. Her hair, pulled back from her face, was wrapped in an elaborate pillbox creation on top of her head, adding to her already imposing height. Miniature pearl earrings and a necklace complemented her flawless skin, a surprising amount of which was visible above the deep V-neck of her black silk dress. I hoped that thinking of her as Mrs. Compton would repress the usual facetious streak in my conversation. I reminded myself not to comment on her Sunday afternoon libation.

"Darlings!" A composite salutation.

What has Jonathan told her about me?

We stepped into the vestibule, and Jonathan gave his mother a peck on the cheek. "Mother, I'd like you to meet Tom Fischer. Tom, this is my mother, Margaret Compton." She leaned over and tilted her head to the side. I mimicked my boyfriend's kiss on her cool-as-ivory cheek. She straightened up, looked into my eyes, smiled again, and turned to lead us into the living room. Not a drop of vodka spilled. Jonathan gave my baby finger a little squeeze. *So far, so good.*

"Walter. Jonathan and Tom are here," she called out quite naturally.

"I'll be right out," a gruff voice responded from another room.

The living room oozed old money. A large oil pastoral scene in an ornate gesso frame dominated the wall over the open fireplace. It looked like an early Turner. I thought I'd try to surreptitiously check it out later. It looked like I would have a great deal of sleuthing to do. Intriguing art hung on every wall, ranging from old European masters to an impressive Rothkoesque painting over the sofa. The principal seating was of the oversized, large-armed variety, upholstered in a soft taupe. A massive oriental carpet covered the floor. It would have been overbearing in most rooms, but the size of the Compton living room accommodated it with ease.

Margaret saw me studying the rug. "Do you like it?" she asked. "Walter and I bought it in Tangiers on our honeymoon. It's more than a hundred years old. It's called a kingdom carpet because it was made for one of the royal family members. The Moroccan royal family, that is," she said, smiling. "All the patterns mean something in Arabic culture. The salesman did explain them to us. He took us through this absolutely lovely tradition of sitting on the carpet in his store and drinking tea together, a symbol of hospitality, as the carpet was about to change hands. We knew it wouldn't fit in our apartment back home, but we figured that when we came to buy a house to start a family, we'd just have to get one with a room large enough to handle the carpet."

I ventured my first intimacy. "I like your sense of priorities, Mrs. Compton."

"Do you now?" she replied noncommittally, and she studied me for a moment.

"Mother, don't bore Tom with stories about all your stuff."

I turned toward Jonathan and, with an expression of contrived horror, said, "You call this 'stuff'? Jonathan, am I to assume that you did not inherit your mother's exquisite taste?"

Not missing a beat, he replied, "Well, I chose you, didn't I?" Jonathan bit his lip.

Okay, that was way too blatant an endearment, way too soon. The following silence was awkward. I glanced at Margaret. She was looking benignly at the two of us, enjoying our moment of discomfort.

"So, where's my scotch, Margaret?" Walter's robust baritone voice broke into the living room's fragile ambiance, his words slightly garbled because of the smouldering cigar clenched in the corner of his mouth.

Margaret, quite deliberately, allowed another few seconds to pass before turning to the butler's table and picking up one of several crystal decanters. "Tom was just complimenting me on our décor, dear. He seems to appreciate its provenance more than our own flesh and blood does." Walter rolled his eyes and tossed his cigar into an ashtray. "Oh God, Margaret. What was it this time? The cloisonné collection? Your grandpa's Matisse?"

Matisse! I glanced furtively around the room. Walter grabbed my hand and started pumping. "Listen, kid. Don't let her seduce you like she has me. Over the years our quote unquote *décor* has cost me a fortune, just to hang on a wall where nobody notices it or to sit on a table and gather dust." He dropped my hand, crossed his arms and rested them on his protruding stomach, and scrutinized me for a moment. "I'm Walter Compton. Who are you again?"

"Yes, uh, sir, very glad to meet you. I'm Tom. Tom Fischer. A friend of Jonathan's."

He turned to Jonathan. "So this is the young thing you've been buggering."

"Walter!"

"Father!"

Margaret lifted the freshly poured scotch as if preparing to throw it into his face, and Jonathan looked ready to punch him.

Walter, laughing, almost choked, his substantial frame bouncing underneath the burgundy velvet smoking jacket. "Just kidding! You should see all your faces. You'd think I had blasphemed the whole cotton-pickin' holy family." He nudged me with such force I almost lost my balance. "You see, my boy. My wife has these social sensitivities, and she seems to have corrupted this son of mine."

"Who exactly is corrupting him?" Margaret said quietly as she crossed the room to hand Walter his drink.

I glanced at Jonathan. He was ignoring her comment.

"Where's my other son, by the way?" said Walter, deftly changing the subject and the atmosphere.

Jonathan looked at me and explained. "Jeremy is notorious for being late."

Walter took a gulp of his drink and, still in the process of swallowing, said, "It's the artistic temperament. Time, deadlines, money mean nothing to the kid. What did I do to deserve this? One son up to his elbows in paint and the other son with his head in the clouds, communing with Socrates and Plato and all those other Greek buggerers." His laugher erupted again, and he spat a few droplets of Glenmorangie onto the kingdom carpet.

"Let it go, Dad," Jonathan chided.

The front door opened. It was clear to me that identical twins don't necessarily observe protocol identically. Jeremy strode into the room, looking stunning in a handsome tailored suit that set off an athletic frame similar to the one with which I was becoming intimately familiar.

"About time, boy. I think I'll institute a system of demerits for every minute you're late."

"Wouldn't work, Pops. Mom would make sure I didn't suffer." Jeremy sauntered over to his mother, gave her a big hug, and planted a sloppy kiss on her cheek.

The Compton sons were the spitting image of each other in stature, hair colour, facial features. I couldn't verify everything. I wasn't close enough to discern the hue of his eyes and was discrete enough not to glance down below the waist.

Margaret put her hands on Jeremy's shoulders, turned him around to face me, and said, "Jeremy, I want you to meet Tom. Jonathan's 'friend.'"

Jeremy strode across the room and clasped my hand in his. We shook hands firmly; his grip was naturally strong, mine consciously so. "Well, well, old man," he said to me. "On behalf of the family, I wish you the best of luck. It's about time that somebody corralled Jonathan and made an honest man of him. I can tell you it will take a load off our minds."

"That's rich," retorted my new boyfriend, "coming from the quintessential non-committer."

"That's my prerogative, indeed my calling. I am betrothed to my art. Also, as your elder, it's my responsibility, my sacred duty, to ensure that you get well and properly shackled. By the way, Tom, you shouldn't count on too much of a dowry from this old geezer," titling his head toward his father, with his gorgeous brown eyes locked on mine.

Ignoring the rapidly accumulating presumption that Jonathan and I were long-as-you-both-shall-live partners, I interjected. "Elder? I thought that the two of you were twins."

"Two minutes," Jeremy replied. "I popped out of Mommy dearest two minutes before the laggard here had finished prepping his hair and was prepared to make his fashionably late entrance."

"But I understood that you are the tardy one in the family," I responded.

"Touché!" Jonathan cried, smiling at me with appreciation. Walter applauded, ashes from his recently retrieved cigar dropping onto the floor. Margaret chuckled as she headed toward the kitchen. Jeremy just looked at me.

Dinner was exquisite. Margaret served the meal in the massive dining room, each dish arriving at just the right moment and temperature. Wine glasses and water goblets were replenished on cue and coffee poured with the dessert. There was such effortless grace in her manner that she accomplished the hosting unobtrusively while maintaining a presence in the conversation. The pearl necklace never wavered.

"Thank you, Mrs. Compton. That was just delicious," I said, touching my lips with the Irish linen napkin to dab any crème brulé residue.

"Tom, for the last time, please call me Margaret. If you don't, I'll start thinking you are a slow learner." Her affectionate glance offset her scolding tone.

"Sorry. Of course. Thank you, Margaret."

Jeremy dropped his fork, letting it clatter loudly on the china dessert plate, and cleared his throat. "So Dad, is your trip to Santiago next week still on?" he asked.

"Yeah. With a side trip to Lima to sew up a few loose threads there." Walter leaned over to the buffet and grabbed a small silver toothpick holder. "Thank God the Chilean project is finally coming together. It's been a hell of a struggle." He paused as he tried to extricate a stubborn fibre of roast beef from between two teeth. "I've got most of the financing in place, but they want me to meet once more with the bankers down there. Fortunately, the mine's new management knows how to cooperate. Not like those former Commie bastards."

"Well, that's good then," Jeremy said. "Makes your clients happy, I suppose."

"The Bay Street boys are feeling more relaxed. I have to watch my tail to make sure that Ottawa doesn't step on it, but so far, so good."

I looked across the table at Jonathan. His head was lowered, eyes fixed intently on his empty plate.

"More coffee for anyone?" Margaret asked.

I swallowed hard. "Sir, may I ask," I ventured tentatively, "how do you find the political situation?"

"Oh, much, much improved. There are the odd skirmishes here and there. Mostly in the countryside."

I waited as Walter struggled again with the toothpick and then gave up. He cocked his head to the side, inserted his thumb and index finger into his mouth for a moment, and then tossed the offending nuisance onto his plate with a triumphant flourish. Jonathan would still not return my glance. Jeremy stared at me, eyebrows raised, a subtle smirk dancing around the corners of his mouth.

I spoke in as matter-of-fact a monotone as I could manage. "Wouldn't they be a bit of a problem, those 'skirmishes'? I assume that your clients' mine sites are in fairly rural areas."

"That's true, my boy. It can cause us a few headaches, but mainly it's just an occasional slowdown in some of the engineering and geological work. Generally, the army is quite adept at clearing away any roadblocks before our construction folk arrive."

I beaded my eyes on Jonathan, trying unsuccessfully to will his head up. I looked again at Walter. "Yes, I've heard about the roadblocks. I understand that some of the indigenous peoples have contested the foreign companies' rights to prospect on their land."

Walter waved his hand dismissively. "Rights? Chile is a sovereign state that has its own laws. The resources are legitimately the property of the people of Chile, duly managed through their government."

I took a deep breath. "I'm sure you know a great deal more about the situation than I do, but isn't that one of the issues? The legitimacy of that government?"

Walter's forehead furrowed. His expression hardened. "Excuse me? The legitimacy of the government? It's the goddamn government. Of course it's legitimate. If the people didn't want it, the people wouldn't keep it."

Jonathan tapped my foot under the table.

Jeremy shifted back in his chair, crossed his arms, and smiled.

Margaret poured herself another cup of coffee.

Stuttering slightly, I said, "But sir, with all due respect, it's not exactly a democratically elected government."

The cutlery rattled as he slammed his fist down onto the table. "Dammit, boy! Pinochet is the best thing that ever happened to that blighted place. It was on its way to hell in a handbasket before he stepped in."

Several days ago I had asked Jonathan about what his father did. He'd replied with a curious ambiguity. *Mystery solved. Do I press on?* My heart raced.

Walter raised his wine glass. "A toast to Augusto Pinochet."

No one moved except to look from Walter to me.

I took hold of my glass, striving to lift it as steadily as possible. I looked at Walter and said, "To the people of Chile." I lifted the wine to my lips and drained the glass, dribbling a bit in the process. I set the empty glass back on the table, staring at it as I wiped my mouth, and without raising my eyes, said, "I am sorry to differ, sir, but is it not something of a euphemism to call what Pinochet did 'stepping in'?" *Jonathan, where are you? Remember your sidewalk promise.*

Walter went quiet and just stared at me. No one spoke. Silence ruled, and not the healing kind. After a few moments, he quietly, repressively, said, "Who the hell do you think you are, coming into my home and lecturing me on the intricacies of political-economic affairs in a country half a world away from here where you've never been?" Sarcastically, he added, "I assume ..." and then continued, "and where I have spent a good portion of my working career?"

I was too far gone to retreat now. I thought, *Jonathan and me, it was nice while it lasted.* In firm, measured tones to match Walter's, I said, "Yes, you are correct, sir. I have never been to Chile. But there are such things as newspapers, magazines, books, and informal networks from which one can glean a lot more information than what is promoted through corporate literature and trade mission communiqués."

Almost inaudibly, he asked, "Informal networks? Please, do tell me about your informal networks."

The tone belying the content, a naïve observer might have assumed that he and I were co-conspirators whispering to each other. "I apologise, sir. I am, no doubt, way out of my depth." A flash of relief crossed Jonathan's face. It didn't last as I added, "It's just, sir, that in the solidarity groups that I participate in at the university we hear quite disconcerting reports. They have close connections with some of the labour and indigenous groups in Latin America. I probably shouldn't say more. I don't want to, um, betray them."

Slowly, Walter placed his hands palms down on the table in front of him. "*Betray.* Interesting choice of words, Tom. Let's forget about Chile for a moment. Who is betraying whom around this table?" I was startled by the change of tack. My resolve to say no more dissipated. "Let's not make this personal, sir. We are having a frank discussion about, as you said, 'political-economic affairs.'"

Walter looked at me for several moments and then rotated his gaze around the table, examining in turn placid Margaret, smirking Jeremy, and flushed Jonathan. Suddenly, Walter leaned back in his chair, clapped his hands, and roared with laughter. "I don't believe it. An intelligent conversation at this table, for a change." Still laughing, he tossed his napkin at Jonathan, and said, "Oh, Johnny boy, you're going to have your hands full with this one."

Chapter 3 ———————————————

The logistics of Jonathan and me moving in together were daunting. I was living in a single room in residence. Jonathan, as befits a graduate student, had his own digs off-campus, a small one-bedroom in an older building. He could have afforded much more sumptuous quarters had he been willing to accept the same living allowance from his father that kept Jeremy in style.

As a couple, we had a problem. He clearly couldn't move into my room. I raised the possibility of moving in with him, but he vetoed that. He argued that to start out in an equitable relationship, we needed a fresh abode that was devoid of our respective histories. I appreciated the sentiment, if not the implied additional work, to be squeezed in between my course work and his dissertation deadlines.

After several weeks scanning the classifieds and visiting the depressing options that would match our combined budget, we happened upon a second-floor flat in a somewhat dilapidated red brick Victorian house in the Annex. I wasn't keen about the mouse droppings in the cupboards, but I loved the eleven-foot ceilings. Jonathan had reservations about the creepy-looking tenant in the basement, but he adored the garden view through the cantilevered windows. More to the point, it had two bedrooms, as well as a large living room. We could use one of the bedrooms as our study, setting up our desks and cramming most of our books into it. That would give us the luxury of using the living room exclusively for living and the second bedroom exclusively for bedding.

We furnished the apartment primarily with Jonathan's belongings. In an attempt to meet my side of Jonathan's criteria for an "equitable start" to our cohabitation, I scavenged around in my parents' attic and came away with a set of Grandma's china dishes, a large, dark oak-framed hall mirror, and a magazine rack that Dad had made. Jonathan effused over them—a bit patronizingly, but with good intentions.

I came home from class on the first official night in the new/old apartment to discover the arborite kitchen table covered in a crocheted cloth that had also been mined from my parents' attic, two place settings of Grandma's china, a lit candle flickering in a Chianti bottle (not ours, heaven forbid, but rescued from a neighbour's garbage), and, as a special treat for my soon-to-be-curbed junk food fetish, a bucket of the Colonel's spicy chicken, french fries, and coleslaw.

We ate with relish, toasting our new abode regularly. Having stuffed ourselves, we sipped the last of the expensive bottle of Chardonnay. The culinary menu may have been intentionally ironic, but there was a standard below which Jonathan could not bring himself to go, hence the accompanying beverage. We had finished recounting our respective day's trials and triumphs and now sat quietly, enjoying the comfortable, newly established domesticity.

Jonathan pushed his chair back from the table and carried his plate and cutlery to the sink.

"Give me about five minutes," he said, "and then come into the bedroom."

"What! This five-star restaurant doesn't provide a choice of gastronomic delicacies for dessert?"

He turned to face me as he walked out of the room and winked.

I stretched my legs out under the table and used my toes to maneuver his recently vacated chair close enough so that I could rest my feet on the seat. I clasped my fingers together and extended my arms up above my head, stretching biceps and triceps in turn. My muscles were still sore from the previous day's move. After a few minutes, I picked up my plate and set it in the sink beside Jonathan's.

When I got to the bedroom, the door was closed. I stood in front of it for a moment and then knocked gently.

A soft "come in" came from the other side.

I opened the door to an almost dark room. Three tall candles flickered on top of the chest of drawers. Small glass bowls with miniature tea candles lit the surface of the nightstands on each side of the bed. I stepped inside. My eyes gradually adjusted to the dimness. On the bed, the top sheet and the comforter had been pushed down to the bottom. I could see the outline of Jonathan's body in the centre of the bed. He was stark naked.

I was immediately hard. Then, just as immediately, confused. My confusion had no impact on my erection.

Jonathan was not lying on his back or on his side or in any other position that he had assumed in our two-month history of nightly love-making. He was lying on his stomach. "Um," I sputtered. "You've really, um, made the room look, um, romantic."

Jonathan chuckled into the pillow in which his head was partially buried and around which he had wrapped his arms. "A comment on the décor is really the best you've got?"

I did not move. I just stared at the back of his head, and then at his shoulder blades, and then slowly down along the crevice in his back to his buns.

Jonathan lifted his head from the pillow, turned, and looked at me. After a moment, he smiled and rolled over onto his side. Patting the edge of the bed, he said, "Come over here."

I walked over to the bed and sat down as instructed. He put his hand on my thigh and then moved it up to my crotch. "Well, it would seem that part of you at least is ready."

I raised my head and looked him in the eyes for the first time since coming into the room. "It's just, well, unexpected."

Jonathan pulled his knees up and swung his legs over the edge of the bed so that we were sitting side by side. He reached over and took hold of my hand, raised it up to his mouth, and planted a gentle kiss on the back. "Don't you want to?" he asked.

"Uh, yeah. It's just we never have before. You had made it pretty clear that … getting fucked … was definitely not your thing."

He leaned over and kissed my cheek. "You're right. It's definitely not my thing. But you definitely are my thing. So …" He read something in my eyes. "Now don't go getting all sentimental." He gave my shoulder a playful punch. "That would be a bit of a mood-changer."

I pushed him back down onto the bed, rolled on top of him, and started kissing him, initially deeply and passionately on the mouth, and then progressively down the length of his body, a body that I was about to possess in all its robust totality.

An hour, or two, later, I slipped out of bed, leaving the gently snoring

Jonathan, and went to the kitchen to get a drink of water. The Kentucky Fried Chicken bag still sat on the counter.

Dessert, as had just been served by Jonathan with such generosity in the bedroom, was something I could never have gotten from any franchise.

Chapter 4 ——————————————————

One of our challenges in setting up house together was to decide whether we'd integrate our respective book collections. Both of us, for good or ill, shared a highly proprietary attitude toward books. None of them were worth a lot of money. But they were priceless to us for their literary richness, as research resources, or for the nostalgic import of what we had experienced when we had read them.

A potent symbolism was attached to the decision. I was shy about explicitly acknowledging it, and I suspected Jonathan was as well. Prosaically, it would make the present living arrangement less complex if we put all our books together. More momentously, it would say something about our future commitment to one another. Of greatest significance, combining our book collections would integrate our pasts. Our respective memories, reflective of a spectrum of precious intellectual and emotional experiences, would rest side-by-side, sometimes even lodged between each other.

We sat on the floor for a long time, drinking wine, surrounded by piles and cartons of those memory-bearers. We looked at the books and at each other. Initially, the conversation focused on pragmatics, such as whether vertical or horizontal stacking would allow for better use of space; if we should place hardcovers on lower shelves to reduce the potential of liability suits from guests were a bank of shelves to topple over on them; and how to create double rows, with taller books behind to leave enough of the spines visible for identification. Such issues weren't quite obfuscation, but they were temporary surrogates for the biggie.

"We've both got books on Marx," I said as I set my copy of *An Introduction to Marxist Economic Theory* on the floor beside Jonathon's *Das Kapital.* "They could obviously be placed together."

"Not so fast, my little one." Jonathan picked up his well-worn volume and slowly paged through it, stopping occasionally to scan notes that he had penciled in the margins. "I read Marx as a social philosopher. My guess is that you were interested in him as a political revolutionary. Right?" He put it back down on the floor.

"I suppose. But Marx is Marx." I leaned forward and pushed my book over so that it was touching his.

"Yes, my dear," Jonathan said as placed his foot on his book and gently eased it a few inches away from mine. "The question that I have to ask myself is whether I want my intellectual rigour contaminated by your guerrilla warfare." I hoped that he was being facetious.

"I've got an easier one," Jonathan said, rummaging through a box by his side and hauling out *A Portrait of the Artist as a Young Man.* "I saw in your piles that you also have a copy. They could go together. Or you could get rid of yours."

"Not on your life!" I yelled. I scrambled to my feet, somewhat unsteady from the multiple glasses of wine. I knocked over a couple piles in a frantic search for the prize. Holding it to my breast, I said, "You have no idea how much impact Stephen Dedalus's spiritual struggles had on me as an impressionable teenager."

Jonathan laughed. "It's just a piece of literature, not sacred scripture, and James Joyce was hardly a friend of the church."

"I didn't say he was." I pouted. "But it's not 'just' a piece of literature. It was a story that was very important to me," I said quietly, with some embarrassment. "At a certain period in my life. When I was young. Younger."

Jonathan looked at me for a few moments and then got to his feet and came over to where I was standing, hugging the reliquary of an earlier time. He took hold of my hand and coaxed me over to the couch. He sat, pulled me down on his lap, and started stroking the back of my head.

"I say we go for it," he whispered in my ear.

"What?" I asked.

"Do I really have to spell it out?" He smiled.

I swallowed. "It's a big step," I replied.

He turned my head toward him, kissed me, and asked, "Does that convince you?"

"Sentiment is cheap," I huffed, an inconsiderate shot after a tender gesture. "I didn't mean that," I quickly added, trying to erase the glimmer of hurt that flashed through his eyes. Then slowly, and more deliberately, I confessed, "I would really, really like it."

I had salvaged the propitious moment. Just.

We got up and began arranging our one library.

Chapter 5

Jeremy had invited himself over to our place for a Saturday night dinner.

I greeted him at the door, where he had knocked and was waiting.

He wore a white linen shirt, beige dress slacks pressed to perfection, and oxblood penny loafers—an appearance that left me, in my jeans and short-sleeves shirt, distinctly underdressed. He held out a bottle of wine.

"Thank you. Come on in," I said, stepping aside to let him pass. "Jonathan, your brother's here," I called toward the study. "Sorry, Jeremy. He'll be right out, hopefully. He's been working at his desk all day."

Scanning the room, Jeremy spoke without looking at me. "No problem. He was always like that. The guy is definitely the brainiac of the two of us." He continued looking around, scowling slightly.

I waited for a comment on our apartment.

Jeremy surveyed the various seating options and settled on the large overstuffed reading chair that had almost defeated our efforts to get it up the staircase on moving day. He sat down and folded his hands in his lap. He looked up at me but said nothing.

I excused myself and went into the kitchen to open the wine. As I returned, balancing three glasses in hand, Jonathan walked into the living room, white T-shirt hanging loosely outside his pants. I handed one glass to each brother.

"So Sis," Jeremy said with a glint in his eye. "Nice of you to join us."

Almost sputtering, Jonathan said, "I swear, if you call me that once more, I'll throw this wine in your face." After a moment, he added more quietly, "Shiraz stains linen, you know." Jeremy took great pride in his Holt Renfrew wardrobe, a sartorial vanity that was exceeded only by his obsession with radiant skin. He had two drawers full of Clinique Men's Skin Care products.

"You wouldn't!" Jeremy blurted before he noticed the "gotcha!" flicker in Jonathan's eyes.

"Good one. So, these are your new digs."

Jonathan took hold of my hand and led us to the sofa. We sat down, and he put his arm around my shoulder. "Yeah. This is our new love-nest. Do you like it?"

Jeremy grunted. "Tell me. Have Tom's folks been here?"

"No, I haven't met them yet. We're going up to Waterloo next weekend for dinner. I'm looking forward to it."

"Really? I thought you said his sisters were wackos."

"Jeremy!" Jonathan turned to me in time to catch my frown. "I didn't tell him that, exactly," he said. "I just said that you said they were a bit strange."

I looked over at Jeremy and said to him, "I'm afraid your brother is getting himself involved in a somewhat different family than yours."

Jeremy crossed his legs and titled his head slightly. "You don't say." He looked at me over the rim of his glass as he took a sip of wine.

"Well, my parents are nice enough. In fact, I think Jonathan will get along quite well with them. Especially Dad."

Jeremy ran his finger slowly around the rim of his glass. "As well as you got on with our father?" he asked, staring into his wine.

"Oh. I'm sorry about that …" I began. Jonathan stopped me by putting his finger up against my lips. He smiled at me as he shook his head back and forth.

Jeremy drained his glass and held it out toward us. "Heh, sis … brother, can you get me more vino while Tom tells me about these interesting sisters of his?"

"Over dinner," Jonathan replied, pushing himself up off the sofa. "Let's head to the table. Tom's casserole will dry out if we don't get to it soon."

Jeremy bounced up out of his chair. "Oh goody. Kraft dinner." He slipped his arm through Jonathan's, and the two of them sauntered arm-in-arm out of the living room. I sat for a moment longer, listening to their laughter in the kitchen.

The salmon and noodles were rather on the dry side. I tried to deflect attention with an animated description of my sisters. I felt considerable trepidation about subjecting Jonathan to Patricia and Carolyn. Both of my sisters were religious fanatics. One believed everything about God. The other believed nothing.

Patricia is four years older than I. When we were kids, she assumed that the age difference endowed her with unfettered authority over my moral education. She had once tried to perform an exorcism on me when she found me masturbating in my bedroom with the Eaton's catalogue opened to the men's underwear section.

When she turned sixteen, Patricia excused herself from the family's pew at our United Church congregation and started participating in a small house church run by the fundamentalist parents of a high school classmate. In university, she was president of the Inter-Varsity Christian Fellowship for three consecutive years. At university she became engaged to Robert, a stunningly handsome football star who kneeled in the end zone to thank God every time he scored a touchdown. They dedicated their first year of married life to helping dig wells in rural Nigeria with the Good News Missionary Society.

Patricia was embarrassed to have me, an unrepentant deviant, as her brother. While we were both living at home, she and I had interminable arguments about the Bible and homosexuality.

Carolyn was by far the brightest of the three of us. She was a gifted student before that was a formally recognized category of brilliant overachievers. She read voraciously. The family's dinner conversation was regularly hijacked by her extemporaneous recitations of William Blake, Emily Dickinson, or E. J. Pratt.

Though she was a year younger than I am, I always saw her as my guardian. Her tongue could wither any adversary who threatened me. I adored her.

By high school, it was apparent that her intelligence and acerbic wit had a shadow side. Being smarter than her classmates, and thinking that she was smarter than her teachers, took a toll. The only person's company that met her exacting standards was her own. She would seclude herself in her room, reading everything from the creators of the Western canon to American avant-garde writers. She became increasingly cynical about the world around her.

For very different reasons than Patricia, Carolyn wanted to stop going to church with us as a family. Mom and Dad dragged her along;

eventually tiring of having to constantly shush her running commentary on the sermons, they acquiesced, with the proviso that she read and report regularly to them on books with religious or ethical themes. Meeting the requirement opened up not only the world of theology for her but also that of its antagonists. She became an articulate, evangelical atheist.

Jeremy reached across the table and took a hold of Jonathan's hand. "God, I'm thankful that we're normal siblings," he said. He paused, and then they both burst out laughing.

Jeremy turned to me. "I can't wait to meet these two winners."

"Sometime," I mumbled. "Maybe sometime."

"And thank you, Chef Thomas, for this wonderful gourmet meal in your fabulous new quarters." He swept one arm around over his head.

"How is it that you sound more gay than your gay brother? What straight man says 'fabulous'?"

"I'll tell you a secret, Tom. Gay-speak is a real chick magnet. Women hear you, think you're a gay man, and become excited by the challenge of seducing and converting a member of the other team. Of course, in catching prey, it helps that I am so hot-looking." He looked over at Jonathan. "Rather, that we are."

Ignoring the inference, I said, "You seem to have this down to a science."

"Now you've insulted me. I am an artist, not a lab rat. Sex is an ecstatic experience, and I want my art to reflect that. Art is a travesty if it can't thrust us into the essence of our humanity. Not just love, but also fear and hate and horror and grief. But right now I'm concentrating on love and sex. The research is a hell of a lot more gratifying," he laughed.

"You've given this a quite a bit of thought," I said.

"The female is my muse. I cannot be creative unless I have regular injections of the elixir of love."

"Sounds rather utilitarian. You use women for stimulation, so to speak, but you're not interested in them beyond that." I smiled at Jonathan, hoping to convey that I was pursuing an agenda of his. "Not interested in a serious relationship, for example. Or so I've heard."

Jeremy nodded toward his brother and inquired, "Did he pay you to ask that?"

Jonathan pushed his chair back from the table and stood up. "Anyone for coffee?" he asked.

"Yes, please," Jeremy and I chirped in unison while Jonathan picked up a few of the dirty dishes from the table and headed into the kitchen.

Jeremy and I sat in uncharacteristic silence, letting the Brahms on the stereo filter through the tranquility, with only the sound of water filling the coffee pot as competition. I looked up to see Jeremy staring at me with intensity quite distinct from his badinage of a moment ago. I raised my eyebrows slightly. *What?* He continued to stare. He leaned over the table toward me, hands clasped together in front of him. His voice was a rapier flourished with a quiet exactitude that pierced my complaisance. He whispered, "I swear if you hurt my brother, I will kill you."

"Uh, excuse me?" I stammered.

"He may seem like a smart, tough cookie to you, but he is a babe in the woods. I have a strong suspicion that you've been around the block quite a few more times than he has, even though he has a few years on you."

"I love Jonathan," I protested.

"Don't give me that crap. You're not talking to your doe-eyed lover boy here. This is only the second time I've met you. I have no basis on which to assess your honesty or your integrity or even how well you know your own mind. But I do know my brother, and he is head over heels in love with you."

I smiled instinctively at this assessment.

"Wipe that smirk off your face. I will cut your balls off and stuff them in any orifice you choose if I think for a second that you might be toying with the 'professor.'"

"What are you two whispering about?" Jonathan called from the kitchen.

"Just getting to know each other a little better," Jeremy replied innocuously.

Steadying my voice to mask the intimidation he had successfully imposed, I said, "Listen, it's true you don't know me from Adam, but this thing between your brother and me is mutual to the hilt. You're going to have to take my word for it. Or ask Jonathan." Still looking at Jeremy but addressing Jonathan, I yelled, "Honey, your brother has something he wants to ask you."

"You little shit," Jeremy muttered.

"What is it?" Jonathan asked, carrying a tray with three cups of coffee back into the dining room. He set them down on the table and looked back and forth between the two of us. "Well?"

Jeremy glared at me.

I stared back.

Without taking his eyes off me, Jeremy said, "What I wanted to ask you is, how do you think you're going to get along with your new sisters-in-law?"

I flinched. *Fuck, he is good.*

Jonathan sat down and replied, "I've been wondering that too. We do think alike, Jeremy."

Hardly.

Chapter 6

It was clear that we were going to be arriving late at Waterloo. We hadn't reckoned on the traffic after the Saturday afternoon Argonauts football game. Because both of us spent most of our time at the university and either walked or biked to the campus from our flat, we had become isolated from the realities of the expressway and the suburbanite commuters.

"Can you imagine people battling this every day?" I commented, squinting into the blinding sun that was setting directly in front us as we headed west, out of the city. The traffic flow alternated between a slow crawl and speed-limit pace, the latter made challenging by frustrated drivers weaving in and out with only feet to spare between them and the cars they were cutting off.

"Huh?" Jonathan was buried in his book. Many people get car sick if they read in a moving vehicle. Not my boyfriend. Just one of his many talents.

"What are you reading?" I asked.

"Just a minute. I want to finish this paragraph."

One of those frustrated drivers passed us on the right, bolted into our lane, and then slammed on the brakes to avoid plowing into the car ahead of them. "Shit!" I hit the horn. "That idiot! Did you see that?"

"Huh?"

I glanced over at the passenger's seat. Jonathan's head hadn't veered from the page. "We just passed Gloria Swanson," I said.

"That's nice."

I had developed little strategies to test if Jonathan was anywhere near my orbit. When he was reading, he was invariably on the far side of Neptune. I was impressed by his capacity to concentrate, oblivious to the world around him—another dimension of the "brainiac" that I had fallen in love with.

"Oh, that's well said, Michel."

Now it was my turn. "Huh?"

"Listen. 'I think that a rigorous, theoretical analysis of the way in which economic, political, and ideological structures function is one of the necessary conditions for political action, insofar as political action is a way of manipulating and possibly changing, drastically disrupting, and transforming structures.' You know, you should look at some of Foucault's writings for your poli sci paper."

"Forget my paper. That sounds like it would be more useful for my next battle with your father."

"Somehow I don't think Father would give much credence to a homosexual French Marxist philosopher," Jonathan laughed. "Which attribute do you think he would find most repugnant?"

"He'd probably find the political positions the most difficult to swallow. Mind you, that's only based on one Sunday dinner. Are you sure that you and Jeremy weren't adopted? Your dad is such a Neanderthal. How is that you could be his offspring?"

An extended pause followed.

"Sorry, I didn't mean to be disrespectful."

"No, you didn't intend to be disrespectful. It just comes naturally to you."

"Ouch."

We drove in silence for a few minutes before Jonathan, in a much lighter tone, asked, "Speaking of families, are there any last-minute orientation tips you want to give me about how to win over your folks?"

I appreciated his rapid shift in focus, a generous pass on my faux pas.

"Any prep? I don't think so. I've already given you the overview. You've got plenty of diplomatic skills. You're not going to provoke an intergenerational incident like I did at your parents' place. Mom's the talker. She'll keep the conversation flowing—something about Mother Nature abhorring a vacuum. Dad will listen politely. Don't hesitate to ask him anything. He's a deep thinker, and he reads a lot. His quietness can be deceptive. I misread him for years. As a teenager, I was so full of myself."

"Really?"

"You're getting to know me too well too quickly," I laughed. "As for Carolyn—well, you'll just have to judge for yourself. I do hope that she deigns to join us for dinner. She's quite a piece of work, and I think you two could get along. Just don't get into a pissing contest with her about which of you has read more. There's no way you'll come out on top."

"A pissing contest with your sister? That's kind of a gross image."

"You know what I mean. I'm just relieved that we're able to procrastinate on the Patricia inquisition. She and Robert are at some function at their church."

Jonathan returned to his reading. I concentrated on avoiding getting us killed.

I rang the doorbell to give them a heads-up and then walked right in. I hoped Jonathan would notice.

"Well, it's about time. Was the traffic bad? I was imagining all kinds of terrible things." Mom gave me a big hug. Her hair was freshly permed. I smelled perfume. She was wearing a light beige pantsuit that I had never seen on her before. "How are you, darling? I miss you. I hate this business of you going to school in Toronto. We have two perfectly good universities here in Waterloo. Anyway, we've been over this a million times—you made your choice."

"Yes, Mom, we have," I mumbled.

"And you must be Jonathan. I'm so very glad to meet you."

Jonathan had brought a small bouquet and somewhat awkwardly offered them to her, simultaneously reaching out to shake her hand. She ignored both gestures and gave him a hug and a kiss on the cheek. The flowers suffered. Still not appearing to notice the proffered hostess gift, Mom grabbed my arm and ushered me into the living room. I glanced back to see Jonathan gallantly handing the flowers to Carolyn. I hadn't even had a chance to introduce them. And there was clearly no need. Carolyn did a modest little curtsy as she accepted them, a gesture that looked even more absurd dressed as she was in jeans and sweatshirt. Carolyn said something to Jonathan. They both laughed.

"Dad, so good to see you." I greeted my father as he entered from the kitchen, a flowery apron tied around his waist. We embraced. He stepped back a pace, both hands resting on my shoulders, looked into my eyes, and smiled. "I'd like you to meet Jonathan," I said.

Jonathan extended his hand. Dad clasped both of his hands around Jonathan's.

"Sorry, Jonathan," Mom interjected, pulling him away from Dad. "We don't have time for lovely hors d'oeuvres like I had planned.

Like you have at your parents' house, I understand." Jonathan shot a suspicious glance at me. "The roast is going to burn if we leave it in any longer, and Tom is always complaining that we never serve roast beef any way short of charcoaled. I can tell you, when we were growing up, we never heard of a rare beef roast. But I guess things change, and I've got to adapt. Isn't it a little dangerous eating beef that's not really well cooked? I'm a nurse. Oh, you probably know that. Well, I've seen enough nasty germs and bacteria for more than one lifetime, and I don't like taking a chance in my own household."

"Mother. Please. Take a valium," were Carolyn's first words, not counting that little vestibule interchange with Jonathan.

"Oh, right. Sorry. I have a tendency to talk a bit more than I should, I suppose."

Carolyn and I rolled our eyes in unison. Dad scolded us gently with his. "Well, come now. Jonathan, you sit on this side. Tom and Carolyn, sit on the other. And no fighting, you two."

As we headed toward our assigned places, Jonathan scurried to pull out and hold Mom's chair, almost tripping her in the process. "What a gentleman," Mom effused.

Jonathan looked to me for a nod of approval. I shook my head. *Cool it, baby. Sorry to disappoint you, but that was a little over the top.* He sighed. We were getting good at nonverbal communication.

We chewed over the well-done roast beef and did the same with the Indian summer weather, our new apartment, Mom's frenetic hospital shifts, and Dad's resistance to the pressure to move him up the institutional hierarchy from classroom to administrative office.

Jonathan turned to Mom and asked, "If it's not too personal, would you mind telling me something of your histories?" He gestured with his fork between Mom and Dad. "The families you came from? How the two of you met?"

I looked down at my plate. His inquiry had come out of the blue. I didn't question that he was sincerely interested, but I was uncertain whether his intention was to please me or chastise me with the contrast with my behaviour at his parents' dinner table.

"How nice of you to be interested." Mom smiled at Jonathan and then she asked Dad, rather unnecessarily, "Shall I start?"

"By all means, dear," Dad chuckled. He turned to Jonathan and said, "She's a much better storyteller than I."

License given, Mom launched into describing how she was the youngest of five girls. In what remains something of a mystery, her father left that household of six women and moved to the other side of the country with a different woman, leaving Grandma to raise the daughters alone, earning money by teaching piano lessons at home and taking in paying roomers.

Mom was talking with surprising candor, given how recently she had met Jonathan. She had always been quite reluctant to talk about what it meant to come from "a broken home."

Because money was so tight, Mom had to leave high school earlier than she wanted and take a clerical job to contribute to the household's survival. She managed to save enough to put herself through nursing school, a dream vocation from her earliest years. Just as she was graduating, word came that her father had died and left his wife and the five girls several thousand dollars each.

Mom's jaw tightened as she said, "One can only speculate about what kind of deathbed conversion would lead a man to bequeath a small fortune to his family, after having deprived us of his personal and financial support for decades."

The table was quiet. Dad picked up the cue.

"My father had been a minister. Unfortunately, his tenure in the church was not a happy one. As in many churches, there was a small but powerful clique of members. Dad preached the word as he saw fit, which included criticizing what he perceived as the hypocrisy of the power elite who professed their faith on Sundays but conducted their personal and business affairs in quite contrary ways. Dad was told to stop. He didn't. He was forced out of his pulpit and was never allowed to work in the church again."

"My goodness," Jonathan said. "Sounds like your father had a lot of guts and integrity."

Dad nodded his head. "Yes, he did. But losing the capacity to exercise his calling broke his heart."

Carolyn shifted around in her chair. "Surely you don't want to hear all this ancient history, Jonathan."

"On the contrary, Carolyn," Jonathan replied, looking at my sister. He glanced over at me as he said, "I am very interested."

Taking him at his word, I turned to Dad and said, "Tell them about your honeymoon."

"Oh, I think your mother would be better to relate that part of our story."

Mom smiled appreciatively. "Lawrence and I met at a church youth social and, very rapidly, fell in love." She paused for a moment and looked back and forth between Jonathan and me, smiling broadly. "Our families assumed that we would follow a path of tradition and security, get jobs, and begin to raise a family. We had other ideas."

I observed the sparkle in her eyes as she described how they announced their plans for an unconventional honeymoon to the stunned households. Drawing on her father's postmortem generosity, they intended to see something of the world before settling down. They were going to travel by bus to Central America, live there for a year, and then return to assume the roles that everyone expected of them.

Mom looked at Dad. "Lawrence, you tell Jonathan about our great adventure."

Carolyn pushed her chair back and got up. "Excuse me, but I have to go to the bathroom. I think I've heard this before. About fifty million times."

"Just don't go off to read in your room, dear," Mom called after her as she headed up the stairs. Carolyn didn't reply.

"So did you spend a year in Central America?" Jonathan asked.

"As we travelled through Mexico," Dad continued, "we were rather overwhelmed. We had never witnessed poverty such as we saw day after day. Nor had we witnessed such exuberance for life. By the time we reached Oaxaca, we could not bring ourselves to pass by another Zapotec child in need of rudimentary health care or pass up another invitation to a spontaneous family celebration where everyone of every age in the community seemed involved. So we set down roots for a year in the small town of Santa Maria del Tule."

"I got nursing experience unlike any of my fellow students back home," Mom interjected. "And my father's monies helped buy resources for the local health clinic. Lawrence made himself useful with the school that the town was building. Every night, we pored over our Spanish books. When the year came to an end, we came home. *C'est tout.*"

"Correction, my dear," Dad chuckled. "*Esta todo.*"

From the fifty million times that I had also heard the story, I knew that their return had not been quite that simple. They had left their new friends with heavy hearts. But they had made a commitment to their families, and they were a woman and a man of their word.

Chapter 7 ————————————————

Carolyn's bathroom break took longer than necessary. Dessert was being served when she returned and plopped herself back down on her chair. Mom cut a slice of apple pie and placed it in front of Carolyn. Jonathan and I were in the midst of recounting the challenges of our moving day.

Fed up with such banalities, Carolyn looked over at Jonathan. "So, professor, tell me about your dissertation."

Jonathan demurred. "I'm a long way from being a professor."

"Well, that's what Tom called you when we talked on the phone. I think he actually said, 'the professor.' Now, let me remember. Was his inflection one of respect and affection, or was it sarcastic and derisive? My brother can be so opaque." She laughed.

"I'm not opaque," I protested.

"You're right, simpleton. You are as easy to read as a second grade primer. Have you no sense of irony?"

I didn't fancy having my intellectual insecurities vis-à-vis my sister on full display, so I deflected the focus back onto Jonathan. "His dissertation explores the intersection among socio-economic developments and political theory within various European philosophical schools in the nineteenth and twentieth centuries."

"Tom, it sounds like you're reading from a syllabus," Carolyn sneered.

Dad sat up. "Sounds ambitious, Jonathan."

"Excuse me, sir," Jonathan slurred, rapidly chewing the piece of pie he had just put in his mouth. He swallowed and set his fork down on his plate. "I'm still in the early stages of sorting out what I want to do, but I'm interested in historical flow." He clasped his hands together and rested his elbows on the table, leaning in so he had a more direct view of Dad at the end of the table. "Generally speaking, theology as a force was waning, while economics was revolutionizing, literally in some countries, the social and political landscape. What were philosophers

33

thinking about those dynamics and how were they contributing to them?"

"I'm not sure that I would agree that theology was being eclipsed." Intentionally or coincidentally, Dad mimicked Jonathan's pose, elbows on table, hands together, leaning into the conversation. "The power and place of the church was certainly changing, but would you not say that significant spiritual and ethical issues were being struggled with post-enlightenment?"

"I have difficulty with the term *spiritual*," Jonathan said with a bit of a grimace. "You're right that there remained big questions, like how we understand existence, thought, perception. But science and philosophy were gaining all the tools needed to address them." Jonathan caught himself. "Sorry, I don't mean to be disrespectful."

Dad smiled. "No offense taken. I guess that I just don't share your optimistic spirit about the capacity of human reason." Tapping his head lightly with his right hand, he said, "I think that we suffer today from dogmatic rationalism as much as from dogmatic theology. Granted, scientists need rigor and detachment in their experiments. But other areas of human endeavour require us to become engaged, subjective—transformed, if you will." He raised his hands and his eyebrows in tandem. "For instance, in how we experience music or understand the nature of God."

Jonathan smiled. "I certainly am no expert on God."

"A philosopher who is not interested in the question of God. Is that possible?" Dad jested.

Jonathan shrugged. "Professionally, yes, it's a legitimate subject. But personally, I'm just not that much into God. Nor he into me, I suspect. Sorry." He looked in my direction just as I frowned.

Carolyn pulled her chair closer to the table. "I agree with you, Jonathan, my boy, about the goddamn God business. You'll have to excuse my family. They're all a bit soft in the head on that subject."

"Don't be blasphemous, Carolyn," Mom scolded.

Waving her hand dismissively in Mom's direction, Carolyn continued more aggressively. "Professor, from the way Tom described your dissertation, assuming he knows what he's talking about—though I hate to break it to you, but he's not all that bright ..." she said, fluttering her eyelids at me. I fluttered mine back. "Anyway, it sounds like you're talking about almost the whole intellectual waterfront for the past two hundred years. Anything that macroscopic is bound to overlook so many complexities. Surely it has to be more focused?" "Well, yes." Jonathan hesitated. Strategically facing Dad rather than Carolyn, he elaborated. "I'm focusing primarily on three philosophers, Kierkegaard, Heidegger, and Foucault."

Carolyn was soaring. "But you've got such confounding variables there, with radically different cultural and political situations. Kierkegaard in nineteenth-century Denmark. Heidegger in Nazi Germany. Foucault in postwar France." She raised three fingers in succession and stared at them with a mocking expression. "A comparison across such disparate contexts is inevitably going to be very superficial." Softening her critique a touch, she added, "Wouldn't it?"

Ignoring my earlier advice, Jonathan turned to her and challenged. "You've read Kierkegaard?"

"Well, not his original writings," Carolyn said without defensiveness. "But Sartre criticizes Kierkegaard quite convincingly in *Being and Nothingness*."

Jonathan crossed his arms and leaned back in his chair. "So you've read about Kierkegaard, but you haven't read Kierkegaard," he said quietly. "Perhaps you're not aware that Sartre's existentialism draws heavily from Kierkegaard, even though Sartre, as an atheist, disagrees intensely with Kierkegaard's Christian faith. And if you consider Sartre's analysis to have merit, then that would suggest that you acknowledge that comparisons of thought across time, cultures, and politics has validity." Jonathan smiled. "Wouldn't it?"

The pissing contest was in full swing.

"Kierkegaard?" Dad had not leaned back. "Interesting choice," he said, his head nodding. "I've been a fan for a long time. May I ask why you chose him? As you acknowledge, he was a person of deep faith, though admittedly he had a tortured struggle with it."

"My main concentration will be on Foucault. For a variety of reasons, he appeals to me." Jonathan managed a subtle wink at me. "I'm intrigued by who influenced him. Kierkegaard is one. It seems to me that his 'tortured struggle' ... I like that phrasing, thank you." Jonathan mimed note-taking on his palm. "Kierkegaard's tortured struggle to understand the nature of the self, his emphases on finding meaning in life through action, his analyses of despair and alienation—all these are influences on Foucault in his own struggles, professional and personal." Jonathan dropped his eyes to his plate. His expression sobered. Mom cleared her throat. Where Dad was an ideas person, Mom was a people person. I could see that she was getting antsy. Her head had been following the three-sided intellectual ping-pong game between her husband, her daughter, and Jonathan. But she took the initiative to move the conversation into less esoteric territory. Reaching out and placing one hand on my arm and her other on my boyfriend's, she said, "So, how did you two meet?"

She had been anxious to pry open my closet door long before I was prepared to. Years earlier, well before we had "the conversation," I and Andy, my boyfriend of the time drove up to their camping trailer one summer Sunday to spend the afternoon with them and to stay on for a couple of days after they returned to the city. Over the barbecue supper, Dad gave us instructions on such essentials as the operation of the propane stove and where to pick up fish bait. Mom interjected. "And if you want to sleep in the same bed, you know that the kitchen table folds down and the seats can be made up into a double bed." Andy froze, his hamburger suspended halfway between plate and mouth. I looked out at the lake and tacked. "Dad, have you had any problems with the boat motor this season?"

I attributed Mom's openness to her nursing life. Her favourite self-description was "a fixer of broken bones and broken hearts."

"Yes, what about that?" prodded Carolyn, smarting from having failed to triumph in the previous round. She was her daddy's child, living mostly in her head, and had never exhibited much sign of having inherited any of Mom's genes, with this one exception: a taste for family gossip. Not that the story of our meeting was particularly racy, but the table didn't know that yet; I knew the women hoped for something spicy.

I glared at Jonathan. He smiled down at the pie crumbs on his plate. I had to make sure that he wouldn't respond with the one-liner he usually offered in answer to that query. "A public urinal" was not what my family needed to hear. Of course, it wasn't true, but Jonathan loved to shock our friends with such a clandestine image. I jumped in. "We met at a disco. We danced that night and then started dating."

Carolyn was pouting. "You mean you dated before you slept

together? I didn't think that was the gay way. I thought that's what lesbians did, not gay men."

"Sorry to disappoint you, sis." I leaned over and nudged her with my elbow. "If it reestablishes our gay creds in your mind, I can confirm that we were living together, more or less, within a week of our first dance."

"That sounds better." She placed her hand on my shoulder and, in a sweeter voice, asked, "Just to be clear, 'living together' does include fucking, right?"

Jonathan guffawed.

"Carolyn," Dad said sternly. "None of that language at the table."

Carolyn turned from me to Dad and, maintaining her feigned tone of innocence, said, "Just trying to ensure historical accuracy, Pops."

"That was hardly your motivation, young woman," Mom said. "Enough."

"Isn't it interesting," Carolyn sighed, "that the golden-haired boy in this family gets to shack up without censure from you two, but you won't even let me go out on a date without imposing a curfew?"

"You want to go on a date?" I asked, throwing my hands up and jolting back in my chair.

"Not funny, you prick," she said, and she punched me on the shoulder. "I'm just interested, sort of clinically curious, about the double standard—no, triple standard—in this house. Patricia never had any rules imposed because she was always such a goody-two-shoes. And you"—she recommenced punching my shoulder, rather more forcefully—"got away with murder because you were the male child who they"—she extended her arm and pointed at Mom and Dad—"always thought would be the propagator of the family name." She retracted her arms and folded her hands on the table in front of her. "Ha! Look how that turned out."

Dad reached over and placed his hand on hers. Without looking at him, she yanked it away from his grasp.

"We don't want to hear about it now," Mom dictated, looking back and forth between her daughter and her husband.

"Carolyn can say what she needs to say," Dad said.

Carolyn folded her arms and stared down into her lap. Without looking up, she mumbled, "You guys are in the city, at university, living together. I'm just impatient for my life to begin."

I looked over at Jonathan, who returned my glance, a smile firmly entrenched.

"I'm sorry, Jonathan," Mom said, turning toward him. "We didn't intend for you, our guest, to have to witness our little family drama."

Carolyn growled quietly, "Mother, please don't patronize me."

Jonathan looked at Mom and replied, "Mrs. Fischer ... Isabel ..." Mom nodded approvingly. "I don't feel like a guest. This has made me feel quite at home." Jonathan glanced at me and continued to address Mom. "Tom can attest to my family having its fair share of drama as well."

I smiled inwardly. *Tonight, I will be rewarding my boyfriend's generosity in the manner Carolyn so subtly alluded to.*

Chapter 8

Jonathan and I felt the need for a let-lose party fix with friends as an antidote to the recent family scenes. The pretext was a housewarming. The subtext was midterm stress relief.

Before anyone arrived, I had fastidiously organized a pile of LPs that represented an evolution in the tempo and genre of music, starting with welcoming jazz, ramping up the energy for mid-party dancing with umpteen disco records, and then easing into a selection of more mellow vocals for later in the party, to match the anticipated fatigue and inebriation of the guests. Jonathan laughed when he noticed what I had planned but wouldn't tell me why. Within the first half hour, there were too many people speaking at too loud a volume for my background ambiance to be discerned. That and my own escalating drunkenness interfered with my attending to the demands of the record player.

A couple of hours into the party, I tried a quick head count. I gave up when I passed fifty. People just wouldn't stand still for my census. Most of the partiers were our friends from school or from the dance clubs. Our new apartment was being inaugurated with a profusion of tie-dyed T-shirts on the straight boys, loose-fitting cotton dresses draped over the girls' braless breasts, and sprayed-on tight jeans on the gay boys intent on advertising.

It was always a smart idea to invite the other residents in the house so that they couldn't complain about party noise. Ulrich and Althena, professors both, owned the house and lived directly below us on the ground floor. They had invited us down for a welcoming glass of wine a few nights after we moved in. Jonathan had talked to them about university politics most of the evening, which gave me dispensation to explore their library. Ulrich's physics books were not of much interest, but Althena's collection of English literature was astounding. She must have had every book ever published on the poets of the Romantic period—every book published before the twentieth century, that is. I knew where I could go if I needed a Byron fix. The stacks reeked of mould, and every time I withdrew a volume, a cloud of dust followed. *I'll have to warn Jonathan. He'll have an allergy attack just walking into the room.*

Our landlords never entertained in their own home, overwhelmed, I gathered, by the logistical challenge of clearing their dining room table of the stacks of papers and undertaking the daunting task of planning a menu. But they loved people and parties and wine and had enthusiastically accepted our invitation. Ulrich exhibited a not very subtle, but ultimately harmless, attraction to the young women in the room, who discretely but effectively eluded his clutches. He was a good conversationalist, but most of our friends were a fraction of his age and unlikely to be attracted to spending time with him, given his corpulence, permanently untrimmed beard, and chronic halitosis. Althena, her statuesque height set off smartly by a navy blue suit, ignored her husband and persisted in her objective of meeting all our friends. She was altruistically interested in the preoccupations of the younger generation. Our friends were polite and perhaps flattered by her attention. I saw many of them leaning into conversations with her at one time or another during the evening, their disheveled dress a marked contrast to her classy appearance. Eventually, though, they would seek to extricate themselves from her grasp to socialize with their contemporaries, using the excuse of wanting another drink or needing to use the bathroom.

The apartment above us was occupied by a sweet and very pregnant couple newly arrived from Nova Scotia. Jonathan and I were nervous about the possibility of a screaming baby in the house, but Jim and Barb were so laid back that we hoped that the child would inherit their temperament. They didn't stay long at the party. Pregnancy made for a good excuse to slip away, though I suspected that they felt a bit overwhelmed by the very diverse crowd. They made a point of searching out both Jonathan and me to express their appreciations and, possibly, to build up goodwill with the couple of potential babysitters in the unit below them.

We didn't invite the creepy tenant from the basement. Since moving in, we had only seen him emerge from his lair once, late at night, with a bag of garbage. He almost ran us over as we came up the walk. We said hello and attempted to introduce ourselves, but he just grunted, dropped his garbage near the curb but nowhere near the garbage cans, and scurried back through his door under the front veranda. It wasn't kind, but the image was just too apt—Jonathan and I started referring to him as Ratman.

Most of our friends abided by poor-student party etiquette and brought a contribution for the bar. Even cheap wine tasted fine after the sixth glass. The beer was consumed before it got warm. Supplies were replenished with every new inundation of guests.

Jonathan, thinking himself politically astute, had invited his dissertation advisors from the Philosophy Department. They and their spouses came dressed for a formal faculty cocktail reception. I caught several of them coming in the door and glancing distastefully around at the other revelers. Besides a brief introduction by Jonathan, I had little contact with them. Our landlords were not keen on spending time with them. Althena, in particular, found her peers boring. So Jonathan was left to entertain his faculty supervisors. Both Jonathan and I were opera buffs and, fortunately, so were several of his professors. They had just seen a production of Handel's *Rinaldo* by the Canadian Opera Company that we had also seen, so that provided Jonathan a subject to help dissipate the social awkwardness. Passing by at one point, I overheard a spouse expressing distaste, fueled by numerous glasses of wine, about being subjected to the disorientation of a countertenor voice. Feeling no pain myself, I was tempted to commiserate and decry the paucity of decent castrati these days. Jonathan noticed the mischievous glint in my eye and warned me off with a glare of his own.

I thought it was a shame that Jonathan felt trapped by the exigencies of future dissertation approval. Quite a few of his friends and fellow grad students had come. I was meeting most of them for the first time and took pride in exuding the dual persona of co-host and their friend's new boyfriend. Jonathan had warned me that they would be scrutinizing me. I had consciously dressed in a tight-fitting T-shirt to exhibit the fruit of my rigorous daily workout regime. I figured that if his crowd was going to dismiss me as not intellectually meriting their friend's infatuation, at least they might grant that Jonathan had found other redeeming qualities.

Sheila, one of his oldest friends, trapped me in a corner almost as soon as she arrived. Her jeans and flannel shirt initially put me at ease. I was on the verge of asking if her girlfriend was here as well. I hesitated, wisely, when I noticed her checking out the attractive men in the room.

I had little chance to find out anything about her. She grilled me with an intensity I usually only saw on Perry Mason reruns. She wanted to know about my family, where I grew up, how much I had travelled. Her habit of tapping her beer bottle against my chest in tandem with every new question was annoying but effectively intimidating. I thought she crossed the line when she demanded to know the size of my student loan debt and the number of previous boyfriends I'd had. But her bulky frame and the aura of being able to take me down at will that she exuded cowed me into answering, more or less accurately.

"What do you think of his dissertation topic?" she asked after having elicited a full description of my course load.

"Somewhat over my head, I'm afraid," I said. Her frown prompted my rather lame backtracking. "I do find it fascinating."

"So you and Jonathan don't have that much in common."

I wished it had been a question rather than a statement. "Oh, I wouldn't say that. Some common interests. Some different." I held up my empty beer bottle, but her eyes pinned me to the wall, and I didn't dare excuse myself. "You're in philosophy too?" I asked.

She cackled. "Oh, God no. Can't stand that airhead shit. Engineering."

"So, you and Jonathan don't have that much in common," I said.

Her eyes narrowed, and she squinted at me for a long moment. Then she smiled and threw her arm around my shoulder and ushered me toward the kitchen. "You're not a very good host, leaving a poor damsel like me without a fresh drink in my hand."

I must have passed the exam. Midway through the party and quite spontaneously, she gave me a big hug and an altogether too sloppy kiss.

Roger, another of Jonathan's friends, was a different case. His interrogations stopped just shy of condescension and were ladled with landmines. I could tell when I had tripped one. His glance would dart to others in the cluster. Initially, I made a vain attempt to respond in kind with the cynical repartee that masqueraded for sophisticated party conversation. I was clearly no match, so after a while, I opted for the naïve innocent. That had a sufficiently disarming effect, particularly when Sheila and others came to my defense, that Roger eventually left to get a drink and ignored me for the rest of the evening.

My former roommates from the dorm were the most undisciplined of the crowd. For the first couple of hours of the party, they remained in the happy zone. I did my best to sequester them in the kitchen, which was at the back of the apartment, down a long hall. This had several advantages. The rest of the guests were somewhat sheltered from their noise. Spilled drinks would do less damage there than in our living room, study, or bedroom. And a door opened from the kitchen out onto a staircase that gave access to the backyard. If alcohol-induced nausea set in amongst the roisterers, I could easily usher them outside to get fresh air and dispose of whatever.

By two in the morning, Althena had woken Ulrich and carted him downstairs. Jonathan's faculty overseers had long since exhausted conversational topics and made their exits. My former dorm buddies had moved their drinking party back to the residence hall, having failed to provoke me to paroxysms of nostalgia.

The party dregs coalesced in the living room. I was on the couch with Sheila, who was leaning up against my friend Paulo in an awkward and unreciprocated cuddle.

Andrew, a former short-term boyfriend of mine, and Susan, his wife, were sitting on floor cushions. They were an attractive and smartly dressed couple. His short, black brush-cut was a perfect foil for her long blond hair. Both still sported tans from having spent all September at their cottage on Cape Cod. They had been married for more than ten years, living in an unconventional relationship, when he picked me up in a bar several years earlier. Despite being a gregarious lover while we were dating, he had made it clear that he was, first and foremost, a husband to Susan and a father to their children. In exchange for her considerable generosity, he had vowed never to leave the marriage and to be honest with her about where he was and who he was with. That arrangement quickly frustrated me. I wasn't cut out to be the other woman, and so I called us quits. But the three of us, somehow, had remained friends.

Jonathan was next to Andrew. This past and present visual made me smile, until Clyde, a dancer friend of Jonathan's, began giving my boyfriend a neck massage. They had had a brief fling a while earlier, before Clyde got a job with the Joffrey Ballet in New York. Jonathan had told me about the stares that they used to get out at clubs. He was never sure whether people were perplexed by Clyde's stiffness on the dance floor because his classical ballet training inhibited him from the loose-limbed style of disco or whether the onlookers were just admiring the handsome biracial couple. I stared at them now for my own reasons.

My ambient music preparations had finally become viable. Judging the laid-back atmosphere of the hour, I stacked three LPs. Cleo Laine would transition into Joni Mitchell, who would then cede air space to Roberta Flack. I hoped that my thousand-plus playing of "The First Time Ever I Saw Your Face" would not have created too many mood-disrupting scratches in the vinyl.

"How about I order some pizza?" Paulo was either hungry or had devised a strategy to extricate himself from amorous Sheila. The beer and wine supplies, supplemented by generous guests, had been sufficient. There were still unopened bottles and cans. But Jonathan and I had underestimated our friends' appetites. The snacking supplies we bought were decimated within the first few hours. Hunger pangs were also exacerbated in the committed few who had smoked more than tobacco out on the back staircase. From time to time throughout the evening, the sweet aroma of their clandestine street corner purchases escaped the kitchen and tempted other under-thirties. Those olfactory skills seemed to be generationally dependent.

"Good idea!" enthused Andrew, not wanting the party to end. He flinched as Susan squeezed his hand. She was fidgeting, telegraphing that she was ready to go home.

"Huh?" Sheila was jarred awake with the sudden removal of her headrest when Paulo stood up.

I reached across the couch and laid my hand on top of hers. "Are you hungry, my dear? Paulo is going to phone for pizza."

"Oh God, yes. I'm famished. There's been no decent food at this party. I thought your type was supposed to have been born with the entertaining gene. You and Johnny, my boy, are a major disappointment. I had expected catering by Daniel et Daniel."

"So you've heard our story of the two Daniels?" I asked.

"No, do tell."

Jonathan rolled his eyes. I ignored him. "We were coming in from the Arches late one night a couple months ago, and Daniel and Daniel happened to be riding up on the elevator at the same time."

"This place has an elevator?" Clyde interjected facetiously.

"Cute. No, this was back at Jonathan's old apartment. Anyway, as I was saying, I guess me and Johnny my boy … I love that, by the way …"

Jonathan pounced. "Forget it. Sheila's the only one who gets to call me that."

"Okay. As I was saying … no one else wants to interrupt? The story isn't going to be as funny now that it's getting dragged out."

"Just tell the *maldita* story so I can find out what people want and order the goddamn pizza." This shard from Paulo, the sound of a sexually frustrated young male libido, startled the room.

The story really wasn't going to seem as funny, I realized, but I carried on "As I was saying …" I continued provocatively slowly, glaring at Paulo. He looked away. "I guess Jonathan and I were a bit in flagrante delicto when one of the Daniels covered his eyes and said, 'Pleeeze, dees ees a puuuuublic place!' "

Silence.

Sheila. "Then what happened?"

"Bitch. That's it. That's the story."

Jonathan got up, came over, plopped himself between me and Sheila, put his arm around me, and said, "That was a lovely story, darling. You can retell it as often as you want, whenever you want, even though I've already heard it, and I was there."

"Now that this party has deteriorated from chi chi to schmaltzy, I've lost my appetite and am going home," Sheila declared, struggling up from the sofa with more than a small wobble. "There's not going to be enough room on this couch for me in a moment anyway. Or any of you," she pronounced with authority, glaring at the others around the room.

Everyone took the cue. Jonathan and I were shortly a party of two, free to transition from schmaltzy to sexy.

Chapter 9

Lunch together most days at Wymilwood Café was another sign of our burgeoning domesticity.

Jonathan's daily routine was quite routine. He spent mornings sequestered in *la dona brutalisima*, his affectionate christening of the Robarts Library because of its strident architecture. He thought that was cleverer than Fort Book, which most undergraduates called it.

From nine until noon, he read background works for his doctoral dissertation. His concentration was astounding. No break for coffee or anything else—phenomenal bladder capacity.

He claimed to be going through a rough patch. His German was not as adequate as he felt it should be for appreciating the nuances in Heidegger's writings, so he was going back and forth between originals and translations. He was fastidious and wanted to be able to compare several translations simultaneously. Neither the desk size of his study carrel nor the university's book-purchase budget met his needs, which left him invariably grumpy by lunchtime.

Vegetable soup and my presence, I liked to think, lightened his mood.

His afternoons were divided between writing analyses of his morning's reading and "babysitting" undergraduates in fulfillment of his TA requirements. "You were an undergraduate too not that long ago," I reminded him when he disparaged the youngsters, "and you're shacked up with one to boot." He wouldn't respond, evidence that he didn't think of me as a member of that underclass, or if he did, he didn't want to be reminded.

My daily routines were much less routine. A double major in history and political science meant a heavy course load. Fourth year was also thesis time for me, though I didn't complain about the amount of work when I witnessed the sweat and tears that Jonathan was investing in his. Not that I had a chosen a Mickey Mouse subject. The legacy of Simón

Bolívar not only required hours of research, but I had to put time into improving my Spanish.

My involvements outside of class were also time-consuming. The year before, I had been a stalwart member of the Latin America Working Group, and I still tried to get to their evening and weekend organizing meetings. Recently my attendance was getting spotty, now that I had someone to come home to. No one had said anything yet, but I was anticipating deprecating comments about my social justice commitment and accusations of bourgeois tendencies.

That term I was also on the executive of SAPS, the winning acronym for the poli sci students' association. We had several fights going on with the department chair.

Plus there was my personal commitment to daily workouts. Healthy body, healthy mind, I would say. Body image vanity might have played a minor supporting role.

"Don't you get tired of tuna fish sandwiches?" Jonathan asked, looking disdainfully at my plate.

"You're to blame. Following your stellar nutritional example, I'm trying to reform my eating habits. Pizza is out. No more french fries or fried chicken. Besides, tuna is supposed to have lots of protein." I parted the bread and pointed the tuna salad contents in his direction, as if the abundant protein molecules would be visible, dancing around the sandwich innards. "I was talking to a guy at the gym who said that eating well and getting sufficient sleep are at least as important in building muscle as are the actual exercises."

Jonathan dangled his spoon over the top of his soup bowl. "A guy at the gym? What guy at the gym?"

"Oh, is somebody jealous?"

"Just curious."

"He's a phys ed major." I paused and took another healthy bite of the sandwich. "So he's learning the theory, as well as keeping in shape."

"Uh huh. And you're just interested in the theory." Jonathan blew gently across the surface of his spoon but then lowered it, letting the soup dribble back into the bowl.

"Don't fret, dear. Between my courses, my comrades, and my concubine, I have no time for those kinds of extracurricular activities." I began munching aggressively through the second half of my sandwich. "How was your morning? Did you have a good time with Martin? Or were you cavorting with Søren? Or Michel? I'm the one who should be jealous."

He stirred his spoon distractedly around his soup bowl, yet to take in a single mouthful. "I'm not sure I'm on the right track."

What's the crisis today? I waited. He was far away. "Hello, Jonathan. Come in, please."

"Huh? Oh, sorry. You don't want to hear about it."

"Yeah, that's why I asked about your morning, because I don't want to hear about it. Tell me."

He looked up, brow deeply furrowed. He'd said that he liked my dimples. I loved his furrows. I touched my fingers to my lips and then placed them gently between his eyebrows. Two girls at the next table giggled.

"Okay. You asked. I'm trying to think up a novel approach to tackling the age-old question of what it means 'to be.' Reams asking how we are aware that we exist have been written. What's the role that our own perceptions play, and what is the role that social conventions play?" He balanced his spoon on its tip and slowly twirled it, staring at it intently as he continued. "I'm trying to stake out new territory, focusing on the relation of the past and the future to the present. How do our personal histories and, intriguingly, our memory of those histories play conscious and unconscious roles in me knowing that I am this confused philosopher-in-waiting"—he lifted his spoon and started wagging it at me—"and knowing that you are an adorable, hot, political activist. You still with me?"

"I like that you think of me as hot. I understood that part. Go on."

Jonathan rolled his eyes. "Then there's the future. We are doing what we are doing, like eating lunch and slogging our brains out at this university, because we have some sense that this present moment is in preparation for a future moment." He laid his spoon beside his untouched bowl and lifted his hands off the table, palms up, moving them up and down in sharp jerks. He continued. "A future that, of course, is totally unknowable and may not even exist, at least for us. We may die in two minutes, poisoned by a tuna sandwich and a bowl of vegetable soup."

"So, your holy grail is to come up with a way of describing how we know we exist in this present moment, as influenced by our perceptions of what the past was and what the future may be." I crossed my arms and smiled with the self-confidence of someone who thought he knew what he was talking about. Jonathan looked at me but said nothing. I ventured on. "The nature of existence is your holy grail, but how does it relate to the three wise men?" I asked.

"You're confusing your religious imagery there, aren't you?" he teased.

"Picky, picky."

He placed his elbows on the table and rested his chin on his clasped fists. "Kierkegaard, Heidegger, and Foucault were all struggling with similar issues. Well, maybe not in the same terms as I am." He scanned the table, reached over, picked up the salt and peppershakers and the napkin holder, and lined them up, side by side. He placed his index finger on top of the saltshaker. "Kierkegaard was wracked by angst about understanding human existence." He tapped the saltshaker, knocking it over and littering the table with fine white pebbles. He grabbed hold of the peppershaker and squeezed it tightly. "Heidegger considered what is it 'to be' the quintessential philosophical and human question. And Foucault ..." Jonathan started pulling napkin after napkin out of the dispenser, scattering them across the table. "Foucault understood existence as having necessary social and political realities and reflected this in his writings and in his life."

He gazed at the cluttered table, took one more napkin, leaned back in his chair, and draped it over his face. His breath billowed the white face-covering into sporadic pulses as he said, "I've probably bitten off far more than I can chew. Furthermore, I'm supposed to be studying their thoughts and their writings, but I keep getting distracted by their lives."

"Something in particular about their lives?" I asked the white shroud, unable to help smiling, glad that he couldn't see what might be misinterpreted as my bemusement over his befuddlement.

"I wish it were that specific. There's Kierkegaard's battles with the church, Heidegger's relations with the Nazis, Foucault's activism." He yanked the napkin from his face and sat up. "I'm trying to find some kind of motif that I can use, but any that I've come up with so far feel forced. The department is giving me grief for not having submitted a comprehensive outline to them yet." He rolled the napkin into a tiny ball and dropped it in his soup bowl.

I thought for a moment. "You're looking at how these guys influenced and were influenced by the changes occurring in their societies. Right?" He frowned. I hazarded a step further, my previous confidence slipping precipitously. "What about looking at them as outsiders? Using their writings to battle against the establishments of their day?"

He shook his head dismissively and said, "Sorry, but that's your agenda, not mine. Anyway, it's not appropriate here. There's too much complexity in their relationships with the establishments of their particular day."

I hesitated. "Um. Then do you think that Carolyn perhaps had a point?"

"Who?"

"My sister. Remember dinner at Mom and Dad's? Before everything fell apart, you and she were talking about your dissertation. She said something about ... what was it? ... difficulty comparing across cultures or different political periods."

His eyebrows morphed from furrows to arches lifting halfway up his forehead. His pupils beaded into my skull. "My God, you're not serious. No offense, but she didn't have the bloodiest idea what she was talking about. If we can't compare thought across cultures and historical periods, why do we read Plato or Augustine or Descartes or Sontag?" His voice was rising. "We might as well blow up all the universities and then drown ourselves in the lake."

The girls next door looked over nervously.

"Okay, calm down. You're right. I'm sure that sometimes she doesn't believe what she says. She just likes to argue and hear herself talk."

He pushed his chair out. "I'm late for a tutorial. I'll see you at home tonight."

I sat for a long moment, picked up both our trays, and headed toward the exit.

Chapter 10 ─────────────────────

Jonathan was a theoretician. I was a strategist. Our combined and complementary skill sets should have vaporized the idea within minutes of it surfacing over supper at the kitchen table, but judgment was clouded by the regret we both felt about the lunch conversation.

"I can't imagine fitting everyone in here," I said, thinking of the modest seating capacity of our apartment. We had managed a standup party of tons of our friends, but a sit-down Christmas dinner for both our families? The logistics boggled the imagination.

Jonathan wasn't thinking about practicalities. In his big-picture mode, he was playing with the concept. "We've got to do it, sooner or later. Well, that's not entirely true. We could never introduce them to each other and probably live happily ever after—more happily ever after. But there's something inauthentic about that."

"Your integrity would be very tiresome if I didn't love you so much. Oh yeah, that's one of the reasons I do love you." I blew a kiss in his direction.

He slapped his cheek as my kiss hit target. "Takes one to know one," he said, winking.

I looked forward to getting past this fragile stage of rebuilding confidence. I preferred mutual playful insults made with impunity.

"Here's a thought. What if we make it a potluck? And a buffet?" I was sticking with the pragmatics.

"That was two thoughts," Jonathan said smiling.

"Which is two hundred percent more than you have offered," I said, reciprocating his smile.

I got up and started clearing our plates off the table.

As I passed by his chair, Jonathan slapped my ass, delivered with a touch more force than a love tap would warrant. "Let's thrash out the advisability a bit more before getting into the viability," he said. "I think that our parents are mature enough to be respectful of each other. I don't see them ever being buddy-buddy, but they could probably coexist in the same room for a few hours."

I placed the plates in the sink, turned around, and leaned against the counter. "Is that a classist assumption?" I asked. "Why is it that you don't think they could become good friends?"

Jonathan hesitated. "Maybe I'm underestimating them. I'm just thinking that they have rather different interests. I'm quite sure they wouldn't agree on much politically."

"Okay, you may be right there. I thought that you were referring to the economic differences."

Jonathan put his wine glass down, squinted at me, and asked in a quiet voice, "Do you think that I care about that?"

"No, I know that you don't care about money. Look at how we live," I said lifting up a yellow melmac saucer from our daily dishware. "I guess I thought that you were thinking that my parents might be intimidated by your family's wealth."

Jonathan laughed. "It stretches the imagination to envisage any circumstances in which your parents would be intimidated."

"Your parents are not exactly shrinking violets either," I said, sitting back down in my chair.

"You're right there. Shall I open another bottle of wine?" Jonathan asked, already up and heading toward the counter.

"Sure." I sipped the residue in my glass and watched his back as he reached up to grab another bottle from our makeshift wine rack on top of the cupboard. I liked tall men. Not too tall. Jonathan tall. "I've got a proposal for you," I suggested. "How about we switch parents?"

"You're going to have to explain that one," he said, filling up my glass.

"Well, at least mothers. I want to keep Dad as my dad, but I think that I'd like to have Margaret as my mother. I can picture having such fun with her, going to the symphony, museums, spending hours wandering around MoMA."

"You and your New York fantasies." He shook his head as he sat back down and topped up his glass. "If we're trading progenitors, I take first dibs on your father. Can you imagine me having the kind of conversation about philosophy with my father as I had with Lawrence? Besides, you and Father have a common interest in Chilean politics. You'd make a good pair."

I guffawed. "Okay, let's call a truce on the parent swapping and get back to the question at hand. I've got an early class, and I'd really like us to make a decision about this gathering of the clans before we go to bed tonight. I think that we can agree that we can risk bringing our parents into the same room together. But—and this is a major 'but'—what are the odds of our pulling it off with our siblings?"

"Well, Jeremy's no problem."

I winced. Jonathan noticed and paused. "What was that about?"

"What?"

"Your little tick just then."

"Nothing." *Diversion, quick.* "I was just trying to visualize the first meeting between Jeremy and Carolyn."

"Good point. Now that's a dynamic duo," he said. "Then there's the still undiscovered Patricia and Robert. I'm really looking forward to that."

"Maybe we can schedule our dinner when they've got a previous commitment," I offered. "Would that look too suspicious?"

"Let's let the chips fall where they may," Jonathan said with finality. We both sipped our wines. "So, I guess we've decided that we're going to do this?"

I clicked his glass with mine. "Onward and upward."

"What a wonderful idea." The words were affirming, but the inflection lacked conviction. "I've always enjoyed novelty," Mom replied in response to our unorthodox proposal for Christmas dinner. I tried to imagine what facial gestures she was making to Dad as she said her reassuring comments into the phone receiver. "Jonathan's parents will probably have reservations. I suspect they have quite formal traditions in their household."

"Actually, they've already agreed," I replied, hesitating. I knew that Mom would be slighted that we hadn't checked with her and Dad first. "Margaret called Jonathan on another matter last night just after he and I had come up with the idea," I hastened to add. "So he asked her then. Their agreement is contingent on Walter going along. He's out of the country on business and won't be back for another few days. We might run into resistance from him." I had to give Mom something.

I stared at the sheet of paper in front of me on the kitchen table. There were two columns, one with the names of each member of the

Fischer family and the other listing the Comptons. I took my pencil and put a big check mark beside Isabel and Lawrence. I looked guiltily over at the check marks already beside Margaret and Walter.

"Have you spoken to Patricia yet?" Mom asked.

"No. I was sort of hoping that you would break the ice for me."

"You know that I don't like getting in the middle of your arguments with your sister."

"I don't have any problem with Patricia," I lied. "She's the one who has the problem with me." I doodled a skull and crossbones beside Patricia's name.

"Whatever. You're both adults, so I think that you should make the call." She was making me pay for having disadvantaged her in the first Isabel-Margaret competition.

"All right, I'll call her. What about Carolyn? Would you be willing to talk to her and soften her up to the idea?"

"Just a minute. Carolyn," she yelled, not making any effort to shield my eardrums. "Your brother wants to talk to you." I inherited my stubborn streak from Mom.

I reached behind my head and switched the phone from one hand to the other. The cord from the wall mount was stretched almost taut. It reached my other ear just as I heard Carolyn's voice calling out faintly, "What about?"

"He'll tell you," Mom shouted, again at an unnecessarily elevated decibel level.

"She's coming." The Waterloo receiver was dropped on the vestibule stand. Carolyn's footsteps sauntered down the stairs. No hurry. Likely, her head was in a book as she walked.

"What do you want? I'm busy."

"What are you reading?"

"Why?"

"I'm just curious."

"You phone me from Toronto to ask what I'm reading? Get real."

I took a deep breath. I penciled an up arrow followed by a question mark beside her name. "I do have something to ask you, but I am genuinely curious about what you're reading these days. I'll show you mine if you show me yours."

"Don't gross me out, Tom. You tell me first. What great work of literature have you just discovered that I likely have read three times already?"

"*The Cartagena Manifesto*. I bet I stump you on that," I said confidently.

"Bolívar's 1814 declaration to the Columbians."

"Damn. How did you know that?"

"Dear woefully undereducated brother of mine, anyone who has even a passing knowledge of Latin American history knows about *The Cartagena Manifesto*." I changed the up arrow to a down arrow as Carolyn continued. "I wrote a series of articles for the school paper on military dictatorships in Latin America and the duplicity of American intervention in the region."

"That sounds like pretty impressive material for a high school newspaper. Don't they usually just cover football, glee club, and prom night?"

"Precisely. That's why the goddamn faculty advisor censored every one of my contributions." I could picture her shaking her clenched fist. "Tell me again what the subject is of your thesis?"

"You know."

"U of T may consider itself Canadian Ivy League, but if a fourth-year history student doing his thesis on Simón Bolívar is just now discovering *The Cartagena Manifesto,* the school's accreditation should be yanked."

"I'm not just now discovering it," I blurted defensively. "I just didn't think that you would know about it. And, anyway, it was 1812, and Columbia wasn't called Columbia yet. It was New Granada. So there." I tried sketching an approximation of South America at the bottom of the page. Neither geography nor art were my strong suits.

"*Fear and Trembling.*" Carolyn would never acknowledge having made a mistake. "I bet I stump you on that," she said, parodying my misplaced self-confidence of a moment ago.

"Kierkegaard."

"Well, you had better know that, or else you and the professor don't communicate other than between the sheets."

"Don't gross me out, Carolyn." My turn for parody. "So, you're mobilizing for the next encounter with Jonathan. Good. I'll give you a timeline. Three weeks from now. Christmas Day. Our place."

"Come again?"

I started writing a series of question marks beside her name. "Jonathan and I are inviting both our families to have Christmas dinner here at our apartment."

"I love it!"

"Pardon me?" The pencil flipped out of my fingers and rolled off the table onto the floor.

"You're telling me that you and the professor are planning to assemble the Squire and Wife of Bath, twin queer boy number two, and our whole dysfunctional family in one place at the same time, and Christmas Day at that! This is too good to be true." She started laughing directly into the phone. I moved the receiver a little distance from my ear. Her enthusiasm was more disquieting than the resistance I had anticipated.

I heard Mom in the background yell, "Carolyn, don't use that word."

"What word, Ma—*Christmas* or *dysfunctional*?"

"Jeremy is not gay," I interjected, hoping to preclude a further diversion in the conversation, which was already starting to run up a serious long-distance charge.

"They're twins, aren't they?"

"Just shows how much you know. Not all twins share the same sexual orientation."

"This I've got to see. Count me in. See you." Click.

"Looks like you have an early Christmas card, Tom." Althena studied the envelope with an archivist's eye, lightly fingering the stamp, squinting at the decal in the opposite corner, and examining the return address on the back. Within a few weeks of our having moved in, I gave up resenting her intrusiveness. She was naturally and innocently inquisitive. It didn't occur to her that people might take umbrage at the invasion of their privacy. "Who are R. and P. Jackson?"

I snatched the envelope. I usually waited patiently for her to hand me our mail after she had finished the inspection. Her question so startled me that I forgot my manners.

"Um. That's my sister."

"She's married? I thought she was younger than you."

I was staring at the envelope. I recognized Patricia's formal teacher penmanship. There was a touch of ornate calligraphy to it that would have been attractive were it slanting fluidly in one direction or the other. Patricia's letters were unwaveringly vertical. Technically, one could say that she had followed Dad into education. But whereas Dad was the kind of teacher who prodded students to think for themselves, who wasn't afraid to admit his own fallibility, and who was idolized by his charges, Patricia was the type who insisted that there was no way but her way in the classroom. She inspired fear, not respect. I thought of the rigidity of her writing style as a window into her soul.

"Okay, you're not getting away without telling me what's going on."

We were squeezed uncomfortably close together in the cluttered front vestibule. An old oak table jutted out into the passageway and was the catchall for advertising flyers, newspapers, and magazines that Althena thought might interest others in the house, though none of us ever picked any up. Each time we came home, we had to excavate through the paraphernalia on the table to see if we had any mail, unless Althena was in the vestibule, already examining what had arrived for us.

The entrance door to Althena and Ulrich's apartment was open, as it was at all hours of day or night, and through it she now dragged me, still transfixed by the letter carrier's delivery.

"How is it that she got married before you did?" Althena paused and then laughed. "Oh, what a silly question. It's sweet that she has sent you a Christmas card. You told me that she was such a voracious reader that I had the impression that she wasn't inclined to such social graces. Is that why you seem to have gone catatonic? You're stunned that she's sent you a card?"

Althena sat on the sofa, and I plopped down in one of the overstuffed living room chairs opposite. I absentmindedly began playing with loose strands of the fraying upholstery on the arms. Why was Patricia sending me a Christmas card? We didn't phone each other and generally avoided each other at family gatherings.

"I would have thought you would be delighted. It's such a cordial custom. Of course, when we were children, we couldn't afford to buy the cards. Mother used to have us make all the family cards to send out. Much more personal. She even had a system for creating handmade envelopes. The Royal Mail was not too keen on that. Sometimes the envelopes came apart, and then the sorters or the carriers would have to carefully reconstruct them. Service here in Canada is not what it was in England, at least as I remember it. Well, aren't you going to open it, Tom? Tom?"

I looked up, startled to see Althena sitting across from me. "Oh, sorry. I am just a little surprised. Patricia and I don't communicate much." I tapped the envelope nervously against my knee.

Althena tilted her head and squinted me. "You told me that she and Jonathan got into a big to-do about his dissertation when you went up to your parents the other weekend."

"Huh? No, that was my other sister, Carolyn. She and I get along fine. Well, she can be a bit of a pain, but at least we're on speaking terms." I waved the envelope in the air. "The card here is from my older sister Patricia. She's married to a fellow named Robert Jackson."

"Oh, I was confused!" Althena laughed. She sat back and crossed her legs. "I don't think that you've mentioned them before. I thought it was just you and, um, Carolyn, in the family. Why don't you talk with Patricia? What's the history there?"

I rolled my eyes. "Do you have five hours?"

Althena sat up straight, resting her elbows on her knees. "Ulrich's due home soon, but he can open a can of soup if he's hungry. I want to know what's between you and Patricia. Do you want to stretch out on the sofa here?"

"No, I'm fine. I can't afford your rates."

"Bollocks. Talk, for heaven's sake. Or at least open the bloody card."

I slipped my index finger under the back flap, gingerly and nervously pried it loose, and pulled the card out. An old master's takeoff of a crèche scene adorned the front, with the header *A Blessed Christmas Greeting*. Hallmark traditional. Inside, the inscription read *May the joys of our Saviour's birth fill your home at this Christmas time*. At the bottom, in black fountain pen ink, Patricia had written, again in her almost calligraphic script, *Robert and I appreciate the invitation. Yours, Patricia.*

I sat staring at it.

"Well? What did she say?"

"I don't know." I shook the card, as if that would extract some greater clarity.

"Steady on, old chap. Let me see it." Althena bounded across the room and tore the card out of my hand. She stepped on the envelope as she walked back to the sofa, engrossed in reading the message.

"That seems pleasant enough," she observed.

"Yeah, but it doesn't say if they are coming or not."

"Coming for what?"

Jonathan and I had succeeded so far in avoiding any comment about our Christmas dinner plans in the presence of Althena and Ulrich. Though we had grown to like them very much, we thought that we would have our hands full with the diplomatic challenges of the first meeting of our families, without having to entertain the two of them as well. As a childless couple, and with no family in Canada that they had ever mentioned, we suspected that they would be alone on Christmas Day. The precedent had been established that they come to our parties. It was an unresolved dilemma in our minds.

A burst of cold wind sent dust bunnies scattering across the living room floor. "Hello, you two. Having a pleasant tête-à-tête?" Ulrich trampled into the room, leaving a trail of melting snow with each footstep, and threw his coat onto the sofa beside Althena. Apparently, the hall tree required too much manipulation to hang it there.

"Hello, Ulrich," I said, leaping to my feet. "Is it that late already? Jonathan will be home soon, and I promised him a decent dinner tonight. He's been slaving so hard on the dissertation. Thanks for the chat, Althena. Have a good evening."

I rushed out their door and bounded up the stairs. Halfway up, I remembered that Althena was still holding Patricia's card.

Chapter 11 —————————

Margaret and Walter were the first to arrive and, apparently they were none too happy about it. I knew that they preferred to make an entrance. I had heard Jonathan tell them on the phone the day before to come in the never-locked front door and up the stairs. Instead, they stood on the veranda ringing the doorbell next to the almost indecipherable *Second Floor* label. The doorbell hadn't worked for years.

"Is someone knocking downstairs?" I called into the living room. My head was ensconced inside the oven. I was a firm believer in basting a turkey frequently during the final hours of cooking. I had to do it surreptitiously. Jonathan had already objected twice, maintaining that if the oven door were repeatedly opened, heat would be lost, and it would take forever to cook the bird.

"What?" he replied distractedly.

I took off the oven mitts and poked my head around the kitchen threshold. I was sweating, as much from nervousness as from the 350-degree oven interior. Jonathan was seated on the sofa, feet up on the hassock, deep into the December issue of the *Atlantic Monthly*. He lifted his head and noticed me. We simultaneously heard Althena's voice in the stairwell.

"We are enjoying having them with us so very much. They are such a delightful pair." Jonathan and I both strained to hear what response would be made by whomever she was escorting upstairs. There was only silence, not likely a good sign. I cocked my head toward the door. He nodded, acknowledging that receiving the guests fell into his column of our division of labour. I ducked back into the kitchen.

"Jonathan, look who I found shivering on the veranda. Some son you are. You should have told your parents just to come in."

"Thank you, Althena. That was negligent of me." I noted his generosity. He clearly believed there was no benefit in squabbling with his parents before they were even in the apartment. "Hello, Mother. Hello, Father. Please come in."

"Do you and Tom need anything else for your dinner? You know how well supplied our kitchen downstairs is." Althena laughed at her own joke.

"No, I think we have everything under control. Thank you," Jonathan replied, with a touch more formality than usually characterized his interactions with her.

"Well, we'll be downstairs if you change your mind." The unmasked desire in her voice was painful. Jonathan closed our door.

"So this is your palace? It's larger than I thought it would be." Margaret sounded enthusiastic. "Oh, are we the first to arrive?" she said, less enthusiastically.

"Here, let me take your coats. This snow might be slowing Tom's family. They're driving in from Waterloo, of course." There was silence when Jonathan abandoned them to take their coats into our bedroom.

I couldn't hide out in the kitchen any longer. As I came into the living room, Margaret and Walter were standing just inside the apartment door, looking awkward in semiformal dinner wear, snow-dappled galoshes still on their feet. Margaret's hands were by her sides, a small beaded purse in the right. Her left hand gripped the cabled cord of a blue velvet bag that I presumed held a pair of shoes. Walter was looking at his wife, his face telegraphing the desperate message, *How soon can we leave?* A bottle of wine lay at his feet, as well as a brown paper bag, out of which protruded the toe of a black patent leather shoe.

I dragged over one of the dining room chairs. "Please, Margaret, have a seat so you can take off your boots." Kneeling on the floor, I said, "Let me help you. I must teach Jonathan some manners. He shouldn't have left you standing here."

"That's quite all right," she replied as she perched herself on the edge of the chair. Her voice was frostier than our uninsulated windows. I bit my tongue. Was my faux pas the offer to grasp my mother-in-law's stockinged leg to aid in boot removal or casting aspersions on the adequacy of the etiquette schooling of her son? Impropriety or presumptuousness? Both capital offenses.

"Heh, boy, think fast!"

Reentering the living room, Jonathan had to dive to catch the wine bottle that Walter picked up and tossed in his direction.

"Nicely done," Walter congratulated, as Jonathan clumsily rose from the floor, bottle intact. "Mmm. Smells good in here. Turkey on Christmas. What a surprise."

"I'm nursing the bird," I said to Walter. Turning to Margaret, I added, "And Jonathan made the dressing, following your recipe exactly. I'm hopeful that everything will turn out well."

"If not, we can order pizza. Now, that would be a holiday novelty," Walter laughed. "Any chance of getting a drink? I don't suppose you've got any single malts."

"Sorry, Father, we don't have the range of options that you do at home. Is Johnny Walker okay?"

"Red or Black?"

"Red."

"Oh. Well, I guess that will have to do. That's what I drink with pizza anyway."

"Walter. You promised that you would behave," Margaret reprimanded. I wondered how much preparatory conversation they had had about tonight.

"Yeah, yeah. So how about a grand tour?"

"I'll just excuse myself, if you don't mind, and get back to my work in the kitchen." Everything was ready except that which could only be done at the last minute.

"Well, this is obviously the living room and will serve as our dining room tonight as well. Down this hallway are the two bedrooms, one of which we use as our joint study." I overheard Jonathan's nervous explanations. His voice became muffled as they moved further into the apartment, away from the kitchen.

One bedroom, one bed.

"You boys certainly do have quite a few books," Margaret was commenting as I emerged back into the living room. Our attempt to sequester our library in the study had been unsuccessful. There were too many books. We had had to devise makeshift shelving in other rooms for the overflow. "How can you find what you need?" she asked Jonathan.

"He's done a great job of organizing them, Margaret," I said. "First by subject, then by author."

"You're giving me too much credit, Tom. But yes, Mother, at least the different subject areas are grouped in the same place. For instance, those piles on the floor just to your left are all art books, including your old ones."

"Mine?"

"The ones from the attic that you let me take when I first moved out, years ago. Remember?"

Margaret rose from the couch as gracefully as our dilapidated sofa would allow and moved to the piles Jonathan had indicated. She stooped over for a moment and then turned to Walter. "Here, hold my wine, dear." Unencumbered, she gathered her skirt in one hand, steadied herself on the couch with the other, and knelt down on the floor. Jonathan and I leapt up and each went for an arm to support her. "I'm fine, boys. Let me go. I want to look at these." We backed up a step. Her fingers moved along the several piles, touching one book after the other. She pulled out the old Faber and Faber volume, *History of Italian Art.* The disintegrating spine was exposed; Jonathan had discarded the dust jacket, which was torn during our move. Margaret ran her hand over the surface of the cover and then opened it. She turned a few pages, stopped, and read something handwritten on the title page. She closed the book, gently placed it on the floor beside her, and returned to her scrutiny of the piles.

"Jonathan, can I have another drink? I'd help myself but I'm trapped ..." Walter held up Margaret's wine glass in one hand, pointing to it with his other in a parody of a model demonstrating glassware at a department store counter or on a TV commercial.

"Oh sure, Father." Jonathan retrieved the lesser quality scotch and topped up Walter's tumbler. I hovered behind Margaret. She had extracted another worn volume, Friedlaender's *Carravagio Studies.* She paged through it, pausing frequently to look at the reproductions. She placed it on the floor with the other and steadied herself as she moved to stand up. I took her arm and helped. She accepted without objection.

Seated again on the sofa, she said quietly, "Son, I would like to borrow those two back if you don't mind." Jonathan made no response, transfixed by the sight of Margaret's moist eyes.

"Jonathan," I said, a bit abruptly.

"Huh? Oh, certainly, Mother."

I opened our apartment door after I heard a polite, firm knock. Patricia, unsmiling, stood on the landing, feet planted stoically about six inches apart, hands clasped firmly around a dark brown leatherette purse that clashed with her grey three-quarter-length wool coat. *Why couldn't the others have been first? Any of the others.*

"Hello, Tom," Patricia greeted me quite matter-of-factly, as if this were an everyday encounter.

A step behind her, Robert stood silently. He was wearing what looked to be a high school athletic jacket. It fit like a glove, highlighting his broad shoulders and powerful chest. He flashed his bright trademark smile at me over Patricia's shoulder. I had forgotten how easy on the eye he was.

"Patricia and Robert. I'm so glad that you could make it. We're so glad. Come in."

"We'll just take our boots off out here in the hall," Patricia said. She put her hand out to her side. Robert's arm was immediately positioned under it to provide my sister stability while she perched on one leg to slip off the first overshoe. "It's okay to leave them here, I suppose. It's safe?" she asked.

"How was the driving?" I inquired, ignoring her condescension. "Mom and Dad haven't arrived yet, and we were getting a bit concerned."

Robert smiled and replied, "No problem. I got a four-wheel drive this year. Terrific traction."

I smiled back. "Come in." I stepped aside, and they strode in. Jonathan approached the doorway and then had to backtrack to make room. I closed the door and cupped my hands on Robert's biceps to maneuver behind his back so that I could get beside Jonathan. "Patricia and Robert, I'd like you to meet Jonathan. Darling, this is my sister Patricia and her husband, Robert."

"Welcome to our home," Jonathan said.

"Thank you. We're so pleased to meet you." Robert and Jonathan shook hands. "We've heard so much ..." Robert hesitated and shot a quick look at his wife. Patricia locked eyes with me and ignored Jonathan.

"Let me take your coats," Jonathan offered. "I'll put them on the bed. They didn't build these old homes with the expectation of needing a hall closet on the second floor."

Patricia turned her back to Robert, whose hands immediately moved to the shoulders of her coat to help her out of it. He handed hers to Jonathan and then removed his own. Jonathan headed away with them.

Walter and Margaret had been sitting quietly on the sofa observing these introductions. Sporting a mischievous smile, Walter stood and approached Patricia and Robert. "Well, hello there. I'm Walter, Jonathan's dad." He started pumping Robert's hand and said, "I think you used to be quite the university football player, didn't you? The Golden Hawks, wasn't it? You got to the Vanier Cup a few years back, 1972 or '73. Too bad you didn't win. University of Alberta had a powerful team that season."

Robert's eyes bulged. "My goodness, how did you know that? It was 1972."

How the hell does Walter know that?

Jonathan returned to the living room. I caught his eye and discretely shrugged my shoulders to signal that I didn't know what was going on.

"Oh, I'm a big football nut. And an alumni of U of A. Went there many, many moons ago. That's where I bagged that little chickie," Walter laughed, cocking his head toward Margaret. "I catch as many university matches as possible. Tons of energy on the field. I like watching up-and-coming talent. I was at Varsity Stadium when you played in the Vanier Cup. Bloody cold day, if I remember correctly."

"It was a hard-fought game and certainly was cold. Started snowing in the second quarter. Mighty difficult to get a good grip on the ball. I should have been able to complete more passes, but our guys just couldn't seem to hold on to it. Slipped right through their hands." Robert was very excited, like a kid talking about the circus with the ringmaster.

"Our Golden Bears managed. We beat you, something like 20 to 7," Walter said, grinning broadly.

"Great memory," Robert enthused. Patricia nudged her husband, not inconspicuously enough. All of us noticed. "Oh, may I introduce my wife. Patricia."

"Well, hello, dearie. Nice to meet you. You must be very proud of your husband. He was quite the star. Great style."

"Yes, well, that was a few years ago." Patricia's jaw muscles were so taut the words sounded frozen.

Walter turned back to Robert, winked, and said, laughing, "Maybe, but you never lose those kinds of moves. Speaking of which, do you two have any little footballers running around?"

"Walter! Please. Hello, I am Margaret." Margaret had joined her husband and extended her hand to Patricia.

"Hello, nice to meet you," Patricia replied, quietly shaking Margaret's hand.

"Robert and Patricia, can I get you a glass of wine?" I asked. "We have white and red open."

"We'll both take ginger ale, please, if you have it in," Patricia said.

"You folks all take a seat," Walter directed. "I'll help Tom get the drinks. I need mine replenished. Not ginger ale, though, I assure you." He laughed and marched ahead of me into the kitchen. He was opening cupboards when I caught up with him. "Did my son think to get more scotch? This bottle is almost empty."

"Yes, Walter, don't worry. There are one or two more. Our liquor cabinet is under the sink." I moved toward the oven to do another basting. "What a coincidence that you've seen Robert play."

"Coincidence be damned," he whispered. "I never saw the game. A bit of info from my intelligence sources, my dear boy. You have your 'informal networks' and I have my sources, which, I bet, are a hell of a lot more effective. They better be, for what it costs me. I know just about everything there is to know about your family. I'm not going to tolerate anything threatening my property. You get their ginger ale. I've got my scotch," he said, and left the kitchen.

I dropped the baster.

Mom, Dad, and Carolyn arrived about fifteen minutes after Patricia and Robert. I did the introductions. Conversation about the weather was the pragmatic icebreaker adopted by the two sets of parents. Carolyn shuffled off into the library. Jonathan and I slipped unobtrusively into the kitchen.

"We're going to have to start eating soon, or everything will be dried out," I complained to Jonathan. "The potatoes are mashed, the dressing is out of the turkey, and the rutabaga is cooked. I'm keeping everything warm as well as I can. You still want to do the macho bit about carving the turkey on the table?" I was standing at the stove stirring the gravy that Jonathan had made. Neither he nor I trusted my limited culinary instincts to get the proportion of flour, water, and drippings correct. He'd prepared it after I had removed the turkey from the roaster. I was making sure it didn't stick and burn. That much I could manage.

Jonathan came closer and stood behind me. He looked over my shoulder, put his hand on my right wrist, and together we moved the wooden spoon around the thick, dark brown, artery-clogging concoction. He kissed my neck. "Do you have any idea how much I love you?" he asked softly.

"Why? Because I am protecting your gravy?"

Jonathan moved to the doorway and peeked out of the kitchen. He surveyed the animated scene in the living room. "So far, so good, I'd say," he said. "I think we've got a remake of *Bob and Carol and Ted and Alice* in the offing."

"What are you talking about?"

"Come over here. Take a look." I abandoned my post at the stove with reluctance and joined him in the kitchen doorway. Dad had replaced Walter on the sofa, sitting beside Margaret as she paged through the art history books. They were in animated and sympathetic conversation, speaking too softly for us to hear. They pointed in turn to different illustrations and seemed to be analyzing them in detail.

Mom and Walter, on the other hand, were not in serious discussion. They were standing together in the front window talking and laughing. Mom looked radiant. She was quite stunning in a shimmering white blouse with an ornately ruffled collar that descended to her waist, where a wide gold belt provided the transition to a floor length dark skirt patterned in a subtle tartan of Christmas red and green. Her hair had been freshly styled with a beige tint that I had never seen her choose. It all had the desired effect. When they'd arrived, Jonathan and I were almost speechless. Margaret was respectful. Walter was effusive and had promptly corralled her at the front end of the living room. Jonathan and I watched as periodic bursts of laughter punctuated their conversation, interspersed with a frequent clinking of glasses.

Patricia and Robert sat quietly on the other side of the room, surveying their elders. Robert looked bemused. Patricia scowled. Carolyn was nowhere to be seen; I thought she was probably in the study, scouting out our library.

I fussed. "That's all well and good that they're getting along, but they're going to be hungry soon. I don't want your father to have more ammunition for giving our meal a scathing review. For God's sake, where is that brother of yours?"

"I think that we should just go ahead. He'll show up. Probably immersed in a project. I wouldn't put it past him to have completely forgotten that this is Christmas."

"Or else he's snogging one of Santa's elfettes," I grumbled, as I scurried back to the percolating gravy.

"Turn the stove off and come out into the living room," Jonathan directed. Before I had a chance to object, he was out of the room. I did as instructed.

"Carolyn, would you join us please?" Jonathan called toward the study.

"In a minute."

"Join us out here now, please," he reiterated, loudly and firmly. Carolyn, looking sullen, stepped out of the study.

"On behalf of Tom and myself, I want to welcome you all to our home." We hadn't scripted this. "A day of firsts. Our first Christmas together, and the first time you have all been able to meet each other." Jonathan's voice cracked a little.

"Almost all. I do believe that you have a brother, or is he a phantom?" Carolyn's acerbic tone could not have contrasted more with Jonathan's. I shot daggers at her.

"Quiet, dear," Dad said.

Jonathan continued, unfazed. "Dinner is ready. We'll bring it out in a moment and put everything on the table, buffet style. Then you can help yourselves. I'm sorry that we don't have a dining room table large enough so that we could have a proper sit-down affair. Before we eat though, I'd like to ask Lawrence if you would say grace."

"Pardon me?" Dad sputtered, caught off guard in the midst of sipping wine. Robert and Patricia stood.

Jonathan looked at me and said, "It's our practice to say grace before meals." I smiled. *More honoured in the breach than in the observance.* He continued, "A practice that Tom tells me was standard in your home as he grew up. So, Lawrence, if you wouldn't mind?"

"Quaint," Carolyn said, only partly under her breath.

Patricia looked in her direction and said, not under her breath, "Shut up, Carolyn, please."

Dad stood and helped Margaret as she moved to stand.

"Let us pray. For this time together, as new friends and as a new family, for the celebration of new life that this day symbolizes, for the food that we are about to eat and the hands that have prepared it, we give you thanks."

Bang. Bang. Bang. "Anybody home?" The apartment door flew open. "Christ, it was so quiet in here, I thought I had gotten the wrong house." Jeremy scanned the room of startled faces and laughed. "What? What? Has somebody died?"

I had been about to turn the handle on the bathroom door when I heard the voices inside. "Just give it a rest, Patricia. Can't you see that he's happy?"

"We came today only because you insisted," Patricia said. "You know that, right, Mother? It sickens me to see them carrying on like a normal couple." My grip tightened on the door handle. "And the rest of you, abetting this deviancy."

"You and your bloody judgmentalism."

"I'm standing up for what's right, that's all. Like you should have done years ago."

"Ahhh!"

I swung the door open just in time to see Mom pummeling the shower curtain.

They both wheeled around, facing the door, Mom's face contorted in frustration, Patricia's hands riveted by her side, fists clenched.

Patricia and I were face-to-face. "You heard that, I suppose," she said flatly.

"Ugh. Yes," I seethed. "You pompous, self-righteous little bitch."

Mom moved quickly away from her surrogate punching bag and tried to maneuver herself between the two of us. Neither Patricia nor I budged from our standoff positions.

Patricia put her arms up to block Mom's access and then, after a moment's hesitation, wrapped them around me. I froze. "I love you, Tom, and it tears me apart to see you damning yourself with your lifestyle. I'll pray for you." She dropped her arms and stiffened her back. She stared at the floor. She swallowed, sighed deeply, and then called toward the living room. "Robert, it's time for us to leave."

I moved aside, saying to her back as she passed me, "I'll get your coats from the bedroom. With pleasure."

Mom stepped backward and sat down on the edge of the tub, her head in her hands. I stepped up and put a hand awkwardly on her shoulder. "I'll send Dad in," I said and headed off to collect Patricia and Robert's coats.

Why is the bedroom door closed? I had the handle in my grip, ready to turn, when I heard noises inside. Moans. I hesitated, nonplussed, and withdrew my hand. The image of my distressed mother in the bathroom was still in my head. *Is there another family crisis behind this door?* I placed my hand gently on the knob again and turned it slowly. I pried the door open. It creaked.

Shit!

In the narrow space between the chest of drawers and the window, only a foot or so wide, Jeremy had Carolyn pinned against the wall. His stripped-off shirt hung down precariously from the waist of his pants, revealing his broad back, the muscles undulating with each thrust of his pelvis. His head, half-covered by her disheveled red hair, was buried in her neck. One of her hands clawed at his right shoulder.

"What the fuck!" I shouted as I lunged across the room. "Get the fuck off my sister, you bastard." I pounced on Jeremy, knocking the three of us off balance. We crashed against the chest, falling onto the floor.

"Ow. Oh, Jesus. Tom, get off. Get off." This was Carolyn. "Oh, Jesus. Shut the door. Quick!"

I stared past Jeremy's squirming head and into Carolyn's flaring eyes. "Tom, will you get off and shut the bloody door," she hissed.

I rolled off the two of them and propped myself up against the window ledge, my mouth gaping.

Carolyn scrambled out from under Jeremy and tore over to the doorway. She closed the door, quickly but quietly. She was fully dressed. She leaned against the door, put her ear up to the jamb, and listened. She turned and faced us, her finger to her mouth. "Shhhh."

Jeremy was stretched out on his back. He started to giggle. I clenched my fist, leaned forward, and punched him in the stomach. He doubled up, wrapping his arms around his chest. "Fuckin' hell," he groaned.

There was a knock on the door. "What's going on?" Jonathan demanded, starting to open the door. Carolyn thrust her full body weight against it from the inside. It slammed shut.

Jeremy started to chortle again and then shot a quick glance at me. He quickly rolled out of reach.

"Open the door," I said to Carolyn, catching my breath. She didn't move. "Open the bloody door. Let him in."

Brushing her hair from her face, she moved away from the door. The knob turned and the door opened. Jonathan stood in the doorway looking at the scene, aghast.

"Come in and close the door," I whispered. He didn't move. "Come in and close the door behind you. Now."

"What are you kids up to?" Dad's voice called down the hallway.

"Nothing," Carolyn and I yelled back, a conditioned response we'd used innumerable times over the course of many years a lifetime ago.

Carolyn and I looked at each other, startled by our instinctive and simultaneous response to Dad, and both burst out laughing.

Jonathan moved across the room and plopped himself down on the floor between Jeremy and me. He turned to me and said, "Well, does this answer our question of whether Jeremy and Carolyn will get along"—he paused as he glanced back and forth between the two of them—"or tear each other apart? Looks to me like a bit of both."

"More than a bit," I chuckled as I scrambled up onto my feet and picked up the coats on the bed to finish my interrupted errand. I looked around at the other three and smiled, saying, "Patricia is going to go ballistic. I love it."

Part Two

1984

Chapter 12

The phone on my desk was ringing as I returned from the cafeteria, carrying my daily tuna fish salad sandwich on sesame seed bagel. It was difficult to tell whose phone was whose. Twenty desks, overflowing with paper, reports, books, and typewriters, were crowded into SB1108, the eleventh floor research office of the Department of Economic and Social Development. Originally intended as one of many meeting rooms when the Secretariat Building was completed in 1950, it had long since been appropriated for office space as the mandate and staffing of the UN burgeoned. Long before my time, a wag had dubbed SB1108 as SAWONECE, pronounced sa-wo-neez, standing for Saving the World Nerve Centre. Though the acronym was dumb and awkward, it had stuck, and we used it with pride. Competition for prestige, political clout, and budget among the various branches of the UN was endemic, everyone believing that their unit was the most important. Only one was right—the Office of the Secretary-General.

I grabbed the receiver and pressed the flashing button. "Hello, Tom Fischer here."

"Mr. Fischer, this is Patricia Hoffstetter. I'm administrative assistant to Fernando Gutiérrez, policy advisor in the Secretary-General's office. Señor Gutiérrez would like to see you, please. Are you free to come to our office now?"

"Yes, certainly."

"Thank you."

I replaced the receiver in its cradle and snatched it back up a second later. "Hello? Hello? Ms. Hoffstetter?" Only the dial tone responded. I didn't know where Gutiérrez's office was.

What can he want? I'm a lowly minion in a sea of minions.

For the past six weeks, three of us had been poring through documents from other UN bodies, company annual reports, and academic papers, preparing a backgrounder for our department head to use in negotiations with his counterpart at the UN Centre on

75

Transnational Corporations, the UNCTC. Our boss, Dr. Mohammed Aziz was building a case for soft law criteria in a revised mandate for the UNCTC—human rights, social and environmental considerations, labour standards. Yvonne, who sat to my right, was the statistician in our little group; her head was buried in spreadsheets for hours every day. It looked mind-numbing to me. Fortunately, it didn't to her. Ichiko, the desk on my left, was collecting data on policy positions of international business and labour organizations. My role was to research cases of major conflicts involving multinationals in developing countries and then to write the composite report for Aziz. The latter task was mine only because English was my first language.

The Centre on Transnational Corporations project was far too low-level to be on Gutiérrez's radar screen, I was sure.

I grabbed a note pad and ran to the hallway. People who worked in the Secretariat Building generally approved of Oscar Neimeyer's architectural design, but there was universal frustration with the engineering of the bank of elevators. While enduring the predictable delay for one to arrive, I tried to imagine what my summons was about. I was baffled. Well-established precedent held that I shouldn't be setting foot in the S-G's thirty-eighth floor suite of offices without my departmental head. Aziz was travelling in Southeast Asia, so that was a nonstarter.

I had never been within twenty floors of the senior management offices. I had been an intern as part of my graduate work, which had allowed me to shadow a number of staff in the department, but I never got higher than the eleventh floor. An unexpected job offer at the end of the internship three years ago interrupted my graduate studies. My tortured acceptance of the offer was not welcomed in a certain Annex house in Toronto. Since becoming a regular staff with attendant security status, I had become more familiar with the building but still had never been anywhere close to heaven.

When I emerged on the thirty-eighth, the security officer at the desk frowned suspiciously.

"Mr. Gutiérrez is on the thirty-seventh," he responded indignantly when I asked for directions.

"Oh, is it okay if I take the stairwell?" I asked.

"Do you really want to set off the alarms?" I guessed that was a no. I pressed a down button. It didn't light up. I pressed it again to no avail and then turned around to see the security officer staring bemusedly. "Do you have an OSG passcard? Didn't think so. Can't use that elevator. Try the button for the one you arrived on."

As instructed, I pressed the correct down button and waited. The doors of the out-of-bounds elevator suddenly opened and out strode Pérez de Cuéllar with three others. I had never been this close. One of his aides was speaking as they moved. "The UN Special Committee against Apartheid has had the text ready for weeks and now, at the last minute, Reagan and Thatcher's people want it watered down. Maybe you could make a couple calls, Mr. Secretary-General?" They disappeared through the large wooden entrance doors that were being held open smartly by the security officer into the inner sanctum. I decided that I preferred my level of stress.

Twenty minutes after her call, I stood in front of the desk of Patricia Hoffstetter, who looked up and asked in a more pleasant voice than my security friend, "May I help you?"

"I'm Tom Fischer. You called. Sorry it took so long. Elevators."

"Mr. Fischer," she repeated to herself as she paged through a steno pad. "Oh, yes—just a moment, please." She lifted her phone, dialed, waited a moment, and then announced me. "You can go in. Second door on your left," she said pointing down a corridor.

The door was slightly ajar. I knocked lightly.

"Entre!"

I pushed the door open and walked in. "Hello, sir, I'm Tom Fischer." Gutiérrez was flipping through a sheaf of documents on his desk.

"Yes. Hello, Fischer. Sit down, please," he said without looking up. He continued scrutinizing papers. He swiveled around and, with an audible sigh, dropped the pile on the cadenza behind him. He turned back and focused on me for the first time.

"So, you know Jim MacNeill," he said.

"Excuse me?"

"Jim MacNeill has recommended you."

"I'm sorry, sir. I don't know Mr. MacNeill." I deflated a bit—all this mystery, and admittedly some excitement, for a case of mistaken identity.

"Mierda!" He retrieved the documents from behind him and flipped through the pile until he found one, which he yanked out.

"You're Tom Fischer, a doctoral student at the University of Toronto. Si?" he said rapid-fire looking at the paper in front of him. "Oh, I read too quickly. MacNeill got your name from a Dr. Stevenson, who I guess is one of your professors. That's who recommended you."

MacNeill had come to Stevenson's seminar class once a couple years ago to do a guest lecture, but I was sure that he wouldn't have remembered me.

"MacNeill has suggested you for the Commission staff. Are you interested?"

"Excuse me, sir. Commission?"

"Has no one spoken to you about this? The Commission on Environment and Development? Gro Harlem Brundtland? Are you with me?" He spoke with the irritation of someone recognizing that a subordinate had not done his or her job.

"I've heard that a commission is being set up, but no one has spoken to me about it." My heart was pounding.

"I have to tell you that I'm not keen on this new environment agenda. I've spent my career on development issues, and then along come you Northern types with your angst about a bit of pollution, and you expect the international community to forget about starving babies and focus instead on protecting your pristine landscapes. A warped set of priorities, if you ask me."

I sat silently.

"You and your Canadian cabal. This MacNeill character getting the OECD all hepped up about linking environment and economy, and then there's your guru Maurice Strong."

"Sir, with all due respect, this is not exactly new. The Stockholm Conference in 1972 started linking environment and development. There were some powerful Southern voices there, most prominently Indira Gandhi."

"Si. And who was pulling the strings in Stockholm? Your compatriot Strong."

It was hardly my place to argue with the S-G's policy advisor. I ventured hesitantly, "From what I've heard of Indira Ghandi, I don't think she was the type to be easily manipulated. There is a legitimate argument to be made that human development and ecological sustainability are inextricably linked."

"Oh, you're right up on the latest jargon, aren't you? *Ecological sustainability,*" he hissed sarcastically. "Well, I don't have much of a say here, unfortunately. I'm just the expeditor. Since you seem to be uninformed about the Commission, you probably are not aware that Brundtland has recruited MacNeill as its secretary general."

"No, I didn't know that."

"Your name rang a bell when I saw it on MacNeill's list. I got a call recently from a guy who used to bug me when I was with Foreign Affairs in Santiago. Whenever he recommended something to me, I listened to his advice and did the exact opposite. I found it was usually the right strategy. He was asking me to keep my eyes open for you. He wouldn't say how he knew you. Have you ever heard of Walter Compton?"

Walter? What was he doing sticking his nose into my business? The prospect of an amazing new job was suddenly tainted.

Chapter 13 —————————————————

We had established a pattern: I went back to Toronto one weekend a month, and Jonathan came down to New York one weekend a month. We had six days out of thirty together. It was an expensive and undesirable arrangement but the best that we could manage while we worked and lived in two different cities.

"Apartment" was an ostentatious word to describe my New York accommodation. Digs, cubbyhole, squalid roof over our heads were better matches. Wood covered three broken panes and plastic two others in the eight-paned street level entrance door. The doorbell module for the six units hung precariously from the socket, hosting dust and weather residue accumulated since the Great Depression. Only half the stairway lights ever functioned. The halls were only cleaned when one of us tenants took the initiative. If there was a superintendent, no one had ever set eyes on him.

There were three locks on our apartment door, one in the door knob plus two deadbolts. It looked impressive, but I had a key for only one. I thought of replacing the locks, but I didn't want to give Jonathan more reasons to doubt the temporary nature of my expatriate status.

The apartment door opened only two-thirds of the way. Behind the door, the foot of the bed impeded a wider swing. The kitchen counter protruded immediately in front of anyone entering. Beside the small arborite table, two plastic chairs provided seating. A formerly white sheet served as a curtain, covering the window that looked out onto the airshaft at the rear of the building. On top of the half-sized fridge, a two-burner hotplate sat. Only one of those prestigious appliances could be plugged into the socket at a time. I had gone through many fuses before discovering the trick. We never ate in on Jonathan's weekends in New York.

Its one redeeming feature was location: it was only a fifteen-minute walk from work. Prosperous New Yorkers or diplomats on expense accounts occupied most apartments close to the UN. Our third-floor walk-up on Lexington, near Thirty-First, was a rare find. When I had arrived in New York as a UN intern, one of the other interns had just found the place and offered to share it with me, half the space for half the rent. Once I graduated from internship to employment, I was too busy to look for anything better. The original intern roommate had left. Since I was now earning a salary, I could afford to carry the apartment on my own, which allowed room for Jonathan on his visits. And a move to a less squalid, more permanent apartment would have suggested that I was planning to stay in New York, an impression I didn't want to give.

When we settled on our pattern of alternating weekends between Toronto and New York, Jonathan insisted that we buy a new New York mattress, our one extravagance.

The attractions New York held for Jonathan, in addition, presumably, to being with me, included the Museum of Modern Art, Central Park, the Metropolitan Museum, Columbia University, Lincoln Center, the occasional Broadway musical, Carnegie Hall, Macy's at Christmastime, the Guggenheim, and West Village bars. The apartment almost offset them all.

I decided to delay broaching the subject of Gutiérrez's offer to Jonathan, because I was sure it was best done in person, face-to-face.

When Jonathan's weekend to be in New York arrived, I was pumped. We had planned the trip for this particular March weekend because the Black Party, New York's contribution to the circuit of mega gay dances, was on Saturday night. I loved those blowout events. Jonathan was not a fan, but for my sake he had agreed to subject himself to the late night, jam-packed venue, ear-splitting club music, and inevitable hangover.

As a tradeoff for his agreeing to the Black Party, I had bought two tickets for the Friday night concert of the New York Philharmonic at Avery Fisher Hall. The concert and dance tickets appropriated the better part of two weeks' salary as an aspiring global civil servant.

I slipped out of the office earlier than usual, to the chagrin of Yvonne and Ichiko. The deadline for our paper for Dr. Aziz was looming, but the apartment needed cleaning before Jonathan's taxi arrived from LaGuardia. I felt a touch self-righteous that I was prioritizing my domestic responsibilities above my international ones. I had no right to feel smug. Jonathan had a catalogue of contrary examples that he had accumulated over the past few years of our relationship.

I was on my knees scrubbing the toilet when I heard the door open. "You're early," I called out.

I was drying my hands on my pants when he grabbed me and clasped his arms around my body. He brought his right hand up behind my head, looked into my eyes for a moment, and then kissed me with a prolonged intensity that would make a Harlequin reader wet. I went limp. He hugged me tighter, supporting my full body weight.

"God, I missed you," he whispered into my ear.

Regaining composure, I hugged him back in response.

"Come here," I said softly, leading him the three steps to the bed, where I welcomed him properly.

Afterwards, we fell asleep, legs and arms intertwined.

A siren woke me up. Trying not to disturb Jonathan, I extricated myself and slipped out of bed. I opened the bottle of wine I had bought at the corner liquor store on the way home from the office and poured two glasses. I sat down on the edge of the bed, shivering slightly as the early spring dusk settled in.

I gently nudged my boyfriend with my elbow, and said, "Here's a second welcome, my dear."

"Huh? Oh, thanks." He took his glass. "Here's to never being apart again," he said as we clinked.

"Pardon?"

"Just a bit of wishful thinking on my part."

"Are you getting hungry?" I said, a little too quickly.

"So did Lenny meet your exacting standards?" I asked, while waiting for my coffee to cool.

The bistro down the block from Lincoln Centre was sparsely populated at that hour. Two couples sat together at a table to our left, dressed in we-drove-in-from-New-Jersey-for-dinner-and-a-show attire. My guess was *Sunday in the Park with George.* I heard one of them make a comment about Bernadette Peters. *Bingo.* A disheveled businessman sat in the window, tie askew, reading the early edition of the *Wall Street Journal,* probably before heading back to the lonely hotel room that was home since his wife kicked him out of their Upper Eastside brownstone.

A single woman at a nearby table eyed Mr. Wall Street Journal. She shifted in her chair, trying to catch his attention, I thought.

Jonathan set down his fork after swallowing a bite of the pie à la mode that he had meticulously divided in half on the plate. "I do enjoy seeing an icon like Bernstein in the flesh. Barbara Hendricks is no slouch either. I guess I am something of a star-fucker, aren't I, and a sucker for Mahler, especially the Second Symphony. How perfect that that's what was scheduled this weekend."

I couldn't resist. "That's you, darling, my pretty little fucker sucker."

"Wash your mouth out, young man! That's no way to talk in public and to your elder and after a lovely cultural evening like this."

"Sorry. I guess I'll have to pay for that."

"In a literal sense, you already have. You've really pulled out all the stops this weekend. Did you rob a bank or get some big boost in pay?"

"Funny you should ask," I responded nonchalantly. I took a sip of coffee. I hadn't touched my share of the pie, protests from the disintegrating scoop of ice cream notwithstanding.

"Uh oh." Jonathan sat up straighter. The corners of his mouth perceptibly tightened, eliminating the relaxed expression evident when he'd relived the concert a moment ago.

He looked at me and waited. I looked back, thinking, *How do I start this?*

"It's possible that our life is about to get more complicated."

Jonathan pushed both the dessert plate and his coffee cup to the side, placed his elbows on the table, and rested his chin on his cupped fists. "Okay, hit me with the details."

I spoke rapidly, sure it was best to get the dreaded moment of disclosure over with quickly. "I've been offered a research position on the staff of what's called the Commission on Environment and Development. It's just now being set up. Former Norwegian prime minister Gro Harlem Brundtland is chairing. If it succeeds with its mandate, this could be a game-changer in international affairs, charting a path to tackling environment and development simultaneously, a North-South collaboration. That's the hope, in any case. Big picture people have been appointed as members of the Commission. It's cutting-edge stuff."

I hesitated to assess the impact. No reaction.

"It would be a huge stimulus to my career, both in the skills that I would develop and the profile I could get." I watched Jonathan. Still no response.

It was time to move on to the benefits for us that I'd itemized in advance. "I'd just be a lowly researcher, but it would pay better. I could contribute more to our Toronto rent. We could do more of the travelling we've wanted to do, for half the price. Most meetings will probably be in Europe. There's some talk about basing the office in Geneva. My travel costs would be covered, so we'd just have to pay for yours. We could spend time with Jeremy and Carolyn in London. They've been bugging us to come over."

Jonathan lifted his head. "No, you can't accept it," he said in a slow, measured tone, looking me directly in the eyes.

I gasped.

After a minute, or ten, during which Jonathan gazed noncommittally at me and my brain sped in disparate directions, he reached across the table and placed his hand on mine. "Does it really matter what I say?"

He paused, withdrew his hand, and dropped his head. "I've got to tell you, though, that this is the shits. I'm having a god-awful hard time being separated as much as we are now."

"I know."

His head jerked up. "No, you don't know." A tear rolled down his cheek. Wiping it away, he whispered, "Goddamn, what a suck I am."

I bit my tongue not to make light of his repetition.

He took a deep breath and looked up again. "I was going to surprise you this weekend with my own news. Good news, I thought."

"You've been offered tenure," I blurted out.

He scowled. I should have remembered that that would not come until much later in an academic career.

"Sorry. I wasn't thinking," I replied penitently. "What is your news?"

He stared at me, mute, making me wait.

"Althena wants to sell us the house."

"What?"

"She says that since Ulrich's death, it's too much for her. So she wants us to buy it."

The two couples had gone. Jonathan looked over at the solitary figure sitting in the window and the other one resignedly slouched at her table. "We could be a real couple, together," he said. "In our own house." He leaned back and crossed his arms. "Shit."

Do I encourage him in his fantasy or ask the hard question? I opted for honesty over fabricated empathy. He would have detected the fake at fifty paces. "That is exciting news, but how could we possibly afford it? Aren't mortgage rates now up around fifteen percent, or something like that?"

"She says that she'd give us a private mortgage at whatever interest rate we can afford. 'Damn those bloody banks. We'll screw them for change.' Quote unquote."

"Yes, I can just hear her."

"She says she's okay financially. Ulrich had a faculty life insurance policy, and she's getting his survivor pension. Plus she's continuing to do some part-time teaching."

Jonathan looked at me, seeming uncertain whether to continue. I raised my eyebrows in encouragement.

"She says that she doesn't need the money. What she needs, she says, is ... family. That's what we are. Her family." He sighed.

There was plenty we could have talked about over breakfast Saturday morning. The previous evening's conversation left a lot unresolved. But we opted to sequester ourselves and read the morning paper.

We lay down in the late afternoon and slept until almost nine that night. Fatigue was a natural byproduct of our intense professional lives and our frenetic personal schedules. We often spent much of our weekends, whether in Toronto or in New York, in bed. Sleeping.

One pronounced exception to this pattern had been the weekend the previous November, when we had been up almost twenty-four/seven for days. I had flown out from New York to San Francisco to join Jonathan and a group of his academic friends at what might best be called a Michel Foucault love-in. In the years since Jonathan's dissertation, he and Foucault had become working colleagues, for the most part separated by the Atlantic Ocean, but nonetheless in regular contact on the phone, exchanging drafts of books they were working on and occasional visits at each other's lectures. In November, Jonathan had gone out to California for a series of lectures that Michel was giving at Berkeley. I flew out from New York for the final weekend of intellectually stimulating seminars that were, for the most part, well beyond my comprehension. They were interspersed with long, riotous nights of overindulgence by the group in the SF gay scene, which definitely was within my zone of expertise. As a reprise of that fun time, Jonathan had tried to convince Michel to come to New York to join us for the Black Party weekend. Michel was tempted, but he couldn't swing it.

I knew that there was no sense in us getting to the Black Party until well after midnight. I had been warned that only trolls and the uninitiated showed up before 1 a.m. or so. I wanted to keep Jonathan in bed as long as possible to help build up our energy reserves for a long night of dancing. I proffered sexual favours as an inducement. Jonathan initially resisted, still carrying resentment about my new job news. But my well-developed skills to rouse his excitement overcame his hesitation. By the time he was ready to shower and dress, he had been satisfied. Three times, I think.

We splurged and took a taxi to the Roseland on West Fifty-Second. Walking into the cavernous dance hall, one felt crowded by ghosts of the ice skaters, roller skaters, disco dancers, concert goers, banquet attendees, political rally participants, fashion show devotees, and countless other partiers who had laughed, loved, and lost on this floor since it opened in 1922. As we arrived at about one thirty, the ghosts far outnumbered the live bodies. A few small groups of friends were dancing together, while others stood drinking, smoking, and cruising around the edges.

"This looks like fun," Jonathan said sarcastically. I had been counting on a wild night to change the mood since yesterday's coffee, pie, and disappointment.

It was the Black Party, so we had come dressed in compliance with the code. I was in black Levis with a white T-shirt and my black leather vest. I was something of a dilettante in the gay leather community. The vest was my sole investment in the uniform of the culture. At least I was more in sync than Jonathan, who didn't own any jeans—blue, black, or otherwise. He had on black dress pants and a black cotton shirt that probably made him more noticeable, in a good way, than me in my clone wear.

The crowd and our moods changed by 3:00 a.m. In the four corners of the hall, hundreds of guys strained to get a glimpse of the current top echelon of raunchy porn stars dancing on stages strategically curtained off behind massive black drapes, intended, presumably, to add to the risqué atmosphere. The dance floor was packed with two to three thousand men gyrating to pounding music. A hefty percentage of the sweating bodies looked to be full-time professional gym rats. Though I was clearly in the bantam division of the league, I discarded my T-shirt to join the bare-chesters. Jonathan didn't follow my lead but nevertheless had turned a temperament corner. The beer, the infectious euphoria, the novelty, and, I hoped, our having fun together, conspired to lift his spirits.

More than anything else, it may have been the unexpected arrival of his old boyfriend Clyde, with a coterie of friends in tow from the New York dance world, that seemed to throw Jonathan psychologically back a decade into a more carefree period of his life. I suppressed my jealousy as he laughed with the ever-expanding party, yelling over the music, grabbing one after the other, pressing his body up against theirs in the unsubtle style of the occasion. His stature, his good looks, his relatively sophisticated attire, and his reputation, as apparently circulated by Clyde, made him very popular in our sector of Roseland.

Jonathan's preoccupation with his admirers freed me to wander around the dance floor, doing a bit of flirting myself, including with a couple of guys that I had hooked up with on other occasions. It hadn't been all work and no play for me during the past months in New York.

Eight a.m. found Jonathan and me back together again, leaning up against each other on one of the tattered, seedy, stained sofas that ringed the perimeter of the lounge. We were feeling our age. The real circuit party aficionados were still hard at it on the dance floor.

"I'm done in," Jonathan mumbled, eyes closed, head resting on my shoulder.

"Okay, let's go," I responded.

We got in a taxi out front, and I said to the driver, "One Forty-Five West Forty-Sixth, please." He complained about the short fare. Jonathan, slouched back in the seat, made no comment.

When the car stopped a few minutes later, he came to. "Are we home already?"

"Well, not quite." I paid the driver, tipping generously, and opened the side door.

"Where are we?" Jonathan asked as he stumbled out of the car holding on to my arm.

"A little surprise."

"I don't want any surprise. I want my bed," he said groggily. He let me lead him up the limestone steps and through the large oak doors. The choir of St. Mary the Virgin Church had begun the 8:30 a.m. Sung Matins. I had been told that their choristers were drawn largely from the Juilliard School. The aural beauty that cascaded over us as we entered the sanctuary confirmed that probability.

We slipped into a pew near the back. Jonathan sat rigidly upright, eyes wide open, mouth slightly agape. I reached over and took his hand in mine.

We sat in silence. Ethereal voices from some distant galaxy enveloped us. Allegri's "Miserere" insinuated its plaintive harmonies into our veins. A protective gossamer descended down upon us from the organ pipes above.

Jonathan slipped down onto the kneeler. I joined him.

He laid his head on the crest of the pew in front of us. I gently massaged his neck. For about ten minutes we didn't move but just stared into each other's eyes, oblivious to the movements of the parishioners scattered throughout the church.

Chapter 14 ─────────────

"I'll take your place," Sheila cackled. "He needs somebody to keep him warm on chilly nights."

"It's June. We're in the midst of a heat wave. We only have a rickety old semi-functioning fan in our bedroom window. It's hot," I protested. "If anything, he needs someone cooling him down at night, not heating him up."

"I can do both," Sheila persisted. "First, the heating up, of course, and then the cooling down. Followed by another heating up. And another. The way he likes it. That's what I hear, in any case."

"What might be your source, perchance?"

"You know. Just the word on the street." She tilted her head slightly and lowered her eyes.

I reached across the table, patted her hand, and said, "I'm sorry, dear. I love you, but I gotta tell you, you don't do coy and demure very convincingly."

Sheila jerked up in her seat and glared at me. "Shit. Damn. Fuck. I've been practicing relentlessly in front of the mirror. I wish the Extension Department offered Emily Post etiquette courses."

"Right," I laughed. "Why don't you offer to teach it? It could be called 'Learning Etiquette by Observing the Antithesis,' taught by Emily Post's nemesis, Ms. Sheila Offrenchuk."

"You really can be quite the little bitchy queen, you know." She dipped her hand in her glass of water and spritzed me.

I lifted my glass and made motions threatening to douse her. "Truce?"

"Okay, for the moment, you bugger."

"By the way, I've always wondered. Doesn't your rather colourful command of the English language ever get you into trouble in the classroom?"

"What do I teach, my dear?"

"I don't know exactly what you teach, other than that you're on the engineering faculty."

"Ta da!" she said, thrusting her hands forward in the ringmaster's gesture. When I just squinted and looked at her, she elaborated, "Do you think that my engineering jock students care if I pepper the lectures with a little 'colourful' language? It gives me more credibility."

I smiled. "Okay. Getting back to the subject under discussion—tell me truthfully, in all seriousness, did you ever fancy Jonathan? You know, in that way?"

She crinkled her brow. "What do you mean 'in that way'? Fella, you don't do coy and demure any better than I do."

I shrugged my shoulders.

"You mean did I ever screw your boyfriend? Hmmm. Let me think. Oh yeah, I remember. Yes, we did have a torrid affair. Just after I dumped Paulo. Rebound sex. While you were gallivanting around in New York."

"I know you're lying," I chortled. "First of all, I don't *gallivant*."

"Give me a break!" she laughed.

Ignoring her, I continued, "More to the point, I know you're lying because you never got it on with Paulo, which means you never dumped Paulo, which means that you didn't need rebound sex, which means you didn't have a torrid affair with Jonathan."

"That little snitch," she sneered. "Paulo, I mean, not Jonathan. What a pity. He had such cute buns. Paulo, I mean, not Jonathan. Not that Jonathan doesn't have cute buns. Actually, come to think of it, I don't know if Jonathan has cute buns or not. I've never seen them in the flesh, so to speak."

"Ah ha! You admit it then," I declared triumphantly. "You haven't gotten it on with my boyfriend."

Sheila exhaled an exaggerated sigh. "Of course not, silly. Yuk! The very idea gives me the creeps." She wiggled, as if shaking off an invasion of crawly insects.

I frowned. "Why the creeps? I'll have you know that my boyfriend is very handsome and very good in bed. And he has cute buns. So there."

"I know all that, dunkleface. Would you have sex with Carolyn?" She hooted as she added, "Or how about Patricia?"

I screwed up my face. "Oh, don't make me sick!"

"That's the point. Jonathan is like a brother to me. I don't think of him as a man. Well, I do think of him as a man, but as a brother-type man, not a lover-type man. Okay? Clear? Can you let it go?"

"Sorry. I know how close you two are and have been since long before I arrived on the scene. I just get a little jealous sometimes. In fact, I suspect that he shares stuff with you that he doesn't with me."

She reached across the table and took hold of my hand. "You're right about that, like this whole business of you going off to Geneva. I know that you know he is upset, but I don't think you realize how deeply upset. He told me the other night that it felt like you were deserting him. Heads up. Here he comes."

Jonathan approached us, grinning broadly, and pulled up a chair beside me. With an exaggerated flourish, he plopped his briefcase down on the table, jostling our glasses in the process and splattering water onto all three of us.

"Well, somebody is in a good mood," Sheila said, addressing me while cocking her head toward Jonathan.

"How are my two favourite people in the world?" Jonathan leaned over, pecked me on the cheek, and then lifted Sheila's hand from the table and bestowed a gallant kiss on it.

Still looking at me, Sheila asked, "Do we know this person?"

"You, my dears ..." Jonathan hesitated for effect. "You, my dears, are looking at the recipient of an extraordinary, unprecedented, one might say, exemption from standard departmental protocol." He sat back, crossed his arms, and smiled.

We waited. Jonathan said nothing, just Cheshire-catted Sheila and me, back and forth, back and forth.

Sheila, short on patience as usual, shouted, "Goddamn it, Jonathan, don't be coy," whereupon she and I looked at each other and hooted in unison.

"What? What's so funny?" Jonathan asked.

"Sorry, dearie, an in-joke," Sheila said. "Never mind. Tell us. What is your news?"

No longer able to sustain the suspense, Jonathan spoke excitedly, "I've just come from Chapman's office. He's reconfigured my fall teaching schedule. I've got a mini-sabbatical. Me, an assistant professor. I pitched this idea about trying to get Foucault to come to U of T as a visiting scholar for a term next year. I played up my connections, the complimentary letter that he sent me on my dissertation, the correspondence that we've had since spending so much time with him last fall when he was lecturing at Berkeley. Chapman bought it, my idea, and has given me the fall off to negotiate with Foucault. In Paris."

"You're serious?" I said.

"He even threw in a modest travel budget. I think he's angling for a higher profile for the department. Maybe he feels underappreciated, with all the new research grants flowing into science and engineering."

"Ta da!" Sheila repeated, grabbing hold of her lapels.

Jonathan rolled his eyes. "That's right. Engineers one, philosophers zero. But just think—if we philosophers weren't around, who would you go to in an existential crisis?"

"Oh, honey," Sheila laughed. "Me in an existential crisis? Boggles the mind. And it would be my priest. Or my friends." She batted her eyes at Jonathan and then at me.

"Your priest? Really."

"My dear Jonathan. You don't know everything there is to know about me. I may act as your confessor-in-chief, but you don't reciprocate the role."

Ignoring the barb, Jonathan turned to me. "So, my dear. Looks like you won't be able to get rid of me as easily as you thought. I'm trailing you to Europe, at least for the first few months."

I wrapped my arms around him and hugged him tightly. This good news diminished my guilt in prioritizing professional advancement higher than time with my lover. Somewhat.

Chapter 15 —————————

Watching a ferry make its way across the inner harbour, gliding in amongst a myriad of sailboats, I realized that Jonathan and I had been neglecting a whole dimension of the Toronto experience. We had never gone for a picnic on Centre Island. Most of our life over the past decade had been spent essentially landlocked in the downtown area, at home, on campus, in neighbourhood restaurants. When scarce time and limited budget allowed, we ventured further afield to exhibitions and concerts, friends' places, and occasionally a bar in the Village. We might as well have been living in the middle of the Prairies, so oblivious were we to the proximity of Lake Ontario.

The view through the floor-to-ceiling windows of Walter's fifty-fifth floor office made such an insular worldview untenable. As I sat in the leather wing chair opposite his desk, sipping on the coffee his secretary had brought me, I envied him the beautiful panorama that was his to enjoy every day—every day that he was in town and at work, that is. According to Margaret's periodic phone conversations with Jonathan, Walter was travelling more than ever, leaving this view, and perhaps his wife, underappreciated.

Margaret was quite circumspect about their domestic life. Jonathan was unable to decipher whether she enjoyed the independence or regretted being alone so much of the time. She certainly had no trouble keeping busy, with her volunteer work at the art gallery and the food bank and chairing the Volunteer Committee of the Toronto Symphony. Currently, according to this week's phone conversation, she was spending a great deal of time with Walter's accountant and lawyer, setting up a philanthropic foundation. It struck me as odd that she referred to them as Walter's advisors, when it was essentially her family's money that she was seeking to donate in a more targeted manner. Presumably, she thought Walter preferred it that way.

He was now twenty minutes late, unusual for him, given his characteristic military precision. I thought it might be a strategic tardiness, intended to increase my anxiety level. His secretary had been quite specific when she called to request that I come to his office at 4:45 p.m. He was flying out somewhere in the evening. Manila, I think she said. Don't mention anything to Jonathan, she had said. She had told me, not asked me.

My coffee cup jumped off the saucer as the booming baritone six inches from my ear protested, "Oh, please, don't get up on my account." There must have been a disguised doorway somewhere. Walter hadn't come through the main entrance that I had been monitoring in tandem with my Toronto Island-view watching. "Gotcha, didn't I?" he laughed, as I dabbed at the coffee stain on my pants.

"Sorry, I didn't hear you come in. Rather clandestine of you."

"I like to keep my prey off guard. What's with the wimpy coffee? You should have told Ursula you wanted a proper afternoon cocktail. Where are your balls, boy?" He sauntered around behind his desk, collapsed into the monster high-backed swivel chair that he probably considered a throne, and immediately leaned down and yanked open a desk drawer, hauling out a half-empty bottle of Chivas and two crystal tumblers. Without asking, he poured generously and slid one across the highly polished mahogany surface toward me. I caught it just before it added further fluid to my beveraged crotch.

"Thank you." I welcomed the bracer.

"*L'chaim!*" he said, raising his glass. We both took a substantial swallow. "Nice of you to arrive early."

"Actually, I got here right on the dot. Four forty-five."

"I had said five fifteen. Not very efficient of you not to be able to tell time," he said straight-faced.

Pick your quarrels, Tom. I let this one pass.

"How's my dear friend Fernando?" he asked, raising his eyebrows.

"He sends his warm regards."

"You have to improve your lying skills, my boy. Fernando hates my guts, so he's unlikely to be blowing kisses to me through you."

"Since you seem ready to plunge right in, may I ask why you contacted him about me?"

"You got offered the job, didn't you?"

"I assume that's a rhetorical question."

"You're right. I know you got the offer. I know that you accepted, probably to Jonathan's consternation. Why he'd be upset, I don't know. Seems to me that marriages prosper if you're not together too much." I couldn't let that pass. "Married?" "You and Jonathan sleep in the same bed, I presume. You fight and make up, I presume. Except for the fact that you've got the same plumbing as each other, I don't see much difference between you two and Maggie and me. Do you?"

"I assume that's a rhetorical question," I repeated impassively.

"Good one!" Walter laughed.

"Anyway, what's it to you whether I take this job?" I asked.

"You're not as bright as I'm giving you credit for. You're not going to be much good to me if you haven't figured that out."

"Your attempts at intimidation have worn a little thin over the years, Walter," I lied. "Just answer my question."

He smiled, carefully wiped a bit of moisture off the bottom of his glass, and set it down gently on the desk. "A little quiz. You like games?"

"I'm not very partial to the ones that you play."

He leaned toward me. "Well, let's give it a go anyway. Which new Canadian corporation was I advising in 1976 when you parachuted into our lives?"

"I haven't the faintest idea."

"Strike one. Okay, let me give you an easier one. What do I do? Professionally? To earn the ton of money that buys the roast beef that you eat on the Sundays when you deign to grace us with your presence and that is going to be paying a hefty chunk of the downpayment on that roof over your head?"

"What? What about the house?" I asked flabbergasted.

"Don't get so easily diverted. Stick with the program, and answer the question. What do I do?"

"Well, you act as a financial advisor to a variety of companies. Primarily, in the resource sector."

"Very good," he applauded.

"Don't patronize me," I said trying to sound firm, not wimpish.

"But it's so easy," he said, taking another hefty gulp of his drink. "I'm getting bored. Okay, who was the CEO of that major new Canadian oil company in 1976 that you couldn't identify, who also dabbled before and after in all sorts of international affairs ... who is going to be one of your new bosses?"

"Maurice Strong."

"Like pulling teeth," Walter sighed.

"So you knew Strong back in his ... Petro-Canada days. No big deal."

"Better late than never, I guess," he said rolling his eyes. "I've kept my eye on dear Maurice over the years and some of the others on your commission."

"It's not my commission."

"I'm not too keen on what I've seen," Walter continued. "They have this global governance fetish. Want to rule the world by international fiat. Throw some sand into the gears of the market. Environmental standards and such. Pretty nefarious stuff, no?"

"Actually, no. It's long overdue that there be some kind of guiding principles that companies, particularly in the resource sector, need to observe for protecting the environment in their operations, whether they be in Canada or, let's say, Chile. Industrial operations that disregard negative environmental impacts not only do damage to ecological systems and the people dependent on them but will also ultimately hurt the companies' own long-term economic viability."

Walter studied me for a moment and then asked quietly, "You really believe all that?"

"Yes, I do."

"And that's the sort of position you will advocate in the Brundtman commission?"

"Brundtland. Brundtland. I'm just going to be a lowly researcher on the commission staff, so I won't have much chance of 'advocating,' but yes, essentially, that is the position that I will be functioning from."

"Good. Then I guess you'll be a credible spy."

"Pardon me?"

"You're going to keep me informed on the deliberations of the commission and give me a heads-up on the kinds of recommendations that they might think of proposing."

I threw my head back, laughing. "In your dreams."

Walter was not laughing. I stopped laughing.

"You see, my dear boy," he continued softly, "you're going to do as I request because I have some interesting laundry that I don't think you'd be too keen on me sharing with Jonathan. Even pictures, courtesy of my Big Apple connections. It seems you don't always go home to your apartment and knit after work. You've been an energetic boy down there. 'Down there' in multiple senses." He roared with laughter at his pun.

"What the hell are you talking about?"

Walter shook his head. "Don't play the naïve innocent with me. I couldn't care less what you do with your dick and your orifices, except"—he paused and glared at me—"except if it were to threaten my family, or if my knowledge of your extracurricular activity were to be of use to me professionally. At the moment, I have no indication of the former, but I do have a specific application for the latter."

My throat was suddenly dry. There was a touch of melted ice in my glass, but I didn't trust that I could lift the glass without my hand trembling. I didn't want to give Walter that satisfaction.

Chapter 16

Mom was tearing up, a rare occurrence. She grabbed a tissue, rubbed her eyes, and blew her nose. Straightening her back and recovering her composure, she turned away from me and faced Dad. In a voice that still wobbled, she asked, "Lawrence, tell me honestly. What have I done that my children all want to move as far as they can to get away from me?"

Dad pulled one of the dining room chairs away from the table and set it in front of her. Sitting down, he took her hands in his, tissue and all. "Don't go there, Isabel. This is modern society. There's a lot more mobility than there used to be. Families don't spend their whole lives in their home community like they used to."

"Bullocks. Look at your brother's family. Five children and they're all married, raising children, and living within half an hour of their parents. We only have three, and they're all going to live in different countries. Explain that to me."

Dad hesitated. "Well, that is true. But if you look at your sisters, their families are much more dispersed."

Mom pulled her hands away and stood up, forcing Dad to shift his chair rapidly to allow her to get by. She needed to pace. "That confirms it," she exclaimed. "It is my fault. My family is the dysfunctional side. My father abandons us as children and all hell breaks loose for generations. The sins of the father ... " she stuttered. "The sins of the father ... whatever, whatever ... however that goes. I know it's not good."

Dad sensed that further rational argument from him would not be heard. He moved back and sat in his reading chair beside the fireplace.

Mom walked around the living room coffee table half a dozen times, hands on her hips, and then abruptly halted in front of me. I had sunk into the tub chair in the bay window, hoping Dad could deal with Mom. Now I was in the direct line of fire. She stood towering over me, glaring down. I felt like a five-year-old about to be reprimanded for a schoolyard incident. My evident cowering started to dissipate her anger. Sorrow took over. The hard-set muscles around her mouth relaxed, and the glowering eyes moistened up again.

She sighed deeply. "First, you left to go to university in Toronto instead of here in Waterloo. Then, you took that position in New York. Even when you came home on weekends to be with Jonathan, we rarely saw you. I don't begrudge you that. I know the separation has been tough on the two of you. But Geneva? Who knows for how long? Jonathan must be apoplectic. Now we'll never see you." Her articulation of the pending reality reignited her resentment. "It's not fair. It's just not fair," she shouted. "What about honouring your father and your mother? That one I know. And it's a commandment. One of the bloody Ten Commandments. Dammit, Tom."

"Mom." I started a defense. "Your honeymoon. You had the travel bug too."

She ignored me. "Patricia was a stubborn child since day one. So single-minded." Mom recommenced her pacing, talking to herself as much as to Dad and me. "I wasn't surprised when she wanted to separate herself from us heathens. No, I don't mean that. She just had her own convictions, strong, strong convictions. Good for her. We raised you kids to think for yourselves. So now she's off with Robert teaching at the Bible College in Dayton. At least we can drive down there, to see the babies. She has given us grandchildren." She shot daggers at me.

I grimaced and looked over at Dad. He shrugged his shoulders.

"Carolyn. Don't get me started on her!" Pace, pace, pace. "My God. She wasn't a stubborn child. She was downright obstinate. She could have really made something of herself. Certainly not the maternal type."

Mom turned back to me. "Then she ran off to shack up with Jeremy. In blimey London."

"Mom, that's not fair. She's been working hard on her doctorate at LSE."

Dad chimed in. "I suspect that she enrolled mainly to get the student visa so she could stay with him."

"You're not helping, Dad."

"Thank you, dear. I appreciate a little support here," Mom said.

Picking up steam again, Mom looked over at me and said, accusingly, "He's probably got her knocked up by now. She's so daft-headed. Two bits she doesn't remember to put in her diaphragm or get herself on the pill. And, he doesn't strike me as a responsible type. I can just hear him in that bloody arrogant tone of his. 'Oh, we don't need to take any precautions. We're not breeding stock. The universe will see to that.' Bloody hell."

She began crying and came over to my chair and walloped my leg.

"Ow! Mom!"

"If anything happens to my baby, I'm going to hold you personally responsible. Getting mixed up with that idiot. Bringing him into our family."

"Jonathan?"

"His brother, you fool," she shouted. "In fact, you can all go to bloody hell as far as I'm concerned. Jeremy, Jonathan, and you. Bunch of selfish, elitist, bloody, bloody ..." She paused and took a deep breath. "Bloody motherfuckers. That's what you all are. So inconsiderate of poor Margaret and me. Damn you."

She stormed out of the room and up the stairs.

Her bedroom door slammed.

I didn't look at Dad.

Chapter 17 —————————————

"**Heads**," Jonathan said, kissing my forehead. "Heads, it's an open mixed party. Tails"—he pushed me on my side and walloped my ass— "tails, it's a gay-men-only party." It was a relief to see him in a playful mood.

I propped a pillow behind my back and maneuvered myself up to lean against the headboard. Jonathan laid his head in my lap. Running my fingers through his bristly hair, I asked, "Flipping a coin is the most sophisticated decision-making mechanism we can come up with? Didn't you teach Logic 101 this term?"

"What do you suggest?"

I hesitated. "Well, this may be the last time for a while that we'll be able to host a party on Gay Pride weekend. The next number of years, who knows what our schedule will be or whether we'll be in Toronto on Pride weekend?"

He turned his head and looked up at me. "You mean, whether *you'll* be in Toronto on Pride weekend. I'll be here." He didn't smile, but there was no edge in his voice. He was stating the reality, not being petulant.

I kissed the top of his head. "Yeah, you're right. So this one is sort of special. Let's do a pros and cons list."

He laughed. "You and your lists. Okay, a Pride Weekend party just for men. Pros and cons."

"I should have a pad and a pen," I said.

Without looking up, Jonathan swung his arm up and cuffed me on the side of the head. Laughing, he reprimanded me, "Don't be so anal. Live on the wild side. Try it extemporaneously."

"Okay," I said, blushing, glad that he wasn't looking at me. "Sorry. I do get annoyingly compulsive sometimes." I thought for a moment and then said, "An all-gay-male party. Pros. Well, some people, like Dwayne and Stefan, will only come if we can guarantee a vagina-free zone. It would probably be more relaxed. No risk of tensions between boys and girls, between breeders and faggots. Less drama."

"Sorry to interrupt your flow, but 'less drama'? An apartment full of queens, gym rats, twinks, leather daddies, aspiring porn stars, and the rest of us uncategorized, boringly normal gay men. You think that is a prescription for 'less drama'? I beg to differ."

"Who do you know who is an aspiring porn star? Have you been holding out on me?" I bit my lip. I could hear Walter chuckling.

Jonathan, his head in my lap, looked up at me.

"Back to the task at hand," I said pretentiously, miming writing on a virtual pad. "Cons. Let me see. Sheila would never speak to us again. Oh, that should be in the pro column."

"Now, be kind."

"Sorry. Yes, a party without Sheila, perish the thought." I paused for a moment and then continued. "Actually, what would bother me, us, is the look on Althena's face when she learned we weren't inviting her. I think that settles it in my mind. I vote that the party be open to any of our friends, regardless of gender, orientation, ethnic origin, economic status—I don't want to discriminate against your aspiring porn stars—eye colour, religion, disability, age, nationality … have I forgotten anything?"

"I would make one category of exception," Jonathan said. "Family. No one allowed who is an immediate member of the family of either one Jonathan Compton or one Tom Fischer."

"Amen."

Jonathan raised his hand. I ducked. "No, dummy,' he laughed. "Just shaking hands on our agreement."

I leaned closer. "No way. This decision deserves to be sealed with a kiss."

On Monday, I phoned our friends, inviting them to the party.

On Wednesday, I phoned our friends, canceling the party.

From time to time, I went into the bedroom, got on the bed, and wrapped my arms around Jonathan. He had been crying for two hours. Then I would leave him alone for a while. He was inconsolable.

Patrick had called our apartment from California about four in the afternoon, while Jonathan was at the university. I was home reading. I remember exactly what: Armistead Maupin's *More Tales of the City*. I had been plowing through so much heavy material about economics, environmental ethics, and international law, in preparation for the Commission work, that I had decided to reward myself with the light fictional fare of Michael Tolliver's San Francisco exploits.

When I first heard Patrick on the phone, I laughed. I had been engrossed in Tolliver's world at 28 Barbary Lane, and here was our friend from just off the Castro on the line. I pictured Patrick, sitting in the window seat of his flat, surrounded by his pots of blooming orchids, phone in one hand and a joint in the other, blowing the smoke out through the open window so that Trevor wouldn't catch wind and scold him. Just to his left would be the door to the guest bedroom that had been Jonathan's home for the three weeks while he was at Berkeley last November and mine for the all-too-short weekend when I joined him. Patrick and Jonathan had been fierce rivals for top marks in graduate school at U of T. Now they were academic collaborators on opposite coasts of the continent.

When I told him that Jonathan wasn't home, he sighed audibly. "I'm relieved. I was dreading how I would tell him."

His tone brought me up short. I stopped laughing. "Tell him what?" I asked.

He hesitated. "I hate to put this on your shoulders, Tom," he said slowly. "It's probably better this way, hearing it from someone, you, face to face and not over a phone line."

"Patrick, you're spooking me. What are you talking about?"

He started to sob. I waited. Then, I couldn't wait anymore. Quietly, I asked, "Patrick, are you sick? Do you have … AIDS?"

After a moment, he replied, "No, honey, I'm okay."

"Trevor?"

"No, he's fine too. At least, we assume we're okay. Who knows these days?" I could hear him starting to cry again.

"Patrick," I said, gently but firmly, the auditory equivalent of grasping him by the shoulders and shaking him. "Tell me. What's the matter?"

The phone banged in my ear as he lay the receiver down. I heard him blow his nose. He came back on the line and said, "Sorry. Okay. This is it. Michel is dead. Michel Foucault."

A cramp in my left calf unpleasantly brought me to consciousness. I slowly straightened my leg and quietly enjoyed the gradual draining of the pain. Pale silver moonlight filtered through the open window. The slightly vacillating sheers produced shadow upon light upon shadow upon light in arrhythmic images that figured from the window across the floor and up onto the bed.

I turned to look at Jonathan, intending to bring his attention to these vaporous patterns if he were awake. His side of the bed was empty. Then I remembered.

I got up and walked out of the bedroom, poking my head first into the empty library, and then stumbling into the living room. The moon's ambient light, whose playfulness I had been enjoying a moment ago, did not reach the windowless corridor.

No sign of him in the living room. As I moved toward the kitchen, I heard the soft clink of ice in a glass. The door leading from the kitchen to the outside back staircase was open. Jonathan was sitting on the top step, gazing down into the tumbler that he was slowly rotating in his hand, sending the ice in relentless circles. A bottle of vodka lay on the step beside him.

I backed up and took a glass out of the cupboard. The freezer door creaked, as always, when I opened it. I broke a few cubes free of the tray and dropped them in my glass. Squeezing past him, I sat on the next lower step, picked up the frosted vodka bottle, and poured a few ounces. I held the bottle up to him. He extended his glass and watched as sluggish clear liquid spilled over the water rocks.

"With this heat, the bottle's not going to stay cold very long. Should I put it back in the freezer?" I asked.

"I don't care."

I put my hand on his knee. "I'm so sorry, my darling. I know how much you idolized him."

Jonathan lifted his eyes from the glass to which they had been riveted and looked into mine. From this angle, the half moon reflected off his corneas, producing tiny dancing crystals, so inconsistent with the bloodshot sclera around his pupils. He lifted his drink-free hand and let it fall gently on top of my head, stroking my prematurely balding scalp. I anticipated that this intimacy would reopen the floodgates, but with a few quick intakes of breath and a perceptible tautening of his stomach muscles, he held the waterworks back.

"Do you know if he's going to be buried or cremated? A funeral?" he asked.

"Patrick didn't say. I don't think he knows many details, other than what he told me on the phone."

"Can you tell me that again? Slowly. Everything's kind of a blur."

"Of course. Somebody called him from Paris this morning. Woke him up, he said. Ghislaine or Geneviève or something like that. Patrick's speech was kind of garbled. Anyway, this person told him that Michel had gone into hospital about two weeks ago with some kind of infection. In the brain, I think he said."

"How appropriate. Or ironic."

"Antibiotics seemed to help, for a while. Then, suddenly, they didn't. He got worse very abruptly, and then, yesterday afternoon"— I paused and then quietly mouthed the dreaded words—"he died. There's some indication, apparently, that it may have been ... AIDS-related."

In tandem, we took another swig of vodka. I poured more into our glasses.

Jonathan spilled a bit on his knee. He absentmindedly massaged it into his skin. "I'm sitting here," he said, "trying to visualize his brain cells as they are at this moment. All that grey matter, inert now, drying up, crinkling, brittle. No more electrical sparks that guided the way he used to massage the pen before attacking the paper to continue writing, or to speak with such animation when he was standing up in front us, giving his Parrhesia lectures last fall at Berkeley."

He stopped and took another swallow.

Jonathan gazed up at the moon, now partially obscured by the newly arrived leaves of the massive chestnut tree whose canopy stretched over three backyards. A few weeks ago when in full bloom, it had looked like a gargantuan spirea, a specimen in the garden of the Queen of Brobdingnag, we the minuscule Gullivers enjoying the shade beneath it. Now those dried fallen flower petals covered the ground, decaying, disintegrating, dead, their purpose served.

"It's not the physical brain cells that I care about," he addressed the fragments of moon that were visible. He was speaking with precision but impassively, as if in a small graduate seminar.

I wondered how shock manifests itself.

"It's the ideas that I'm trying to find. Those essences of light or energy that swamped us when we were listening to him. It was like we were having one prolonged, ecstatic communal intellectual orgasm that never dissipated in intensity."

I gently squeezed his knee. He came down off the moon and looked at me with a glance that conveyed surprise that I was there. Not missing a beat, he continued, "The weekend that you came out, I think you were there for the concluding lecture. Do you remember?"

I had reentered Jonathan's psychic universe. I was anxious to support his buoyancy, like an adult, arms outstretched underneath the body of a youngster in the swimming pool, determined to keep him afloat, a child who, despite flailing slightly, was splashing in the unaccustomed sensation of weightlessness.

"I do remember," I said. "He was summarizing what you and Patrick and the other lucky ones had been hearing from him during the previous lectures. What I remember most was that he was talking about the role of truth-telling in societies. Based on some Greek word. You just mentioned it a moment ago."

"Parrhesia."

"Yeah. It struck me because I thought of it in terms of the UN. How truth-telling is recognized or ignored or suppressed by powers that are threatened."

"Yes, yes, and how the truth-telling activity evolves as social or political or conceptual changes occur in a society. He talked about how the Greeks explored the problems raised by the process or activity of truth-telling. Problematization—he liked that term. Who has the legitimacy to be a truth-teller? What are legitimate topics for truth-telling? What are the consequences and what are the problems that are created?"

"I remember you being excited because you said that it gave a new dimension to your interest in 'historical flow.'"

Jonathan didn't respond but just gazed ahead. Maybe he was back in that lecture hall at Berkeley. I was nervous that I had let him drop, that he was starting to sink.

He came back, looking at me again in the present time and space. He smiled and asked, "Do you remember where we went afterwards?"

"Umm. Probably out to a bar, I suppose. It was a Friday night."

"That's right. Some shady place on Market Street, I think. His choice, no doubt. I felt a little guilty. I sort of abandoned you. Patrick and I and a couple others sat in a booth near the back talking with him for a long time. He was really consumed with the problematization of sexuality, as he called it. The same way that he had looked at the problematization of criminology and mental health. We were all so excited because he was so excited. He loved being there in the middle of such a vibrant, sexualized city. Applied research, we teased him."

"Yeah, I do remember you eggheads going at it. I don't think that I was bored though. There was enough else going on in the place to distract me."

Jonathan gave my head a lenient cuff. "Doing some of your own applied research?" he teased.

I looked up and was about to continue the jibing when the moonlight resurfaced through the tree branches, illuminating his face. His expression was in the discernible process of plunging back into the depths.

"That's gone now, all gone now," he said. "We can't talk to him again, ever. It's not only in the past. There's something fundamental and essential that is gone because he's gone. Michel is fucking gone. His life is gone. That brain has stopped. Forever. Gone."

Jonathan began massaging his abdomen. He looked down at his waist and with a kind of clinical scrutiny said, "And it's taken something away from inside me. Something's gone ... a piece of me ... what?" He rubbed his stomach. "So much of what I think, who I am, came from my connections to him. He was such a god for me. Gods don't die. How can he be fucking dead?"

I moved up to sit on the same step, beside him. I put my arms around him and whispered, "Oh, babe, I'm so sorry."

"Oh, my gut aches," he moaned, suddenly wrapping his arms around his stomach, dropping his glass. It went clattering down the wooden steps.

Chapter 18 ————————————

We got off the Tube at Westminster Station so that we could have a short walk along the Thames. It was a very low-tide day, the exposed muddy terraces leading down to a modest brown rivulet crammed in the middle with only those smaller boats that were still able to manage. Great London looked less great with its aquatic lifeline so constrained.

As we approached the Tate, we saw the long line waiting to get in. It stretched out the door, down the stairs, and onto Millbank. It was July, the height of the tourist season.

"I'm glad you've got connections," I said to Jonathan. The stroll had been pleasant, but the sun at high noon was blistering, and I didn't fancy a long, sweaty wait to get in. "Which side did he say we should go to?"

"He said the staff access is around the back, off John Islip Street," he replied. We walked past the imposing columned façade, down Atterbury, and then along the back to the staff entrance.

A bus passed just as we approached the security booth. "We're here to see Jeremy Compton," Jonathan yelled through the small grill in the concierge's window.

"That's okay, mate. I can hear you fine. What department does he work in?"

"Installations."

"Just a moment, please." He opened a large loose-leaf binder and turned one page at a time, licking his finger on each occasion to gain traction. Once he had found the sought-after page, he ran the same index finger down the list of names, pulled out a pencil, and wrote a number on the pad on his desk. He picked up the receiver of a vintage-era black phone, dialed, and then spoke into the mouthpiece. A moment later, he put his hand over the receiver and said back through the grill. "Name, please?"

"Jeremy Compton." This time Jonathan used a conversational volume.

"Beg your pardon, sir—your names. I've got Mr. Jeremy on the line here. He's wanting to know who's asking after him."

"Tell him it's his brother."

"My, my. I should have guessed that," he said grinning. "You do look alike." He lifted his hand from the receiver and spoke again. After he hung up, he gestured to the right. It took him a moment to exit from his cubicle office, but soon enough the heavy metal door swung open and he said, "Do come in. Welcome. Mr. Jeremy will be here promptly."

"Imagine, *Jeremy* and *promptly* in the same sentence," I said to Jonathan. "I'll have to make a note of this in my diary." He grinned.

"Oh, it's so good to see you guys!" Jeremy's voice reverberated against the high ceiling as he hollered his greeting and jogged down the long hallway toward us. Jonathan walked toward him. They crashed into each other's embrace, hugging and swaying back and forth, almost losing their balance. I stood a step back. Eventually, they disengaged their bodies but not their eyes.

"It is so good to have you here," Jeremy said quietly to Jonathan, hands resting on his shoulders.

Jeremy took a deep breath, smiled broadly, and stepped toward me. "Hello, Tom. Welcome to London," he said warmly as he put his arms around me.

"Thank you, Jeremy."

"So, you're screening your visitors?" Jonathan asked, as Jeremy and I separated.

"Come again?"

"You asked the concierge to ask us who we were."

"Oh, yeah. I knew you were coming today but I thought maybe later in the afternoon. I figured you'd be sleeping in late to get over the jet lag. I'm regularly getting petitioners, like some of my former buddies from OCA, wanting to pick my brains about how they can break into modern art circles here. Gets a bit tiresome."

Jonathan fingered him in the ribs. "Is my brother getting world weary? This highfalutin' job at the Tate gone to his head?"

"It's hardly highfalutin'," Jeremy scoffed. "I'm a glorified carpenter and mover and painter and lightbulb changer. Get the picture? No pun intended."

"Well, we're still very impressed," I said. "Associate Director, Installations Department, Tate Museum. It has a nice ring."

Jeremy rolled his eyes.

"Well, Mother is very proud of you," Jonathan said. "She's told you about the scholarship, right?"

"What?"

"Oh, what a sneak she is," Jonathan laughed. "She probably thought that you would forbid her if you knew. This whole gig she is on setting up the foundation. Well, one of her initial endowments is for a scholarship for a first-year fine arts student at OCA, named the Ontario College of Art Jeremy Compton Scholarship."

"Oh, Jesus!" Jeremy slapped his palm to his forehead. "Listen, we don't have to stand here in the hallway all day. How about lunch? Have you eaten?"

"No."

"Okay, let's go to the café. We can get a sandwich or salad. Is that okay? The Rex Whistler Restaurant is kind of pricey for a lunch. Carolyn and I will take you out to a fancy restaurant tonight if you're up for it."

"Fine," I replied for us both. "How is my sister doing?"

Jeremy looked at me for a moment as we started off down the hall. "I'll need you to tell me. She's been in a mute mood lately. I can't get a thing out of her. I'm counting on you to open her up in one of your tête-à-têtes while you're here. I'll haul Brother off to the pub for an evening."

"I'm sure I can get her to talk to me if I have her all to myself."

"Be my guest," Jeremy huffed.

Jeremy slipped the three of us, trays in hand, through an unmarked door. The staff dining room was prosaic-looking but much quieter than the public café. Jeremy steered us to an unoccupied table in the corner.

"I want to show Tom your collection of Hockneys after lunch." Jonathan smiled and corrected himself. "I mean the museum's collection."

"Sure wish they were mine. Selling one would pay our rent for many a year. I could free myself from my indenture to Dad. We're in the early stages of negotiations for a major Hockney retrospective, probably to coincide with his fiftieth birthday in 1988."

"Did I tell you I met him last fall in San Francisco?"

"The great Saint David," Jeremy said caustically.

Ignoring him, Jonathan continued, "A cocktail party at our friends Patrick and Trevor's. Hockney and Isherwood were there, and, of course, their cute American boyfriends. For some reason, these Brit artistic ex-pats prefer California's sun to England's rain. I can't understand that."

Jeremy turned to me. "So my brother is thoroughly corrupting your proletariat values by exposing you to such elitists?"

"Funny. That's how my mom referred to the three of us recently."

"What?" Jonathan and Jeremy in unison.

"Never mind," I said. "No, I'm afraid that I didn't get the chance to drink martinis with, ahem, David and Christopher. I was only out in San Francisco for one weekend. Jonathan was there for three weeks. With Michel."

Jeremy reached his hand across the table and took hold of his brother's. "I was really sorry to hear about Foucault. How well did you know him?"

Jonathan set his fork down. Gazing at the intertwined Compton hands, he replied quietly, "I certainly wasn't part of his inner circle. We were in regular contact over the past few years. Academic stuff. Then last November, I was at Berkeley for three weeks for his lectures, and we socialized quite a bit." He paused. Jeremy and I both watched the twitching muscles around his mouth. "Just days before he died, my department head had given me the go-ahead to negotiate a visiting scholar arrangement with him. I was going to be spending most of the fall with him in Paris getting that organized. Since that's off, to state the obvious, I'm going to Paris now for a few days to meet with some of his former colleagues and see if we can set up some sort of memorial lecture series at U of T next year. On our way to Geneva to get Tom settled for his new job."

Jeremy, still holding his brother's hand, turned and looked at me, crinkling his brow. "Geneva?"

"Yes, I'm taking up an assignment with a new UN commission

dealing with environment and development. It's time-limited, maybe a couple years based in Geneva."

"Whoa!" Jeremy let go of Jonathan's hand. "That raises a shitload of questions. You're just packing up and leaving my brother alone in Toronto? Does Carolyn know about this?"

The latter was the easier one. "Yes," I said. "I wrote her about it a couple weeks ago. She didn't tell you?"

"No." Pointing with both hands toward his face, he said, "Excuse me. Does this expression not convey surprise? You and your sister. You and both your sisters. My God. What did your parents do to deserve the three of you? Fucking hell, Jonathan, what do you think about this?"

Jonathan sat, not answering, staring down at his abandoned hand.

"I guess it slipped my mind," Carolyn mumbled, sipping her tea. We were sitting on the roof patio of the tenement next door to their Earls Court apartment. We'd cautiously accessed the patio via the rusting wrought iron fire escape that led from their apartment to the next-door roof on a circuitous route down to street level.

Patio was something of a hyperbole. Four wooden folding chairs, silvered by years of exposure to the elements, framed an upside-down plastic crate that was now enjoying a second career as a coffee table, having been absconded from a nearby green grocers after being retired from its previous life of transporting milk cartons or olive oil bottles. This scrounged furniture set was situated next to the north-facing wall of their apartment building, affording the users of the facilities some measure of shade at almost any time of the day. Against the base of the wall were several terracotta pots that held emaciated geranium plants, clearly suffering from both this year's dry summer weather and communal neglect. The gravel under our feet radiated the warmth absorbed from today's scorching temperatures.

None of the four of us had had the energy for an extravagant dinner out. Take-out fish and chips were the consensus option, eaten around the kitchen table that doubled as Carolyn's desk. I was relieved that we hadn't asked if they could put us up during our few days in London. Nor had they offered. The small apartment would have felt claustrophobic housing four adults. The pullout couch in the sitting room would have been our bed, or theirs if they had insisted on being hospitable hosts. Though a bit larger than my New York apartment, it reminded me very much of it in decrepitude and lack of redeeming ambiance. With Walter's financial assistance, Jeremy could have afforded more comfortable lodgings in London. He'd opted to rent this Collingham Road apartment so that he would have funds remaining to lease the small shed around the corner on Hesper Mews as his studio.

After they ate, the Compton brothers had excused themselves to wash down the batter grease with a pint or three at the nearby Coleherne.

I stretched out my legs and rested them on top of the coffee table. It's ridged, faded blue surface gave slightly under the weight, a protest against not being allowed an undisturbed retirement. "Do you suppose your forgetfulness in sharing my news is because I'm not very important to you or because Jeremy is not very important to you?" I asked.

Carolyn placed her feet on the crate, playfully tapping my toes. Her eyes twinkled as she looked at me. "Let's see. What's the game here? Dr. Freud or Miss Marple?"

It was good to be together again.

"Just curiosity. It would have seemed to me that a big change in my life that has big implications for Jonathan's life would have been of interest to you and that you would have assumed that it would be of interest to Jeremy."

"Well …" She paused and looked up at the sky. "I've had a bit on my mind lately."

"Ah, that's intended to satisfy my curiosity?" My tea had cooled enough to start sipping. I had never been one to add milk or cream, not so much because of taste as aesthetics. A pallid liquid the colour of dishwater just did not appeal. A consequence was that I was usually slower to drink than a tea-with-milk companion. "Well, I've got to tell you," I said. "I'm not hurt. But Jeremy is not very happy with you at the moment."

Carolyn yanked her feet off the stool. "Why does everything have to be about Jeremy? I suppose he delegated you to pry me open."

"Not quite in those words. But yes, bottom line."

"So, how about we start this conversation that I bet he called a tête-à-tête …"

I nodded sheepishly.

"... how about we begin in a different place? Perhaps, 'dear sister Carolyn, how are you doing?'"

"Fair enough. Carolyn, dearest sister of mine, how are you doing?"

She repositioned her feet back on the crate and smiled. "Actually, it should be 'dearer' sister. Comparative, not superlative. I appreciate it when you trash Patricia, though, even when grammatically incorrect."

"You're welcome." I reciprocated her smile. "Now, how are you doing?"

Carolyn took a long, slow sip of tea and looked around the terrace at the flowerpots. Her hesitance was uncharacteristic, but I didn't press her.

After a few minutes, she said, "It is the best of times. It is the worst of times."

"A little hackneyed and melodramatic. But that's not virgin territory for you, my dear."

"Listen, dear brother of mine, you've always been the drama queen of our family."

"Oh, I beg to differ. Maybe that's true in title but not in substance. Mild-mannered, balding Tom can't hold a candle to volcanic, red-headed Carolyn in the drama department. But let's move on. Start with 'the best of times' please."

"Well. There's the sex. And, let's see, did I mention the sex?"

"Ah, yeah, I think you did."

In much greater detail than appealed to me, Carolyn described the morning sex when Jeremy would come back from an early visit to the loo and start ravishing her body. Then there was usually shower sex. That happened when they were fighting over who had the more pressing schedule that day and thus deserved priority in the shower, except that it usually ended up with both of them in there together, and one thing leads to another. Sometimes she went over to the museum between classes, and they did it in a back room near a few of the Lichtensteins in storage. Apparently, Roy's work gave off so much energy it stimulated them both. Then of course in his studio. Jeremy went there right from the museum, and when Carolyn brought his supper over, they would always start with the hors d'oeuvres, so to speak. By the time he got back to the apartment, she was usually in bed reading, and he was too tired to get it up. So they would just cuddle and fall off to sleep.

"Thank goodness for that. I was starting to worry about chafing, yours and his."

Carolyn reached over and swatted my arm, spilling some of my tea. *The rustic floor covering has another advantage*, I thought to myself with a smile.

"So nothing has changed on that score, eh? When you moved in with him in his Toronto apartment, we could never get you on the phone. And it wasn't because you weren't in."

"Yes, well, I can confirm that Jeremy was the one who was in. Always in. Wherever."

"You naughty girl. How you speak. May we move on from this subject to other areas of the relationship?"

Fanning herself with her napkin, Carolyn looked skyward again, and sighed, "We may, but I'm not sure we can. You will have to give me a moment to catch my breath. This tea seems to be making me sweat a little."

It was my turn to lean over and swat her arm.

With our teas drained, we tackled the perilous reentry route to access the bottle of wine that Jonathan and I had picked up on our way from the hotel. All through dinner, it had sat on the kitchen counter, begging to be opened. But Merlot with haddock didn't seem to appeal. Carolyn propped a fan in the window through which we had just crawled, and we sat within range of its breezy oscillations.

"There are likely more locales and occasions around Metropolitan London where and when you two have done it …"

"There are."

"But since I get the picture, all too vividly for my tastes …"

"Such a prude."

"No, just squeamish. It's not the kind of visual I want occupying that part of my brain. Let's move on. I hope that there are different types of entries in the 'best of times' column, but for a change of pace, give me one of your top-of-the-list 'worst of times.'"

Carolyn placed her wine glass against her lips, gazed out the window, and took a very slow sip. With both hands cupping the glass, she brought it down into her lap and stared into it.

I allowed her a few moments to pick up the conversation. After no response, I prodded. "It looks like you're trying to divine some meaning in tea leaves, except that chance evaporated when we switched beverages."

She grimaced and looked over at me with tears in her eyes.

Startled at her shift in mood, I moved my chair closer, reached out for her hand, and asked, "What is it, babes?"

Carolyn flinched. Looking away from me, she released a rather unconvincing giggle and mumbled something indiscernible before her voice trailed off.

"Pardon?"

She took a sip of wine, looked back at me, and then said brightly, "Sorry. Where were we?"

"Ah. I don't know exactly. You were going to tell me, I thought, what was on your 'worst of times' list."

"Right. Okay. Let me see. Worst of times. Worst of times. Um. Okay, here's one. I'm getting bored."

Taken aback, I said, "Oh. Sorry. I can leave, if you want."

"Not with you, dumbo. I mean that I'm bored with my life here in London."

"When do you have time to be bored?" I asked, attempting to recapture the earlier playful ambiance.

She took a deep breath and exhaled slowly.

"You're bored with Jeremy?"

Her head jerked up. "Oh God, no." Pause. "Well, he's not the principal source." Pause. "Well, he is partly the source. But not really."

"Excuse me. Did you see where that articulate young woman went who I was just talking to?"

Carolyn set her wine glass down. Her explanation was clearly going to require supplementary hand gestures. "You see," she said, tapping the tips of her fingers against each other in rapid succession. "I love living with him. The sex is fantastic."

"Yes, I think that we've established that."

"But we, well, we don't talk enough."

"You don't talk enough?"

"And when we do it's always about either of two subjects."

I waited.

His art. Carolyn told me how Jeremy talked incessantly about whatever project he was working on: why he loved it, why he hated it, why he was frustrated because he wasn't making progress. Why he was frustrated because he was progressing too quickly and wanted to relish the creativity and not have it finished. Why no one would ever want to buy his work. Why those who might want to buy his art were boors and didn't deserve to buy it because they wouldn't truly appreciate what he was trying to express with it. Why he hated having to spend his days doing such menial work at the museum, instead of being in his studio. Why landing the job at the museum had opened up great contacts for him that he would never have gotten if they had stayed in Toronto. Why he was going to lose all credibility as a Canadian artist because he wasn't working there. Why he would only get credibility as a Canadian artist if he could make a big splash here in London …

"Yeah, I think I'm getting the picture."

"I love that he's so enthusiastic about his work," she said, gesturing to emphasize the point. "He's determined to come as close as art can to replicating the most intense human experiences. He was part of a group show at a small gallery out in the Docklands. But there was only space for one of his pieces, and the one he chose, *The Kiss*—much more explicit and engaging than Rodin's, I'll tell you—well, it so overwhelmed the other artists' pieces that they were hugely jealous. He lost a couple friends because of it. The whole show flew under the radar—not one review. So he thinks he failed. He was depressed for weeks. I tell him that there is a real buzz developing around town about him, whether he's ready to acknowledge that or not."

She picked up her glass, took a sip, and then leaned in toward me, staring directly into my eyes. "And, Tom, you've got to believe me. I really, really love him. Beyond the sex. Beyond his creativity. I love him. Never thought you'd hear me utter those words, eh? I never thought I'd hear myself utter them." She smiled.

I smiled back. "I love that you're in love, sweetie. I always thought that you would be, eventually. Hadn't quite pictured a scenario where you would fall in love with the brother of my lover—his twin brother. But what the heck. If I've got great taste, then stands to reason that you would too."

I picked up the bottle and poured more wine into each of our glasses. I was getting anxious about the time. I wanted to make further progress before our twin lover boys came crashing up the stairs. "So, you love Jeremy but you find the communication between the two of you a little limited?"

Carolyn squirmed in her chair. "I hate to say that, but yes."

"What's the other one?" I asked.

"The other what?"

"You said that there were two subjects that you mainly talk about. His art is one. What's the other?"

"How I'm wasting my time at LSE."

"He thinks you're wasting your time there?"

"I think I'm wasting my time there. It's the only thing I ever talk about. I'm so bored hearing myself complain about it. Back in Toronto, I had this big romantic image. London School of Economics. Rigorous scholastic standards. History of cutting-edge, socio-economic analyses. Socialist politics. Steppingstone to changing the world, intelligently. I thought it would be fantastically exciting. I've got to tell you, Tom— maybe for some people it is fantastically exciting, but not for this ... babe. I am so totally, fantastically bored."

I reached out and put my hand on her knee. "I'm really sorry to hear that, sweetie. What's the problem with it?"

"It may not be LSE as much as me. I think that I am getting a bit more mature, self-aware, as I age. Believe it or not."

I raised my eyebrows and bit my tongue.

"I saw that," she laughed. She then continued, seriously. "I've got so many interests and ideas that I want to pursue. Simultaneously. I get frustrated when I have to restrict myself to the specific requirements of the courses that I'm taking."

"Any idea what you can do about it?"

"Well, I've made some contacts here at LSE. The place has been great for that." I remembered that she had written in a letter to me sometime over the past few months about a couple, Thomas and Alexandra, whom she had been helping while they scoped out possible subjects for documentary films, mainly global justice issues. Once they had a viable proposal, she'd explained, they'd then pitched it to production companies and TV networks. Most of the proposals didn't get picked up, but every once in a while one did, and then they pulled together financing and dedicated the next year or so to producing it. "I'm telling you, Tom, it would be such an exciting way to live. Exciting intellectually, politically, interculturally. The work takes them all over the world."

Carolyn stared at me out of the corner of her eye, intentionally, provocatively.

"What? What does that look mean?"

She took a sip. "It would mean I'd have to make some changes."

Another sip.

"And? That might be what, exactly?"

"That would mean I'd have to leave."

"Leave LSE."

"Leave LSE ... and London, and hence Jeremy for months at a time when on projects."

"Jesus!"

"Oh, I left him long ago."

Chapter 19 ———————————

Several days later, the morning broke softly into our Paris hotel room. A soft tapping at the door signaled the arrival of breakfast. I hesitated to move. The wafting of the sheers had hypnotized me. The whitest of light cascaded into the room when they parted, to be supplanted a moment later by diffused amber as the drapes reasserted their responsibility. This sedating visual performance was unaccompanied by any sound of its own. What muffled noise did reach into our bedroom emanated from the morning's commercial dealings of the small shopkeepers up and down Rue Saint André des Arts.

Jonathan was asleep on his side, facing me. His head was barely visible, ensconced within the depths of an oversized down pillow. He released an occasional, almost inaudible, snore. The night had been so warm we had used only a light cotton sheet, most of which was now crumpled near the bed's baseboard, exposing the full length of his lean frame and the full length of his morning erection. I admired the aesthetics and then bent down and gently mouthed it. It grew to even greater attention. He moaned softly but didn't awake. With effort, I resisted further engagement lest I disturb his tranquility.

If he was dreaming, there were no evident signs. His expression, what I could see of it around the folds of the pillow, was placid, relaxed. His body's stillness was undisrupted by any flinching, its only movement a slight but perceptible rise and fall of the chest. His left arm was gathered under the pillow; his right was lying across his chest with the hand, palm up, next to me.

I placed my hand gently next to his so that our silver bands touched. We had bought them years earlier in Taxco, Mexico, from a merchant whom we thought seemed delighted to be sanctioning our relationship. We were probably over-romanticizing the transaction. More likely it was just a case of "any business is good business." We chose to wear them on our ring fingers to testify to our coupling, but on our right hands, to assert our unorthodoxy.

I slipped out of bed and into the vestibule and drew back the bolt on the ten-foot double doors. The age of the lock and the hinges frustrated my effort to avoid any noise. I opened the doors slowly to ensure that Madelaine, the young maid who daily delivered our breakfast tray, was not still in the hall. On the floor, right outside, lay a large wooden platter, covered in linen, bleached white except for a few uncooperative stains. Near the handles on either side were two sets of cutlery rolled in napkins framing the white porcelain dishware. Two coffee cups and two small plates. Two large coffee pots, one with hot black coffee and the other with steaming milk. Sculpted butter molds lay on one saucer and another balanced several ramekins of jam. The whicker basket, a deviant amongst the porcelain, cradled four large croissants.

I tiptoed back inside, setting the tray down on the round table by the window, and then fluffed the seat cushions on the two adjacent chairs before turning toward the bed. Jonathan was awake, watching me, smiling. I sat on the edge of the bed and kissed his forehead.

"*Bon matin*, mon chérie," I said.

"*Bon matin*, mon amour," he replied.

He lay back and pulled me toward him. I pulled him up vertically. "*Plus tard. Maintenant, le petit déjeuner avant que le café se refroidit.*"

"*D'accord*," he said, with an exaggerated sigh.

As we drained the last of the coffee, Jonathan said, "I don't understand why Jeremy isn't more upset about Carolyn's plans."

That had taken me by surprise as well. When the Compton brothers returned from the pub the other night, Carolyn broke the news, having tested the waters first by sharing it with me. Once Jeremy got through his initial explosion, he seemed to reconcile himself rather easily to the idea of them being apart a lot of the time.

"Maybe he had seen it coming?"

"I don't know," Jonathan replied. "He didn't breathe a word to me when we were out drinking. If he thought things were going to change between them, he hid it well."

"Jeremy can do that," I said before thinking.

"Can do what?"

"Well, you know. What you see is not always what's there."

"He's my brother, been so for thirty-two years."

"Thirty-three, my dear."

"Whatever. I think that I can read him pretty well. I would know if he were hiding something."

"You think so?"

"Yes, I know so. Why?"

I paused, weighing respective transgressions. "Well, do you know, for instance, that Jeremy is sleeping around? Quite a bit." Die cast.

"No way. He's a highly sexed person." He tapped my foot under the table. "Runs in the family."

"You don't say?"

"But he's not cheating on Carolyn, I'm sure of it. It's obvious. They're so affectionate with each other, almost to the point of embarrassment."

I laughed. "It did make you uncomfortable when they started making out on the sofa. My darling little prude."

"Well, we were guests, for heaven's sake," Jonathan said. "Anyway, he's much too busy at the gallery, with his own art at the studio, and then getting it on with Carolyn, to have any energy left. He can't be having other relationships. He's not cheating on her. He's monogamous, much to his own surprise, I'm sure"

"Right, right, right, and wrong."

"Huh?"

"You're right that he's super busy. You're right that he's not having other relationships. You're right that he's not cheating on Carolyn. And you're wrong that he's monogamous."

Jonathan squinted at me for a moment. "Okay, I can't decipher that," he said. "Tell me what you know."

"Well, they've got an arrangement, an understanding. Carolyn told me."

I tore off another fragment of fibrous white perfection from the interior of my croissant, popped it into my mouth before the butter base melted in my hand, and then licked my fingers.

"An arrangement? Meaning what?"

"They love each other. They really do. Wholeheartedly. But Jeremy has needs. You know what he always says about women being his muse. Women, in the plural. So he screws around. And that's okay with Carolyn. It's a very modern relationship they have."

Jonathan made a face.

I continued. "She says that he can do what he wants to meet his 'inspirational needs,' as they apparently call it, as long as he doesn't fall in love with someone else. Then she'd cut his balls off."

"My God."

"So my guess is, to answer your question about his being okay with her traipsing around the world, that he thinks that he'll keep busy with his art and his work, get laid whenever he wants—with his great looks he has no limit to his options ..." At this reference, Jonathan smiled, puffed out his chest, fluffed his hair, and batted his eyes. "Yes, yes, like brother, like brother. As I was saying before your ego intervened, he probably figures that when Carolyn comes through London or they reconnect somewhere else, they then pick up where they left off and recharge their love affair."

Jonathan sat for a moment looking at me and then asked quietly, sadly, "Is that you and me, too?"

Jonathan came scurrying down the gallery. "I'm sorry I'm late. I don't believe the line to get in. Remind me not to come to Paris in July again."

"That's all right. I've been in good company."

Jonathan glanced around.

I tipped my head toward the wall.

"Oh, gotcha. It helped me find you when you told me that you'd be with Giotto. Why Giotto?"

"Just look at it," I replied. We stood gazing at *Saint Francis of Assisi receives the stigmata*.

"But it's just an old painting," Jonathan said.

"What?" I virtually screamed, before looking at him and seeing the glint in his eye. "Oh, you bugger."

"Teasing, but seriously, tell me what attracts you to him?"

"Do we have three weeks?"

"Let's sit down here on the bench," he said, pulling me toward the leather couch in the middle of the gallery. "I'm exhausted. We can rest and talk at the same time."

"Oh, I'm sorry. You've been running all over town. I should have asked. How did it go at the Sorbonne?"

"Collège de France, across the street."

"I thought Foucault taught at the Sorbonne," I said.

"Common misperception of illiterates," Jonathan jibed as he tickled me in the ribs. A pair of tourists passing by us frowned at such irreverence in this cathedral to the Early Renaissance. "It looks promising, a memorial lecture series. We can talk about it over dinner. Answer my question about you and Giotto. I'm curious."

Returning my gaze to St. Francis, I leaned against the small rise in the middle of the couch. Jonathan moved closer and rested his arm behind me, his hand lightly caressing the small of my back. After a few moments of silence, he whispered, "Why the hesitation?"

"What I'm inclined to say, what's in my head, I think would sound affected if I were to say it out loud."

"Then pretend I'm not here. Just talk to yourself, but out loud."

I looked at him. "No, I don't want to pretend that you're not here. You're the one person that I should be able to say anything to, even if it feels embarrassing."

Jonathan smiled.

I took a deep breath, looked back to the painting, and said, hesitantly, "Okay. I feel a connection to Giotto and his work, what I've seen of it. Especially this one."

"Go on. You don't have to be so defensive."

"When I first saw this, back during the summer that I was hitchhiking around Europe, I didn't know anything about Giotto. I spent days here in the Louvre, and I kept coming back to this painting."

"I so wish we had known each other then," Jonathan said. "I would have loved to watch you discovering Europe, Paris, the Louvre, for the first time."

I didn't respond. It had been a lonely time for me and having had someone, Jonathan, to share everything with would have been wonderful. But being alone then had also its pluses. I didn't have to worry about another person's agenda. I sat in Notre Dame for hours listening to organ recitals. I spent whole days reading in the shade of Jardin des Tuileries plane trees. I had time to think, to write. I'd thrived on the solitude.

"Two things in particular hooked me about this work. One was the way he painted—the intensity and the humanity of St. Francis's expression, the sense of perspective in the drawing of the buildings and the landscape, the beautiful lifelike birds with him in the small panel at the bottom."

"Astute observations for a teenager. How old were you?"

"Um. Let's see. Summer of 1973. I would have been eighteen, I guess."

"Giotto was one of the key figures in ushering in the Renaissance; he broke new ground, was more naturalistic than the rigid formalism of Gothic and Byzantine art."

"So I discovered. I started reading up on him. He came to it largely intuitively. Not much in the way of training. He just did it. Instinct. I liked that."

"And what was the second thing?"

I hesitated again, reluctant to sound affected, and something more.

"Well," I continued. "I like what he painted. Not only how, but also what."

"Explain."

"St. Francis. Giotto did many paintings and frescoes of him. St. Francis was a very humble man, not some big whoop-de-do in the religious establishment."

Jonathan laughed. "'Whoop-de-do.' Now that's quite the ecclesiastical terminology."

I elbowed him in the ribs. "You know what I mean."

"Yes, technically."

"Well ..." I got up and walked up as close to the painting as I thought I could without provoking a tackle from a security guard. "Look at the expression on St. Francis' face. He's in awe, somewhere between fear and ecstasy. Christ is appearing to him, imbuing him with the very symbols of his own suffering and death." I stared at the upturned, bearded face.

An anxious on-a-tight-schedule-before-the-bus-leaves tourist nudged me to move me out of his way. Startled, I glanced back at Jonathan. He was leaning forward, watching me. His eyes conveyed no reaction to my exposition. I ventured on. "Then Giotto shows him communing with those birds. God, Francis, the birds—all interconnected at some profound spiritual level. How moving is that? It touches me very deeply, and not just aesthetically. It's like a metaphor for what I covet for my own life."

I sat back beside Jonathan. I continued to look at the painting, but I could see peripherally that Jonathan was looking at me. *Shut up, Tom. You've said enough, too much.*

"Hungry?" I asked lightheartedly. "You ready to go?"

"Okay."

We got up and quietly made our way through the noisy crowds.

Chapter 20 ——————————

It was hard to disguise my disappointment. The studio apartment was tiny and sterile. The third-floor unit sat halfway down a long hallway in a featureless building, one of five identical sisters in an underwhelming complex, squeezed by similar nondescript mega-residences near the Geneva Airport. On the positive side, there were a surprising number of mature trees that would provide some green colour contrast in this cinderblock jungle in seasons other than winter, and there was a trolley stop right outside my door. The route five bus connected to most other lines at Cornavin, allowing me access to every area of the city.

Jonathan was delighted, twice: once by the dramatic contrast of this accommodation with our Toronto house and neighbourhood, which were so replete with character, and secondly by my evident distress upon discovering the barracks that the UN office had lined up for me. His eyes and smirk said it all. "Serves you right."

"It is depressing, isn't it?" I observed, after dropping my suitcase at the door and wandering for a few minutes around the apartment, hoping in vain to discover some fabulous alcove that I could make into an intimate reading nook or a view out a window that would afford something more than the adjacent nondescript buildings staring back at me.

"Well, look on the bright side," Jonathan replied, with all too much giddiness in his voice. "You clearly don't have room for the amount of stuff that you had intended to ship over from home. So you'll save on boxes and shipping."

"There's not even a tiny balcony where I could periodically escape from this interior dreariness," I whimpered as I pirouetted, my outstretched arm taking in the full sweep of my new mini-home.

"I noticed a little café just down the block. Let me take you there for an espresso, and then we can return to find this hovel magically transformed into a castle in our absence. Cinderella-like."

"Ah, I don't think it was her habitation that got transformed."

"No? Well, you would be more up on fairy tales than I."

The café did produce wonderful espressos. I made mine a double, since Jonathan was paying. We were one of three couples sitting on the small outdoor terrace. A light breeze with a hint of coolness wafted down from the regional mountains and filtered in across Lake Léman. The August evening sun had disappeared behind the monoliths that now constituted my neighbourhood.

We brainstormed about a daytrip that we might take while Jonathan was there, perhaps somewhere around the Swiss countryside or over into France. My mind kept wandering back to the dreary cell that was to confine me over the coming months.

"You are in altogether too buoyant a mood," I complained.

"What? Oh, your apartment. It's not ideal, I'll grant you that," he said. Jonathan started scrutinizing me, his eyes narrowing, his brow furrowed. "When you were trying to convince me that we wouldn't be separated all that much, you emphasized that it was a temporary assignment and that you would be back on the our side of the pond frequently." He gazed distractedly at a couple wheeling a stroller with two infants, perhaps twins, along the sidewalk. "So I don't know why you're so upset, unless those were more rationalizations than reality."

The sudden disappearance of his effervescence caught me off guard.

"That's all true. But," I protested, "I've been so excited that you were going to be here in Europe all fall. And now you're not." I pouted.

Jonathan jerked his head up and glared at me. "You're blaming Michel for dying and interfering with our plans? Fuck you." He pushed his chair back from the table, spilling the remainder of my coffee, got up, and headed back toward my building. I was destined to a single espresso after all.

Gutiérrez had led me to believe that the Commission would have a large staff. Either he didn't know what he was talking about or funding dynamics had changed considerably in the six months since the March day when I was summoned to his office. A large personnel complement, in my mind, meant considerably more than the five of us in the room.

We five were dwarfed by the massive mahogany boardroom table at our first staff meeting. Morning sun flooded in through the large windows along the end of the room that faced east toward the lake. Balding Jim MacNeill, in a dark blue suit, white shirt, and striped tie, sat at the head, looking every inch a conservative economist. Obviously, looks could be deceiving. To his right was his Swiss administrative assistant, Felicia, files neatly piled on the table in front of her, steno pad and pen in hand. Sunita, the deputy researcher, wore an attractive green sari that revealed too much of her excess weight, a byproduct of her long career in Geneva. Senior researcher Janos, sporting his trademark turtleneck sweater under a tweed jacket, sat next to her. Both Sunita and Janos had their doctorates: international affairs at Oxford and political economics from Stanford, respectively.

I was across the table from them, beside Felicia. I had chosen to wear nondescript business attire, hoping to simultaneously appear professional and inconspicuous.

Of the executive staff, I was the most junior—organizationally, educationally, experientially, chronologically.

The CVs of the Commission board were even more intimidating. The twenty-one members, drawn from every region, were all heavyweights chosen for their expertise in areas such as environmental policy, economic analysis, poverty and development, and international law. Some had decades of experience in running international organizations. Others had published more research than all my former professors combined. It was an impressive roster, and scary. We, as staff, were to do their bidding.

I anticipated that I might be subject to some geographical prejudice. Canada was punching considerably above its weight already. Maurice Strong was a Commission member and revered, as Fernando had noted without enthusiasm, for his role as the secretary-general of the 1972 Stockholm Conference on the Human Environment. MacNeill was respected as an intellectual powerhouse in understanding the linkages of environment, development, and economics, and he had a proven record as an international diplomat. I wondered, might I be perceived as one maple leaf too many? My personal insecurity meter was registering off the scale.

MacNeill began the staff meeting by inviting each of us to describe our background and our interest in working for the Commission. I came off as an inarticulate underachiever.

After the round of introductions, the boss initiated a brainstorming session, asking each of us to identify what we thought to be the most critical issues that the Commission should address. My seniors proposed a long list of crises: hunger and malnutrition; access to clean water; industrial pollution; population growth; the debt crisis.

I decided to take a gamble, something to make my mark. When it came my turn, I proposed climate change. An awkward silence filled the room, and then came the questions. What was the scientific evidence? How could we justify focusing on such a long-term issue in the face of much more immediate crises? What were my sources?

That last question was the only question for which I had a definitive answer, but it was one that I was hesitant to share. To date, there had been very little written about the subject in academic literature. I had, though, read a compelling article about climate change recently in the *New York Times*. Confessing that the *NYT* was my authoritative source did not strike me as a way to impress these colleagues with my research skills.

Not an auspicious first day.

Chapter 21 ⸻⸻⸻⸻⸻⸻⸻

Still ruminating on how I could have performed more professionally at the staff meeting, I emerged from the elevator in my apartment building and headed toward my depressing den. I did a double-take. I had never seen a homeless person on the streets of Geneva. Now there was one propped up against my apartment door, sound asleep, legs sprawled halfway across the hallway, head covered with a soiled blue slicker.

"Pardon. Excusez-moi, monsieur." Nothing. Nudging him with my foot would have been decidedly uncharitable, so I leaned down and took hold of his shoulder and gave it a modest shake.

"Huh?" A hand emerged and slowly began to pull down the nylon head covering.

"Carolyn! Oh, my God. What are you doing here?" My sister looked pale, gaunt.

She stretched her hand out. "Help me up, please."

I stepped in front of her and placed my hands gently under her armpits. I pulled her up and toward me. She groaned, winced, and collapsed into my embrace. I fumbled to get the keys from my pants pocket and unlock the door without letting go of her nearly limp body. We did an awkward two-step into the apartment, and I eased her into the armchair that I had salvaged from the basement garbage room the previous week.

She immediately fell asleep.

I went back into the hallway to retrieve my briefcase and then quietly closed and locked the door. Taking off my overcoat and suit jacket, I hung them up in the clothes closet and stood for a few moments, staring into that repository of my current apparel, sparsely furnished until my next trip to Toronto, when I would bring more of my belongings. I somehow suspected that once I turned around, the armchair would be as empty as I had left it this morning.

But Carolyn was there, slouched down in the chair. An almost imperceptible snore emanated from the same mouth out of which a sliver of drool hung, suspended, waiting for the appropriate moment to drop onto her chest.

I moved toward the sink, filled the kettle with water, placed it on the stove, and lit the element. I opened the cupboard door, relieved that the meager provisions that I had bought so far included a box of tea bags. I grabbed two mugs and put one bag in each. Once the water started to boil, I filled one of the mugs for myself. Carolyn wouldn't be ready for hers for some time.

I sat down on a wooden chair at the table and placed the mug in front of me. I raised it to my lips, nearly scalding myself. I put it down and looked over at frail, wispy Carolyn—a novelty, and not a good one.

I lunged to grab the phone before it had a chance to ring twice. Carolyn's body flinched but she didn't wake. Cupping my hand around the receiver, I whispered, "Hello."

"Have you heard from Carolyn?" Jeremy's voice was subdued. I was too flustered to respond. "Tom," he said firmly. "Tell me the truth. Have you heard from Carolyn?"

"She's here."

Jeremy mumbled something. Perhaps it was, "Thank God." Or maybe, "Fuck her."

"I just got home from work. She was lying in front of my door. What happened?"

"You tell me. What has she said?"

"Nothing yet. She's asleep. Right out of it. She looks awful." Suddenly, anger exploded from somewhere inside. "Jeremy. What did you do to her?" I yelled into the phone before catching myself.

Too late. Her eyes were open, fixed on the receiver in my hand.

"Can you put her on, please?" Jeremy requested, his tone flat.

I looked at Carolyn. Our eyes met. I pointed at the receiver. She remained unresponsive and unmoving, curled up in the chair, her gaze as devoid of expression as Jeremy's voice. She was as far away from me in this room as was her lover on the line somewhere across the channel. Her ex-lover?

I felt a weight on my chest. Oppressiveness pervaded the apartment, vacuuming the oxygen, replacing it with something suffocating, noxious. I needed to inhale to survive but feared the toxicity would doom me, and Carolyn. She sat, catatonic.

"Tom? Are you still there?" I held the receiver in front me, staring at it.

Unremitting silence surrounded us, the audio not absent but rather overwhelmed by the intensity of the atmosphere.

"Tom?"

From somewhere, I found my voice. "I'll call you back."

"Ouch."

I opened my eyes. My arms were wrapped around the pillows that, curiously, seemed slighter than usual. There was only one. *Where is the other?* The room was dark. I rolled onto my back and then saw my sister.

Carolyn was sitting at the table, hands clasped around a mug in front of her.

"Sorry, I woke you," she said. "Almost burned my tongue on the tea." Like brother, like sister.

"What time is it?"

"Don't know. I forgot my watch. Middle of the night, I would guess, unless the continent has a different helio cycle than we do in the UK."

I swung my legs off the futon and manipulated my feet into slippers. Standing up was always a bit of a challenge, the bed being too low to get an easy footing. The modest ambient light from the street coming through my blind-less window was of no assistance in finding the housecoat that I usually left piled beside the slippers, until I looked back at Carolyn.

"Well, you've made yourself at home, I see."

"I never pictured you as the silk dressing gown type."

"It's Jonathan's. Mine's terrycloth, as you probably assumed. I didn't have room for it in my luggage. Next trip."

The conversant sister, who was such a welcome contrast to the corpse on my doorstep a few hours earlier, was suddenly mute and staring at the sleeve of her garment. Jonathan's dressing gown, my lover's, brother of her lover.

I sat down in the chair opposite her and waited. After a few moments, nervous that she might slide back into catalepsy, I reached over, touched her arm, and asked, "So are you going to tell me what this is all about?"

She raised her head and looked at me. Her eyes were silent but not void, like earlier. I didn't press, just waited. She dropped her gaze as she put her hand on top of my hand, on top of her arm, on top of Jonathan's dress gown sleeve, and said, slowly, "How do you feel about Luke and Naomi?"

"Excuse me?"

She didn't respond but just sat staring at the sleeve, her arm, my hand, her hand.

"I don't see them much," I said. "Periodically at home, in Waterloo. I've never been to Dayton. They're certainly cute kids."

Carolyn raised her head and asked, "Did you ever want kids?"

I laughed. "Right. Can't you just see that? Not in this universe. Why do you ask?"

She said nothing.

Keep her engaged, Tom. Don't let her slip away. "Do you?" I asked.

She looked up at the ceiling. "I did … have a kid."

"What?"

"For eight weeks. About."

"Carolyn. What are you saying? Oh, my God. You were pregnant? You miscarried?"

Carolyn dropped her gaze from the ceiling and looked directly into my eyes and said, quietly, unflinchingly, sorrowfully, "Yes. No."

Jeremy said he would take the earliest morning departure from London. That would get him into Geneva about two thirty in the afternoon. I suggested that we meet in the Mirror Bar at the Swissôtel Métropole at five. That would allow him time to find a cheap hotel room near the train station.

None of the three of us were Métropole-class clientele. I calculated that the ambiance of the Mirror Bar might exact a sedating influence on the discussion. I was prepared to spring for a bottle of wine.

Carolyn put up no resistance to the plan, her reaction a complicated amalgam of trepidation and resignation.

Jeremy was seated at a table facing the door, his back to the window, more interested in watching for our arrival than enjoying the vista. Carolyn and I held hands as we walked toward him, both with sweaty palms. Her grip tightened. Jeremy rose when he saw us. His brow was slightly furrowed, his eyes locked on Carolyn. He bumped one of the other chairs at the table as he moved toward us. It made an intrusive clatter in the quiet atmosphere of the bar, still sparsely peopled at this pre-dinner hour.

Carolyn stopped walking. Jeremy halted about three feet in front of us. The two of them looked at each other. I didn't exist.

"Hello, Jeremy," Carolyn said in a subdued voice.

My palpitating heart beat out fifteen seconds, thirty, more.

Jeremy's chest moved in and out in tandem with my pulse, a sprinter's pace.

Carolyn loosened her grip and dropped my hand. Slowly, she raised her arm and placed her palm gently against Jeremy's cheek. His body flinched. He shut his eyes. When he opened them, his eyeballs were missing, only the whites visible. His body wavered and toppled away from us, crashing against a table scattering vase, flower, water, and ashtray.

The waiter initially resisted my order, hoping that the provision of a glass of water and cold face cloth would exhaust our expectations. I would have to tip well. He acquiesced after ensconcing us at a table in the farthest corner. He acknowledged me as taster, and I did my best sommelier impression. I nodded without looking at him.

We each took several sips without any conversation.

"How bloody embarrassing," Jeremy mumbled, methodically swirling the Pinot Noir around in his glass.

"Granted, it wasn't the reception that I expected," Carolyn responded.

Jeremy set his glass down and looked across the table at his lover. "A million questions," he said with a solicitude that I had not witnessed before.

"Fire away," Carolyn replied quietly, maintaining her role as the calmest and most self-assured presence at the table.

"I don't know where to begin. When did you find out? Why didn't you tell me?"

"Somewhere around the beginning of July."

"Oh, my God," I blurted. "You knew that you were pregnant when Jonathan and I were there?"

"I suspected so. Yes."

"Why didn't you tell me?" My mind flashed back to our conversation in their flat.

Jeremy turned to me. "With all due respect, Tom, I think that is more my question than yours."

"He's right." Carolyn smiled at me, as consolation, before turning back to Jeremy. "Because I love you so much."

"Keeping it secret that you, that we, are pregnant?" Jeremy's voice rose for the first time. "That's your idea of showing me how much you love me?"

Carolyn let a few moments pass before responding.

"It was a foregone conclusion that we could never have children. Well, we could biologically. I guess we proved that. But we both know perfectly well that neither of us is the parental type."

"We never talked about it," Jeremy protested.

"Precisely. When we're together, we are all-consuming," she continued. "And when we're not together, we are both totally consumed in the other things that matter in our lives."

Carolyn reached across the table and placed her hand on Jeremy's.

"And, my dear, there is not and never would be room in our private life nor in our professional lives to accommodate children. We both knew that, instinctively. The fact that we both take protection, doesn't that tell you something pretty clearly about us wanting to avoid me, us, getting pregnant?"

"You do?" I asked.

They both looked at me quizzically.

"Nothing." I brushed the moment off. The glimmer of satisfaction of being able to tell Mom that she was wrong was immediately squelched by the prospect of how this conversation would inevitably have to be replayed for the four non-grandparents-to-be.

Jeremy stopped just as he was about to pour more wine into his glass; instead, he offered to pour for Carolyn first.

"Yes, please," she said lightly. "I don't have any reason to avoid alcohol. Now."

"You're right, I suppose," Jeremy acknowledged. "We were never destined to grace the cover of *Family Circle Magazine*. But when you knew you were pregnant, which I don't understand how, what with all the 'protection' ..."

"Things happen, I guess. Nothing is a hundred percent secure."

"But why didn't you tell me?"

Carolyn's placidness started to slip. Her hands were clenching the wine glass in a grip more befitting a Swiss beer stein. She stared at the table. Without looking up, she said, "You want the truth?"

"That's why I got up in the middle of the night and travelled umpteen hours to get here. Yes, I want the truth."

Speaking to some imperfection in the table surface, Carolyn confided, "I didn't trust you. I thought that if I told you that I was pregnant, you would get all these romantic and totally impractical ideas about us having a baby. You would get carried away with the fantasy of having created this new life force, a little Jeremy or Jeremina. You would see it as another manifestation of your artist genius, carrying on the Compton line of arts aficionados."

"Mother," Jeremy said reflectively.

"See. Exactly. That's where your heart would have led you ..."

Carolyn's voice was now the raised one.

"And then I would have had to be the one to talk sense into you about diapers and finances and schooling and travel limitations and lifelong commitments to your child. It was hard enough being your baby-killer. I couldn't handle being your dream-killer as well."

The imagery froze me in my seat.

"And if I had relented and we'd had the child, it's my life, not yours, that would have changed. You would have continued working at one of the world's most prestigious museums and creating your art and having exhibitions and getting famous, and I would have been at home nursing and cooking and doing shifts in the daycare centre and not having time to read and not taking further classes and not working with Thomas and Alexandra on groundbreaking documentary films around the world and not making a name for myself ... except as the mother of Jeremy Compton's child."

Carolyn started sobbing into a damask Swissôtel napkin.

"So I knew that I had to do it all alone, without you. Once I made the decision that I, we, couldn't keep it, Alexandra helped me find a good clinic, and she came with me. The procedure was done on Wednesday."

Carolyn closed her eyes and took several deep breaths before continuing quietly and slowly.

"I underestimated how weak I would feel afterwards. I was afraid that if I went home, you would figure it out. So I got on a train and came to Geneva. But now here you are, so that was a shit plan."

The sound of the waiter clearing his voice reached our family conference.

"So I've killed our baby. Our-baby-to-be. Our-baby-that-we-never-would-have-been-able-to-care-for-properly-anyway baby."

She looked back and forth between Jeremy and me, both sitting in dazed silence.

"Please, say something," she pleaded.

We sat mute.

With an aggressively challenging glare directed alternatively between the two closest men in her life, she continued, "Well, God in whom I don't believe, it seems that I was right. I am alone in this. These bastards have damned me. You, if you existed, would condemn me. So it's unanimous. I'm to be confined to my own hell, to find a way to live with my decision."

Carolyn picked up her glass and emptied it in one long, deliberate swallow. Slowly, she pushed her chair back and stood up.

Looking down at me, she said without expression, "Thank you for the bed last night. I'll let you know where you can send the bill."

Turning to Jeremy, she paused, and she stared at him for a few moments. Leaning in toward him, she dabbed at the tears streaming down his cheeks with her already moist napkin. "Goodbye, Jeremy," she whispered. "I'll give you my forwarding address, once I know where I'm going."

She straightened up, turned, and walked out of the bar with no backward glance.

Chapter 22

"**My** poor baby. Why didn't she come home? I would have looked after her." Mom was pacing around our flat. She plopped down on the sofa beside Dad, whose attempt to comfort her with a shoulder hug was sabotaged by her leaping back up on her feet.

She marched over to the chair where I was sitting. I flinched. Her body language bespoke an imminent assault. "What! You think I'm going to hit you? Name one time in your life when I or your father have ever struck you."

It wasn't a rhetorical question.

"Never," I replied quietly.

"Maybe this should be the first time. Why, for heaven's sake, did you not call to let us know? It doesn't surprise me that Carolyn didn't call. She so bloody independent-minded. But you? You should have telephoned the minute you found out. Don't you think that I ..." She hesitated and glanced over at her husband. "That *we* would have wanted to know?"

"It was just a week ago that she broke the news to me in Geneva. I already had plans to come home this weekend, and I thought it better that we have this conversation face to face."

"That does make sense, Isabel," Dad said. "There's nothing we could have done anyway, even if Tom had called earlier."

"That's not the point, Lawrence," she practically screamed. "This is my daughter we are talking about."

"Our daughter."

"I'm her mother! You don't get a more female issue than abortion."

"Ohhh."

We all turned as Margaret buried her head in her hands. She had been sitting placidly in the large reading chair. Mom's declaration of the A-word shattered her apparent tranquility. Jonathan, who was sitting on a stool beside her, moved closer to offer some consolation. Mother and son did not often display physical expressions of affection. The juxtaposed seats exasperated the awkwardness. He settled for a limp hand on her shoulder.

Mom had no such reserve. She immediately moved over in front of Margaret's chair, kneeled on the floor, and wrapped her arms around the lowered, well-coiffed head.

"I'm sorry, Margaret. I didn't mean to upset you. I'm a nurse and have dealt with hundreds of women before, during, and after an ... an intentional termination of a pregnancy." She paused. "I know that ... abortion ... is against the teachings of your church."

Margaret, her hands still covering her face, made no response.

"I don't have the same religious reservations about it as I assume you do," Mom continued quietly. "For me, it's a medical procedure, almost always an unhappy and regrettable medical procedure for all parties. Nevertheless, usually necessary, given the circumstances. But this is my daughter we're talking about. I'm sure that you can appreciate that this is much, much more personal and distressing for me."

"Excuse me." Margaret stood up abruptly, knocking Mom off balance and sending her toppling over on the floor. Without comment, Margaret stepped over her and scurried off toward the bathroom.

Dad, Jonathan, and I were immediately at Mom's side, simultaneously grasping at her arms to help her up. Mom brusquely shook us all off.

"Leave me alone. I can get up fine on my own."

Brushing herself off, she turned and addressed Jonathan. "I was just trying to comfort her, for goodness sake. She was upset." Extracting herself from our still-hovering circle and moving toward the window, she continued, "We all are upset, for heaven's sake. Seems to me, though, that I have the greatest right to sympathy and am the one receiving the least." She glared at the three of us and then riveted around and looked out the window.

Jonathan brought his stool over beside my chair, and the two of us sat back down. He took hold of my hand. Dad walked over to the window, took Mom's hand, and said, "We all know how upset you are, darling. And you have every right to be. Tom made a judgment call to wait until his next trip back to this side of the Atlantic to share the information with us. Maybe that was the wrong decision, but his intentions were good. Come sit back on the sofa with me."

He pulled at her hand, encouraging her to follow his lead.

"No, thank you," she said withdrawing her hand from his, not withdrawing her gaze from out the window.

Dad knew enough not to persist. He sat down.

A few minutes of silence passed inside the room. A siren wailed somewhere in the distance.

Mom turned and walked past us. "I'm going to see if Margaret is okay."

Jonathan started to speak, "I think ..." He stopped when I squeezed his hand.

The three of us sat silently.

After about five minutes, Mom walked back into the living room, followed by Margaret. Neither looked at us. Margaret sat back in the armchair, folded her hands on her lap, and gazed calmly down at them. Mom moved to the window, arranged the cushions on the window seat, and sat down facing into the room.

"Margaret has something to say to all of us," Mom announced. "Please give her your full attention." That seemed an unnecessary request.

Margaret lifted her head and looked at each of us in turn. With the quiet dignity that I had years earlier misinterpreted as hauteur, a way of holding herself that was so much in contrast to the unfettered effervescence that I associated with maternal presence, Margaret began, "Isabel and Lawrence, I realize that you both must be very stressed about the well-being of your daughter. Carolyn is a high-spirited young woman ..."

Her lips twitched in what might have been an inadvertent smile.

"... but she is your youngest daughter, and I expect that you do now and probably always will consider her as your baby, your vulnerable baby. Lawrence, I told Isabel that, though I do not have a daughter of my own, I appreciate how concerned she must be. Believe me, as a woman, I can very much understand her anxiety. Any pregnancy, and any terminated pregnancy, carries with it the possibility of complications. My religious convictions notwithstanding, I sympathize with your distress."

She dropped her head, looked down again at her lap, and then continued. "I want to be honest. Your distress is not my major preoccupation. I'm sorry that Walter is out of the country, though maybe it's for the best. You know how Walter is ..."

She smiled rather inscrutably.

"When Jonathan called to ask me to come over and said that the two of you were on your way in from Waterloo and that Tom had just flown in and had some news to share, I let my imagination run away with me."

She lifted her head and gazed around the room, making eye contact with each of us in turn.

Margaret shifted in her chair so that she was directly facing me. "Tom," she began. "You haven't mentioned about Jeremy's role in this decision."

Caught off guard, I stuttered, "Yes, of course, Margaret. I'm sorry. Jeremy came to Geneva. We met together. The three of us."

"And?" Margaret asked unflinching.

"Well, I would say that he was quite upset."

"About?"

"Pardon?"

Margaret's eyes narrowed. "Tom, don't obfuscate. What was he upset about?"

"Well, that Carolyn had had an abortion."

"Are you telling us that he did not know that she was going to terminate the pregnancy?"

Mom jumped up from the window seat. "Tom, is that right? Did Carolyn do this totally on her own?"

I looked at Jonathan. He nodded.

Mom frightened me. I addressed Margaret. "Yes, that is correct. Carolyn made the decision on her own. She left after it was done and came to Geneva."

Mom collapsed back onto the window seat. "Oh, my poor baby, so alone."

Dad shook his head. "Oh, Jesus," he muttered.

Margaret cleared her throat. "And Jeremy?"

"He came to Geneva immediately on learning that Carolyn was with me."

We all watched as Margaret stood up and walked toward the apartment door. She reached for the doorknob and then paused.

Turning around, she faced us, looking at none of us in particular, staring through us, into a vanishing fantasy.

After three deep breaths, she said, "My grandchild. Your daughter has killed my only hope of a grandchild."

She lowered her head and stared directly at Jonathan and me. "My only hope of a grandchild. That dream is dead."

She turned and let herself out.

Chapter 23

I was supposed to be in New York by Sunday evening. Jim MacNeill was making a presentation on Monday to departmental chiefs at UN Headquarters. The meeting would be critical, and MacNeill was determined that we be well prepared.

As the staff functionary charged with maintaining efficient communication between the New York departments and our Commission office in Geneva, my participation in the Monday meeting was a sine qua non. I didn't want to set a new record for briefest UN appointment.

But there was a competing command performance.

Walter had issued a summons to Jonathan and me—his office, Monday morning. The call from Manila was short and unequivocal.

After intense brainstorming, frantic on my part, resignedly on Jonathan's, we phoned him back with a counterproposal—Sunday, in New York. Walter was flying into JFK from Manila in the morning. If Jonathan and I went down to New York, we could meet with him at the airport Sunday afternoon. Then, father and son could fly back to Toronto together, and I could get to my preparatory meeting with MacNeill in the evening.

I tried to make a case for Jonathan staying on in New York for a few extra days to give us more time together. Jonathan asserted, forcefully, that it wasn't an option. Chapman had reassigned him a full course load when the fall mini-sabbatical in Paris fell through. I argued that surely he could negotiate coverage of his classes for a couple days. He wasn't disposed to try.

"Why should your schedule be immutable and mine not?"

Back off, Tom.

With the transfer from New York to Geneva, I had given up our Lexington Avenue apartment, "the hole," in Jonathan's parlance. Now, whenever in New York, I could stay in a hotel. Jonathan agreed to let me treat him to Saturday night in the city, something to make the quick trip a bit more palatable. Neither of us was relishing the Walter conversation on Sunday.

By most standard's, Ty's should not have qualified as one of my favourite bars in New York. There were others that had much cuter patrons and bartenders. It was small, so it could get uncomfortably crowded on weekends, leading to the inevitable spilt drinks. You often had to line up to use the small grubby washroom. But I invariably found myself in Ty's at some point on my nights out when I was living in the city, and it was there that Jonathan and I went after eating at the diner just a few doors up on Christopher Street.

Ty's was a place to relax. The music was not of earsplitting intensity, thus allowing for easy conversations. The atmosphere was not intense either. Not that there wasn't any cruising. The massive framed mirror over the bar was strategically hung at the perfect titled angle so that everyone could see everyone else in the room, without being blatant about checking them out. The drinks were cheap and generous. One might describe the patrons as unpretentious. The younger crowd in the city considered the whole scene tragic, but that was okay with me, and obviously quite a few others. Less attitude was always a good thing.

I had paid for dinner, so Jonathan insisted on buying the drinks. As he maneuvered through the pack balancing two beers, headed toward the window seat to which I had laid claim, I watched, both in my line of vision and in the mirror, the number of heads turning to stare at him. A good-looking man, both coming and going. My good-looking man.

I shuffled some gay tourist magazines and assorted brochures advertising dances and AIDS seminars out of the way, brushed dirt off the section of bench beside me which one of the unpretentious had apparently used as a foot rest, and Jonathan sat down. He passed one of the frothy pints to me.

"Thanks," I said.

"Cheers."

We clinked glasses, and each took a long, refreshing swallow. The evening air at eleven o'clock that night was unseasonably warm and humid for the beginning of October. We gazed into the street and watched the passing hordes of Saturday night Village pedestrians. I had grabbed the window seat because it was such a good perch from which to enjoy the visuals outside, as well as inside.

"There's something I want to ask you and something I want to say to you."

I was startled by the seriousness of the statement and the sobriety of the tone. I decided against a flippant rejoinder.

"What?"

"No. Changed my mind."

"Huh?"

"Switched order. I'll say what I want to say to you first, and then I'll ask the question."

"Whatever."

I waited. Jonathan looked at me and then down at his beer. Then out at the street.

Suddenly, a fight erupted on the sidewalk just outside the bar window. Six or so young toughs were yelling at each other and starting to throw punches. One body was hurled against the window, which rattled ominously. All the guys in the bar turned and looked for a moment and then went back to their drinks. A few passersby walked around the fracas without interrupting their conversations. Then, just as quickly the melee was over, and the kids were tearing down the street.

"New York, and nobody gives a damn," Jonathan said, smiling.

We drank in silence, with Cher providing the background vocals.

"You were saying ..." I prodded.

He set his drink down on the bench. "I want you to know that I appreciate what you're doing."

"What do you mean?"

"You're better at it than the rest of us, and I want you to know that it has not gone unnoticed. By me, at least."

It sounded like I was getting complimented, but I had no idea about what, which made me distrust my perceptions. "Can you be more specific?" I asked.

Jonathan picked up his glass and took another swig.

He looked at me and replied, "You're the one who picks up the pieces in our families. For me and for the others."

I waited.

"I don't think you're even aware of it. It just comes naturally to you."

"Jonathan, that's very sweet of you to say, but I still don't understand. What are you referring to?"

He leaned over and planted a kiss on my forehead. "For someone who is so smart, you demonstrate remarkably limited self-awareness sometimes," he laughed.

I stared at him.

"Okay," he said. "If you're going to force me to cite chapter and verse. Me, through the long, torturous years of my graduate work when I was having existential crises every other day."

"I thought those were just your practicum so that you could internalize the Kierkegaardian angst that you were studying."

He cuffed me on the side of my head.

"Ow," I cried.

"Behave, or I'll shut up and leave you in suspense."

"Sorry. Please. Continue."

"And so many other times over the years, most noticeably this June when Michel died."

Jonathan inhaled deeply and exhaled in kind. "Then there is your sister. You're the one she ran to. You're the one who mediated Carolyn and Jeremy's reconciliation."

"Whoa," I jumped in. "You're wildly overstating the case. Both the current state of their relationship and my role."

"Not according to my brother."

"Pardon me?"

"On the phone last night."

"He called you?"

"No, I called him. After Mom and your parents had all left, I phoned him. You had gone to bed and were out cold. Still jet-lagged. Anyway, I called Jeremy."

"That would have been the middle of the night in London."

"He was waiting for my call. He knew I would call. Carolyn came home a couple nights ago. They're talking. Trying to sort something out. She's still intent on taking up international journalism ..."

"Documentary film-making," I corrected.

"Whatever. It seems likely that they'll be living apart. She'll be travelling most of the time. Jeremy's tiring of London. He thinks he'll move to the continent. Who knows what will happen with them? At least, they still consider themselves a couple. Somehow. Sure wouldn't work for me."

Jonathan flinched. He looked at me. I pretended not to notice as I took another sip of beer.

"Maybe the sex will bring them back together," I offered, continuing the diversion.

"What do you know about their sex life?"

"More than you, apparently."

"Do tell. No, on second thought, don't. I don't want to visualize all that panting and groaning."

"Queasy, are you?" I kidded. "We do our fair share of panting and groaning, I would say."

"Yes, but we, at least, understand the plumbing," he teased, as he made a grab for my crotch.

"Puleeeese, thees ees a peublic place," I scolded, as I brought my legs quickly together.

A couple standing at a nearby bar table laughed. Jonathan and I had been oblivious to our entertainment value.

"Anyway, Jeremy said to tell you thanks. For whatever."

My God. Things change. In life.

"And then there are our parents."

"Come again?"

"Catch-up North Bay. We were talking, before getting diverted by your lascivious sex talk ..."

"... and your lascivious hands," I interrupted.

"We were talking, I was talking, about your"—Jonathan reiterated, suddenly seriously—"your care-giving. I see the way that you care about and for your mom and dad. You're the one that they turn to."

"I'm sorry, but I don't see that." I took another long sip of beer to cover my cringe. I could be pretty disingenuous at times.

"I'm not surprised that you don't see it. But I do. And I know they do."

"What does that mean?" I asked.

"We talk. Your parents and me."

I coughed as a bit of beer slid down my windpipe. "Behind my back."

"Well, you're hardly around. Your parents know that they can't count on Carolyn. As much as they love her, she's too much of a free spirit to have much real life connection to Isabel and Lawrence. Your parents are nothing if not pragmatists. And then there is Patricia."

"Yes, dear, sweet Patricia," I said rolling my eyes. "Isn't it some sort of sacrilege to invoke her name here in the bowels of a New York gay bar?"

I glanced around, fantasizing Patricia immobilized in the midst of the leather, the cowboy hats, the torn T-shirts.

"Though she is our resident familial alien, she has provided your parents with grandchildren," Jonathan noted reflectively.

"That certainly is something not to be scoffed at," I said, "as Margaret made crystal clear last night." Jonathan looked at me. "Sorry, I didn't mean that to sound insensitive," I recanted.

"Apology accepted. Dad and you are the one major conundrum that I still haven't figured out."

"You are sounding a lot more like a psychologist than a philosopher tonight," I observed.

Ignoring me, Jonathan continued, "There's kind of a subtext in your interactions." He looked me squarely in the eyes, as if trying to pierce the veil.

"I think your sleuthing is off-base," I dissembled. "Anyway, we should call it a night. We're both fagged, so to speak, and we have an appointment with Der Fuehrer tomorrow, for which we'll need to be in top form."

Jonathan sighed, finished off his beer, and headed for the door. I followed.

Chapter 24

"Excuse me, Walter. Could I see your pen?"

Walter had been writing notes on a pad when we found his table in a far corner of the airport bar. Files were spread out across the table, and his carry-on lay open on the chair beside him. We shook hands, sat down, and started with informal chitchat, as much as Walter was capable of informal chitchat. Jonathan was describing his fall course load in response to his father's query that, to my ears, sounded like feigned interest. My eyes drifted over the materials in front of us. The pen leapt out at me.

Walter picked it up and, as if examining it for the first time, asked, "What about it?"

"Does that say 'Placer Development'?"

Walter rotated it horizontally so that he could read the lettering running the length of the expensive-looking pen. "Yes. I guess I picked it up on the trip, or maybe back in Canada. I don't remember. They're clients."

"Marcopper," I said.

Walter squinted at me.

It was a name I knew well. Marcopper was a big mining project in the Philippines that had been dumping toxic mine tailings for years into Calancan Bay, just off the island of Marinduque, poisoning the water and devastating the livelihood of the local fishermen.

"Who is Marcopper?" Jonathan asked, piqued that I had interrupted the father-son conversation.

"What about it?" Walter demanded, fixing me with those hard eyes. Jonathan might as well have been back in Toronto.

"An interesting coincidence. That's all."

"How so?"

"Well, it just happens to be one of the case studies that we're considering."

"Jesus Christ."

"Who is Marcopper?" Jonathan repeated, inserting himself into the table discussion.

I turned to him. "What, not who, darling." I glanced back at Walter to see if my use of the affectionate appellation provoked any response.

"Marcopper," I said, turning back to Jonathan, "is not going to win any prizes for corporate responsibility."

"God, you can be a pompous asshole," Walter said, throwing the offending pen down on the table, where it bounced and slid off onto the floor. No one took the initiative to pick it up. "There is no documented evidence for your claims."

"Why is there no documented evidence for the devastation? Oh yeah, there's been no environmental assessment. And why no environmental assessment? Oh yeah, Marcos and his cronies won't allow one. Nor will your client, the esteemed Canadian mining company Placer Development."

"Someday, young man, your misinformation and prejudices are going to trip you up royally. But I'll save you the embarrassment on this occasion by setting you straight on a few little details."

I massaged my chin and said reflectively, "My misinformation and prejudices? Hmmm."

"Don't be so cheeky. The Philippine Government is the major owner of Marcopper, not Marcos. Placer is only a minority shareholder."

"Ah, yes, President Ferdinand Marcos. Such a great democrat. Very open, transparent, non-authoritarian, and incorruptible. I'm sure that he doesn't have any say at all in the economic decisions of Philippine Government corporations. Arms length and all that. As for Placer, forty percent is a pretty significant minority status."

"Thirty-nine point nine percent."

"Sorry, I stand corrected. You're right. I am propagating misinformation. But then there's also that management role. Just so that I'm accurate, can you clarify who it is that actually manages the operation?"

"Well, that is Placer, but under contract to the Philippine Government. They have the final say."

"Right."

"By the way, what are the sources of your misinformation?" Walter pried.

"My information."

"Your misinformation that you misconstrue as accurate information."

"You think I would tell you who our sources are? You're likely to arrange for them to be taken out by some of your hired goon squads."

Jonathan snapped his head in my direction.

I stepped back. "Sorry. That was uncalled for. I apologize. It's just that I'm concerned for the safety of our local contacts in the Philippines. They've already been harassed by Marcos's 'associates.' I will say that some of our research comes from the International Marine Alliance. In Canada, we have been in touch with the Taskforce on the Churches and Corporate Responsibility, who have been in dialogue with Placer management."

"Oh, I'm familiar with the tree-huggers at IMA, or perhaps I should say dolphin-coddlers, and the TCCR folk in Canada are a royal pain in the ecclesiastical ass. That description, by the way, if you'll respect confidences, comes straight from the Archbishop's office. And what did you mean by you're considering Marcopper as a case study?"

"The Commission," I explained. "We're thinking of using various case studies around the world to illuminate particular issues of environmental destruction, unsustainable development, that sort of thing."

"Jesus Christ." Walter brushed the back of his hand across his forehead. "Why didn't you tell me this before? That's a contravention of our agreement."

"What agreement?" Jonathan asked.

"I never signed on to any such agreement. You dictated what you wanted me to do. I never agreed."

"What agreement?" Jonathan repeated.

"Well, you didn't decline." Nodding in Jonathan's direction, Walter added, "I thought we had a quid pro quo."

"Play your cards as you wish," I gambled.

"What bloody agreement?" Jonathan demanded.

I put my hand on his arm. "We'll talk about it later."

Jonathan took hold of my hand, lifted it off his arm, and placed it back on the table in front of me.

"Tom, I just ask that you reconsider using Marcopper. Surely there are plenty of other corporate screw-ups to choose from."

Walter caught my smile at the unintended indictment of his client. "Oh, bloody hell. Waiter, can I get another Bloody Mary over here?" Walter bellowed.

Catching himself, he paused, looked at us, and said, "Sorry, I've forgotten my manners." He laughed at himself. I smiled. Jonathan sat glumly. "What would you boys like to drink? It's on me."

"Coffee's fine for me. I'm due at the office this afternoon," I replied. "Jonathan, you're not working today. You can drink."

"Like I need your permission," he growled.

"Now boys, play nicely," Walter teased.

"Bloody Mary."

"Good," Walter hooted. "Waiter, make that two Bloody Marys. Strong ones."

The nervous waiter brought the beverages in record time. The three of us sat in silence, sipping or guzzling, depending. The Walter volcano, as usual, had subsided as rapidly as it had erupted.

"Listen, boys." Walter began speaking almost at a whisper, as if taking us into his confidence. "I obviously didn't call you to meet with me to argue about some mining project halfway around the world. I've spoken to Margaret. She called after your Friday night family conflab."

"Yes, we gathered," Jonathan said, reasserting his role as having the greater claim to his father's attention. I demurred, gladly.

"She's very upset," Walter explained, as if we didn't know.

Jonathan said, "We realize that."

"It's a bigger issue for her than for me. The grandchildren bit. Future generations are an irrelevant abstraction as far as I'm concerned." He gazed back and forth between Jonathan and me. "Lucky for you boys, eh?"

Without even looking at Jonathan, I could feel the intensity of his blush. I just smiled.

"I'll spend some quality time with Margaret over the next while. Give her some good loving."

Neither Jonathan nor I commented, the image of Margaret's tearstained face in the forefront of our minds.

"I'll take care of your mother. What I wanted to talk to you two about are your siblings. You were both with them in London a month or so ago. And, Tom, obviously, you were with them very recently in Geneva."

He turned and faced me. "Tom, my first question is, just out of interest, how do you, as a religious person, though from my observations and according to my standards you're really some kind of heretical liberal when it comes to tradition and theology as I understand it, but whatever—as a person with a spiritual inclination of some warped degree, how do you feel about your sister having had an abortion?"

"Yeah," Jonathan leapt in. "You haven't said anything about how you feel about what your sister has done. That's what I meant to ask you last night."

Walter's question had been asked with almost benign curiosity, Jonathan's with a hundredfold more affect.

I shifted from Walter's modestly smirking expression to his son's plaintive earnestness and decided to respond to the latter.

"Darling," I said quietly, not looking or caring about any paternal reaction, "I don't know."

"That's it? You, who always has so much to say—that's all you've got?" Jonathan demanded aggressively.

I hesitated, struggling to formulate an adequate response for Jonathan and Walter that I had been unsuccessful in articulating for myself.

"On the one hand, I can see the dilemma that Carolyn was in, just as I related her struggle to you the other night. On the other hand, I can appreciate how devastated your brother and your mother are." I trusted that Walter noted the omission.

Jonathan rotated in his chair to allow sufficient range of motion, brought his arm up, and slapped me across the face.

"Stop being so bloody analytical. Tell me how you feel that your sister killed her foetus!"

I placed my palm against the stinging cheek and sat for a moment. "I don't know, you bastard," I said quietly. "I don't know how I bloody feel. I don't have all the bloody answers. Is that bloody unanalytical enough for you?" Heat radiated from my cheek onto the palm of my hand as I held it there, partly to sooth, partly for defense.

After a few moments in which we sat in silence, Walter said in a cold monotone, "I sympathize with your dilemma, Tom, but I don't really give a damn. I sympathize with Carolyn's dilemma, as you euphemistically phrase it, but I really don't care about that either."

Both Jonathan and I stared at Walter.

"What is important to me is my son, Jeremy. He's no irrelevant abstraction for me. Jonathan, you I don't worry about. Much. Perverted to hell and back, as the Archbishop would say, which I don't care about, and head-in-the-clouds flaky most of the time, but you've got a decent head on your shoulders and you have this little bastard here to keep you grounded. That much, I'll grant him. Deep down, Jonathan, you're strong. Willow strong. Jeremy's not. Well, he is strong. But it's tough oak strong. That makes him a hell of a lot more vulnerable, more brittle than you."

Walter reached across the table, and for the first time that I could ever recall, he gently took hold of my hand in what seemed a gesture of affection.

His grip tightened. My hand started turning red.

His glare burrowed into my skull. "You may be good for my one son, but if you and your sister fracture my other son, so help me God, I'll kill you both."

He dropped my hand, put his papers into his carry-on, and stood up.

The pen remained, untouched, on the floor under the table.

"Come on, Jonathan," he said as he tossed a twenty dollar bill on the table. "You and I have a plane to catch."

Jonathan got up and, without saying good-bye to me, started trailing after his father. As he reached the doorway, he paused. He looked over his shoulder and scowled at me for a moment. Still not smiling, he mimed a reluctant kiss. He turned and left.

Part Three
1993

Chapter 25 —————————————

Málaga wasn't as warm as we had presumed it would be. The sun was beating down and there was almost no breeze coming off the sea, but still the air was chilly. Jonathan and I had to walk along the beach for quite awhile before we found an open seafood kiosk where we could buy lunch. Being the only customers, we had the choice of any of the rather dilapidated tables that stretched out for a few metres from the boardwalk toward the Mediterranean. We chose one close to the water.

This short mid-winter trip had been scheduled, of necessity, to coincide with the university's reading week when Jonathan could get away. He needed the break. We both did.

Jonathan was firmly on the tenure track and hence a member of the publish-or-perish community. He had published a few articles in journals but preferred to sequester his energies for more ambitious and less transitory projects—books. He now had three to his name, two as solo author and one as editor of a collection. The effort of cowing friends and colleagues to contribute to the latter was far more taxing than writing a volume himself. He vowed not to repeat that mistake.

My work on the Brundtland Commission had, as I anticipated, increased my experience and profile, eventually landing me a permanent position on the UN staff. Permanent in that I was a regularized employee, but not permanent as to the department in which I was placed. Since the publishing in 1987 of *Our Common Future*, the Commission's report, I had been variously assigned to projects in United Nations Environment Programme, United Nations Development Programme, and the Non-Government Organization Liaison Office. I had a low threshold for boredom, so I didn't mind the transient work style.

The biggest challenge had been serving as part of the planning staff for the 1992 Rio Earth Summit. Apparently, I had acquitted myself sufficiently on the Brundtland Commission staff that Maurice Strong had wanted me in his office to help prepare the environment and development mega-conference. The intensity of the work leading up to and at Rio was stimulating and nearly killed me. Now we were into follow-up, organizing the new Commission on Sustainable Development agreed upon at Rio. This assignment had me regularly commuting back and forth between the New York and Geneva offices, with side trips to the home hearth as frequently as I could manage—though not nearly as frequently as one's lover would have liked. Fortunately, we had both been prescient enough to get our schedules organized to give us this coinciding break together in Spain.

I had finished up with a set of meetings in Geneva and flew into Barcelona on Friday evening. Jonathan arrived at our hotel on Las Ramblas Saturday morning. Both of us were tired from work and travel, and so we slept for most of the day, oblivious to the vibrant life below our window. On Sunday and Monday we ravaged Barcelona's frenetic Gaudi architecture and devoured the glorious Joan Miró Foundation. Tuesday, we scaled the topographical and aesthetic heights to the Benedictine Abbey at Montserrat.

Travelling by train from Barcelona to Málaga took up most of Wednesday. The hotel concierge was able to score us a couple good tickets for Marilyn Horne at the opera house in the evening. We tipped him at the time for his assistance. I doubled the tip after we returned to the hotel; such was our lingering exuberance over the diva's concert.

Now, on Thursday, we had already visited Picasso's Casa Natal in the morning, more out of a sense of cultural obligation than genuine interest, and we planned to hit the Picasso Museum for real aesthetic nourishment after lunch. Except that we were exhausted from the week's whirlwind activities, and I had a cold. Málaga had been a miscalculation if we were hoping to include a warm beach segment in our vacation. February clearly wasn't beach weather on the north side of the Mediterranean. Everyone else apparently knew that.

"Here, put my coat around your shoulders," Jonathan said, passing his jacket over to me. "You're shivering."

"But you need it," I said, accepting his offer. He smiled at my feeble protest. He licked a bit of grease from his fingers and looked with a disappointed expression at the empty plate that had moments earlier teamed with fried calamari. I pushed my still half-full platter across the table. The fever that was starting to announce itself had diminished my appetite.

"But you need it," he said as he dug in.

I leaned back in the chair, carefully balancing my body so as not to tip, stretched my legs out in front of me, turned my head toward the sun, and closed my eyes, letting the rays bathe my face with their modest warmth. At least our ill-timed beach holiday had the benefit of providing this quiet space for Jonathan to savour his lunch in peace and me to doze, undisturbed by chattering tourists.

I came to just in time to avoid toppling over onto the sand. Our table was clean, and Jonathan's chair was empty. I looked around and saw him, elbows leaning on the counter of the kiosk, with his back to me. Our used plates and cutlery were piled beside him.

Jonathan was talking to the Alejandro, or so his nametag read— the young man who had taken our order, prepared our calamari, and delivered it and the accompanying cerveza to our table. He was probably in his mid-twenties, though his ruddy complexion, a product of a life spent in the Mediterranean sun, made him look older than he was. Jonathan said something, and his new friend laughed. They were too far away for me to make out the conversation. Jonathan had more facility in Spanish than I did, so I might not have been able to follow them even if I were within hearing range.

Jonathan turned around and saw me watching them. He waved. He spoke again to Alejandro, who then blew me a kiss.

Maybe there was a plan in the works? Not likely. Jonathan had never initiated a threesome. When I had tentatively suggested such an idea the few times over the years when the opportunity seemed to present itself, he had shut me down in two seconds flat. Anyways, Alejandro was working, and I was not feeling well.

Forget the fantasy, Tom. It's not going to happen.

And it didn't.

We had a good time in Málaga. We didn't have that good a time.

Chapter 26 ──────────────

My parents broke the news over dessert.

"I'm so pleased!" I enthused with genuine delight.

"Mom and Dad, that's great," Patricia echoed. "You've worked so hard, you deserve to take it easy. Early retirement. Wish I could envisage that for Robert and me. But don't worry about us. Any of us," she said, glancing at me. "What savings you may have acquired and the equity in the house are for you to use for your own leisure and relaxation. We're not counting on any inheritance."

Patricia, with a mortgage, two kids, a husband with a modest salary as an assistant football coach at a small Mid-western college that no one had ever heard of, meant exactly the opposite.

"You make us sound like we're cascading into our dotage years," Dad chuckled.

"Far from it," I replied, intent on reasserting authenticity in the conversation. "You've got your health, physically and mentally …"

"You better believe it," Mom interjected.

I smiled. "Absolutely. So good for you for getting out of the rat race."

"We're both nervous about the next number of years here. The recession is wreaking havoc with public finances, and if Harris and the Conservatives win the next election, they'll bring a sledgehammer to education and health budgets. I don't have to worry about losing my job, but with growing class sizes, I won't be able to teach the way I want to, the way the kids deserve."

"I hear you, Dad," Patricia chimed in. "The recession has been brutal for us at the Bible College. Our donations are way down, and, of course, we don't get the level of public funding that other American universities get, certainly nowhere near what Canadian universities get."

The arrow was shot without even a glance in my direction.

"Lawrence and I have both come to the conclusion that now is a good time for us to make our exits from the systems here." Mom smiled at Dad.

"We'll get a reduced pension, of course, since we're taking early retirement, but it will be sufficient. Our living costs will be lower." Dad smiled at Mom.

Patricia and I were looking at Mom and Dad, who were looking at each other, smiling.

The sound of the backdoor being jerked open and slamming shut broke the silence that had descended on the living room conversation.

"Luke! Take your boots off first." Robert's voice, even in disciplinary mode, exuded good-heartedness.

Bootless Luke came tearing into the living room. "Grandma, do you have a toboggan or a sled or something that we could take to the park? I hope, I hope, I hope."

"You think there will be enough snow, sweetie?"

"You've got more snow left than we do at home," Naomi said, having caught up to her brother. "Of course, this is Canada," she added with a smile that hovered precariously between whimsical and condescending.

"We're not quite at the Arctic Circle, my dear," Dad corrected.

"Of course. I know that, Grandpa. Waterloo is at forty-three degrees latitude and the Arctic Circle is at sixty-six degrees. Dayton is only at thirty-nine degrees. It's not the latitude that affects the snow levels so much, though. It's more the lake effect precipitation that you get here in Southwestern Ontario. The late March storms that you had were quite intense. So, lucky for us, this is going to be one of those Easters when you've still got snow on the ground."

"Thank you for the geography lesson, Miss Precocious. Since you two munchkins are so keen on the snow, why weren't you here last week to help me with the shoveling?"

"We were in school, silly," Luke teased.

"Luke, don't call your grandfather silly," Patricia scolded, for real.

"I'm called much worse by the kids at school, I'm sure. Particularly behind my back," Dad sighed.

"What do you think, Lawrence?" Mom asked. "Is there something down in the basement or in the attic that they could use?"

Dad turned to Patricia and me. "Do you two remember the flying saucers you had?"

"Oh, my God, they were so much fun," I replied. "They flew like the wind but were so unstable you couldn't help but get thrown off before you got halfway down the hill."

"They were awful things," Patricia said. "My little bum was so sore every time I used it."

"Mommy, you said *bum*," Luke giggled.

"That's enough, son," Robert chided. Then he added, "When she was a little girl, she did have a little bum. Now that she's a big woman, she has a ..."

"That's far enough," Patricia intervened.

"Yes, well—I'm sure we still have the flying saucers downstairs somewhere," Dad said. "Robert, will you help me pull them out?"

"Will you come with us, Uncle Tom? Please, please, please."

As if on cue, my throat seized up, and I coughed several times, a sign of the malingering cold that I hadn't been able to shake. I had a doctor's appointment tomorrow for a check-up.

"I'd love to Luke, but I don't think that I should. I have to drive back to Toronto tonight, so I think I should have a bit of a nap before dinner."

"What? You're not staying overnight?" Mom's disappointment hurt. "We see so little of you as it is—I thought that you would stay longer."

"That doesn't leave us much time to talk," Dad said.

Patricia looked at me. "Jonathan has you on a short leash, does he?"

Mom was fretting. Dad was fidgety.

Dinner was over. There was an hour or two before the kids' bedtime, perhaps more if they could leverage the holiday trip to the grandparents for some extra leniency.

"Did Luke and Naomi bring some books to read or games they could play upstairs?" Mom asked Patricia.

"We'll stay downstairs with you, thank you," Naomi declared.

Mom looked at Dad, who turned to Naomi and Luke. "Would you kids mind busying yourself upstairs for a while? Grandma and I want to talk to your mom and dad and Uncle Tom about something important. In private."

Patricia and I glanced at each other, eyebrows raised in tandem.

"Did we do something wrong?" Luke worried, staring up from the floor where he was nestled against Mom's legs.

"No, no, dear. Nothing at all." Mom kissed the top of his head. "It's just adult stuff."

"I am a young adult," Naomi asserted, so much her mother's daughter.

"Come on, kids," Robert said as he grabbed Luke and thrust him up on his shoulders. Luke giggled. "We've got some books that we can read as Grandma suggests." Naomi didn't budge.

"Naomi, go with your father," Patricia said sternly.

Pouting, Naomi got up and marched out of the room. "Nancy Drew will be more interesting than your adult stuff anyway," she called as she ascended the stairs.

"I hope Robert can rejoin us," Dad said.

"It's okay. I'll fill him in on anything that he needs to know. Now, what's this about?"

Mom and Dad looked back and forth at each other. Mom stood up, grabbed a dining room chair, put it beside Dad's recliner, and sat down on it, taking his hand in hers.

"Oh, Jesus, what's wrong," I blurted.

"We've made some decisions," Dad started.

"Yes, yes. The early retirement. Have you forgotten that you already told us? Maybe some early dementia," Patricia laughed with uncharacteristic nervousness.

"There's more," Mom responded, not in kind.

"We're going to sell the house," Dad said.

"Wow."

"You think that's wise, Dad?" I asked. "Won't you need projects like the garden and house maintenance to keep you active?"

Dad and Mom chuckled together. Patricia and I did not.

"Keeping active will not be a problem."

"Father, Mother, stopped being so coy. What is this about?" Patricia spoke for us both, for once.

"Gee, I wish Carolyn could have been here for this," Mom lamented.

"For what?" Patricia almost shouted.

"Is everything all right down here?" Robert asked, having appeared unnoticed in the doorway.

"We don't know, honey. Mom and Dad are selling the house."

"Great idea," Robert congratulated them.

Patricia glowered at him. "And where will we stay on visits?"

"Oh yeah," Robert back-pedaled.

"Mom and Dad," I said with deliberate calmness. "What is it that prompted you to make this decision?"

"Your mother and I ..." Dad turned to her and placed his left palm on top of their clasped hands. She reciprocated.

"Now you're getting melodramatic," Patricia scolded.

"Sorry, dear. Your father and I are taking early retirement from our current jobs and selling the house because we are going to take up volunteer work."

"Overseas," Dad added, grinning.

"Wonderful," Robert responded

"No." Patricia was on her feet. "No, it is definitely not wonderful. You're too old for something like this. Look at you. Dad had the heart scare last year. You, Mom, are not as slight and agile as you used to be. Not obese, but overweight. You're in no condition to start traipsing around the world."

Mom leapt up and tried to hug her eldest. Patricia pushed her away. "We've given this a great deal of serious thought. It's not something that we're entering into lightly."

"Let us explain, dear," Dad said.

"Indeed, you have a lot to explain."

"Patricia." Robert was by her side and clasped her hand.

"Don't shush me."

"Patricia, sit down," Robert commanded.

Patricia sat down.

Mom returned to her seat beside Dad. "We really didn't want to upset you kids."

"That's okay, we're all adults here," I said, glancing through the doorway to see if Naomi was eavesdropping. "Spill the beans."

"It's a second honeymoon," Dad said.

"How sweet," Robert gushed.

"What do you know about their first honeymoon?" Patricia was a step ahead of the rest of us.

"You're going back to Mexico?" I speculated.

"No, but you're on the right track."

"This isn't twenty questions, for God's sake." Patricia maintained her earlier tone but at a lower volume.

"Remember last year when we went on that church-sponsored visit to Kenya and they took us up to the camp with all the displaced Sudanese refugees? Well, that was quite an eye-opener." He looked at Patricia and said, "Eye-opening, just as our honeymoon had been in Mexico. We want to give something more back, for all the blessings that we have experienced in life."

Mom took hold of Dad's hand, adding, "We've both got skills that could be useful. We've got no responsibilities here, what with you kids all living productive, independent lives on your own."

"And what about your grandchildren?" Patricia snarled. "You don't care about seeing them growing up?"

"We will be back on furlough from time to time, darling," Dad responded.

"We will be helping many Lukes and Naomis who don't have the privileges that our own do," Mom added. "But in truth, that is our biggest regret."

We heard children's laughter upstairs. Mom looked down at the floor.

"I was so proud of them," I said as Jonathan squirmed a bit behind me. "They even had a comeback for Patricia. 'Well, dear, you and Robert did missionary service in Africa. We're just following your example.' That took at least some of the air out of Patricia's balloon."

Jonathan moved again. "Can you sit up for a moment? My arm's a little cramped."

We were lying in bed, propped up against the headboard, Jonathan's arm around my shoulders, my head resting on his chest.

"True, but your parents are considerably older than Patricia and Robert were when they were over there."

"And, hence, much more experienced." I explained that that was one of the things the church apparently found interesting about them as candidates. Mom had years of both practical nursing experience and administrative work. Dad had been a teacher forever, had a proven capacity to learn languages and dialects, and was a talented carpenter, untrained, granted, but he could build just about anything he put his mind to. All told, they presented an attractive package of "enthusiasm and experience," to quote the description of the interviewer.

"You have no reservations about this plan?"

I sat up and took a drink from the water glass on the nightstand. "Yes, I am concerned, of course. It's a huge life change for them. But they also claim to have been inspired in part by us. All of us."

"How so?"

I readjusted myself on the edge of the bed and turned to face Jonathan. "Well, the comment about 'following your example' was mainly strategic, I think, but they are genuinely impressed by Patricia and Robert's long-term involvement in the Nigerian development projects. They are immensely proud of Carolyn's doc films. They've got a whole video library that they keep lending out to all their friends, ad nausea, I suspect. And my work at the Earth Summit and now setting up the new Commission. They say that they've been listening over the years to all my blather—my word, not theirs—about the issues in developing countries."

"*Blather* is not a bad descriptor."

I picked up my pillow and whacked him on the head.

"Don't get self-righteous, professor. They cited your latest book as an inspiration as well."

"Oh, now you're talking sense. Tell me more."

I took aim with the pillow, but this time he was prepared, his own in hand, threatening retaliation. After a few moments of standoff, we both slowly lowered our weapons.

"Dad has read it twice and apparently has tried to explain it to Mom. She said it was very thought-provoking."

"Thought-provoking. That's sort of like *interesting*. Meaning that they didn't understand it. Limited comprehension skills run in the family."

Pillows engaged. With equal odds, Jonathan resorted to his surefire conquering tactic—tickling.

"Stop ... no fair ..." I screamed, when I could catch my breath.

"All's fair in love and any chance to prick your ego," he replied, in total self-control.

Damn people who aren't ticklish.

"We'll wake the tenants." I appealed breathlessly to his landlord proprietorship. "Or Althena's ghost."

That stopped him cold.

Sobered, after a moment he asked, "How is it that my book inspired them?"

Forgoing a sarcastic rejoinder, I tried to repeat Dad's comments. "He said something to the effect that he liked very much your analysis of the responsibility for social engagement as a fundamental dimension of being human."

"Nothing novel there. That's Heidegger and Foucault," Jonathan said dismissively. I found his prodding for more specifics about the compliment transparent and endearing.

"Yeah, but then you applied the analysis to the case studies. He particularly liked the critique of Western educational paradigms and the appraisal of the World Bank structural adjustment programs. He thought the sexual liberation one was a little stretched."

"I see."

"The point is that my work, your books, Carolyn's films, and Patricia and Robert's Africa projects have tapped into their midlife crisis assessment of what they have accomplished in life. They want to contribute more."

"Can't fault that."

"So it's hard for us to object."

I got up and walked to the window. We had a more expansive view of the back garden since we'd moved down to the main floor. Low cloud cover obstructed the moonlight but also reflected the ambient light of the city. The late winter scene appeared like, well, late winter, ghostly grey, deadly dormant. I hadn't been around enough last fall to do a pre-winter cleanup. Jonathan hadn't had the inclination. The raggedy tentacles of the clematis that scaled the back fence protested our negligence. Toppled stocks of sunflowers, hydrangeas, and delphiniums stuck accusingly out of the residual snow.

Jonathan came up behind me and wrapped his arms around my slightly shivering body.

"You okay?" he whispered in my ear, after having given it a little nibble.

"A bit nervous for them, I guess."

"Ditto."

Chapter 27

"**Well,** it's about time we saw you in here. It's been a while."

I had lucked into getting Alan as my GP a few years ago when my original Toronto doctor retired. Alan was smart and very personable, and his office was within walking distance of the university and our house. In contrast to my previous doctor, Alan was gay. I liked that. It felt more comfortable.

"Sorry. I'm hardly ever in town. Then when I do get home, I usually haven't thought far enough ahead to phone for an appointment. I was surprised that I could get in today. I thought that you might be taking an extended Easter break."

"Well, the office is officially closed today. I'm not seeing any patients. A long-planned quiet day so that Jennifer and I can get caught up on paperwork."

"Really? How come she booked me in then?"

Alan laughed. "She thinks of you as something of a celebrity."

"What?"

"Ask her to show you her Tom Fischer scrapbook sometime. No, on second thought, that might embarrass her. It's full of articles from when you were in the papers at the time of that big UN event in Rio last year. She even has several videotapes. She kept her VCR primed to record whenever you came on any of the news reports."

"The Earth Summit? I was just the Secretariat's media spokesperson. I wasn't making the news, just reporting the progress, or lack thereof, in the negotiations."

"Didn't matter in her eyes. You were on TV almost nightly for two weeks, and that was enough for her."

"Well, I'll have to disabuse her," I said. "Working the Summit was a bitch. I got the media assignment by being the staff who pulled the short straw."

"I kind of doubt that. You're very articulate, and you were fast on your feet when peppered by hostile reporters in the news conferences."

"Ah ha!" I crowed. "So Jennifer wasn't the only one watching for me to show up on her TV screen."

Alan blushed. "I follow the news," he protested.

"Anyway, that was almost a year ago. Now I'm back to being a faceless functionary. I do apologize for intruding on your filing day," I said halfheartedly.

"Yeah, right," he laughed. "Is there something specific that you wanted me to check besides a general exam after so long an absence?"

"Yes. I've had a persistent low-grade cold that has hung on for months. I haven't been able to shake it. It's probably nothing—a product of not enough sleep and too much travel across too many time zones. But it is unusual for me."

Alan got up from his desk and walked over to his counter to pick up his stethoscope. "Shirt off and up on the examining table here," he commanded.

"Yes, sir! Brrr. Hasn't modern medical science figured out a way to warm the ends of stethoscopes?"

"Just sit here like a good boy and breathe deeply. In and out. Slowly."

Though the examination brought those beautiful brown eyes within inches of my face, I gazed past his head and out his office window.

"Everything sounds clear." He put down the stethoscope, whose function was always self-evident, and started the double hand-tapping around my chest and back, a procedure I never understood the purpose of.

"Okay, tell me more about the history of this cold. How long have you had it and what exactly have the symptoms been?"

I thought back for a moment. "I guess it has been almost a year, ever since a horrible flu I had just after the Summit."

"A horrible flu?"

"Yeah. Jonathan came down to Rio at the end of the conference. We had planned to spend some time in Rio and then go to Buenos Aires. Oh, and stopping in Iguazu Falls ..."

"Get back to the flu."

"Well, I remember starting to feel unwell during our one night stay at Iguazu. By the time we got to Buenos Aires, I was sick as a dog. I'm sure it was because I had just spent over two weeks at the Summit, working eighteen-hour days without a break. I was completely whacked. I went straight to bed when we got to the hotel in Buenos Aires. Jonathan was so pissed. 'All I get of you is the dregs.' He has said that repeatedly over our years together, with reason, I'm afraid."

"And the flu symptoms?"

"It was really intense. I'd never felt so sick—fever, headache, chills, achy all over." I remembered back to how I had gotten into the shower with the water as hot as I could stand to stop the shivering. I felt so weak it was difficult to keep upright. I think I sat down in the shower because I was afraid of falling. I was glad that Jonathan had gone out to do some sightseeing. He would have wanted to take me to the hospital because I appeared so sick.

"How long did it last?" Alan had picked up my chart and scribbled notes.

"That was the weird thing. It seemed to break almost as quickly as it had hit me. I felt better the next day, or at least was well enough that I could fake it and go out with Jonathan. He wanted to take me to the antique shops in San Telmo."

Alan sat at his desk. He continued writing. I took that as a signal that the examination was over. I put my shirt back on. I crossed over and sat in the chair opposite him.

He put down his pen and leafed through my chart for a few moments before looking up at me.

"Tom. When was the last time you got tested for HIV?"

I wrinkled my brow. "Why do you ask?"

"When was the last time?"

"Oh, Jonathan and I have gotten tested regularly over the years. My results are in the chart, right? Always negative."

"And the most recent time was when?"

I couldn't remember. It had been a while. Maybe a year. Or more. I looked out the window and didn't respond.

"Tom," Alan said. "Tom, look at me."

I left the struggling early spring buds on the tree outside to fend for themselves and refocused on Alan.

"A flu like you describe is a bit suspicious," he was saying. "But we won't know anything for sure until we do the blood work and get the results back. There very well could be another explanation, so we'll do other tests as well."

I leaned back in the chair, the fingers of my right hand drumming frenetically on my knee.

"Under the circumstances, I think we need to talk," Alan began quietly, "about your recent sexual history. What about Jonathan?"

"What about him?"

"Does he have other sexual partners that you know of?"

"Jonathan? Oh God, no. Mr. Monogamous."

From day one, Jonathan had expected that we would be exclusive. He had no interest in recreational sex with others and assumed that I would feel likewise—a misconception that I let ride. My coming clean with him years ago, after Walter had forced my hand, had not been a pleasant scene. Jonathan couldn't understand why I found it hard to replicate his standard, and he was pissed off that my meanderings meant that we needed, of necessity, to always practice safe sex. He exacted a certain justifiable revenge by circumscribing the repertoire of our activity in the bedroom. The opportunities for me to be the fucker as opposed to the fuckee, infrequent as they had been, evaporated altogether.

I placed one hand on top of the other to steady the fidgeting.

Alan was quiet for a few moments before asking, "What about you?"

"Well, there have been a few times since my last test." My mind tore through the calendar, the places, the men. "But they've been of the non-risky sort, with appropriate protection."

My memory scan suddenly screeched to a halt. "Oh, Jesus. There's one possibility."

Shit. It only takes one.

"What about it?"

I looked back out the window at the prematurely opened buds on the tree, naked and exposed, with a dusting of snow on them.

"Well, I had been drinking so I can't be sure. But I'm not certain that the guy used a safe. He had one. I saw him open it. But"—I paused and swallowed—"afterwards, I wasn't sure that he had used it."

"Do you remember when?"

"Um, let me think," I said. "Yeah, it was at one of the planning sessions a few months before the Summit. It would have been, um, November or December, 1991."

"That would make it six months before your bad flu when you were in Buenos Aires."

"Yes," I said. "That's right. Is that significant? Six months?"

Alan closed my file and folded his hands together on top of it. "As I said, we won't know anything for sure until we do the blood work." He paused. "But yes, it does fit a pattern that we're seeing."

Another pause.

"I'm sorry, Tom."

Chapter 28

It took little coaxing to get Jonathan to agree to attend St. Thomas for the Maundy Thursday Eucharist. Sheila and I, allied in a common cause, proved a formidable force in reinforcing his intrinsic interest.

Jonathan was a classical music connoisseur and acknowledged the prodigious library of sacred music. However, his agnosticism had long ago stripped his appreciation of any dimension other than the aesthetic. St. Thomas had one of the best choirs and organists in the city, so he was up for attending a fine "concert."

Sheila had a personal, decidedly unliturgical, interest. For the past several years, she had been seeing the baritone soloist. Markus was a professional structural engineer, having graduated from Sheila's department. Against university protocol, they had started dating when he was in his final year. The increasing stale ribbing we subjected him to questioned the structural integrity of buildings on which he'd worked, given the suspect nature of his high scholastic marks. He expressed his artistic aptitude through his love of architecture, but it was in his unquenchable passion for music that it truly thrived. He paid the rent through his job in his family's construction business. He nourished his soul at choir practice.

My reasons were complex. In my hierarchy of musical tastes, organ and choral music were the ultimate. Attendance at church had become sporadic in my adult years, but sacred ritual retained meaning, and prayer was more than episodic. After my discussion with Alan earlier in the day, I needed it all—the art, the liturgy, and the spirituality.

I had said nothing to Jonathan. After all, we wouldn't know anything for sure until the blood work results. Meanwhile, I would keep my suppressed angst to myself.

As we moved down the centre aisle, scanning the rapidly filling pews for room for two, we didn't notice Sheila standing and motioning to us. An inappropriately loud "Pssst!" accompanied by vigorous pointing at the places beside her draped with her coat finally caught our attention. Smart, boisterous, lovable Sheila was chronically unaware of the appropriate decorum for settings in which she found herself, high Anglican churches included. Ignoring the sucking teeth around us, we squeezed by the regular parishioners to make our way to the seats she was holding for us.

"About time!" she said in a loud stage whisper.

Jonathan and I both grimaced in apology and remained silent in a futile effort to model the expected behaviour.

"What? Were you two doing the naughties and lost track of time?" she giggled.

Jonathan put his arm around her shoulder, kissed her cheek, and mimed a *shush*.

Still giggling, she rolled her eyes and put her finger to her lips in acquiescence. Jonathan looked at me, smiling, and rolled his eyes, a silent acknowledgment between us that it had likely been Sheila and Markus most recently doing the naughties, fueled by after-work cocktails.

I eased myself down onto the kneeler, trying vainly for inconspicuousness, ignoring the commotion next to me while my companions poked each other in the ribs. I concentrated, emptying my senses of any awareness of my surroundings and my mind of the cacophony that had consumed it all day. As I reached a point of tranquility, I jumped when the organ pipes vibrated with the discordant strains of Jean Langlais's modernist "Médiation Suite Médiévale." However proficiently played, it was not Gregorian. I sat back up, disgruntled.

Giggling and rib-poking resurfaced next to me as the choir processed down the aisle with the opening hymn. Markus stared directly ahead toward the altar as he passed the end of our aisle. Sheila sighed, part disappointment, part lust. I closed my eyes and drifted with the interwoven strains of choir and organ. *Alone thou goest forth, O Lord.* This was more like it.

The service progressed. I heard but didn't hear the readings, familiar from years of repetition. The sixteenth-century "Pange Lingua" choral mass of Josquin dea Pres was taking me where I wanted to go. I was vaguely aware my eyes were moist. I was back with Alan, who reassuringly massaged my forearm. An unexpectedly sharp pinch brought me back. I opened my eyes. Jonathan had his hand on my arm, his eyebrows raised in query. I patted his hand and smiled to throw him off the scent.

The privacy I yearned for was granted at the point of the Eucharist. Awkwardly, I nudged past Jonathan and Sheila's knees out into the aisle to join the line slowly making its way toward the altar rail. In the middle of a crowd, I was thankful to be alone. Step, pause. Step, pause. *Ubi caritas et amor.* As I slowly paced into the chancel, voices encompassed me, disembodied beauty emanating from vocal chords within arm's reach, including a familiar resonant baritone.

I steadied myself on the altar rail as I knelt.

"The Body of our Lord Jesus Christ, which was given for thee, preserve thy body and soul unto everlasting life: Take, and eat this, in remembrance that Christ died for thee, and feed on him in thy heart, by faith, with thanksgiving."

I crossed myself and extended my tongue to receive the wafer. I pulled it back in and clumsily raised my cupped hands. *Bodily fluids. Different world now. Maybe.*

Gnarled priestly fingers gently placed the wafer in my palm and hesitated. A warm hand cupped my cheek, for just a moment, and moved on.

"The Blood of our Lord Jesus Christ, which was shed for thee, preserve thy body and soul unto everlasting life: drink this in remembrance that Christ's Blood was shed for thee, and be thankful."

Christ's blood. My blood. Thankful?

I sipped.

He wiped the rim, not just after me.

I pressed my arms against the rail to stand up and followed the pair of feet ahead of me through the left door of the chancel and headed toward the opening, out into the sanctuary. Just before I moved through the doorway, a hand touched my elbow. I stopped and turned around. A profusion of silver white, delicately coifed hair filled my view as I looked down on her five-foot frame. The wrinkles coating her face could not disguise the tensed muscles as her searching eyes looked up at me.

"Are you okay?" she whispered.

Other communicants gently squeezed past us in the narrow passageway.

"Oh. Yes, I'm sorry," I stuttered.

"Are you sure?" she persisted.

I brushed the moisture from my cheeks. "Yes, just mourning a loss. Thank you. That's very kind."

She took my damp hand in hers. "God bless," she said, and headed back to her seat.

Chapter 29 ————————————

Fernando Gutiérrez got up from his desk and walked over to the window. A tug was maneuvering a barge teeming with garbage down the East River.

"You think that I don't appreciate the strain that this type of work places on our home life? My wife refused to move to New York. Her elderly parents live just outside of Santiago, and she wanted to stay close to them as they aged. She didn't want our kids growing up in New York City. I get home four times a year, if I'm lucky. My family comes to New York once or twice a year. Believe me, Tom, I know about sacrifices. You want to know about the divorce rate at the UN? HR keeps statistics. It's not a pretty picture. I've come close to being an additional digit in their column of losers."

Without turning around, he continued, somewhat less rant-like.

"We do it, we put up with the sacrifices, we place intolerable burdens on our families, because we believe in what we're doing—the peacekeeping missions, the development work, human rights issues, conflict mediation. Many failures, but some important achievements."

"What have you done with the cynical Fernando that I knew and loved?" I asked.

Still with his back to me, I could hear him smiling as he carried on.

"And what all you folks accomplished with the Earth Summit. Environmental issues are now firmly on the inter-governmental table. Climate change, for God's sake. You had a big hand in moving that issue forward."

"Now I know you're manipulating me," I interjected. "You were never enthusiastic about the emergence of the environmental agenda. What was it you called it? 'A Northern middle class diversion while the impoverished South continues to suffer.' Something like that. Besides, you know me better than that. I don't care about saving the world. I'm just in it for the money and the glory."

Fernando wheeled around. His smile was gone. "Don't mock me, son. And you're far too young to become a professional cynic. Cynicism is a luxury we can't afford."

He turned back to the window, adding in a quieter voice, "That's a lesson that I learned the hard way. Hopefully not too late."

I sat in silence, sobered by the tone of his lecture.

Fernando sat back down in his chair, rested his elbows on his cluttered desk, and stared at me. "Okay, I suppose that I need to humour you. You've developed quite a little fan club among senior management. They want to keep you around. Beats me why. So give me the full scoop."

"What do you mean?"

"You said that you had strong reservations about taking the job to help set up the Climate Change Secretariat because of 'family concerns.' What family concerns?"

"Well ..." I hesitated. "Geneva, to start with. I lived apart from Jonathan during the three years of the Brundtland Commission. That was not easy."

"Pfft! It's a shorter flight from Geneva to Toronto than from New York to Santiago. If I can do it, why can't you? You're younger. Besides, there's word in the corridors that in a couple years the Climate Change Secretariat may move from Geneva to Bonn. The Germans are going to have plenty of empty facilities once they relocate the government back to Berlin."

"As if Bonn is substantially closer to Toronto than Geneva?" I scoffed.

"No, true," he smiled mischievously. "But think of the nightlife."

I guffawed. "There's only one European town that has a quieter nightlife than Geneva, and that's Bonn."

"*Si*, but it's a short tram ride to Köln."

I wrinkled my forehead. "And what do you know about the nightlife in Cologne?"

"A man has his needs. Particularly when he is thousands of miles from his wife's bed."

I threw up my hands.

After a few moments of silence, Fernando, still staring at me asked, "And ...?"

"And what?"

"Come on, Tom. We've known each other for a decade. I can tell when you're holding back."

I can't go there. Still don't know the test results. Won't until next Monday.

"There are my parents. You said that your wife made a decision that she wanted and needed to be close to her parents. Well, I've got some of the same issues."

"I don't see the problem. You can visit them every time that you come back to Toronto to see Jonathan. They live near you, don't they?"

"Not in Toronto, but in a town nearby. Yes, except they are going to leave Canada."

"Oh, yeah? Retiring to Florida, like other Canadian snowbirds?"

"Not exactly. They are retiring from their current jobs in Canada, but they have enlisted with a church-based NGO. They're going to be doing development work, teaching and healthcare activities, overseas."

"No shit. Good for them. Do they know where they are going?"

I looked out the window. The barge had disappeared.

"Sudan."

"Oh, my God. You've got to talk them out of it," Fernando stormed. "There's been a civil war going on for ten years, you know. The last thing we need is naïve Western do-gooders, who we have to protect, diverting our scarce resources from the real victims, the Sudanese civilians who need our protection."

I bristled. "They are not naïve do-gooders," I protested, hoping it was convincing enough to mask my own lack of conviction. "They know what they are getting into. They'll be working on humanitarian projects with the Council of Churches in Sudan. Mom and Dad's church, the United Church of Canada, has been a development partner with the Sudanese churches for years."

"And you're okay with this plan?"

I didn't respond.

"I see." Fernando paused for a few moments and then chuckled.

"Well, at some point, I guess you have to let them grow up, fly the nest, and make their own decisions, for better or worse."

Continuing in a bright tone, he said, "Listen, there are better flight connections to Khartoum from Europe than from Toronto or New York. If you want to keep an eye on them, it would make sense to be working in Geneva. Ah ha. Checkmate." He clapped his hands together.

"There's other stuff, other reasons that I'm reluctant to move away from home."

"You are such a hard sell," Fernando grumbled.

He started leafing distractedly through the mound of correspondence sitting in front of him on his desk. "You know, there is this little situation developing in Rwanda." He stared down through his papers, through his desk, through the floor and the building and the ground beneath, all the way to hell.

"I'm supposed to be working on the draft Security Council resolution. Boutros Boutros-Ghali wants to hear from me before the end of the day." He sighed and then said abruptly, "I don't have the time to hold your hand indefinitely." His frustration was genuine.

"Yes, I realize that. I apologize."

Neither of us said anything for a few moments. I watched him. He did not return the gesture.

Hesitantly, I said, "Can I propose an alternate role?"

He jerked his head up. "I'm offering you a plum job in a new cutting-edge international organization that just happens to be what you've been working your butt off to create, and now you want to negotiate a counterproposal? *Caradura!*"

I squinted.

He smiled. "Chutzpah. Spanish for *chutzpah*."

"Oh, thank you."

He pushed the correspondence pile off-centre, reached over for a pad, picked up his pen, and glared at me. "Okay, professor. What are your terms?"

"Jonathan is the professor," I corrected.

The glare intensified.

"Okay, sorry," I blurted. "Not funny."

I took a deep breath.

"How about a consultancy role?"

Now it was Fernando's turn to squint. "You're willing to sacrifice a permanent regular position, complete with benefits, for a consultancy with less security and considerably fewer benefits?" He set his pen down and leaned back in his chair. "Explain, please."

"Well, the key attraction would be the flexibility." I was winging it. The option hadn't really occurred to me until moments before. "I could take on some specific projects with the Climate Change Secretariat that would not require my full time presence in Geneva. Or Bonn. Wherever. Sacrificing the benefits wouldn't be a big deal. I'm healthy."

That might be about to change. My mind raced. Maybe I could get covered under Jonathan's healthcare plan. The university recently altered its policies to allow for coverage for same-sex partners of their employees.

I plowed on. "Since Rio, I've also been receiving more requests to lecture, which I can't really do while working full-time for the UN."

"So I was right," Fernando laughed triumphantly. "I can call you *professor.*"

"No. Nothing grandiose. Just some guest lecturing," I replied, hoping he would press me.

"Cut the false modesty, Tom," he said. "What invitations? What non-grandiose guest lecturing?"

I blushed. "I related to many of the NGOs in the planning leading up to the Earth Summit. I got particularly close to the World Council of Churches folks. Now, I've gotten some invitations from theological colleges to do some lecturing on the outcomes of Rio, the challenges for the UN to implement the agreements, the struggles, focusing on the ethical dimensions of the environment and development linkage."

"Cushy campus life. Oxford? Harvard? Sorbonne?"

"No," I responded with undisguised satisfaction in my voice. "The two specific invitations are from theological colleges in Bangalore and San Jose, Costa Rica."

"I know where San Jose is, *pendejo.* That's Spanish for ..."

"I can guess."

"What's that sound?" Jonathan's voice rapidly escalated from lighthearted conversation to paramedic emergency response. "Are you in the bathtub?"

"Ah, yes, I am."

"Don't you know that you could get electrocuted?"

"I don't think so," I responded. "Maybe in the old days, but surely with modern phones that's not a problem. Is it?"

"I'm a philosopher, not a physicist, but I have the strong impression that it is never a good idea to mix electricity and water—not in the old days, not today."

"Well, why do they put telephones in bathrooms in hotels these days if it's so dangerous?"

"If you're sitting on the toilet having a crap, you're not in contact with water," Jonathan lectured. "Unless you've fallen in."

"Well, you know me. I like living on the edge." I slid further down so that warm water and soap bubbles covered my chest. I loved a full-size bathtub. Now that my UN expense account was such that I could stay in a half-decent hotel while in New York, I was intent on making use of all the free amenities. I usually disciplined myself to keep the minibar out of bounds. But tonight, three little bottles of scotch balanced precariously on the edge of the tub, one empty, two to go. "I promise not to drop the receiver. Okay?"

"Remind me. Where is your life insurance policy?"

"It all goes to starving children in Africa, remember?"

"Not according to our joint wills. I made sure of that. With you flying all over the world, there's a much higher probability that I'm going to be able to collect than you will. So far, walking from the house to the university does not constitute a serious life-threatening activity."

I was twiddling my toes near the faucet, creating little waves up and down the length of the tub. My receiver-holding hand was suddenly covered with bubbles. I jerked myself up, grabbed a towel, and began furiously wiping the phone dry.

"Next time you talk to Sheila, ask her to enlighten us."

"About?"

"About whether it's safe to talk on the phone while luxuriating in a bathtub. What a short attention span. You've already forgotten that a moment ago you were panicking about my mortality." *Did I really just say that?* "How were your classes today?" I asked, moving my head to safer ground.

"Okay. They're all nervous about the finals. I enjoy inducing such anxiety."

"You're a bit of a sadist, aren't you? What kind of questions are you putting on the exams?"

"In which course?"

"Um, your favourite." I realized, with embarrassment, that I couldn't name what courses my lover was teaching this term. I gambled with Phil 101.

Jonathan was one of the few in the department who enjoyed the intro courses. As a professor, he had discovered a real pleasure in opening young minds to the skills and rewards of critical thinking.

"Tell me what difficult questions you're going to be asking."

"Why? Are you planning to sell them at the student union to make some extra weed money?" he laughed.

"Yeah, right. Tell me. I'm interested." I manipulated the hot water faucet gingerly with my foot to warm up the tub water, but slowly enough not to make noise that would re-provoke Jonathan's safety lecture.

Jonathan went into detail, enthusiastically, about his plans. He had prepared questions on epistemology, the nature of free will, and the merits and limitations of arguments for and against proving the existence of God. He included the trademark Professor Compton requirement. The students had to apply the issues to something from their own personal experience in addition to describing the ideas of traditional philosophers.

With the receiver lodged between my head and shoulder, I opened the last of the scotches and downed it in one gulp.

"Can I pose a personal question?" I asked.

"Bored with the professional already?"

"No, this is a personal question about your professional work. It seems strange that I've never asked you this before. I have wondered about it. Do you have any difficulties teaching classes about proofs or disproofs ... is that a word? ... for the existence of God?" I was slightly aware that my speech was slurring.

"They are intellectual subjects, open to critical analysis and evaluation. Why do you ask? You think because I don't subscribe to a certain Western theological tradition that I'm going to be a biased interpreter of the issues to the impressionable minds in my care?"

"Well ..."

"If that's what you're thinking, which I suspect is what you are thinking," he continued, "one could argue logically, and just as easily, that a Christian should not be allowed to teach philosophy, especially questions such as proofs for the existence or nonexistence of God, because a Christian couldn't be trusted to treat the subject objectively without trying to evangelize their students. Right?"

"Yup. I guess that makes sense."

"Have you been drinking?"

"Just a little after-work relaxer." I giggled, probably not as inaudibly as I intended. "Well, three little after-work relaxers."

"While you've been soaking in the tub."

"I can multitask."

"I wish I were there and could push your head under the water."

"You are a sadist. You know, life insurance is invalidated if the death can be proven to be homicide."

"You need to go to bed, Tom." I heard him sigh.

I wished he were here.

"Before I let you go, tell me, how was your day? You had a meeting with Gutiérrez, didn't you?"

"Yes, and I have some news."

"I don't like the sound of that," Jonathan said anxiously.

"No, it's good news. Well, it's not official yet. It has to go through multiple channels. Anytime there is a deviation from the norm, the bureaucracy gets all in a tizzy," I rambled.

"Well, tell me. What is it?"

"Um, no. I think I'll make you wait until I'm home on the weekend. I'm learning a bit of your sadistic skill."

"Sounds fine with me. I always liked your delayed gratification techniques."

"*Puto!* See you Friday evening."

"Good night. *Puta.*"

I hung up and slid down, submerging my head under the water for a moment.

Chapter 30

"**Well,** I'll have to check with Tom when he gets in." I heard Jonathan on the phone in the study as I walked in the front door. "I don't know what his summer schedule is. There are some changes in the works."

I quietly set my bag and briefcase down and walked to the study door, stepping over a week's worth of newspapers left strewn by his living room reading chair. The end table beside it sported the current *Atlantic Monthly,* a sandwich plate sparsely dotted with desiccated breadcrumbs and jam droppings, and a stained teacup, the fossilized teabag on the accompanying saucer. In the study, Jonathan had his feet up on the desk, looking out the window, receiver to his ear, listening. His back to the doorway, he was unaware of my arrival. I leaned against the door jamb, eavesdropping on the conversation.

"No, Jeremy, I do not have to ask his permission. It would just be better if we could coordinate schedules and come over together."

Jonathan repeatedly curled and uncurled and recurled the phone cord around his finger as he listened. The desk was littered with books, files, journals, a couple of used wine glasses, and a coffee mug, out of which he now took a sip. I smiled. I had been able to catch an earlier Friday afternoon flight than he had expected. He had evidently assumed that he would have time to clean up the clutter before my arrival.

"Maybe you don't, but I do, and Mother, of course, is ecstatic. Did she send you a copy of the AGO members' magazine with her article about the Venice Biennale, where she just happened to drop a reference about your role?"

I debated announcing my presence. I started to walk into the room, when Jonathan suddenly yanked his feet off the desk, sending a couple files flying off the side.

"Settle down, Jeremy!" he hollered into the phone. "She's proud of you. That's all. Surely you can understand that."

I stopped in my tracks.

"Well, it is a big deal. Isn't it?"

Jonathan caught sight of me out of the corner of his eye and pivoted around in his chair. He held the receiver a little away from his ear, pointed toward it, mouthed "Jeremy," rolled his eyes, mouthed "Crazy," and turned back to his desk.

"Yeah, well, maybe next time you will be selected. I know squat about your world, but the competition to be a featured artist must be ferocious, I would imagine. In the meantime, as curator, surely you're making great contacts and people are getting to know you."

Jonathan put both elbows on the desk and rested his head on his available fist.

"Sorry, okay. Assistant curator."

He swung around in his chair again to face me and slumped, listening, with evidently diminishing patience. His long legs stretched out in front of him. He crossed one foot over the other, switched, and then switched back.

"Listen, I can't talk any longer right now. Tom will be home soon, and I have to clean up the house or he'll tan my hide."

He looked at me and winked.

"Yes, I'm sure that we should be able to work out something. Yuk. August in Venice. Tourists and stinking canals. Whatever. I'll suffer for the sake of fraternal solidarity."

Pause.

"Christ, Jeremy. That was a joke. I'll be back in touch soon. Now, take it easy and don't get yourself into such a state."

Pause.

"Promise?"

Pause.

"Okay, bye, brother. Love you."

Jonathan turned back to his desk and, with exaggerated gentleness, placed the receiver back on the base, done with effort to check his desire to slam it down.

I went over to his chair and stood behind him, massaging the tensed muscles in his shoulders.

"What was that all about?" I asked.

"Quote, always the bridesmaid, never the bride, unquote."

The weekend disappeared in something of a fog. Jonathan and I did stuff. We talked. I have no recollection of what. My concentration was on Monday's pending appointment.

Monday, post-appointment, I sat waiting for Jonathan to return home from the university. Despite the heavy padding in our living room armchair, I could feel the bulky papers with the test results in my hip pocket, pressing against my right cheek. Alan had deciphered the numbers for me. Silently, I had returned the material to the envelope, stuffed it into my back pants' pocket, and immediately left his office, ignoring his offer to talk.

I looked at the generous portion of scotch in the glass. How close could I get it to the rim without spilling?

I rotated the tumbler around and around and around. Each cycle, the mahogany essence lapped upward at a fresh spot. My wrist was in absolute control, the uniformity of the circulations unwavering. I paused out of curiosity to see if there was any quivering from fatigue or cramping or shock. Nothing. Trembling was nonexistent.

Gratified, I lifted the glass to my nose and inhaled deeply.

I took a sip. Molten gold. I loved the smoky, peaty taste.

Jonathan called my Laphroaig "ashtray scotch."

I took another sip and rested the tumbler on the arm of the chair, studying the beautiful cuttings in the crystal. Carrera by Da Vinci, bought in one of our first years together. Jonathan had selected it at Ashley's because of the design. I seconded his choice because of the name. What a plebeian I was. Am. It had seemed such an extravagance at the time, eight wine glasses and eight tumblers.

"We need eight for dinner parties," he had explained with intentional condescension. "And it's essential that we have crystal that will compliment the good china ..."

I'd raised my eyebrows.

"... that we'll be buying next year," he had smiled. "When we can afford it."

The tumblers were anchored by a half-inch of solid glass. Seven slender obelisks, interspersed with seven miniature replicas, rose from the base, intersected by two grooves running the circumference, comfortably deep, now securing my grasp. The wine glasses mimicked the same pattern, except that they felt and looked completely different, delicate instead of robust, the incising curving gently along the convex bowl, in contrast to the solidity and linearity of the tumbler.

I raised my glass and took another sip. An inappropriately timed sigh escaped my throat just as I was swallowing, almost instigating a coughing spell, which would have been such a waste of good scotch. I paused and let the two countervailing throat movements run their course.

"The crystal may seem expensive now," Jonathan had said at the time, continuing to make his case. "But neither of us are coming into this relationship with a trousseau." Two smiles, one each. "Besides, we'll have them for the rest of our lives."

The rest of our lives.

I placed the glass back down on the arm again and studied the room. So many acquisitions in the intervening years. Comfortable furniture, a decent sound system, art and sculpture, often bought compulsively in the euphoric haze of travel, and, of course, more—many more—books. And innumerable memories, purchased, gifted, bestowed, or thrust upon us.

I heard Sheila's cackle.

Damn.

The whole scenario in my mind featured Jonathan and me, alone.

The two of them came through the door, arm in arm, for support more than camaraderie.

"Geez, Tom, you startled me. I thought you were flying back to New York this afternoon."

"Hi, Sheila."

"Tommy boy. Now we have a party of three. Your dashing boyfriend and I have spent the last two hours toasting the near end of term. Martinis with beer chasers."

"No, my dear," corrected Jonathan. "Beer with martini chasers."

"Picky, picky," Sheila retorted, punching him in the shoulder before turning back to me. "The only ones in the faculty club who appreciated our newly inaugurated tradition were Philippe and Jocelyn, the bartenders. Our peers are such poobahs. They clearly disapprove of Monday afternoon inebriation."

"I'm glad you're here, Sheila," I said.

"I'm glad I'm here too, because I'm not nearly as drunk as I intend to be before the evening is out, and the drinks will be much cheaper here. That's your cue, boy. I know that you make a mean martini. I have had one, or a million, of yours before."

"You're also in party mode, I see," Jonathan observed, crossing the room to me. "Pulled out the good scotch. What's the occasion?" He gave me a peck on the top of my head and then spun around.

Before I could respond, he plumped himself on the couch beside Sheila. Putting his arm around her shoulder, he leaned toward her, and in a stage whisper, bragged, "Darling, see my little boy wonder over there? He's got the UN wrapped around his little ingenious finger. They're going to pay him half of his salary to do what they want him to do, and they're going to pay him the other half of his salary to do what he wants to do, which he has convinced them is what they need him to do. Clever, eh?"

"I haven't the faintest idea what you just said, sweetie dear, but if it makes Tom happy, and if it makes you happy, then I'm happy. Now, where's my drink? Our drinks," she added, looking at me while pointing back and forth between Jonathan and herself.

Sheila and Jonathan both looked at me expectantly.

"I'll get your drinks in a moment. But first we need to talk. I've got something to tell you. Then we'll all be able to use a drink."

Jonathan jumped up. "Shit, I forgot. What did Alan say?"

"Sit down, Jonathan," I said quietly.

He didn't move.

"Sit down, please."

He did. "Oh, no. Please God, no," he whimpered.

We stared at each other. I slowly nodded my head.

I counted out five seconds. I raised the glass to my mouth to take another sip. Suddenly, Jonathan was on his feet, in front of my chair, towering over me. His hand rose over his head and came slashing down across my face, searing my cheek and sending the tumbler flying across the room, where it shattered against the marble fireplace. Sheila screamed. I sat numbly and watched as Jonathan's foot pummeled the leg of my chair.

Chapter 31

My stomach was in knots as I got off the plane. A quick perusal of my carry-on bag would reveal my medications. When completing the visa application at the Indian consulate, I had lied to the question about whether I had ever tested positive for HIV.

The immigration officer stamped my passport without looking up from his desk. His exhausted body language reflected my own fatigue after our 2:00 a.m. arrival. I anticipated a long wait for my bag at the luggage carrousel. Contrary to expectations, the conveyor belt soon creaked into action, and bags started appearing immediately. I found mine. The customs inspections area was devoid of any official personnel. I headed through the sliding glass doors and started breathing again.

The hot, humid night air hit me full force. The pickup area was open to the elements, a corrugated and rusting roof the only protection from sun and monsoon rains, neither of which was of concern at this hour. No protection was available against humidity and heat, day or night.

The platform was crammed with shouting, straining, sign-holding workers and families, anxious to meet those for whom they had been waiting.

I stopped, put my bag down, and reached for a handkerchief to wipe my perspiring forehead, neck, and arms. Thirty seconds in Bangalore's August temperatures had left me soaking. The pause was a miscalculation. A dozen taxi drivers immediately beset me, intent on making a decent fare out of this disoriented and disheveled newcomer. The sensation of hands on my shoulder bag ratcheted me into action, and I grabbed my larger bag as two young boys struggled to wheel it toward their father's taxi.

"No, no. No need. Thank you very much. I'm being picked up." I yelled to be heard above the commotion. To prove the point, I began scanning the crowd and calling out. "Mr. Fischer. Tom Fischer here."

My left hand securely grasping the shoulder strap of my one bag and my right hand locked onto the handle of my suitcase, I elbowed my way toward the curb. Anil abandoned his relaxed perch leaning against the green, unmarked older model Tata which served as the Centre's hospitality coach and came scurrying in my direction.

"Welcome, Mr. Tom. Good flight? Sorry it is so hot. My name is Anil. First time in India? Wonderful country, but too many flies like these," he said as he helped me with my bags and simultaneously swatted away the persistent, disappointed taxi drivers and their helpers.

On the half-hour bumpy ride from the airport to the Centre, Anil kept up a running commentary on the richness of India's multi-faith history, Bangalore's growing reputation as a hub of new technology, his wife's chronic asthma, the deplorable neglect of the city's road maintenance, political tensions with Pakistan, his hopes for an imminent agreement with his daughter's boyfriend's family on a marriage proposal, the new muffler system that he had installed last week in the Tata, the problem with all the distressed farmers moving into the city and competing for jobs, the flooding over the past few weeks from the monsoon rains, and the guests from around the world that he had the great privilege of chauffeuring in from the airport.

I was slouched in the backseat, struggling to keep my eyes open by concentrating on the patterns that the passing streetlights splayed on the car window, dappled on the outside by a light drizzle and fogged on the inside by our sweating bodies.

The car lurched to the left and, as rapidly, careened to the right.

"No worry. Dog okay. What is it that you're lecturing?"

"Huh? Oh, pardon me. Sorry, Anil. I started to doze off. Long flight, you know. What was your question?"

"My apologies, sir. It won't be long. We are near the Centre. Then you can have a good sleep. The other teachers arrived yesterday, and most of the students are here too. Dr. Schultz came on an earlier flight tonight. My, my, my. What a pretty woman, and a professor too. Seems hard to believe. A woman so attractive, spending her time as a teacher. She should be in Bollywood."

Anil burst out laughing.

"How stupid I am. A German woman in Bollywood. But a pretty woman is a pretty woman, no? Sorry, maybe I should not say so. But we are two men. I asked her what she was teaching, but I could not understand. Can you explain better? What is the course here this week?"

I took off my glasses and with both index fingers and thumbs forced my eyelids as wide apart as possible; I blinked several times and shook my head vigorously.

"Well, the title of the course is Ethical Dimensions of Environment and Development."

"And what does that mean?"

Good question, Anil.

"Well ..." I took a deep breath. "We have some big problems in the world that are getting worse."

"Uh huh?"

"For instance, pollution. From cars and trucks and factories ..."

"Oh, my goodness, yes. That's why I think Fatima has so much more trouble these days breathing. It's not so bad when we go to visit her father in the country, but here in the city ... my, oh my, oh my. Or, maybe, it's just that she's getting old," he cackled.

"Yes, you're right Anil. Pollution in the air and in water and even on the land where we grow our food is causing health problems for many people. And then there is the big problem of what we call 'climate change.'"

I was gratified as he excitedly replied, "Oh, Mr. Tom, I heard of that ...," veering precipitously close to a group of pedestrians as he sped through an intersection with non-functional traffic lights. "The sun is getting closer."

"Um, no. Sorry, Anil. I don't think that's quite what is happening."

"Tell me the course title again, please? I'm sorry to be pestering you, Mr. Tom. If you want me to be quiet, I will stop."

"No, that's okay, Anil. It's called Ethical Dimensions of Environment and Development. I was mentioning some of the environmental problems, like pollution, but we also have serious development challenges."

"... serious development challenges?"

"Yes, like poverty."

"Excuse me, sir, but we've always had poverty in my country. And the nuns told us that Jesus said in the Holy Bible that the poor you will always have with you."

I almost toppled over in the seat when Anil made a sharp right turn through an open wrought iron gate and brought the car to a sudden stop in front of a dark, austere building.

"Yessiree, Mr. Tom. Your servant Anil gets you here nice and safe. All ready for bed, I bet?" He leapt out of the front seat of the car. I stumbled out of the back.

Handing me my bags from the trunk, he smiled and said, "I really enjoyed talking to you, sir. I learned a lot. You are very smart. Good teacher."

Maybe not. I grimaced.

"Thank you very much for the ride, Anil. You're a very good driver."

He beamed.

I looked around the spartan room. The Catholic Retreat Centre was chosen because it could accommodate all the participants but more importantly, I had been told, its modest facilities were in keeping with the seminar's theme.

It was modest.

A single light bulb hung from the ceiling, illuminating the mosquito net suspended over the narrow bed. An uncovered pitcher of water sat on the desk, a frosted glass beside it, the floral design barely discernable from age. Through a small archway, I could see the private toilet—a hole in the floor and a plastic bucket of water in the corner, a ladle floating on the surface.

I had done considerably more international travelling in my career than had Jonathan, and yet he anticipated, considerably more accurately, the challenges that I would face with my new health status.

"Your compromised immune system leaves you very vulnerable."

Compromised immune system was his adopted mantra, recited in conversation after conversation over the past six months, argument after argument.

I didn't have AIDS. I was just HIV positive, and asymptomatic at that. Hopefully, with the meds, I would remain so. The addition of 3TC to the AZT regime was yielding encouraging results, and scientists were on the cusp of a whole new generation of drugs. Jonathan refused to buy my attempts at reassurance.

"Alan says that the research looks very positive. Sorry, no pun intended."

My attempt at humour failed to impress.

"Alan, Alan, Alan. He's a GP. He's not a specialist. What does he know?"

"He follows the literature and is on top of all the new research. He's got a significant roster of AIDS patients. I mean HIV-positive patients," I corrected myself.

"No, you were right the first time. AIDS patients. Many of whom have died, I might remind you."

"I know that."

"Think of our own circle. How many friends have died so far?"

"I'm not keeping count."

"My own cousin. You and I were the only family who deigned to visit Jackson once he was admitted to Casey House. Oh, and Mother, grudgingly. I practically had to shame her into coming with us."

Margaret's brother and sister-in-law had disowned their son when he broke the dual news of being gay and being sick. Jonathan and I knew about Jackson because we had run into him at a bar a few years ago, and he told us over a weepy beer. He made us swear not to spill the beans in the family.

"Margaret visited him more than you are aware."

"How do you know that?" Jonathan demanded.

"The nursing staff told me. They thought she was his mother. I put two and two together."

"Why didn't you tell me?"

"Your mother is a proud and private person. I thought that it was her right to tell you or not tell you."

"Oh." Jonathan was quiet for a moment. "But why can't you just stick around home until we have a better idea of how this is going to progress?"

Progress. With a viral load result of 168,000 on the early test results, Alan had cautioned that I could be a "fast progressor." I had not shared that part of the picture with Jonathan.

"These opportunities for lecturing about Rio and the work on climate change are just too exciting to pass up. If I'm careful about what I eat and make sure that I only drink clean water, I should be fine. I don't want to stop living, Jonathan. I mean, I want to continue my career," I rephrased.

"Gives a whole new meaning to risky behaviour, doesn't it?" Jonathan said ruefully.

I was grateful that he was not standing beside me, looking at the jug and the glass and the hole in the floor and the pail.

I was neither fish nor fowl here. I was an employee of the UN, but was at the seminar under the sponsorship of the World Council of Churches. Gutiérrez had made it clear that I could not present myself as an official UN spokesperson.

I loved the ambiguity of the role—significant informal autonomy and insignificant formal accountability, as long as I didn't screw up.

My good intentions to be present for the opening morning session succumbed to jet lag. It was 11:30 a.m. when I woke up. I scurried down the hall to wash up in the communal shower stall and then dressed quickly.

The seminar participants were passing by the front of the dormitory as I came out the door. One session already under their belts, they were heading to lunch. I struggled to blink away my fatigue-fueled disorientation, exacerbated by the stunning glare of the noonday sun. Dr. Kumar intercepted me when I nearly slipped on the disintegrating concrete stairway.

"Welcome, Dr. Fischer. I'm so glad you made it okay. Anil reported that your flight was delayed. I hope that you were able to get some sleep. Not too much trouble with jet lag?"

"Thank you, Dr. Kumar. Yes, I slept very well." It would have been inhospitable to acknowledge the fitfulness of my first night. "And, by the way, it's Mister Fischer, not doctor. Better yet, please call me Tom."

"Oh," Kumar replied, looking genuinely surprised, or maybe disappointed. Deciding not to pursue my unexpectedly diminished academic status, he advised, "Addressing you as Mr. Fischer is better than just your first name. Helps maintain appropriate respect between students and faculty." He reconsidered. "Invited resource persons."

"Well, I'm very glad to be here. Thank you so much for the invitation."

He took hold of my arm, fraternally or paternally, and guided me through the chattering student body toward a separate entrance to the dining hall.

In the privacy of the moment, I decided to pose my prepared entreaty. "I am sorry to bother you with a little, hopefully little, request, but I have been having some intestinal sensitivities lately, and I was wondering if the Centre has sterilized or bottled water available that I could use while here." A little white lie was easier than a complicated explanation that would likely raise much redder flags than the missing PhD.

"Yes, of course," he smiled indulgently. "We are well prepared for our Western visitors and their 'sensitivities.' I'll ask Sister Serena to make sure you have a supply at meals and in your room."

"Thank you very much."

Kumar reached into his satchel and pulled out a sheath of papers, rummaging through them as we walked. He pulled out one page, frowned at it, and then thrust it into my hand, saying, "I hope we're not imposing too much on you, but we have had to do some juggling of the agenda."

"I'm at your disposal," I replied nonchalantly as I glanced at the week's schedule, covered with scribbling that obliterated some names and added others over them. Arrows ran from one session to another, crossing days and timeslots. I nearly tripped on an outcropping of tree roots.

"Unfortunately, Dr. Gupta from Calcutta has discovered that he has a schedule conflict," he said pointing to several places on the crumpled sheet, "and I think you already know that Professor Johannson from Stockholm has had to cancel."

"No, I hadn't heard that," I said, startled. "Henrik, Dr. Johannson, and I were together in Geneva just last week. I hope nothing serious has happened."

"Well, I don't know how serious. His wife has taken ill quite suddenly. He called two days ago and begged our indulgence. I told him, by all means, family comes first."

"Yes, absolutely." My stomach twitched.

"I was so impressed by your eloquence in Rio, I felt confident that you could help us out with this little problem."

I didn't trust Kumar's assessment of the size of the problem.

"So instead of two lectures, I need you to deliver six. Okay?"

"Six?"

We had entered the bustling dining hall. Kumar steered me toward the faculty table, introduced me around to the other lecturers, and then graciously pulled out a chair for me.

As I sat down, he leaned in and whispered in my ear. "And we'll keep you well supplied with sterilized water." He chuckled and headed through a swinging door into the kitchen.

It wasn't what Kumar expected.

It wasn't what I had planned.

It was better.

The two lectures that I had anticipated delivering were logically interrelated. The first would review the Earth Summit and the treaties that emerged. The second would follow with an analysis of the challenges for implementing those agreements, including the role civil society groups could play, such as the ones represented here at the seminar.

Now, instead of two sessions of two hours each separated by a day, I had to fill twelve hours spread over the whole week.

I get bored quickly enough hearing myself talk. I could only imagine how tired the seminar participants would be if they had to sit through six sessions listening to me.

I had some information, analysis, and experience that I could share, which I decided would still be helpful for setting the context. The real experts in the room, though, were the thirty participants, whose small and underfunded organizations had sent them for this continuing education event. For a week, they had left their work with farmers losing their land to mega-dams, with Dalits suffering in India's rigid caste system, with fishermen finding less fish as a result of pollution and large factory fleets, with rural residents facing water shortages from the increasingly frequent droughts, with slum dwellers whose health was threatened by toxic chemicals.

I could offer some of the theory regarding the ethical dimensions of environment and development, but they brought lived, day-to-day experiences of how those issues played out on the ground. They could learn from me. I could learn from them. They could learn from each other.

I tweaked my first session, introducing some of the context-setting material that I had prepared, but then described the plan that I had conceived over the lunch curry and naan. The thirty participants would choose one of five working groups that were focused on specific ethical principles that had relevance to environment and development: justice, equity, solidarity, sufficiency, and sustainability. In their group of peers, they would select a few case stories from the communities with whom they worked and then develop strategies for how that particular principle could be implemented to improve the lives of their peoples and the environment. What would have to change? What public policies or corporate practices would have to be challenged? How could people be mobilized for action?

Over the course of the week, each working group had the opportunity to present to the whole seminar. I moderated the lively plenary discussions that ensued. I congratulated them on their narratives and analyses. I masked how much their commitment made me feel like a dilettante, a poseur.

Kumar was somewhat miffed. He didn't think he got his value out of my UN connections.

The participants loved it. That's what mattered to me.

I faxed Gutiérrez: "Relax. I didn't screw up."

Chapter 32 ——————————

Getting from Bangalore to Venice proved complicated.

Having to stay at the seminar for the full week instead of the three days that I originally intended required rescheduling flights. Jonathan had proposed that we meet up in Rome for a brief romantic holiday before joining his parents and Jeremy in Venice. But that plan was blown out of the water by my unexpected additional responsibilities at Kumar's behest.

Family always comes first. Right.

Jonathan went on to Venice ahead of me, and I got there as quickly as I could. That turned out to be days later than we had planned, given the idiosyncrasies of the standby world and already complex connecting flights between a non-hub Asian city and a non-hub European city.

Jonathan was correct about the downside of Venice in August. We had been there twice before, once in a cold, rainy, and blustery February and once in the azure perfection of a balmy, softly sunny October. As I headed from the airport to the hotel in the combination of terrestrial and amphibian taxis, the heat, noise, and smells felt as oppressive as my introduction to Bangalore.

But here I wasn't working. I had no responsibilities other than to enthuse over Jeremy's prestigious role at the Biennale, spar with Walter, ogle with Margaret at the genius of Bellini, Piranesi, and Titian, sip espressos with my in-laws in Piazza San Marco, and fall asleep in the arms of my lover after a day of making love to him and to the Paradise of Cities.

Walter, in an exhibit of gracious generosity, had booked us into the Bauer Il Palazzo, a luxury boutique hotel operating for over one hundred years in a converted eighteenth century palazzo. Margaret and Walter were in a suite with a spectacular view onto the Grand Canal; period furnishings; ornate inlaid wood flooring in the living area and decorative mosaic designs in the bathroom; Italian marble vanity; and a white floral Murano glass chandelier in the living room. Our room was smaller by half but with many of the same exquisite features. Less grand but more intimately romantic, it faced onto a quiet courtyard flush with vines, marble statuary, and profuse flowering plantings in large terracotta vessels. Jonathan was delighted that we too had our own Murano chandelier.

I didn't dwell on the contrast between my accommodation now and with the Sisters days earlier in Bangalore.

Jeremy was not staying with us but in his own apartment. He had come to Italy from London four years earlier, spending the first two years in Florence and then moving to Venice after being recruited onto the staff of the Biennale. He was evasive about the location and nature of his lodgings, except to confirm that it combined living and art studio facilities and was in Sant Elena, just east of the Giardini, site of the Biennale. Margaret took his reticence to mean it was chaotic and messy. Walter interpreted it as signifying that it was far too extravagant for his budget. Jonathan and I conjectured, to each other, that Jeremy wanted to protect his amorous privacy. He had told us on the phone earlier in the summer that just as Byron had reputedly out-Casanovaed Casanova, so he was well on his way to out-Byroning Byron. Venice seemed to have that lothario-type effect on testosterone-rich heterosexual males.

I was not so gauche as to mention it to Margaret and Walter, but the prospect of dinner in La Terrazza restaurant at the Excelsior Hotel Lido was a life-imitating-art fantasy for me.

Visconti's *Death in Venice* held first place as my favourite movie of all time. The melancholy and the Mahler plucked the strings of my soul. On a previous trip to Venice, Jonathan had me stage a Tadzio impression, looking as beguiling as I could, swinging on a pole on the beach in front of the hotel. Jonathan bridled his chronic aversion to taking pictures and snapped one for posterity.

We could afford little more in those days than a cappuccino and pastry while sitting on the hotel balcony and gazing out at the Adriatic in the pale late afternoon light. Jonathan shocked me by absconding with an ashtray featuring the emblematic four horses of Basilica di San Marco, an ill-gotten souvenir that still rested in a display case at home.

Now, on Walter's tab, we were having a candlelight family dinner in La Terrazza, the fading rays of the sun reflecting off the sea.

"It took years for many great artists to be recognized." Margaret was building her case. "But they kept producing, creating, because they had to. You have to as well, and I have every confidence that you will."

"Don't patronize me, Mother. Please."

"That's not at all what I intended."

Stung by her wounded tone and assaulted by the glares from around the table, Jeremy backtracked. "Sorry, Mother. I know you mean well. I'm impatient. I can't help it."

He waved his napkin over his head and added sardonically, "You know, it's the artistic temperament. It seems so obvious to me. Art should, must, reflect the physical, ecstatic, intense experience of human existence and emotion. That's what I've been trying to do. I want some sense that I'm getting through. I want people to be aroused, assaulted, connected to life in all its fullness."

Jeremy fiddled impatiently with the escargot utensils. The shells kept slipping around in the tongs, making it difficult for him to fork the snails.

Walter watched his son's struggle with amusement. "For someone who makes his living from his hands, you're not very dexterous."

"What living?" Jeremy snarled. He tossed the tongs on the table and grabbed one of the shells, speared a snail, and popped it in his mouth.

"Jeremy!" Margaret scolded.

Jeremy sat back, visibly tonguing the morsel back and forth into each cheek while his jaw muscles did a slow dance of decimation. His eyes glowed with contentment. "They're so sensuous," he exuded. "Firm, supple, the almost nondescript flavour rescued by the abrasive garlic butter. Modesty and fireworks in one mouthful."

"Ah hah," laughed Walter. "You can become a food critic if you can't sell enough art to support your decadent Venetian lifestyle."

Jeremy spoke to his mother, pointedly ignoring his father. "Take Rothko. He once said that the fact that people break down and cry when confronted with his pictures shows that he is being successful in communicating basic human emotions with them. Why don't people break down and cry or fall on the floor and make love to each other when they encounter my work?"

Jonathan cleared his throat.

Jeremy glared at him. "Don't condescend to me, Mr. Professor. You can be so ... so ... condescending with your perfect academic life, and your perfect publishing reputation, and your perfect Victorian house in perfect little Toronto, where you fuck your perfect little boyfriend."

"Jeremy, stop that," said Walter.

Jeremy caught himself. His facial expression dissipated into an innocuous smile, the fire in his eyes replaced by a glaze. He turned to Margaret and asked lightheartedly, "Speaking of Rothko, when did Grandfather buy his? Well, yours now, of course. God rest his soul," Jeremy chuckled and crossed himself. "Their souls." Another crossing.

Perhaps the fading sunlight and candles were playing tricks, but it looked like Margaret was either flushed or blushing. I looked at Jonathan. He had noticed too.

Jeremy was oblivious. "Did you know Rothko was invited to exhibit at the Biennale?" He addressed no one in particular. "In 1958, or somewhere around then."

"Come on, my dear," said Walter. "Tell the boys."

Until Jeremy's little tirade, Walter had been in a more buoyant mood than I had seen him in a very long time. Being together again with his wife and his two sons, his family, seemed to give him more pleasure than any of his recent successful megadeals. Maybe I had misperceived his priorities.

Margaret gazed out through the windows at the flickering play of pastels on the glistening sea. After a moment, she returned to the present company, looked at Jeremy, and then turned her head and smiled at Jonathan. One son sat on either side of her. She put down her knife and fork, rested her arms on the table, and said, "Give me your hands."

"Are we going to have a séance?" Jeremy giggled.

Jonathan, placing his hand in his mother's, said quietly, "Jeremy. Do as she has asked."

"Okay." Jeremy complied, still snickering.

"It was a gift to me, to Walter and me, from my father on the occasion of your births. Daddy came upon Rothko's work through some business associates in New York. He met him at a gallery that was displaying his work."

She looked back and forth between her sons and squeezed their hands. Jonathan smiled in response. Jeremy didn't.

"Daddy told Rothko that he was buying the piece for his daughter and her new twin baby boys. Rothko said that he hoped the piece would inspire the boys."

Silence.

One of the hovering waiters approached the table, prepared to refill wine glasses, but discretely backed away.

Jonathan lifted his mother's hand and lightly kissed it. "That's beautiful. Why didn't you ever tell us that?"

"You never asked."

Jeremy had gone pale. He sat immobilized, his hand still resting in Margaret's.

The tiny interior of the Canadian pavilion was crammed with milling guests, wine glass in one hand and reception program in the other—art tourists, fashionistas, legitimate artists or artist wannabes, Canadian officials, media encumbered by oversized cameras, Biennale staff looking stressed, and a couple obvious security staff. The cool evening breeze blowing in off the water did not reach us, pressed up against each other within the glass and wood walls of the small building. The hot, humid air was in part seasonal, in part generated by too many people in too small a space. The grand oak, whose trunk was encased in glass when the pavilion was built around it, reached up through the roof into the evening sky, its waving branches taunting us as it enjoyed the fresh air inaccessible to us.

No one seemed to be paying much attention to Robin Collyer's urban scene photography and minimalist sculptures. Jeremy led us around the room to ensure that we experienced Canada's chosen representative.

"Art? Well, you decide," he said, gritting his teeth.

A commotion at the entrance signaled the arrival of the deputy minister. A brief speech praising Collyer's work as an exemplar of Canada's vibrant contribution to the international modern art scene was followed by a defense of the Canadian Government's support for the arts. I was too removed from the politics of Jeremy's world to know how to accurately interpret his and others' coughs and rolling eyes.

Just as the deputy minister was winding up, one of his aides handed him a note.

"Ah, yes," he said. "We want to also express our appreciation to

Canada's Jeremy Compton, who we understand has been doing a fine job on the curatorial staff for this year's Biennale. Clearly, in Canada, we produce not only excellent artists like Collyer but excellent arts administrators like Compton as well. Now, everyone please enjoy the evening and the fine Niagara and Okanagan Valley wines."

Walter and Margaret and Jonathan and I simultaneously pivoted around, searching the crowd for Jeremy.

He was gone.

Chapter 33

I grabbed the phone on the first ring. Jonathan had finally fallen off to sleep.

Cupping my hand around the receiver, I whispered, "Yes?"

The hotel receptionist spoke words that I could not understand. I could, literally, but they did not make any sense. "Your sister is waiting for you in the lobby."

"I'm sorry, you must have the wrong room." Irritation at her mistake compounded my anxiety about Jonathan being disturbed. I was about to hang up when she said a word that I did understand.

"Carolyn?" I asked too loudly. "Did you say that the woman downstairs is named Carolyn?"

My mind raced as she confirmed, now with a hint of irritation in her voice.

"Tell her to wait in the bar. I'll be right down."

I hung up but didn't move from the desk. Out the window, the early morning light was illuminating the tile roofs of the adjacent building. I looked down at the courtyard that remained shrouded in the chilly shadows of night. Someone had already been around to water the plants. Little streams seeped out from the base of the planters, heading in erratic but coordinated rivulets toward the narrow passageway that would lead them, eventually but inevitably, between the buildings to a burst of light and noise at the canal's edge. Not far, yet another world.

I quickly dressed and, as quietly as possible, unlocked the door and stepped out into the hall. As I relocked it from the outside, I remembered the envelope. Cursing myself, I reentered, retrieved it from my bag, and reenacted my exit.

Carolyn was sitting at the window of the bar gazing out at the Grand Canal. Still too early for the bar to be open, the room's lights were off, leaving her back in darkness, emphasizing the contrast of her illuminated profile. Dancing rays off the water swept across her face like reflections from an oscillating mirror. Her hair was cut extremely short, masking its natural auburn. The light made the front appear blond and the back brunette.

The hotel staff had considerately brought her a coffee, which made me guilty about my recent sharpness on the phone. Over the past few days, they had been very considerate, helping all of us with big details and initiating many small, unrequested, and appreciated gestures of comfort.

My footsteps across the centuries-old floor alerted Carolyn, and she turned and smiled. Her beauty, a mature, robust, self-assured radiance emanating from her eyes, stunned me. We hadn't seen each other for several years. Both of us had been crisscrossing the globe, but we had not succeeded at connecting at the same place at the same time.

She got off the stool and took a few steps to intercept me with open arms. We hugged for a long time.

Leaning back from each other but still keeping our embrace, we looked into each other's eyes and spoke simultaneously.

"What are you doing here?" I asked.

"I'm so, so sorry," she said.

"You first," I said.

"Come, sit down with me. Do you want some coffee? I'll share mine, or we can get some fresh for you."

"No, dear, that's fine."

She leaned across the table and took my hands in hers.

"I'm so sorry, my darling, that I haven't been in touch before now. After Mom told me about your diagnosis, I just couldn't pick up the phone. Somehow, it wasn't the right way to have the first conversation. You must have thought that I was horrifically callous. When I learned that you and Jonathan were going to be here, I decided that I would wait until I could see you in person. For once, the timing worked out perfectly. Mom had said that Margaret and Walter were leaving by this past weekend. I really wasn't up to seeing them. I'm sure the feeling would have been mutual. So I figured that the four of us could have some wonderful time together."

She clapped her hands.

"You know that I have never been in Venice before? So you're all going to have to treat me with consideration as I gawk at all the splendours. Jeremy doesn't know I was coming, right? I made Mom swear that she wouldn't breathe a word to you."

I just looked at her.

"Oh, shit," she said. "I just did exactly what I intended not to do. I even practiced this on the plane."

She inhaled and exhaled several deep breaths.

I wasn't breathing at all.

She took hold of my hand again, looked into my eyes, and said, "I'm so sorry, darling. When Mom told me, I cried for three days. But then I figured, well, at least you're not a mother of five in Kinshasa who hasn't got a doctor, who hasn't access to the most rudimentary of medications. You are getting good care, aren't you? You have a doctor you trust?"

I nodded.

"Good. Well, I know that you're going to be okay. I just know it. And you've got Jonathan. Such a brick."

She glanced toward the vacant door.

"Where is he? How's he been taking it?"

"… um, in bed asleep … um, not well …"

"The poor dear."

She diverted her eyes from me, looked out the window, then back at me, and then away again. She started to bawl.

Marco poked his head in the doorway and caught my eye. He raised his eyebrows as if to discreetly say, "Can I help you?"

"*Due espressi per favore*, Marco." I looked at Carolyn, wiping her tears and blowing her nose, and turned back just as Marco was disappearing. "*Doppio*, Marco."

"*Sì*, signóre."

"*Grazie*."

I got up off my stool, moved behind her, and wrapped my arms around her. She took hold of my clasped hands and raised them to her lips and gave them a prolonged kiss.

After a moment, Carolyn sat up straight, shook her head vigorously a couple times, and said, "Okay, enough of that. Sit down, dear."

I obeyed and returned to my perch.

Contrary to her self-admonition, she leaned across the round bar table, grabbed my hands, teared up again, and said, "I'm supposed to be the one comforting you, not the other way around."

I sighed. "No, I think you had it right."

"You're too generous."

"Listen, Carolyn." Better get it over sooner than later. "There's something I need to tell you."

"You're not sick, are you?" She looked alarmed. "I thought you just tested positive. Do you have some opportunistic infection or something?"

"It's not about me. I'm fine. Yes, I'm HIV positive but I'm healthy and on the appropriate medications and getting good medical care. So we don't have to talk about that anymore. For the time being."

"Okay," she conceded warily and let go of my hands.

I paused. I hadn't anticipated seeing her and had no strategy prepared for how best to proceed. *Slowly, Tom*, I counseled myself. *Ease into it.*

"Jeremy is dead."

Carolyn didn't flinch. She just stared at me.

Marco arrived and placed the two coffees on the table. Glancing at the two of us staring at each other, he read the cue and slipped away, leaving us in silence.

"He drowned the other night after a reception at the Canadian Pavilion. Apparently, he tripped on the way home, hit his head, knocked himself out, and fell into the canal. That's what the police and coroner assume."

Carolyn made no response.

"He was alone. We assume. Nobody saw it happen. At least no one has come forward yet. His body was discovered the following morning in a small canal near where he lives. Lived."

Almost whispering, in measured monotone, Carolyn asked, "Is this ... is this some kind of sick joke?"

"No, I'm afraid not."

She shifted her eyes and looked out the window at the emerging morning bustle.

I reached into my pocket and pulled out the envelope and placed it on the table beside the coffees.

"A couple nights ago, we were all out for dinner together, and he gave me this to give to you. He said that he didn't have a current address for you, and he figured that I would likely see you. He wasn't sure when he would."

She rotated her head slowly back to look at me and asked quietly, "He said that? He wasn't sure when he would see me?"

Oh God. "Yes, that's what he said."

Carolyn looked down at the envelope in front of her. She picked it up, gingerly, as if handling an antiquated parchment that could disintegrate in her hands at any moment. She stared at the large scripted *C* on the outside. Turning it over, she placed her finger under the sealed flap and, centimetre by centimetre, pausing for a deep breath between each, she incrementally unlocked the sacred adhesive. Once complete, she laid the envelope flat and repeatedly ran her palm over the flap until it remained flush with the table surface, no longer struggling to lean up, as if to postpone her access. The folded top of the enclosed note lay exposed, inviting or daring or pleading to be withdrawn.

Carolyn drew it out and slowly unfolded it.

I watched as her eyes moved down the page. They eventually stopped and rested at the base and stayed there. Stared there.

A breeze wafted in through the window, effortlessly lifting the paper from her dissipated grasp. Like a feather, it fluttered across the table, teetering on the edge of the table before reluctantly succumbing to gravity and drifting slowly to the floor.

We both watched it fall. Her body was motionless, her hand still positioned as if holding Jeremy's message. Carolyn turned her head and looked back out the window.

After a moment, I slipped off my stool and picked up the note. I scanned Carolyn's face for any signal regarding the propriety of reading it. Nothing.

I laid it on the table and read.

My dearest,
> *You were the only one,*
>> *Ever.*
>>> *Sorry, my love,*
>>>> *J.*

I shuffled into the dark narthex of the Chiesa di San Moisè. After escaping the blinding noonday sun, my eyes gradually adjusted. Thankfully, the rows of pews were deserted.

Just inside the door, a half dozen votives in each of the tiered rows flickered through the red glass holders. I stared at one struggling against the inevitable. Its flame was barely visible. There was no perceptible wax left. I watched, but its stamina vanquished my patience. I lit a fresh one immediately beside it, mine bursting forth in brilliance and then calming to the placid, trembling, norm. Its neighbour's resilience persisted—consoled, I hoped, by the company.

Carolyn was asleep, sedated, next door at the hotel; Margaret and Walter traumatized on a plane somewhere over the Atlantic; Jonathan at the Canadian consulate making final arrangements for the transportation of Jeremy's body back to Toronto tomorrow. I had offered to accompany him. He declined. He wanted, needed, to do this for his brother. Alone.

I chose a pew halfway up the narthex, decreasing the chances of being disturbed by a tourist who might enter the main doors at the back or a priest who might suddenly appear from behind the alter. I sat. I drew down the kneeler and dropped to my knees.

Half an hour later, before opening the doors and passing into the burning sunlight, I paused at the flickering candles. My votive burned alone. Its neighbour was out. Dead.

"It's quite extraordinary." Jonathan was lying on the bed, staring at the ceiling light fixture. Neither of us would ever again be able to appreciate a Murano chandelier without nuance.

"Extraordinary." He wasn't talking about the Murano. "It might have been the last thing he was working on. I didn't notice it at first. The studio is so cluttered. Geez, I don't know how we're going to be able to deal with it all. Or who should."

"Roll over," I urged him. "I'll give you a back rub. We can worry about that another day."

Jonathan turned over, pulled a couple pillows toward him, wrapped his arms around them, and buried his head deep into them.

I straddled his back and applied my hands to the knots around his neck.

He mumbled something I couldn't understand and then tilted his head slightly to the side. "It was hanging from the rafters up near the roof, right in the middle of the room, a single wire holding what looked like an empty light socket. Below it, about a foot or so, suspended somehow, maybe with fine metal rods, I don't remember, there was a circular piece of clear glass or plexiglass."

"A piece of glass? Like a disk?"

"No, no. It wasn't horizontal. It was cylindrical. The glass or plexiglass or whatever was about ten inches tall and wrapped around and below this light socket affair. The cylinder was maybe two feet in diameter."

I was having difficulty visualizing what he was describing, but I didn't interrupt.

"I walked around it, looking at it from below. Couldn't figure out what the hell it was supposed to be or mean."

"It has to have a meaning?" I asked, immediately regretting my tone.

Jonathan let it pass.

"Then I noticed that a cord from the light socket thing was draped over a chair near an outlet, so I plugged it in. That lit up a bright light inside the socket. Now, it was a bit more interesting but not Biennale grade. Oh, shit. Did I just say that?"

He plowed his head back into the pillow to suffocate a sob. I sat back for a moment and then slowly returned to massaging.

He continued. "Here's the kicker. Beside the electrical cord, there was a rope that was attached to a makeshift pulley. The rope held up the whole contraption, the light socket and cylindrical glasswork. I loosened the rope and slowly began to lower it all down until I figured it was at about eye level. I thought that I could examine it better at that height."

He went silent. I massaged.

He suddenly turned over, almost throwing me off the bed.

He sat up and buried his head in his hands. A few muffled sobs.

I sat facing him and rested my hand on his knee.

Jonathan raised his head and looked at me. "You won't believe it until you see it, Tom," he said quietly. "It's him."

I waited, but he added nothing. "What do you mean, darling? What's him?"

His eyes staring off into some distant art studio, he raised his hands and started moving them in slow motion, like a mechanical doll, an animated figure in a Christmas window.

"It's Jeremy. As a beautiful, iridescent hologram. About six inches high. In the middle of the cylinder. It only becomes visible with the cylinder at eye level, when you're looking directly through the glass. Somehow it's created by that suspended light socket above. It's Jeremy, going around, and around. It's small, but you can fairly well make out the figure. It's moving or dancing or waving. He throws his head back from time to time, laughing."

"It sounds amazing," I said softly, so as not to break the trance.

Jonathan was still far, far away, moving his arms in pantomime, mimicking the spirit figure.

Then he lay down on his back and slowly closed his eyes.

Just before the snoring began, he said something. Something like, "Maybe ... the AGO."

Chapter 34 —————————

Patricia was restocking a sandwich tray with a selection of miniature pinwheels and rectangular delicacies made from coloured breads. *Whoever invented these?* Patricia had taken command of the Compton house kitchen. Mom, with characteristic no-nonsense efficiency, would fly through the swinging door, drop an empty tray, pick up a fresh one, and vanish back into the teeming reception. With half the frequency, Naomi followed the same path. Circulating with plates of mini-sweets was her responsibility, executed with studied grace well beyond her years.

The ladies of the Catholic Women's League were delegated to monitor the side buffet with the tea and coffee and juices, a minor role they accepted without complaint once Margaret had made it clear that Mom was the stage manager. A number of them took up proprietary positions at the entrance door, to welcome visitors and ensure that the guest book was signed, and in the parlour, to channel the mourners and to respond to any need of the parents of the deceased for a glass of water or a tissue.

Each time I passed the study door, Jonathan was where he had been since returning from the funeral, sitting on the leather sofa, staring at an unopened picture album on the coffee table in front of him, one hand grasping Sheila's and the other gripping a handkerchief. Neither of them spoke. Markus stood nearby. Sheila would look up when she saw me, smile wanly, and nod. "You can keep greeting folks, I'll stay with him," she telegraphed.

Robert and Luke were in the backyard playing a deliberately low-key game of catch.

Carolyn, cigarette in hand, was at the far end of the garden under the magnolia tree watching Robert and Luke. *When did she take up smoking?*

I was appreciative of my family's presence and pleased with their contributions and pleasantly surprised at Margaret's unhesitating acceptance of their offers.

I walked into the kitchen and sidled up beside Patricia. I gave her a little peck on the cheek.

"What's that for?" she asked innocently.

"I'm glad you're here, you and Robert and the kids. I didn't think that you would make the trip. I appreciate that you did."

"Well, family is family," she said peering at me over her glasses as her hands continued their hospitality provision.

"Thank you."

"A death like this must be just horrible for parents. Your child dies before you. How awful."

"Yeah, that's not the way it's supposed to happen."

"And Jonathan." She stopped her organizing, looked at me, and smiled. "I'm glad he's got you."

I gave her a second peck on the cheek. "Thank you. That's very generous of you to say, all things considered."

She returned to the task at hand. Without looking up, she said, "I am frankly a little surprised that they had the funeral in the church instead of the funeral home chapel."

"Really? The funeral home wouldn't have accommodated all the people and, of course, Margaret and Walter wanted a funeral mass."

Mom came in for more sandwiches. "My goodness, grief builds an appetite," she said to neither of us in particular. "I hope we ordered enough." Then she was off again.

"Yes, well, that's just it," Patricia said picking up her thread. "Surely they must realize that they're deluding themselves."

Those hairs on the back of my neck started doing their thing.

"Come again?" I asked in a monotone.

"Well, surely they understand ... under the circumstances ..."

"Patricia, what the hell are you talking about?"

Naomi had slipped in and was standing behind me. "Uncle Tom. You shouldn't be swearing. Especially on an occasion like this."

I wheeled around. "Sorry, Precious. You're absolutely right. I was just thanking your mom for the work that you and she are doing for us."

"Oh?" Naomi looked up at me over her glasses. "The tone didn't sound like that's what you were saying."

"Here, darling." Patricia intervened, handing her a fresh supply. "More waiting customers out there," she said, patting her gently on the bum and scooting her out of the kitchen.

We both allowed a few moments to pass.

Patricia was determined to state her case. "I'm no expert on Catholic doctrine, but I assume that they are not keen on it. I know that they have refused church funerals in the past, under these circumstances. Certainly, it's what we believe in our church, which doesn't mean anything to you, I'm sure, since you think we're out on the fundie fringe. Our pastor would not allow a religious funeral. Under these circumstances. Comfort to the nth degree, of course, for the family, but … 'your body is a temple of the Holy Spirit' …"

I set my coffee cup down and counted to ten.

I stared at her. "Stop what you're doing. Patricia. Please stop what you are doing."

She brushed a few crumbs off her hands and turned to face me.

I didn't know what to say.

She saved me the trouble. "Carolyn showed me the note."

I grabbed Patricia's wrist and marched us toward the patio doors. She almost lost her balance, and she banged her hip against the countertop.

"Ouch! Tom, for heaven's sake, let me go."

With my free hand I yanked open the screen door and barreled through, Patricia firmly in my vice grip.

"Tom. Stop, for heaven's sake."

Robert, Luke, and Carolyn heard the commotion and looked up simultaneously. Luke started to head toward mommy-in-distress, but Robert scooped him up and carried him in the opposite direction. Carolyn stood her ground, anxiety on her face but no surprise in her eyes.

Patricia ceased resisting my lock on her wrist and sprinted along beside me at the quick pace I had set. We reached the magnolia.

I glared at Carolyn. "What the fuck, Carolyn! What have you done?"

She looked down at the ground, dropped her cigarette, and stubbed it into the grass. She said nothing.

With my other hand, I grabbed her wrist, now holding both of my sisters' arms together in front of my chest. They both winced, but neither spoke. I looked back and forth between them. I tightened my grip. They winced again.

"Start talking," I breathed fire.

Carolyn began to cry. "I had to. I had to talk to somebody. I had nobody. You said I couldn't breathe a word about it to Jonathan. I sure couldn't talk to his parents even if I had wanted to. Mom and Dad would have been all sympathy and support, but that would have been like publishing it in the newspaper. They would have talked. Eventually. To somebody."

"But why did you tell"—I glared at Patricia—"her?"

"She was the only one I thought I could trust. Please, Tom, you're really hurting me." She looked at her sister. "Us."

I released their wrists. They both began massaging the red bruises.

I paced around the tree and took a swipe at an opulent hydrangea, sending snowy white petals scattering.

"Tom. Tom, look at me." Patricia spoke almost conspiratorially.

I stopped in front of them, breathing hard, my mouth quivering.

"One thing you should know about me is that I'm tough."

I rolled my eyes.

"Never mind. In this case, it works in your favour," she continued. "Yes, Carolyn showed me the note. She also told me how adamant you were that no one should ever know of its existence. I respect that. I know your intentions, and I respect them. As much as I can't respect what Jeremy did."

I threw up my hands. "But we don't know what Jeremy did," I said, louder than I should have. I did a quick scan around the yard. No sign of Robert and Luke. Margaret, though, stood on the patio looking at us.

"Shit," I said in hushed tone. I turned my back toward the house. "The note is ambiguous. It doesn't say explicitly that … what you are implying it says. The note is a love letter. Period. To Carolyn. Period. No one is ever, ever, ever to know anything about it. Right?"

Patricia took hold of my hand. "Yes, that is right."

Carolyn dabbed at her eyes and, facing Patricia, asked, "But what about Robert?"

"Sweetie," Patricia responded. "We all love Robert and think he is a dear husband and a dear father. But we also all know that he's not the sharpest knife in the drawer."

Carolyn gasped and then giggled.

"I have no intention," Patricia continued unfazed, "of ever breathing a word about this to him. Or to anyone else. What happened, happened. It has nothing to do with us. Jeremy is the one who now has to face the consequences."

"Face the consequences?" My mind started reeling. "Are you telling me …" I was struggling for air.

"Yes. Because that is the truth. For what he's done, well, there are consequences for his … soul."

"Patricia!" Carolyn's voice rose. "What the fuck are you saying?"

Patricia leaned in toward Carolyn and said softly, "Do I really have to spell it out for you, dear?"

Carolyn grabbed Patricia's hair and yanked her head within six inches of her own. "You fucker," she spit out. "There is no hell. There is no heaven. There is no God. That is the truth. You're creating a hell on earth by spouting this shit. I loved that man. The kind of love you'll never know, obviously, from what you just confessed about your own husband." She spit on the ground for real and rubbed her shoe over the spot. "That's where your fucking vindictive God belongs." She let go of Patricia's hair and vigorously wiped her hand on her dress.

Patricia straightened herself and took a deep breath. She looked back and forth at the two of us and said, with composure inaccessible to Carolyn or me, "You poor, naïve children. I'll pray for you." She looked over my shoulder and whispered, "Attention, everyone. Mother-in-law approaching."

"A rather intense-looking family chat going on here, it would seem," Margaret understated as she reached us.

"We don't often have the chance to be together," Patricia said.

"And so you fight like five-year-olds when you do?" None of us responded. "Never mind, I'm glad that I've caught you all together."

"I should get back to the kitchen." Patricia began excusing herself.

"Your mother is upset with your delinquency, but don't go just yet. There's something that I want to say to the three of you. Well, several things."

We were children summoned to the principal's office.

"First," the elegant but stern schoolmarm began. "About your parents. Don't let our ... family crisis ..." She turned her head and blinked several times. "Make sure that your mother and father follow through on their plans. Both of them are having second thoughts."

"They are?" the three of us said in unison, too enthusiastically.

Margaret scowled at us. "Shame on you. Think of them, for once, not of yourselves all the time. They've gotten it into their heads that we, Walter and I, need them here, in light of everything. They've very fine people. I don't have to tell you that. And we appreciate their concern and generosity. But Walter and I are better off alone."

She turned to me, and said, a statement without inflection, "We still have Jonathan and Tom. What's more important," she soldiered on, "is they have the opportunity to do something that they really want to do with their skills and energy in the time that they have left ..."

Strange choice of words, I thought.

"... and they will do a great deal more good for people in Sudan than they would sitting here holding our hands. So I want you to persuade them to follow through on their plans. Their dream. Okay?"

We nodded.

"Tom." She pulled back her shoulders, looked directly in my eyes, and spoke without stammer. "Take good care of my baby. My remaining baby. And yourself."

She turned toward my younger sister. "Carolyn."

Carolyn looked down, partly to guide her foot to cover the cigarette residue in the carefully manicured lawn, partly to avoid eye contact.

"Carolyn, darling." Carolyn raised her head. "We haven't always been on the best of terms," Margaret said, and then she smiled, briefly. "But I know that Jeremy loved you. Passionately. And you were the best thing in his life." She paused. "After me, of course," she added, without irony. "Patricia, take good care of those children of yours. You have no idea how precious they are."

"Oh, I think that I do, Margaret."

"You have no idea how very precious they are," Margaret repeated, as if she hadn't heard. "To this whole family." She waved her hand in a circle that encompassed the manor. "Do you know that Naomi and Luke came to me earlier and asked if we would be their surrogate grandparents while your parents are away? Well, that's not exactly how they phrased it. But that is what they were asking. And that request means a world to me."

Patricia was stunned silent. Carolyn dropped her head. I blinked back tears, impressed and in love with my mother-in-law.

"Now, Patricia, go back in and help your mother. Tom, go to Jonathan. He needs you."

Margaret took a step toward Carolyn, who stepped back defensively. "Carolyn," she said quietly. "Have another cigarette and enjoy the peace of the garden."

Margaret pivoted and headed back to the house.

Part Four
2002

Chapter 35

The afternoon heat was starting to yield to a typically balmy Puerto Vallarta evening. The breeze often seemed to pick up at that point in the day, reinforcing the pleasant comfort level.

"How much longer are you going to be working on that?" Jonathan asked impatiently. "We're going to miss the sunset from their terrace if we don't leave soon."

"Sorry. It's still going to be a while. Bob and Luis's sunset is the same as ours anyway."

"Yes, but it's more spectacular at their penthouse level with Bob's martinis and Luis' canapés, and more fun watching it while debating American politics with Ralph and Edward."

"All right, all right, I get the picture," I laughed. "Listen. Why don't you go on ahead? I promised Bonn that I would e-mail this tonight."

"What is it?" Jonathan asked, setting down his gin and tonic on the dining room table that acted as my desk. He sat in a chair opposite me.

"My report from the Christian-Islamic dialogue that I organized at the Marrakech climate negotiations last month. Given the post-9/11 tensions and this being the first negotiations hosted in an Islamic state, the UN folk want to look at it as something of a model."

"Oh, la-di-da," he said raising his glass in a mock toast. I glanced past him and out toward Banderas Bay. To see the sun, I had to lean down. It was still high enough in the sky to be hidden by the palapa roof on our suite. It wasn't as late as he had implied. Sunset was more than an hour away.

"Is Morocco really an 'Islamic state'?" Jonathan stuck a finger in his glass and pushed the ice cubes around. "There's an elected parliament, a monarch, and certainly access to alcohol. Some fine wines, as I well recall."

"Yes, my little lush," I said, starting to play footsies with him under the table. "Islam is the official state religion, but functionally,

225

it is quite a secular country. And as for the wine, there was more than one night that I had to carry you off to bed, which you probably don't even remember."

"I do remember fine dinners, with course after course after course, relaxing on a bank of Kilim cushions under starry skies, all complimented by many bottles of … what was the name of that one that I fell in love with? Riad Jamil, that was it."

"I seem to remember you falling in love with more than red wine."

"I haven't the faintest idea what you're talking about," Jonathan protested, reciprocating my foot play from his side of the table. "Ah, Abdelmoumen …"

I returned to my laptop, typing as he wandered off into lusty reveries.

"Your wet dream vibes are making it difficult for me to concentrate here." I migrated from amorous foot tapping to more vigorous jabbing.

"Ow." Jonathan retracted his leg. "You were jealous then as well, if I recall. By the way, did you see him when you were there last month?"

I looked up from my screen. The emerging sunrays poking below the wispy fronds of the roofline were framing Jonathan's profile.

"No, darling. Sorry to disappoint you. Moumen wasn't waiting for me at the airport, hoping that I had you in tow this time. Remember, it was three, or was it four, years ago when we were there last. He's probably off travelling the world now under some lucrative modeling agency contract."

"Or under some lucrative sugar daddy."

"Now who's jealous? You wouldn't have been able to afford to keep him on your professor's salary."

"What do you think the royalties from my books are dedicated to?"

I picked up the glass of water and threatened to toss it at him, my gesture not as feigned as I had intended.

He leapt up from his chair, brushing off the sprinkles that had hit their mark. "Nice! Now I'm going to have to change my shirt. This is linen."

"Okay, okay," I laughed. "You win." I pressed the return button and powered down. "I'll finish this when I get home. Which means that I won't be able to drink a lot. Nothing new there though," I added, as I slipped the laptop into the carrying case. "If history repeats itself tonight, as at every other of their New Year's dinner parties over the years, I'll be the one pouring you into a cab at the end of the evening and then hauling you up the stairs here."

"Admit it. You love taking care of me."

Puerto Vallarta had become our post-Christmas retreat of choice.

We were tied to Toronto until at least December 26 each year. Jonathan and I both felt the need to be with Margaret and Walter on Christmas Day. The Compton dinner had become a quiet affair. The dearth of a particularly boisterous personality haunted all of us, acknowledged only by the extra place setting that Margaret always set. No one ever commented.

My parent's contract provided for up to a month of furlough every other year. To date, they had not scheduled it at Christmastime. They chose to spend Christmas in the refugee camp, where festive occasions were considerably less resourced than ours in Toronto, or at Patricia and Robert's in Dayton, or wherever Carolyn found herself. Not that she celebrated the holiday anyway.

Jonathan craved sun and heat as an antidote to the grey, cold, blustery Toronto winter. His teaching schedule, compounded by his new role as department chair, restricted him being absent from campus for more than a week, or two at most. We took as much time as we dared before the January term began and occasionally a few additional days during March break.

My travel schedule allowed me to avoid the November to March Canadian doldrums with more frequency, spending a week or so in warm and sunny climes several times a winter. All of these were working trips, of course, with a very occasional bit of R and R playtime squeezed in. Our friends were jealous. I found it hard to convince them that ninety-nine percent of my time was spent in windowless conference rooms, translation earphones glued to my head, or in governmental receptions trying to affect interest in another turgid speech, or in airport lounges struggling to stay awake so as not to miss the boarding call.

Travel had lost its romance long ago. Now, it was increasingly a health hazard. My body was not responding with its former elasticity to the endless time zone changes.

Jonathan took pains to disguise what I knew he was thinking—
serves you right. Instead, he laid the blame on the pace of work. He held
the UN criminally responsible for shaving years off my longevity.

This year was already filling up quickly with my responsibilities for
coordinating the climate change portion of the UN's World Summit on
Sustainable Development in August in Johannesburg and planning the
World Council of Churches's consultation on solidarity with victims of
climate change in October in Geneva.

Maybe next year I would slow down.

Bob, our host for tonight's annual New Year's Day party, would have
been a good example for me to follow. After his heart attack last year,
he had taken early retirement at the ripe old age of fifty.

Retirement was something of a misnomer. Being president and
CEO of his own successful real estate development company in Seattle
gave Bob options. He kept an eye on the business from atop his luxury
condo in PV but assigned the day-to-day operations to his son Peter and
daughter Bessie. In the divorce settlement, Bob retained the business,
and his ex-wife got the house and a generous alimony. The divorce came
about when Bob decided that he preferred to sleep with thirty-year-old
architect-cum-actor-cum-model Luis instead of Stephanie. It was all
very amicable. Unless appearances were deceiving, Bob and Stephanie
were still the best of friends, and both of them adored Luis. Bob
always held his grand seasonal gay party on New Year's Day because
the previous week the condo was filled with Stephanie, along with
Peter and Bessie and their spouses and children, and Luis was with his
parents and siblings. Bob willingly hosted the family Christmas but was
ready for a strong dose of all-gay male company afterwards—a potent
palate cleanser, he would say.

We arrived fashionably late, courtesy of my afternoon work
compulsiveness.

Luis opened the door, a brilliant welcoming sparkle in his eyes and
an overflowing platter of hors d'oeuvres in his hands.

"*Juanita y Tom! Bienvenidos.*" He loved to irritate Jonathan, who
never appreciated a femmie greeting. Jonathan grunted and headed
toward Bob at the bar. I winked at Luis and helped myself to a couple
of his delicacies.

The usual crowd was there, freshened by a few new faces.

The spacious living and dining room opened onto a terrace that provided an unobstructed western view of the nearly setting sun and then wrapped around along the north side of the suite to showcase the city, sparkling with dusky luminescence. The floor-to-ceiling glass doors were all pocketed, making the outside space part of the inside and giving the impression that not only the infinity pool in the corner lacked an outer boundary.

Most of the guests were in animated conversation on the terrace or in transit between it and bartender Bob, somewhat like parallel lines of industrious ants moving to and from the queen.

Opting to wait until the crowd at the bar thinned a little, I headed over to a cluster of old friends and unfamiliar faces. Jonathan sidled up a few moments later with his gin martini and passed me my dirty-vodka-shaken-not-stirred-three-olive martini. He interlocked his glass-holding arm with my glass-holding arm, and we clinked glasses—a sweet touch of proprietary exhibitionism on his part.

"I recognize you," exclaimed a tall, balding man, sporting one of those goatees that seemed to be returning to fashion, a century after their late Victorian golden age. Interrupting the flow of chitchat, he raised his highball glass in Jonathan's direction and continued. "You're that media philosopher guy. The one CBC enlists to have some egghead expound on the big-picture dimension of the latest global crisis." "Big picture" was emphasized with a two-handed, double finger simulation of quotation marks, an exaggerated gesture that cost him a third of his drink when it spilled over the railing.

"Who is CBC?" Andrew, a PV regular whom we had known for years, asked in his deep Southern drawl. His father owned a bank in Kentucky, an occupation that we as Canadians were never able to adequately get our heads around. Andrew was a sweet Southern belle whose mannerisms Jonathan found infinitely charming and who, despite his familial connection to the world of finance, was incapable of understanding the concept of foreign currency exchange rates; as a consequence he always and only used American dollars when in Mexico.

I put my arm around Andrew and in a stage whisper revealed that the CBC was a Canadian socialist public institution that we supported and mandated, primarily for the purposes of trashing George Bush.

"Don't tell Daddy, but I say here's to the CBC and trashing George

Bush." Andrew beamed as he raised his glass, and in return, received enthusiastic endorsements from around the circle.

Mr. Goatee persisted. "It is you, isn't it? Geez. I can't stand your pretentious politics, but I love it that you're queer. Never would have guessed."

"Where are you from?" I intervened.

"Calgary."

"You don't say," Jonathan responded.

Serge, a retired schoolteacher from Philadelphia whom we had met a couple times at Bob and Luis's turned to Jonathan and asked, "What is he talking about? Your media role? The philosopher business?"

"Oh, it's nothing," said Jonathan, a little curtly, uninterested in starting the evening off with shoptalk, particularly as so charmingly introduced by our compatriot.

"No, seriously, I am intrigued," said Serge with genuine curiosity. "If you don't mind."

"Maybe he'll be less reticent if you pay him," Mr. Calgary offered. "What kind of fees do they fork over for those sound bites? Or, rather, that we taxpayers pay you, as your boyfriend here so helpfully clarified."

The entire group had begun shifting slightly, turning backs discretely but perceptibly toward the unwelcomed tension-generator. I took hold of Jonathan's hand and gave it a little squeeze. He looked at me and then addressed Serge, ignoring Calgary.

"It really is nothing to speak of. I teach philosophy at the University of Toronto and have a particular interest in contemporary issues— the nature of global citizenship, threats to civic democracy from corporatism. That sort of thing. I get called upon from time to time to do media interviews …"

Jonathan turned toward Calgary, "… by various media, including private, as well as public, broadcasters …"

Facing Serge again, he continued, as if to conclude the conversation, " … when they are interested in setting the story in a broader context, looking at historical antecedents, social norms, competing ethical values. No big deal."

"Fascinating. I think that it is a big deal. Would you mind if we continued this conversation over dinner?"

"Sure, that would be fine," said Jonathan without enthusiasm, judging Serge a better seating companion than the alternate interrogator.

"Well, at least give me some credit for watching the CBC from time to time," we heard over our shoulders as we moved in from the terrace.

"Buenos días. Is everybody decent up there? Is the coffee on?"

I leapt up from the table and stuck my head out over the wrought iron circular staircase that wound up to our unit from the pool area. I put my fingers to my lips and then motioned Maria to come up. For almost a decade, Jonathan and I had been perennial guests at Maria's house, perched high in the hills above old Vallarta. She had three units that she rented out, largely to gay clientele. Ours was the most charming, with its two giant palapa roofs over the dining room and over the living area, both of which opened to an unobstructed bay view.

"Come on in," I said in a hushed tone as she reached the front entrance. "Coffee is on, but His Highness is still sleeping. Bit of a hangover, I'm afraid."

"Again?" she whispered back.

I shrugged and picked the coffee pot up from the stove to pour two cups.

"You working?" she asked, leaning over my empty chair and squinting to read the laptop screen.

"Nothing new about that either," I responded, gently nudging her toward an adjacent chair while I sat down in mine. "A report that I need to finish and email as soon as possible." I hoped that the implied urgency would shorten the usual morning gossip session.

"The house seems quiet."

"You're telling me. Business is way down. Since 9/11, everyone seems to be afraid of travelling. So stop doing foolish stuff on the computer, like work, and send SOS e-mails to your friends to get them down here. Speaking of your friends, how was Bob and Luis's party last night?"

I gave her a crib note version of the food, the gossip, and who ended up leaving with whom.

"Dammit all. I would have a lot more fun and action in this town if I were a faggot."

"Don't go there," I responded quietly. I glanced toward the bedroom door, hoping that the volume of her conversation hadn't woken Jonathan.

Maria caught my glance. She whispered, "While we have a moment alone, tell me. How is he doing?"

"Okay. Why?"

She took a sip of coffee. "I mean with the whole brother thing. He never mentions him. Ever. As long as I can remember."

"Oh, that." I took a deep breath and listened for any sounds of movement. All remained quiet. "It's been a while now, of course. Let's see. Nine years in August. Memories fade. Life goes on."

Maria furrowed her brow and said, "Cut the crap, Tom. This is Momma Maria you're talking to. Those kinds of memories don't fade. Life does not go on after something like that—losing your twin brother." She crossed herself. "*El nombre del Padre, y del Hijo, y del Espíritu Santo.* You never get over that sort of thing."

"Well, we talk about it. Somewhat. But Jonathan is a very private person. He doesn't display his feelings in public."

"I'm public?" Maria asked, with an offended frown.

I shrugged and sipped.

"What about his parents? How are they coping?"

I hesitated. Maria did not understand the concept of boundaries. It wasn't in her DNA. She had a heart as big as the Pacific and considered everyone who entered her house as family. I didn't want her to misinterpret my Canadian reticence.

So I continued, certainly beyond where Jonathan would have wanted me to go.

"His father, Walter, I think it really broke him. He sublimates it by keeping himself busy with work."

"And Mother?" Maria encouraged.

I winced.

"What?"

"Well. She's also, obviously, been deeply, deeply scarred by Jeremy's death. I thought that she might have been able to find solace in her faith. She's quite religious. Catholic."

Maria smiled and nodded approvingly.

"But that doesn't seem to have been adequate. She's become quite attracted to some other ... some other types of spiritual support."

Maria sat upright. "Wackos?"

I giggled. "I don't think that that's the technical description."

"Gurus? New Age?" Maria persisted, almost spitting the words as she spoke them.

"No, nothing really weird," I backtracked, feeling that I had been disrespectful of Margaret's quest. I took hold of Maria's hand. "You must not breath a word of this conversation to Jonathan. Promise?"

Maria frowned and shook her head. "Yes, of course. You people. You're so afraid."

"Of what?" I said, a bit piqued.

"Everything. Feelings. Pain. Talking about pain."

"Tom, is the coffee on?" Jonathan called groggily from the bedroom.

"Yes, dear," I replied while giving Maria a stern warning look. "Maria's here. I'm giving her a report about last night's dinner party. Come out and join us."

"*Claro que sí!*" Maria yelled. "Tom's not very good at giving me all the dirt on Bob and Luis and your other friends. I want to hear it from you. I'm pouring your coffee right now," she said as she moved toward the stove. "You have to come out here to get it. Unless you want me to bring it in and see you *desnudo.*"

"I'll be right there."

Chapter 36

"We don't often have a philosopher on the program. I suspect many people aren't aware that there are still philosophers around these days." Even the slight electrical whine and occasional static from the speakers in the small clock radio on the nightstand in my room at the Ottawa Ramada Hotel could not mask the self-assured velvet resonance of Marion Tonkin's voice.

Though disembodied at my end, I had no difficulty summoning an image to accompany the dialogue—Marion and Jonathan sitting across from each other at a desk in CBC's Toronto studios, large ear phones wrapped around their heads and boom microphones poised six inches from their mouths. Marion had Jonathan's latest book, *The Life of Engagement*, open in front of her and a foolscap pad of notes beside it. Her pen lay on the paper, ready to scribble additional ideas or questions as they arose out of the conversation. Jonathan sat with his hands folded on the desk in front of him. No book, no pad or pen, just a relaxed smile on his lips, his eyes focused intently on Marion, ready to follow the discussion wherever.

Radio interviews with Jonathan were less satisfying than TV versions to me. Getting the audio without the visual was like having to do with only half a sandwich. The radio microphone could transmit his crisp one-liners and eloquent paragraph-length dissertations, all delivered in an animated baritone voice. Missing was a view of that swarthy, yet patrician, head, his copious hair now slightly greying, and his piercing, dark brown eyes, whose gaze extended, unfettered, into your darkest secrets but without threat because of the modulating effect of the generous smile that never smirked or frowned. At least on camera.

I pushed the file off my lap so that I could enjoy the interview undistracted. It slid partway across the bed. A few papers slipped out of the folder, as if the notes for my morning speech at the Ottawa Press Club were eager to be delivered and to celebrate the emerging signs that

Prime Minister Chrétien would soon announce that Canada would ratify the Kyoto Protocol. I crammed them back in the folder with the frustrated energy of knowing that a policy without an implementation strategy is not much to celebrate.

"You're probably right," Jonathan responded to Marion with a chuckle. "Mention *philosopher* and people see Rodin's *The Thinker* in their mind's eye or Socrates drinking a cup of hemlock. I assure you that I'm quite a bit more vigorous than either of them."

"I bet you are," Marion said.

"What are you doing after the program?"

"I think we should get back to discussing the book, for the moment."

"Spoil-sport."

They were incorrigible, both of them. Good for ratings, though, and book sales.

"I'd like to read a short paragraph from your first chapter, as a place to start."

"My words in your mouth. How delicious."

"Okay, okay," Marion laughed. "Sit there like a good boy and don't distract me. The first chapter, for the information of our listeners, is called 'Forces of Disengagement' and includes this observation:

> *The amorphous 'they' out there don't want us to be critical thinkers, let alone actively engaged in social, political, or environmental issues. 'They' benefit when we are compliant consumers and apathetic citizens. In the post-9/11 context, 'they' foster our disengagement with strategies of fear promotion, some of which are blatant and some of which are subtle and insidious. 'They' don't want us making life difficult for them by asking uncomfortable questions. 'They' don't want us assuming our legitimate civic roles and responsibilities—globally, nationally, and locally.*

"I suppose the obvious first question is, who are you referring to as '*the amorphous "they" out there*'?" Marion asked, reassuming her serious interviewer tone.

"If that's the obvious first question, how about we begin with the less obvious second question?" Jonathan countered, assuming a playfully serious interviewee tone. "For instance, how did we get to the situation where we have such a division between those who lead, or purport to lead, and those who are led? What happened to the ancient Greek ideal of democracy, where every citizen in the state had the right to speak and vote in the assembly that made the laws?"

"So we're switching roles here, are we?" Marion said. "I thought I was the one who was supposed to be asking the questions and you answering."

Jonathon assumed a faux-pretentious tone as he gently chastised Marion about, first, being wed to sterile interviewer/interviewee roles and, second, not having mentioned for a couple minutes the title of his new book.

One could hear Marion's smile of enjoyment through the airwaves as she said, "We're talking today with University of Toronto philosophy professor Jonathan Compton about his new book, his fascinating new book, *The Life of Engagement* ... how's that?"

"Very nice. I like the subtlety."

"... in which Professor Compton ..."

"Please, just call me Jonathan."

"... in which Jonathan discusses the importance of civic responsibility. So, Jonathan, do I hear you idealizing Athenian Greek democracy as the standard that we should emulate? True, all citizens had the rights of participation that you describe, but there were strict criteria on who could be a citizen. No women, for instance."

"And the reason that we're not still stuck with that model of the right of citizens to full participation but very limited right of citizenship is that women wouldn't stand for it." Jonathan's voice rose with his enthusiasm. "They demanded the same rights of citizenship. They became engaged in the civic process."

"It was an awfully long wait from the fourth century BC," Marion challenged. "It was only in the early 1900s that women had the right to vote in Canada, thanks to the persistence of Nellie McClung and others."

"And during those ... how many centuries is that? I'm a philosopher, not a mathematician."

"Twenty-four, I guess," Marion laughed. "Depending on how you're counting."

"Thanks. During those long, long twenty-four centuries, why is it that women did not have the right to vote and full participation in the running of the state? Because—I'll answer my own question—it's fun being both interviewer and interviewee."

"I can see you enjoy it."

Jonathan, usually an ideal guest who gave short, crisp answers, went on at some length about the strong, male-dominated institutions, such as government, the Church, the military, the academy, the family, business and corporations as they evolved, having vested interest in preserving their privileges and limiting access to the decision-making process, keeping whole sectors of the community, in this case, women, disengaged. His disciplined discussion style was slipping. I wondered if he had been drinking before he went to the studio.

Marion interrupted him mid-sentence. "But surely, and I can't believe that I'm about to make a defense of patriarchal history," she said with a chuckle, "surely, during those twenty-four centuries, those same male-dominated institutions were responsible for many advances in the well-being of persons in society."

"At what cost during all that time? Society is healthier now that women and men have, for the most part, equitable rights and responsibilities."

I glanced at my watch. The typical time allotted for interviews was running out. Jonathan started speaking more rapidly, arguing that his focus on the negative costs of the historical exclusion of women had been an illustrative microcosm of a much more pervasive dynamic of strong elites disenfranchising many within and across societies. With oratorical flourish, he wound up making the case that so-called advanced Western nations are hugely compromised ethically by the disenfranchising that is done by more insidious forms of manipulation than that of restricting access to the voting booth. "It is our ethical civic responsibility to resist," he pronounced with the authority of a protest leader.

"You make our situation sound rather depressing," Marion observed in a move toward wrap-up, her producer no doubt giving her the T signal through the glass.

"Are you saying that you found this discussion depressing?" Jonathan asked.

"No, on the contrary. It was energizing," she responded.

"Or, you might say, engaging? As in the energy derived from 'a life of engagement'?"

"Touché," she laughed.

I switched off the radio, retrieved my speech notes, and added text about commitment, perseverance, and integrity.

There were disappointingly few people in the Great Hall of Hart House when I arrived a couple minutes after the publicized 5:00 p.m. start of the reception. About twenty or so, ranging in age from undergraduate to retired faculty, were gathered around the table at the far end, behind which a young woman and young man, both nattily attired, stood smartly pouring wine.

On the stage at the other end of the room, Jonathan was perched on the corner of a massive desk that was stacked high with copies of his book. His free leg swung lazily, as if buffeted by a breeze. He was talking with Dominic, his editor, and a couple of others, probably from the publishing house, I assumed. Jonathan noticed me enter, lifted his wine glass in salute, and almost lost his balance in the process. Someone said something, and they all laughed. None of them evidenced concern about the small attendance.

They had more experience with book launches than I. Within thirty minutes, the room was filled with a few hundred people.

Jonathan certainly did not have the draw of a Margaret Atwood or a John Ralston Saul. He was younger than they were, had written fewer books, and had not won any literary prizes. But he had several dynamics working in his favour. Being a professor meant that he had students who felt it to be in their self-interest to acknowledge the power assigning them grades, and he had insecure colleagues who did not want an absence to be interpreted as jealousy.

More to the point for the publisher wanting to sell books was Jonathan's increasing media profile; he had been adopted as something of an intellectual guru by a range of protest movements grouped informally under the anti-globalization banner. They discovered a philosophical and ethical grounding for their social activism in his writings, and they were grateful.

Dominic tapped on the microphone beside the lectern, and a harsh crackle echoed through the august chamber.

"I encourage you, ladies and gentlemen, to take a seat. We're about to begin," he shouted a bit too loudly, making it sound more like a summons than an invitation.

Dominic's intervention into the wine-sipping discussions did have the intended effect of diminishing the hubbub bouncing around the room, just in time to hear glass breaking.

I looked up from the bar and saw Jonathan sprawled out on the floor beside the desk, a couple of piles of books scattered on top of and around him. The jarring noise startled and further silenced the attendees. Jonathan let loose a stream of profanity.

I rushed toward the stage but hesitated when I saw that he was being offered more assistance than he could use. He brusquely swatted the extended arms away and got up off the floor on his own, noticeably unsteadily. Someone handed him a couple napkins. He swiped at the splattered Merlot on his sports coat and shirt. *Of course, he would be drinking red*, I observed to myself. One of the publisher's staff was attempting, as inconspicuously as possible, to pick up and restack the books that had fallen over.

Dominic pulled out a chair for Jonathan behind the desk. Jonathan grabbed hold of the crown of the chair back, yanking it out of Dominic's hands, jerked it closer, and crashed down on it. After a moment, and with slow deliberation, he lifted his arms and placed both hands, palms down, on the desk, shoulder-width apart. He raised his head and glared directly, unwaveringly, at the assembled audience, his mouth frozen in a defiant scowl.

Some returned his gaze. Others diverted their eyes.

Into the awkward silence, a female voice near the rear erupted in laughter, supplemented by vigorous clapping.

Without taking his eyes off the crowd, Jonathan pushed against the table and rose slowly with majestic aplomb. He paused for a moment, his six-foot-four self fully erect, and he bowed deeply from the waist.

A smattering of applause joined Sheila's.

Most sat on their hands.

Chapter 37 ———————————

"**Vancouver** Island? By yourself, Margaret? For how long?" Walter was clearly not pleased with his wife's nonchalant announcement of the impending trip.

Jonathan and I simultaneously laid our knives and forks quietly on our dinner plates, looked at each other and then at flustered Walter, who had tossed his utensils with an unnerving clatter on the bone china, and then at Margaret, who sat serenely placing in her mouth a speared morsel of roast beef done to medium-rare perfection. She gazed at her husband at the opposite end of the ten-foot Compton dining room table, with its exquisite inlaid wood designs, acquired a few years ago from an antique shop in San Telmo, Buenos Aires, as recommended by their son.

Margaret chewed her meat with demure nonchalance, a slight smile interplaying with her working mouth muscles.

"For God's sake, Margaret."

Margaret laid her fork down, picked up her wine glass, and sipped last fall's best Beaujolais.

"Margaret!"

"My dear, you don't want me to speak with my mouth full, surely." Pause. "British Columbia is lovely in April."

"Of course it is. It's the fucking West Coast, for God's sake."

"I have a friend there. He has invited me to come out and stay with him for a little while." Margaret returned to her meal with a resolute smile. She maneuvered a dab of parsley-sprinkled mashed potato onto the back of her fork, and then lapped a touch of gravy over it before raising it to her mouth.

Walter was sputtering. "A friend? Invited you to stay with him?"

"Yes, dear." She swallowed her food and sipped her wine. "That's correct."

"Boys, boys, boys," Walter entreated, his arms extended out

toward Jonathan and me, beckoning with his hands to his enlisted reinforcements. "What the hell is your mother talking about?"

I shrugged.

Jonathan looked at Margaret and reached his hand toward her, resting it on the table palm up. "Yes, Mother, what are you talking about?"

She glanced down at Jonathan's hand, smiled, and then resumed cutting another piece of prime rib. Jonathan withdrew his arm.

Margaret lifted her fork slightly off the plate and rotated it, studying the small slice of beef from various angles. "Beautiful, isn't it. Nutritious and delicious—such a transformation from the cow to the butcher to my kitchen to this table." Looking up at three perplexed faces, she added, "We shouldn't take the little things for granted, you know," and she then inserted the thing of beauty in her mouth. She closed her eyes and savored the moment.

Walter threw his napkin on the table. "Bonkers! You've gone absolutely bonkers. I need a drink. A real one, not this highfalutin', overpriced grape juice." He took a disparaging swipe at the wine goblet, sending it into a teetering spiral dance around on its delicate pedestal. We all watched as it eventually succumbed to gravity and tipped over, the residual Beaujolais trickling out and pooling around the base of the meat platter.

Walter pushed his chair back from the table and headed into the study.

While glaring at his mother, Jonathan spoke to the departing back of his father. "I'll join you," and he did.

Margaret watched them leave and then rose and moved to the far end of the table. Picking up Walter's discarded napkin, she dabbed at the spilt wine and said, "Hazel can do her best with the stain tomorrow." She returned to her seat and continued eating.

I sat on my hands.

After a few minutes, Margaret spoke without looking up. "Yes, Tom?"

"Pardon?"

"Is there something that you want to ask me?" Margaret said before taking another sip of wine. She gently placed the glass back on the table, folded her hands in her lap, and looked at me.

"Well, I guess I'm as perplexed as Walter and Jonathan about what's going on."

"Are you? I'd be surprised if that were the case."

"Pardon me?"

"Tom," she answered in an admonishing tone.

I lifted my glass and took a substantial drink that did not do justice to the fine wine that it was, Walter's critique notwithstanding. I set it down and looked at Margaret, who was waiting patiently, expectantly.

"Eckhart Tolle?"

"You think?" Margaret responded in a partially successful imitation of the inflection popular among kids the age of her grandchildren, if she'd had any.

"He's invited you to stay with him?"

Margaret giggled. "That was a bit of a hyperbole. Just to get Walter's goat."

"So?"

"So—he does run seminars and retreats. I've decided to go out for one next week."

"And he's invited you to stay with him?"

"Aw, no," she giggled, as she flicked her napkin at me. "Eckhart doesn't know me from Adam. Or Eve. I'm just enrolling in his seminar at the retreat centre on the Island. That's the extent of our relationship, to date. Simply a commercial transaction of the most prosaic kind, you must understand."

"You must forgive me, Margaret, if I'm being a bit obtuse. If that's what this is about, why all the cloak and dagger? Why don't you just tell Walter what you're doing?"

Margaret smiled benignly at me, adding after a moment, "Maybe I've given you too much credit."

"Try me again."

"Okay. First, I presume that you can tell how much pleasure it gives me to tease my husband."

"'The little wicked vixen,' we call you around our house," I lied. It was harmless flattery.

"How sweet. I love it," she enthused.

Turning somber and looking through the hallway in the direction of the study, she said, "Seems for some time now there's precious little I have been able to do to get a rise out of him."

The sudden cloud in the room suffocated my instinct for the crude pun.

Reverting her attention to me, she continued, "But seriously. Can you really expect me to talk about *The Power of Now* with him? Or with Jonathan, for that matter?"

"Ah."

"Have you read it?"

I sighed. "Yes, I picked up a copy after our conversation at Christmas."

"And?"

"I don't think that you're going to like my review."

"You're not going to go all judgmental on me, are you, Tom? I thought you were the one person in this family ..." Margaret sighed and looked toward the hall.

I sat quietly, waiting for her return.

She looked back at me, a touch of fire in her eyes. "Well? Tell me. What did you think?"

I opted for the brutal thrust, rather than the cautious incision.

"It's crap, Margaret. I have two big problems with it. He writes that the greater part of human pain is unnecessary. He says it is self-created. Come on. Give me a break. I travel around the world a great deal and see an awful lot of human suffering and pain, and it sure as hell is not some self-imposed delusional state."

"Why don't you tell me what you really think?" Margaret said softly.

I plowed on. "The second thing that really grated me was his dismissal of the past and the future. Sure, I can agree that it's unhealthy to be so obsessed with either the past or the future that you become dysfunctional in daily living. But Tolle goes way beyond that. He denigrates the importance of memory and of working for a better future. At least, the way I read him. I think memory, and our honouring of those who have gone before, and respecting the lessons of history are hugely important."

I stopped.

Margaret hadn't taken her eyes off me, nor had they displayed any reaction to my diatribe. "Well," she said slowly. "Is that what we would call a dispassionate analysis?"

"No, you're right," I replied quietly. "I'm afraid that reading it and thinking about it a great deal ... I've been anticipating this conversation for some time ... I just got very angry. It struck me as so ... self-absorbed."

"I see."

"I apologize, Margaret. If you find it helpful, I should not be so critical. I'm sorry that I told you what I thought so ... so ..."

"Bluntly? Callously? Self-righteously?"

I braced for the counter-volley.

Margaret placed her hand on the table, palm up, just as Jonathan had earlier. I laid mine in hers. With her other hand she started to stroke the back of my fingers, slowly outlining each one in turn, her eyes riveted on them.

"Let me tell you, my dear, I think that I know something about pain."

She paused for a long time before continuing.

She tossed her eyes up and around the dining room, visually cursing everything in view. "Fancy house, I have. A home with a family, I do not. No children present. No husband present. Physically, sometimes. Emotionally, never."

"Margaret ..."

"Shhh, my little man," she interrupted, quietly starting to squeeze my hand more tightly, still stroking the back, still staring at it.

In a soft, affectionate voice that belied her words, she continued. "You probably think that I am a pathetic, self-pitying, over-indulged, affluent housewife."

Her grip tightened further, her eyes looking at or through our intertwined hands.

"I had a son. His name was Jeremy. Perhaps you have heard of him."

My hand was cramping under her intensifying vice grip.

"I had another son. His name was Jonathan. Perhaps you have heard of him. From what I observe, he is drinking himself to an early grave. Why? I can only conjecture. I don't get to see him much. And he doesn't talk to me about anything important, anything real."

Margaret lifted her head and looked directly into my eyes, her expression as placid as her words were not.

"So the pain that I feel every day—I can tell you it's not fabricated. I have tried many different avenues to assuage it. Let's just say that nothing has worked particularly well so far."

She slowly released her grip.

"Tolle's writings are based, as you should know, on Buddhist teachings. I know some refer to him, disparagingly, as Buddhism Light." She smiled for the first time in the conversation. "There's something to that. But there are some elements that do resonate for me. He writes in the chapter on pain in *The Power of Now*, 'allow the present moment to be. This will give you a taste of the state of inner freedom from external conditions, the state of true inner peace.'"

My eyebrows rose involuntarily. Margaret noticed.

"I'll interpret that reaction as you being impressed that I can quote him word for word. My dear, I've been preparing for this conversation as well."

Her grip tightened again, squeezing my hand beyond the comfort level.

"On the other hand, if your raised eyebrows were another manifestation of your condescension toward Tolle, and toward me in seeking some solace through him, well then, you are not the sympathetic son-in-law than I have given you credit for. On your better days." She glared at me for a moment and then down again at our clasped hands.

I shrank back in my chair.

"As for your stunningly lucid critique of Eckhart's perspective on the past and the future." She moved her gaze from the table up to her breast, where a broken heart resided. "My past is not going anywhere." She raised her head and stared into the depths of her empty home. "As to my future, not a pretty picture from what I can see." She turned and faced me. "Don't begrudge me this new option."

She lifted my hand up and laid it gently against her cheek, holding it there for a moment. And then she dropped it and shook her hands a few times, as if to cleanse them.

"Now, how about you help me clear the table, and then we'll join our men. The news should be coming on soon. We can all watch it together, like a nice little family."

Chapter 38

"For heaven's sake, Walter. Dad is there, on the ground. He knows what he's talking about."

I kept my voice controlled. I needed this discussion to go well. I wanted to be able to respond to Dad's letter with something tangible.

It was complicated for all of us. A wrong step could compromise Mom and Dad's safety, or could open Walter to charges of violating his confidentiality agreement as a member of the Talisman Board of Directors, or could land me in hot water for perceived UN interference in private sector and member state affairs.

Any or all of the above, I knew. Yeah. Complicated.

"Tom, I like your father. You know that. I very much respect what he and your mom have been doing in the refugee camp. But he should stick with that. Teaching and helping build shelters is one thing. Shoving his nose into geopolitics, big oil, and a very nasty civil war is something altogether different. He's way out of his depth."

Walter was pacing his response, which I appreciated. Though our politics had grown even farther apart over the years, we had united of late in mutual concern for Margaret and Jonathan's emotional health. At least, that's what we told ourselves, and each other. Perhaps our partners' coping strategies were more efficacious than our own, which consisted principally of burying ourselves in our work.

I took a deep breath. "It's hard for him to avoid. They were supposed to be working in southern Sudan, but the civil war has made that too dangerous. That's why they are stationed in the refugee camp across the border in Kenya."

"I realize that."

I offered a quick recap of the current phase of the civil war, with over two million people dead of war-related causes and between four and five million uprooted. The Sudanese Government's determination to control the oil-rich regions in the south had been a source of an increasing number of those casualties.

"You're telling me something I don't know?" Walter said dismissively, and then he glared.

"There is plenty of credible evidence that Khartoum has been executing a systematic scorched-earth policy to drive people out of these areas, many of them fleeing to Kenya as refugees. Thousands of women and children in the south have been captured and transported to the north as slaves."

"'Plenty of credible evidence'?"

"Yes. Plenty. UN sources. Agencies. The refugees themselves."

"So you and I are going to solve all the world's problems?"

"We're talking about Sudan. And about Talisman. As recently as 1998, Buckee acknowledged to Foreign Affairs that two hundred and fifty million dollars of the original Talisman investment when he bought into Arakis's operations in Sudan would have directly benefitted the Sudanese Government."

"You think you're telling me something I don't know?" he repeated, parodying himself. "For God's sake, I prepared a good part of that presentation when I was still consulting for them, before Jim drafted me to the Board. Jim Buckee can be a bloody-minded stubborn SOB, but he's a damn good CEO, and Talisman has been lucky to have him at the helm during all the mess that your lefty protest friends have created."

"But that initial investment money, plus the oil revenues since then, have gone a long way to financing the government's war effort against the southern forces. And by the way, the mess, as you euphemistically call it, is hardly the work of any lefty protest friends that I may have."

Walter swung around and pulled the Glenmorangie off the cadenza; he held it up and asked, "Refill?"

"Please."

I placed my tumbler on the coaster and pushed it toward his side of the desk. He poured liberally and then topped up his own. He didn't bother with a coaster under his glass. It was his desk.

"From what Dad and Mom see in Kakuma, there's a clear logic. The kids that Dad is teaching in the classroom, and the sick, pregnant women whose lives and babies Mom is trying to save at the clinic, are largely displaced southern Sudanese. This includes families who have been forced, and that's another euphemism, from the area of Talisman's oil concession. If you cut off those petrodollars, you decrease the capacity of Khartoum to continue the war and increase the likelihood of them agreeing to negotiate a peace agreement. The refugees could then leave Kenya, return to Sudan, and rebuild their homes and lives."

Walter smiled, which I took as a better sign than him hurling his drink at me. "You make it sound so simple." He twirled his glass on his index finger with a proficiency that would rival a Harlem Globetrotter. With a sudden thrust, he sent the tumbler straight up a good six inches, and then he swept his left arm across its descending path, grabbing it in mid-air. Not a drop spilt. "Not bad, eh? You know who taught me how to do that?"

I shrugged.

"A lady of the night in a bar in Singapore."

I did a double take. Walter roared with laughter. "I love to shock you, you little son-of-a-bitch."

As worldly wise as I liked to consider myself, he could shock me, and he regularly did. "Can we get back to the topic at hand?"

Walter took a big gulp, emptying his recently filled glass in one swoop. He slammed the tumbler down on the desk. I jumped.

"For God's sake, what's there to talk about?" he yelled. "There's nothing we can do. This is a country that's had a god-awful civil war of one sort or another going on non-stop for almost fifty years. And there's nothing that you or I or Lawrence or Isabel or anyone else can do to unravel decades of hostilities, ethnic rivalries, cultural schisms, and religious animosities."

"We don't agree on that. There is a whole international effort that is trying to facilitate a peace negotiation process. There are some hopeful signs. Certainly, it is a complex, multifaceted situation. Everyone agrees on that. The oil money component, moving back to the reason for this conversation, is one important element."

"So we're just going to wave some sort of magic, or should I say fairy, wand, and everyone over there will start loving each other? You and your do-gooding family and the rest of your ilk risk making things even more desperate for the poor Sudanese people that you claim to care so much about."

"How so?"

Walter stopped. He swung his chair around and looked out the window. I followed his gaze. A few small sailboats were peacefully drifting back toward the yacht club. Dusk was sufficiently settling in that the lights on the CN Tower had become visible. Their methodical pulsing thrust a stark rhythmic contrast into the acoustically chaotic atmosphere that occupied every square centimetre of Walter's office.

I waited.

Without turning around, he asked quietly, "What does your father think we should be doing?"

His sudden tack change took my breath away for a moment.

"Well," I began, speaking to his back, trying to mimic his tone, which I hoped presaged a conciliatory shift, "he thinks we—you that is—could be putting pressure on the Talisman Board. Dad quoted the report of last year's Canadian Ecumenical Commission to Sudan, something to the effect that oil companies, including Talisman Energy, engaged in the exploration and production of Sudanese oil, should immediately suspend operations until peace has been achieved and the victims of forced displacements in the oil concessions have been safely returned to their places of origin."

"A just and lasting peace," Walter said as he slowly swiveled his chair back to face me.

"Pardon?"

"The report that you and your father are condescendingly quoting to me," he replied with an affectless sigh, "says that Talisman, blah, blah, blah, should immediately suspend operations until a 'just and lasting' peace has been achieved, blah, blah, blah."

I tried to read Walter's eyes.

"Oh. Thank you. You're obviously more familiar with it than am I."

Walter smirked. "And that surprises you? How long have we known each other?"

"Right. Point taken. Then you should be more aware than any of us of the evidence that military forces of the Sudanese Government have bombed villages in Talisman's oil concession area to drive out inhabitants and that the company is"—I hesitated in order to choose my words carefully—"complicit in various ways with Khartoum's aggression against the Southerners."

Walter didn't react to my phrasing. "There are things, Tom"—he paused before continuing—"confidential things that I cannot talk about with you." He stared intently at me.

"Yes, I understand," I replied, hoping that he would do just that.

"I suppose your friends are gearing up for the annual meeting?"

"Um. Yes, I suppose. I'm not as directly tied into those networks as I used to be, but I presume that the Taskforce on the Churches and Corporate Responsibility is working with churches and religious orders and the southern Sudan solidarity groups to prepare shareholder resolutions, as they have in the past."

"Well, how should I put this?" He tapped his fingers together. "Let's play one of my quizzes. Canada is a democracy. Right or wrong?" He smiled a toothy grin.

I stared back at him.

"And in this democracy, citizens have certain rights of protest. Right or wrong?"

I said nothing.

"And in this democracy with its rights of protest, citizens, including, shall we say just for the sake of argument, organizations such as churches, have certain rights and channels to express their concerns about the operations of Canadian corporations within and outside of this country. Right or wrong?"

Walter's quiz questions were progressively more debatable. It went against my grain to reply without qualification. I suppressed my ambivalence in anticipation of a greater good down the road.

"Er, right. More or less." My resolve weakened.

"You lose half a point for that. Now, say a hypothetical corporation, domiciled within a democratic country whose citizens have the right to object to that corporation's foreign activities, was, after well-intentioned but naïve protests, to leave that foreign country by selling its holdings to another corporation from another country whose citizens had considerably fewer channels to object to the nature of its foreign operations. Do you suppose that that would improve the situation of the residents of the foreign country in question? Yes or no?"

"That's a trick question." I held his stare and tried to hold my ground. "Knowingly making profits from an operation that feeds a civil conflict in which innocent people are being killed, raped, and displaced from their ancestral lands cannot be justified ethically." I paused. "Even if in the short term, one loses some of one's leverage in that conflict."

Walter sighed. "Even if, in that short term, countless more people are killed, raped, and displaced?"

I didn't respond.

Walter shook his head. "If I believed in reincarnation," he said, "I would hope to come back in your world. Life would be a helluva lot easier."

He stood up.

I stood up.

"Oh, I almost forgot," I said, reaching for my wallet. "Since we're driving up in separate cars, Jonathan wanted me to give you your and Margaret's Stratford tickets, in case we don't see each other before the performance."

I passed them to him over the desk. He looked down and frowned.

"Something wrong?" I asked.

"I thought we were seeing one of the musicals."

"No, sorry. *Richard III.* Jonathan was supposed to have told you. Friends of ours are involved in the production, so we're anxious to see it."

"*Richard III*, eh? 'And if King Edward be as true and just, As I am subtle, false and treacherous' … odds are you're not casting me as Edward."

"That's a trick question."

"It's not a question at all."

Chapter 39

I was exhausted from the eighteen-hour days that I had been putting in at the Sustainable Development Summit and was looking forward to a change of scene by getting out of negotiating meetings and into the street to meet real people. Not that the diplomats and officials weren't real people. Well, maybe there was some question.

"The march is supposed to start at one, which means it will get underway by two," I said, glancing at my watch. "I particularly want to be part of it at the beginning, when it winds through the shanty towns in Alexander. That should be a reality check, after being cooped up here all week in Jo'burg's fancy convention centre."

"When will you have the draft finished?" Fernando asked, not looking up from his desk, burgeoning with piles of documents. "We've got to allow time for the translation."

"It's finished now. I just want to pass it by the Americans before sending it to the translators. They've been such bastards about any reference to the Kyoto Protocol. Uganda, Norway, and Samoa made a suggestion that I think, I hope, will satisfy them."

"Let me see it." Gutiérrez extended his left arm out over his desk, twiddling his fingers in a gimme-gimme gesture. With his right hand, he continued scratching out and rewriting his draft for the secretary-general's speech. He claimed that pen and paper allowed him to create diplomatic text that could pass for poetry. In his view, with a computer keyboard no such artistry was possible.

I pulled the paper out of the printer and placed my decidedly non-poetic draft paragraph in his fidgeting fingers, where it rested, suspended, as his muse struggled for just the right phrase. After a few moments, he threw his pen down in frustration and looked at my work.

"*States that have ratified the Kyoto Protocol strongly urge States that have not already done so to ratify the Kyoto Protocol in a timely manner,*" he read in a mockingly deliberative tone. He thought for a moment.

"Good. The European Union and the G-77 developing nations get to reaffirm their moral high ground, and the Americans and the Aussies aren't bound to do anything. That should fly." He tossed it back in my general direction, lowered his head, and reached for his pen to attack his foolscap afresh. I picked my precious twenty-five-word nonentity up off the floor.

With his eyes still glued to his paper, he asked, "What do you hear in the corridors about the Canucks and the Ruskies?" I had grown accustomed to Fernando's voice seeming to emanate from the balding spot on the top of his head. I stared at it; his head remained buried in the papers on his desk. At times I fantasized a little mouth, with vibrating lips, opening and closing, dead centre between his ears on the hairless scalp.

"It's the worst-kept secret in Ottawa and here in Jo'burg that Chrétien will declare Canada's intention to ratify the Protocol when he speaks during the high-level segment."

"That must make you happy."

"Not bloody likely."

Fernando looked up, surprised by the intensity of my negativity. "You're getting what you want, aren't you?" he asked. He put down his pen and leaned back in his chair, studying me.

I lifted my right hand and depressed each finger in turn as I enumerated the reasons that I wasn't in rapture.

"One, Kyoto was five years ago. Lot's of other countries have found the time to enact the ratification legislation by now.

"Two, the federal government has sponsored umpteen consultation processes and is still nowhere near a credible plan for meeting reduction targets under Kyoto."

I looked at my hand. Thumb and index down, three to go. Aggressively, my left hand jerked down the right middle.

"Three, the lack of a plan is in large part due to Alberta, where the oil companies, especially the oil sands behemoths, intimidate the Liberals, and there's no sign that that's going to change anytime soon.

"Four, in the meantime, the right-wing Alliance is gaining strength and may unite with the Progressive Conservatives and have enough support to win the next federal election, which is really scary because they've got plenty of dinosaurs who completely dispute the climate change science.

"And fifth ... there's got to be a fifth," I said losing my momentum and waving around my right hand, its illustrative task unfinished.

Fernando applauded. "See, no fifth," he laughed. "There's hope because there's no fifth reason to be depressed."

"I'll give you a fifth," I triumphed. "A huge fifth."

"Okay."

"The Russians." I folded my arms and kicked my legs out in turn, hitting the back of Fernando's desk in a poor parody of a Russian dance. *Or was that Ukrainian?* He scowled at me as I retrieved my dignity and train of thought. "Putin's own advisor, Andrei Illarionav, is fiercely opposed to ratifying, and he speaks for a powerful economic elite in the Kremlin. I've heard him. Scary man. Putin will probably override him and push the Duma to ratify Kyoto. That would trigger the formula to bring the Protocol into effect. But Russia only looks good in terms of emissions reductions because of the collapse of their heavy industry since 1992. The lower emission levels will give them all these credits that they can sell, but it's just hot air. No tangible benefit to the atmosphere, just a sophisticated accounting sham."

The only sound in the room came from the humming air conditioning system. Fernando looked at me. I looked back and then looked down at the twenty-five-word sentence in my hand that was going to change nothing.

He picked up his pen, stared down at his draft of the soon-to-be speech of Kofi Annan. He started writing.

"Thank you, Tom."

"Huh?"

"You just reminded me of something." He spoke slowly as he wrote. "Cynicism is a luxury we cannot afford."

Chapter 40

From: jonathan.compton@utoronto.ca
Subject: Missing you
Date: September 2, 2002 11:58:26 PM EDT
To: tfischer@unosg.int

My darling,

I hate, hate, hate these long separations. I know three weeks is not long by some people's standards, but it is by mine. Always has been. Always will. There. Now I've told you something of which you were totally oblivious. LOL. (If you are ignorant of what that stands for, it's because you don't get to spend a good proportion of your time around pimply faced undergraduates, pretentious post-graduates, and tech-savvy computer nerds.)

It makes sense for you to see your parents since you are in the neighbourhood. Don't swear at me. My African geography is not what it should be, but I am aware that Kenya is not a quick bicycle ride from South Africa. But it is in the same part of the world. Generally speaking. And you haven't seen them since they were home last year. It's good timing, since Carolyn is still in the country finishing her film and because Patricia was able to schedule a visit to coincide with yours. See—I was listening when you made the pitch to take the extra week. But none of that rational scheduling and propitious use of resources reduces my loneliness for you one iota.

I trust you can sense the massive pout on my face. Wouldn't it be amazing if we could see each other on the computer screen and talk to each other in real time? Maybe not. You'd scold me about how I look. That I haven't shaved in two days. That I'm still in my dressing gown. That I'm typing with one hand while sipping on a wonderful fifteen-year-old Glenmorangie that my father gave me. Strangest conversation though. He dropped in unannounced. Handed me this expensive nectar of the gods. And then started a rambling conversation in the course of which he happened to mention, at least two or three times, friends and colleagues of his who have started attending AA. Funny thing, eh? He was very uncomfortable. Mother probably put him up to it. Or was it you, my little double agent?

Don't worry. I still have tomorrow to sober up, get shaved and showered, and maybe even clean up a bit around this pigsty. Do they have Labour Day in Africa? How silly of me—every day is an arduous labour day for the poor bastards.

I was in the office for a few days this past week. The university is switching to a new program that's supposed to make it easier to compute students' schedules and faculty assignments. But Mildred was pulling her hair out. She had a screaming fit with one of the IT guys. So I just slunk out. I'm sure it will still be in chaos when I go in on Tuesday. (Orientation week—oh, what joy.) Anyway, I wanted to cocoon here at home with the music on and the blinds drawn, so that I could indulge my full Greta Garbo angst in missing you. "I vant to be alone." I watched Grand Hotel *last night for the thousandth time.*

So how did the UN thing go? I know you've told me a hundred times what it was, but I never remember what you're going to. You walk out the door and my mind goes blank. When people ask me where you are, I've taken to saying Djibouti. It sounds exotic, and I like the way it rolls off the tongue. Djibouti. Djibouti. Some of our less bright friends have said "what, again? Wasn't he just there recently?" We've got some real winners in our social circle, you know. But they're pretty to look at, I guess.

Anyway, I hope it went well for you. There. I've done my supportive domestic partner bit.

NOW GET THE FUCK HOME!

Oh, yeah, I forgot. You're off on your way to get a little titty. Sorry. Give my best to your mom and your dad. My God, where do they find the stamina to do what they're doing? You sure as hell better not inherit their energy genes. When we're their age, I want us sitting in the garden with our feet up, reading Milton to each other, or cruising around Antarctica, or lingering over a fine Courvoisier as we float down the Seine admiring the new lights on the Eiffel Tower (yes, I am one of the boors who likes what they've done, even though the haute couture types thinks that it's sooooo gauche).

Shit, why aren't we having this conversation together here in bed, you with your head on my chest (or lower), and me running my fingers through your ever-thinning hair? I love it that you're balding. It makes us look closer in age. No, the age thing doesn't bother me. LOL.

Get home soon. Please.

For now and forever,
Your love,
Jonathan

P.S. Almost forgot. Dominic called. He's gotten confirmation that my book is on the reading list of courses this semester at four Canadian schools and at least twelve in the United States. Negotiations for the French publication are going on with the folks at Armand Colin. Wish an interested German publisher would surface.

P.P.S. Do you remember my graduate student Okechuku? When I was in the office last week, he told me that he had heard that Carolyn's film was going to be screened at the Toronto Film Festival. He's part of a Darfur solidarity group, and he said that they had heard about it and were very excited. I told him that I didn't think that that could be right because I understood that it wasn't finished. Isn't that what she's doing in Nairobi? Still editing? Oops! I hope I haven't let some secret out of the bag that she was planning as a surprise. Better not say anything until she does.

Chapter 41 ——————————

Nairobi's Jomo Kenyatta International Airport has seen many family reunions. The Fischers of Waterloo, Ontario, could now almost be added to the list.

It helped that I could get away from Johannesburg a day early. The section on climate change in the Summit text was dispensed with early enough that I was able to catch a flight before the masses started their exit.

The previous week Patricia had flown from the United States to Nigeria and spent time renewing acquaintances with staff at the Good News Missionary Society. Her flight from Lagos arrived in Nairobi within an hour of mine.

Carolyn was at the airport waiting for us, having torn herself away from the feverish final editing work on her new documentary *Boy Soldiers of Sudan*. Jonathan's intelligence had been accurate. The movie about the plight of children caught up in the civil war would be premièring at the Toronto International Film Festival in two weeks, an honour that Carolyn, with uncharacteristic modesty, had been hesitant to reveal to her family.

We three siblings had never been together at the same time in any place other than Waterloo or Toronto. Standing together in the arrivals hall of the Nairobi airport was slightly surrealistic, an experience of simultaneous familiarity and dislocation. We didn't dwell on its unusualness. We were distracted by the absence of Mom and Dad. They were supposed to have flown in from Kakuma Refugee Camp earlier in the day, but there was no sign of them.

Fortunately, we had a backup plan in case any one of us had been delayed. Arrangements had been made for Patricia and me to stay for the night at the guesthouse of the All Africa Conference of Churches. Mom and Dad had a small one-bedroom apartment just around the corner on Wayaki Way, but there wouldn't be room enough for us there. Carolyn had already staked her claim to their living room futon, a squatter's occupation while she worked on the film. If something happened so that we didn't all meet at the airport, we had agreed to head to the guesthouse and wait for the others to arrive.

Patricia, Carolyn, and I lingered over our after-dinner tea in the dining room, talking with Jesse Mugambi, a friend of mine and a longtime colleague within the World Council of Churches network. A technology autodidact, he knew all the key contacts around town and had helped Carolyn get the local help that she needed for the film editing.

Suddenly, Mom burst into the room and came careening toward our corner table.

"My babies, my babies." Her arms were spread wide; tears rolled down her cheeks as she descended on us, initiating an awkward collective embrace when we were only halfway up out of our chairs. Dad's quieter entrance helped stabilize us; he sensed just the right position to assume to support his teetering family—a lifelong skill of his.

"My darlings. My darlings." Mom's robust voice ricocheted off the concrete walls and ceiling, filling the entire room. The guests at other tables, a mixture of Africans and foreigners, greeted the boisterous Canadian family reunion with spontaneous applause.

"Hi, Jesse, dear. You've been keeping an eye on my brood here for me?"

"You've got a talented group of youngsters, Isabel. But then I'm not surprised. The apples don't fall far from the tree. If you'll excuse me, I've got a lecture to write. See you in a few weeks in Geneva, Tom."

"Geneva? Oh, you're going to the WCC event. Right. That's great. See you then."

As he turned to leave, he leaned down and whispered in Dad's ear. Dad smiled and shook his hand.

"We're so sorry we couldn't be at the airport when you arrived. Amukak Major had a touch of orneriness this morning. Nothing serious. But she does give us a few problems when we push her too much, which we have been lately. This morning she decided that she wanted to sleep in," Mom said with a giggle, wiping her tears and blowing her nose all at the same time.

"Who is Major Amukak?" I asked.

"Amukak Major. A little camp humour," Dad said with a smile.

"Kakuma spelled backwards," Mom interjected. "Our little Cessna

Caravan. It had been a UNHCR plane originally. It was mothballed for a while, until they let us begin using it a few years ago. It's sort of a permanent loan. We hope. We pray. It's been a godsend. Even though she's well past retirement age, we would be lost without her. We keep fixing up dear Amukak Major with a combination of bubble gum and duct tape and hope that we can squeeze a few more years out of the old girl." More maternal giggles. "Oh gosh, it's so wonderful to have you all here." She reached out and managed to grab hold of all of our hands. I was aware of the residual teary wetness on her fingers, the firmness of her grip, and the calluses.

"Isn't that dangerous, Mom?" Patricia asked, more than a little anxiety in her voice.

"Pish-tish, my dear. She's a good girl, our Amukak Major is. Anyway, no option. Now, tell us everything about everything. Are Luke and Naomi looking forward to their new school year? I can't believe my grandchildren are in university. Does Naomi still have that nice boyfriend? How was the Johannesburg conference, Tom? Whatever it was. You've all got to tell me everything. Except for Carolyn."

Mom gave Carolyn's wrist a playful tap and, addressing Patricia and me, explained, "We know everything there is to know about Carolyn's life these days. Which is not much. All she does is work, work, work. Gone early in the morning and home late at night, she and that crew of hers. We do know that they drink a lot of beer when they use the apartment for scripting conferences or editing fights or whatever their shouting matches are about. The place is such a mess when we get in. My God, worse than the camp. Unless Wajdi has a suspicion that we're coming back. Then he always makes sure the place is tidy."

She picked up Carolyn's hand and gave it a quick buzz with her lips. "And I wouldn't have it any other way, my darling."

Carolyn smiled.

"Wajdi?" I asked Carolyn. "And who might Wajdi be?"

"Oh, he's her cameraman," Mom replied. "And boyfriend and hopefully father of my next grandchildren."

"Mother!" Carolyn wasn't smiling.

"Why," Patricia asked, "don't you stay with your crew ... Wajdi and whoever ... in a hotel? Isn't it imposing on Mom and Dad to take over their place?"

"It's no imposition at all," Dad intervened. "We're only in Nairobi about half the time. Usually we are up in Kakuma or Loki or somewhere else. It's been good to have Carolyn in the apartment. There's a little more security when someone is coming and going regularly."

"The building you live in is dangerous?" Patricia asked, returning to her earlier theme.

"No, it's not much of a problem, dear," Dad replied with a twinkle in his eye. "We had a few break-ins early on, but once the neighbourhood entrepreneurs realized that we didn't have much to steal, they pretty much left us alone."

The manager of the Centre approached the table carrying a platter of cups and saucers, a pot of tea, and plate of pastry.

"Thank you, Philip, how kind," Mom said, taking the plate of pastries and passing them around the table. "*Biskuti ya nazi*'," she explained to us. "They're sort of coconut macaroons. Absolutely delicious."

Philip turned to Dad. "I'm sorry that your family will only be here with us for one night."

"Yes. Assuming that Amukak Major cooperates, we're taking them all up to the camp in the morning for a few days."

"Sorry, Dad," Carolyn interjected. "I won't be going with you. I'm up against a very pressing deadline."

"What?" cried Mom. "I thought we would all be able to spend the time together."

I looked at Carolyn. "You haven't told them either?"

"Told us what?"

Carolyn dropped her head.

"Carolyn has some exciting news," I said, extending my arm across the table.

Carolyn smiled and said, "You tell them. Please." She was actually blushing.

"*Boy Soldiers of Sudan* is going to have its world première in two weeks at the Toronto International Film Festival."

Dad was on his feet and behind her chair in a flash. He wrapped his arms around her and hugged her, rocking back and forth. Caught off guard, Carolyn almost lost her balance. She brought her hands up and laid them on Dad's clasped embrace. "Thanks, Dad," she whispered.

"Oh, fuddy duddy," pouted Mom.

Chapter 42 ———————————

Thousands of small brown dots strung along in rippling wave patterns below us. Sporadic green flecks of vegetation were placed within, surrounded by, a vast, endless eternal sea of beige. *Kakuma* in Swahili means "nowhere," an apt descriptor for our first sight of the setting of the camp, a barren stretch near the Sudanese border that the Kenyan Government had designated for the refugees, being of little use for any other purpose. The local Turkana peoples took strong exception to that assessment.

As we dropped in altitude, the dots grew into discernible huts, some round and thatched, others rectangular, sunlight reflecting off the corrugated metal roofs. Large wooden structures, interspersed with white canvas tents, stood grouped in several clusters. The tranquility of the view belied the reality of the teeming population of displaced and desperate lives. Twenty thousand was the official figure. The actual number was closer to one hundred thousand.

Patricia and I could only stare out the window and occasionally gesture. Amukak Major's noisy engines prevented conversation. Mom and Dad watched us watching the view, slight smiles on their faces, pleased to be sharing their life with us.

Kwasi's head bounced in the pilot's seat in time with his singing, which occasionally surmounted even the deafening mechanical racket. Two of our parents' colleagues, one from the National Council of Churches of Kenya and the other from the Lutheran World Federation, nodded, half asleep, in the rear seats, the two-hour flight from Nairobi being an opportunity to garner a bit of rest, a rare and precious commodity for humanitarian workers.

The cloudless sky with its blazing sun made everything below us acutely visible until the plane approached the landing strip. Gradually and then suddenly, nothing was visible, our side windows blanketed with an impenetrable screen of desert dust. I resisted looking up front, counting on Kwasi's years of flying experience to land us safely if his view was anywhere near as obstructed as ours.

Mom and Dad unbuckled and moved toward the door. Dad stepped out first and reached back to help Mom. Patricia and I watched as they slowly limbered the leg muscles that had cramped during the flight in the constricted cabin and as they wavered slightly in the 40C degrees that slammed us all once the door was opened. They had discernibly less energy than when they began this new phase of their lives with such enthusiasm eight years earlier.

We all pitched in to unload the supplies that had been crammed into the small cargo area and packed in and around our seats, no doubt counter to all safety regulations. We shook hands goodbye with the NCCK and LWF folk.

Dad patted the hood of the Land Rover that was already several years past the usual survival life of vehicles navigating the uncompromising terrain of this border region of Kenya and Sudan.

"Kids, I want to introduce you to Amukak Minor." Turning to the van, he leaned over it and, speaking in a loud whisper, said, "Now, dear Amukak Minor. These are two of our children, Patricia and Tom. You met Carolyn earlier. Remember? Well, we're going to be travelling around with these two for a few days, so I want you to behave yourself and be good to them. Okay?" He put his ear up to the hood for a moment and then stepped back. "Good girl. Thanks."

Mom rolled her eyes. "It's from too much time in the sun."

Patricia and I looked at each other and smiled. Dad and Mom hopped into the front seats. Patricia and I slid into the back.

Mom was responsible for a small maternal health project in one part of the camp. Throughout her nursing career, she had loved bringing new life into the world and was painstakingly trying to increase the odds that the Sudanese mothers and infants would survive a birth that was predictably traumatic, given the endemic malnutrition and severely compromised hygiene. Dad oversaw a couple of struggling schools for younger kids in the same section of the camp, *school* being something of a misnomer for the one-room facility with a few chairs, a blackboard but precious little chalk, and only as many scribblers and pencils as Dad was able to eke out of his strained budget. Today's cargo had included a few hardcover readers, a real luxury.

They both supervised a small staff, made up of a couple of Kenyans and supplemented by a few volunteers from among the refugees, primarily women and young people, anxious for something, anything, constructive to do. Mom and Dad would spend a week or so in the camp before having to travel up the road for meetings in Lokichogio, where most of the agencies were headquartered, or back to Nairobi, to the desk that they shared in the NCCK office, to tackle the endless proposal and project assessment writing that was the bane of all relief and development project coordinators.

As Dad drove into the camp, necessarily slowly, given the omnipresent, axel-threatening potholes, we passed a constant stream of people walking or riding bicycles in both directions and groups of young children darting around in improvised games. Our vehicle with four white faces was not an unusual sight in the camp, but everyone looked at us with eyes at once vacant and accusing. Any novelty, even that which was not particularly novel, helped to break the numbing boredom of camp existence.

Our first stop was an embarrassment for me—a protocol visit to the UNHCR office. My parents proudly introduced their son, the UN staffer who was a member of the secretary-general's office. I masked my recurrent unease about feeling an impostor, someone credited with status as a function of the level of the bureaucracy to which I related. Mom and Dad and those with whom we were amiably chatting changed people's lives. I pushed paper.

Manute was among the first babies that Mom had delivered, one of the lucky ones who survived. Now eight years old, he was in Dad's class. Manute had known no life beyond the refugee camp.

He was sitting on the classroom step as we approached on our walkabout. Stick in hand, he was concentrating intently on the forms that he was drawing in the dusty ground. He would make a marking, rub it out, make a new one, rub that out, and create a fresh one.

"His numbers," Dad whispered to us as we stood a few feet back.

Manute heard his voice and shouted, *"Mwalimu!"* He was up off the step like a bolt of lightning and propelled himself in three long strides toward us and up into Dad's arms. Dad had braced himself for this anticipated greeting, but he still staggered a bit as he caught the twenty kilos of childhood.

"What are you doing here today, my boy? Did you forget that we don't have school today?"

Manute didn't respond but gazed over Dad's shoulders at the two strangers standing beside Mom. I smiled back. He covered his eyes with his hands and buried his head in Dad's neck. Slowly, he separated a few fingers and peered back. I made a little wave and then quickly covered my eyes. When I lowered one hand, his fingers snapped closed. Our mutual game of peek-a-boo went on for a few more moments before Patricia took charge and came around in front of Dad.

Thrusting her arms around him, she maneuvered him out of Dad's grasp in one quick extrication. "Here, young man. I want one of those great hugs of yours. Mwamilu is my father, and he's really nice and all but he gets to have your hugs a lot, I bet. I'm Patricia, one of his and Mrs. Fischer's daughters, and this is my first visit here. I want a greeting like this too. My, you're a skinny little boy. We've got to fatten you up, get some meat on these bones. Goodness me, I can feel your ribs under here. Are you ticklish? I bet you are. All little boys are ticklish."

Manute squirmed and leaned as far back from Patricia as he could manage in her lock-hold.

"What did I say?" Patricia continued in a scolding voice. "I want one of those hugs. I think that you've got lots and lots and lots of hugs inside you just itching to get out, and I really, really, really want one of them."

Manute shot a glance at Dad, who nodded, and then he looked over at Mom, who winked. He stared into Patricia's eyes for a long moment. His tensed muscles relaxed bit by bit, and he delicately laid his arms on her shoulders. She gently massaged her arms around his back and then gave him a kiss on his neck before setting him down on the ground.

"Thank you, Manute. I knew you are a good hugger." He looked up and smiled. Then he took her hand.

"So, this is one of our classrooms," Dad interjected, something of a wobble in his voice. He walked though the doorless entrance, and we all followed. Manute watched Dad point out the limited highlights of the school, the same proud proprietary expression on both their faces.

Inside, Mom took hold of Manute's hand and led him toward one of the few chairs. She plopped herself down and hauled the boy up onto her lap.

"Where's your mama? Does she know that you're here?" Mom

turned to Patricia and me. "Sittina, his mother, is one of my best nurses. Well, not really a nurse. But, my God, she's a quick study. We'd be lost without her at the clinic."

Mom placed her index finger on Manute's chin and redirected his gaze back to herself. "Does your mama know where you are?"

Manute looked down at the dirt floor and used his toe to outline Mom's foot. "They were fighting. I ran out."

"Who was fighting?"

Manute looked up at Mom, tilted his head, and opened his eyes wide in a frustrated "you know" expression.

"Oh, your mom and Akuemuk? They were arguing?"

He looked at the floor again and recommenced the foot design. "Yes."

"What about?"

"The same. Always the same."

"Tell me."

Manute looked hesitatingly at us new strangers in the room.

Dad picked up. "It's okay, Manute. Patricia and Tom are our family. We argue sometimes too." Dad flashed a smile at us and then covered it quickly, noticing Manute's suspiciousness.

"What were they arguing about?" Mom persisted, and then she turned to Patricia and me. "Akuemuk is Manute's older brother. How old is he, Manute?"

"I dunno."

"Probably about thirteen or fourteen?"

"I guess."

"So what were they fighting about … sorry, arguing about?"

"The same stuff."

"What same stuff?"

Manute again looked at Patricia and me with uncertainty. He leaned into Mom's body, and said, softly, "The booze, the guns, and the fighting. He didn't come home all night, until this morning."

Dad turned to us and explained that there was really nothing for the older boys to do in the camp. They were old enough to realize how bleak their future was. The civil war kept dragging on, so there was no chance of them going home any time soon. They couldn't leave the camp, according Kenyan Government rules. So they couldn't go looking for work or any kind of education or skill training. They were bored and frustrated and angry. Gangs had been coalescing in the different zones, pitting the various ethnic groups of refugees against each other. They found access to cheap beer and guns—never a pretty combination.

Patricia glared at Dad. "That must be dangerous for you and Mother," she snapped. "At your age."

"Please, dear." Dad took hold of Patricia's hand. "It's a lot more dangerous for them."

She yanked her hand out of his. "They have to be here. You don't, for God's sake."

She stomped out of the building.

Chapter 43 ──────────────

Dad steered Amukak Minor carefully around another pothole and eased it slowly down an embankment into the riverbed that functioned as the main road leading up toward the border. Patricia grabbed hold of the armrest and closed her eyes.

The sun had been beating down on the vehicle with relentless intensity. We would have been farther along by now if it hadn't been for a morning crisis in the clinic that demanded Mom's presence. Dad had intended that we leave at first light. It was now late afternoon.

Clearly, we would not make it as far as Dad had planned by nightfall. We were carrying a precious cargo—a small package of provisions for Sittina's mother, who had not had the stamina to make it out of southern Sudan to Kakuma with her daughter. But the expedition was less to deliver these supplies than to find her and ensure that she was still alive. Sittina had had no news of her mother for quite a while and had grown increasingly panicky. Mom and Dad had promised to make the informal reconnaissance trip some time before but had not been able to extricate themselves from more pressing needs in the camp and in Nairobi. Their intention to take Patricia and me up into southern Sudan provided them the necessary rationale.

For the umpteenth time, I checked my back pocket to reassure myself of the security of my passport and visa papers. Dad had arranged for us to gain access into southern Sudan through the Nairobi offices of the New Sudan Council of Churches. The NSCC collaborated with the Sudan Peoples' Liberation Movement, the administrative and diplomatic counterpart to the liberation army, the SPLA.

Mom reached into the glove compartment and pulled a handkerchief out.

"Are you okay?" I asked.

"Just a bit of dust in my eye."

Her muted sobbing said otherwise.

I unbuckled my seatbelt and edged far enough forward to place my hand on her arm. "What's wrong?"

Dad glanced at his wife and then said over his shoulder to Patricia and me, "Happens every time we leave camp, a bit of predictable water works."

"It's just stupid me," Mom sputtered. Keeping her focus glued to the passing barren landscape, she eventually confided, "I always feel horribly guilty every time we leave the camp."

"What in heaven's sake is there for you to feel guilty about?" Patricia asked.

Still looking out her window, Mom said quietly, "I feel guilty because I'm so relieved to be getting out of that stinking, oppressive hellhole. And then I immediately feel awful about all the people I love who are locked in that stinking, oppressive hellhole."

"For God's sake, Mom and Dad, don't you think that it's about time that you came home?" Patricia said.

"I agree with her," I echoed, speaking to the back of my parents' heads but looking at my sister. "You have gone far, far beyond the call of duty."

"Duty?" Dad shouted. Everyone jumped. "You think our time here has been about duty?"

Mom reached across and laid her hand on her husband's trembling arm. "We have been talking about coming home," she said quietly. "But we can't. Not quite yet."

The four of us sat in silence as the Rover bungled along, an occasional loud scraping against the chassis underneath signaling the presence of a rock bigger than Dad had estimated.

Suddenly, Dad braked to a stop, throwing us all forward.

"What is it, dear?" Mom asked in a totally controlled voice.

Dad nodded toward his left. We looked in the direction and saw a cloud of dust speeding toward us.

"You kids just stay calm," he said quietly. "Let me do the talking."

"What is it? Who is it?" Patricia demanded.

"Shhh," Mom replied.

In a few moments, the outline of a jeep came into view. It slowed and pulled past us up on the bank above. Patricia and I craned our heads around and looked out the back window, watching it descend into the gully and ease up behind our vehicle. It stopped. Nothing happened. We waited.

"Oh, Jesus," Patricia whispered. "Are they going to kill us?"

"Quiet, dear," said Dad.

"Listen to your father. Do as he says," Mom added.

Two men in army fatigues stepped out and slowly approached. One had an intimidating automatic rifle slung over his shoulder. The other held a pistol aimed at our vehicle. Bandanas covered their faces up to their eyes.

Dad cautiously rolled down his window. "Hello," he called out as the two reached us, one on each side of our vehicle.

No reply. They stared into the Rover. The one on the passenger side knocked on the window with his pistol and made a circular motion with his hand. Mom rolled down her window. "Open your windows, kids," she said quietly. "It'll be okay."

Dad spoke again in a quiet, measured tone. "Hello. We are heading up into Sudan for a brief visit. We have SPLM visas if you would like to see. This is my wife. The two of us work in Kakuma. These are our children. They're visiting us." Only the essentials.

The one with the pistol was scrutinizing Patricia. She shifted over slightly toward me. He spoke. "Rich Yankees."

"No, no, no," Patricia shrieked. "We're Canadians! Canadians! Canadians!"

I guffawed. I had never heard any nationalist fervour from my expat sister.

"Shut up," yelled the one now holding his rifle within a few inches of Dad's head.

"Canadians?" he asked Dad quietly.

"Yes," Dad replied.

He took a step back from the vehicle. All eyes were riveted on him, except for Patricia, who had squeezed hers tightly shut.

He spit on the ground and said disgustedly, "Canadians. Eh?"

He spit again and then wrapped his index and middle fingers together, thrust his hand through the window, and waved it in front of Dad's face.

"Talisman and Khartoum and Janjaweed. Like that."

He spit again.

"You ain't going on any bloody tourist trip to my people's country.

Turn around." He looked through the car at his comrade and jerked his head. They both took a step back from the jeep.

"Okay," Dad said. He sighed deeply.

It took several minutes for Dad to maneuver the vehicle around and head south, back down the gully.

We drove in silence, leaving several missions unaccomplished.

Chapter 44 ⎯⎯⎯⎯⎯⎯⎯⎯⎯⎯

A familiar cloud of dust rose on the horizon as the convoy of vehicles came into view. Two jeeps were followed by four lumbering trucks, the heads and bayonets of dozens of troops poking above the canvas sidings. Two more jeeps brought up the rear.

Instinctively, I grabbed Jonathan's arm. He placed his hand gently on my sweaty grip, leaned over, and looked into my eyes. I watched the flickering light of the screen dance off his corneas. I relaxed and smiled my appreciation.

The Isabel Bader Theatre on the U of T campus was half a world away from that riverbed road, but the experience of two weeks ago still rattled my nerves.

I glanced past him and studied Margaret's face. She had sat frozen since the film began, her eyes glued to the frightening, disturbing, heart-rending images. This was a world foreign to any experience in her life. That it involved the brutalization of children verged on the incomprehensible. Tears might come later. Currently, she was in shock.

Many people in the capacity audience gasped during footage of interviews with kids who had escaped or deserted from the northern Sudan Government forces and their Janjaweed militia allies. The boys' nihilism and callousness was surreal, as they described firing on elderly women, raping young girls, being raped themselves by their own commanders. The film also profiled a few children who had been in the SPLA.

My sister had told me that this was her most apolitical political documentary to date. She knew many people would be unhappy with it. The film assumed no position on the merits of one side or the other in the civil war. Her focus was exclusively on the children—the forced recruitment and subjugation of boys as young as eight years old to fight in a grown-ups' war. For Carolyn, it was a crime against humanity, a crime against young humanity.

At the end of the showing, there was a protracted period of stunned silence in the theatre and then muted applause. In the Q&A, some people expressed ambivalence.

Carolyn had anticipated this reaction and accepted it with equanimity.

"I'm going to blow Adam Sandler before the night is out. I'll bet you fifty bucks." Sheila had her right hand out, ready for us to cough up our wager, Bloody Mary in the left.

"Ah, darling," replied Jonathan, holding up his tumbler of vodka on the rocks, wedge of lime. "I'll toast to your effort, but I'm not going to put any money down. The odds are all in your favour."

"Well, thank you, sweetie. What a nice vote of confidence." She and Jonathan clinked their glasses.

"I hate to be the skeptic …" I said hesitantly, while eyeing the crowd of blond twenty-somethings buzzing around Sandler.

"Tom, you are always the skeptic. Let the old girl have her fantasy," Jonathan chuckled.

"Oh, you bitch. Give with one hand and then take away with the other. I'll have you know I've already pinched his ass. He liked it."

"You did not," I protested.

"My sweetie," Jonathan leaned over and gave me a peck on the cheek. "Not only are you a chronic skeptic, but you're a jealous one at that."

"I admit it," I said, staring toward Sandler leaning against the windows in Stop 33. The penthouse suite in the Sutton Place was crammed well beyond legal capacity for the Absolut party. "I could fantasize doing a thing or two to that hunky little bod." The groupies around him parted for a moment, and I got a fresh look at the buns that Sheila claimed to have molested. I turned back to her. "When and where and how did you pinch his ass? I want details."

"What can I say?" Sheila shrugged. "I was coming out of the powder room. He was going into the men's. I reached out and gave him a good firm squeeze. He turned around, smiled, and thanked me. Perfect gentleman. I asked, 'Can I get more later?' He replied, 'Maybe, we'll see.' He winked and was gone."

I sighed. "That's good enough for me. I'm ninety-nine percent sure you're full of shit, but I'll savour the other one percent as fantasy."

"I intend to savour more than one percent before the night is out," Sheila sighed.

"Enough, already. Markus is returning with your refill."

"There you are, babe," Markus said, handing Sheila a fresh drink and taking her empty glass. "What did I miss?"

"Nothing yet," chuckled Jonathan. "But better stay tuned."

Markus had long ago given up trying to decipher the coded banter between Jonathan and Sheila, a lesson I should have emulated.

"Then who are we dissing at the moment?" Markus asked.

"Adam Sandler," all three of us replied in unison.

"I see. Okay," he replied. "So what are your reviews of his *Punch-Drunk Love*?"

Sheila and Jonathan rolled their eyes. "There are so many things wrong with that sentence, my love," Sheila said, putting her arm through Markus's, touchingly, affectionately. "You know that I'm a TIFF Patrons Circle member only so that I can get into the parties, and you should know that Johnny and Tom never condescend to anything so lowbrow."

"Ah, right," Markus smiled. "How silly of me. Speaking of the non-lowbrow, where's your sister?"

"She said that she would try and get here at some point," I replied, scanning the room in vain. "She's off having a tête-à-tête with one Mr. Michael Moore."

"Are you serious?"

"Yeah," I responded, aiming for nonchalance. "A couple of his people were at *Boy Soldiers of Sudan* this afternoon. He couldn't attend because it conflicted with a showing of *Bowling for Columbine*. Afterwards, they were enthusing to him about it and Moore told them to get in touch with her people."

"Carolyn has 'people'?" Jonathan interrupted.

"Well, 'person.' Wajdi. I guess he's doing his triple-threat bit. Camera man extraordinaire, producer, and her cell phone receptionist when she's tied up. She's been doing a ton of interviews today."

"What's their tête-à-tête about?" Markus asked.

"I don't know."

"I'm bored," interjected Sheila with a slightly slurpy pout. "Can we go somewhere to dance?"

"Don't you have a date?" Jonathan inquired.

"Exactly," she said, kissing Markus. "And that's who is going to take me dancing."

"Let's go somewhere close by," I suggested. "How about Woody's over on Church Street?"

"How about woodies?" Jonathan said, reaching over to grope me.

Chapter 45

"Do you still have family in Egypt?" Margaret inquired as she sipped on ginger ale, a hospitable gesture that she had assumed unobtrusively. Wajdi was in her home for the first time. Margaret's sensitivity was all the more impressive given whose chair Wajdi was occupying at the table, and in Carolyn's life, and in the Compton family.

The rest of us infidels stuck to our wine.

"My mother, yes. She lives in Cairo."

"And your father?" Walter asked.

"Unfortunately, he is no longer alive." Wajdi paused. "He was killed in the Six Days War."

"Along with a helluva lot of your countrymen."

"Walter!"

"Well, it's true, my dear. Israel caught the Arabs flat-footed. Mighty massacre, eh, Wajdi?"

"Yes, that is quite true." Wajdi turned to Margaret. "It's okay, Mrs. Compton. Your husband is correct. The war was a disaster for Egypt militarily. Our political leaders did not serve us well."

"The whole region has such a fucked-up history of such crappy political leadership." Walter was warming to the discussion.

"On all sides," Wajdi noted.

"And," Walter said, looking down the table at me, "the mess spills over into neighbouring countries, as Tom and I were discussing recently. Right, Tom?"

I nodded cautiously.

"Interesting," Carolyn observed, "how religions figure so prominently in all these conflicts, both the inter-state and the intra-state ones."

Walter waved his hand dismissively. "Religions are only a cover for the real issues of political and economic conflicts."

Carolyn countered. "I think they're a big part of the problem."

"You want to get rid of religions?" Walter laughed. "Good luck with that."

"That would be a helpful start," Carolyn replied, smiling. "Then we could concentrate on the 'real issues of political and economic conflicts.'"

"Oh, dear," mumbled Margaret, clearly regretting her alcohol-free beverage.

"Let's take a vote," proposed Walter. "All those in favour of getting rid of religions, raise your hand."

Carolyn raised her hand.

Walter raised his.

"Walter, please. Don't be absurd," Margaret demanded.

"Why? I agree with Carolyn, in theory. I think the world would be a far healthier and happier place without them."

"I don't," said Wajdi.

"Neither do I," I added, smiling at my very attractive unofficial brother-in-law, who smiled back.

"Walter, you and Carolyn are being ludicrous," Margaret said with authority. "Tell them, Jonathan." Why she looked to Jonathan for support baffled me.

"Well," Jonathan said, leaning into the table and into the discussion, "religion has been a critical dimension of the human psyche for millennia."

"This is an argument from an agnostic?" perplexed Walter asked.

"People who can't handle the rough spots in life," Jonathan continued, "are helped to get through by leaning on what they call God."

Jonathan didn't notice, or ignored, his mother's glare.

"And though the dogmas are not true or verifiable, at least the moral codes and ethical principles of most of the religions help, for the most part, to keep people living in some semblance of harmony with their neighbours. That's where I disagree with you, Carolyn. Sure, there are the odd atrocities perpetrated by the extremist fringes, but overall, religions are a force for good in maintaining social order."

"I don't think that 9/11, or the Israeli occupation of the West Bank, or the Srebrenica genocide, qualify as 'the odd atrocities.'"

"Or the destroyed lives of the boy soldiers of Sudan," added Wajdi.

"Granted, those are all horrific chapters in recent human history," Jonathan said. "But Father is right. Religion was a subtext, not the real issue."

"You're being naïve, Jonathan," Carolyn said firmly, not aggressively. "The religious component exacerbates conflicts that could be managed if their roots in political and economic inequities were addressed into full-scale atrocities, odd or otherwise."

"Speaking of the boy soldiers of Sudan," interjected Walter, somewhat piqued at being left behind by the younger generation, "when can I get to see the film? So sorry that I was out of town when you had your big première. I'm sure I will find it … interesting," he added, looking at me again.

Wajdi turned to him. "We could bring a copy here to the house sometime in the next day or so before we leave."

"Yes, I would like you to see it," Carolyn said. "I'm sure that we could have a good discussion."

"You two are leaving town? So soon?" Margaret was disappointed at the news.

"Yes, I'm afraid so," Wajdi replied. "Distributor meetings in L.A. and New York. Carolyn made some promising contacts during the film festival."

"Tom, would you be free to join us?" Walter asked. "We could pick up our earlier conversation from where we left off."

"Sorry," I replied, giving him an innocent smile. "Off to Geneva tomorrow."

Jonathan abruptly pushed his chair back from the table. "I need a drink. Anyone join me?"

"I will," said Carolyn.

"Pour one for me, son." Walter said as he rose, a slightly discernible twinge crossing his face.

Wajdi, Margaret, and I sat looking at each other.

Margaret raised her glass. "To the believers' circle."

We raised ours.

Chapter 46

AS I walked into the room, Lukas Vischer turned to me and said, "You wouldn't mind chairing, would you?" This was his way of making a decision sound like an invitation. An initial hello would have been nice, but that's just me.

Chairing was really his role, since it was a World Council of Churches event. As a UN resource person, I had been looking forward to having no responsibility other than my presentation analyzing the Jo'burg Summit results.

But I knew two things about Lukas and me as a result of our collaboration over the past decade since the Rio Earth Summit. One was that I was a better chair than him. The other was that he was a more profound thinker than me.

I didn't really have the energy. It had been a hectic six weeks between Johannesburg, the time with Mom and Dad in Kakuma, an intended period of R&R with Jonathan in Toronto that had been ambushed by errand-running for Carolyn at the film festival, and now another transatlantic flight to Geneva. And there was the little matter of the daily fatigue from that resident virus in my body and the toxic chemicals that I was taking to attack it; both prey and pursuer demanding ever more of my limited energy.

But this WCC consultation was important, and I wanted it to be successful. The consultation was among the initial efforts to focus on adaptation—what needs to be done to help people, particularly the most vulnerable, adapt to the climate change that is inevitably going to happen, that is already happening.

So I made the ultimate sacrifice. I stayed awake enough to chair the meeting.

I cracked a gentle whip, allowed the cogent points to be made, kept the presentations moving along at a brisk pace, didn't let any of the succinctly challenged hog a disproportionate amount of air time, and carefully monitored the writing subgroups to ensure that by the final day we would have a coherent first draft of a report. Someone proposed the title *Solidarity with Victims of Climate Change*.

It would have been child's play if it weren't that we felt the weight of the millions of children and their families who were suffering and dying in vulnerable areas because of the droughts and the floods, the destroyed crops and the disappearing water sources, the increasingly frequent and intense tropical storms—manifestations of the human-induced climate change that was exacerbating natural climate variability into an extreme and deadly parody of itself.

I looked across the table at Lukas toying with the residual food on his plate. Our numbers were diminishing as people left to catch their flights home. There was a relaxed ambiance around the dining room table, a sense of four days of hard work having culminated in a draft document of which we were all justly proud.

Such satisfaction was not evident in Lukas's eyes.

I had learned that it's not a good idea to poke a morose-looking Swiss German Protestant theologian. You're likely to get a depressing sermon just when you thought that you had gotten slightly ahead of the curve on tackling life's dilemmas. My curiosity trumped my fatigue-laden better sense.

"What's up, Lukas?"

"Pardon?"

"Are you rewriting some of our recommendations in your head as you massacre those cauliflower florets?"

"We haven't gone deeply enough."

"I didn't think it was bad for the four days that we had," I replied, feeling my consultation facilitation being judged a little harshly.

"We did some decent work, I grant you. But the climate change issue is getting worse year by year. Society's response cannot be limited to technical fixes. That won't cut it. We have to find profound spiritual resources to draw upon as well. We stayed at too superficial a level."

The sermon's momentum built. "Our societies are demonstrating a death wish by ignoring the human and environmental costs of our present trajectory." Drawing on Proverbs 8, he launched into a description of the folly of ignoring wisdom, symbolized as a woman, and then exhorted us, his dining companions, to summon faith communities to mount the barricades of resistance.

Everyone around the table was listening intently, the residual food on our plates left untouched. But just as rapidly as his energy had drawn us in, so it seemed to dissipate, leaving us hanging.

Lukas looked up and down the table. He paused and then said softly, "If we are to demonstrate resistance to this societal death wish, it implies the readiness for change. But the change that is required may perhaps not entail ever-improving living conditions. I am becoming convinced that the struggle is now principally against the wholesale degradation of the natural world. Human development is not, as we believed, an inevitable and consistent upward movement. We may have to be content in containing the process of degradation and in maintaining a sense of solidarity among nations and their people."

The table was silent, the collective sense of accomplishment from the week's work dampened by Lukas's jarring reality check.

Chapter 47 ——————————

"**Monsieur** Fischer."

The Centre's receptionist stood behind my chair, hesitant to intervene in the sombre conversation that followed Lukas's post-dinner reflections. I turned around, slightly annoyed at the interruption but aware of the tone of urgency in her voice.

"Monsieur Fischer, there is someone who is eager to speak to you. Would you please accompany me?"

I excused myself and followed Mme Rénaud to the front entrance, where she turned and said, "I have placed her in the director's office. You will have privacy there."

She opened the office door and I strode in, to be greeted by an outstretched hand and a taut expression.

"Bonjour. My name is Jocelyn DuBois. I am with the Canadian Permanent Mission here in Geneva."

"Hello. Glad to meet you. I'm Tom Fischer. Is there some problem?"

"Let us sit down, please."

I sat down in one of the chairs next to the oak coffee table by the windows. DuBois sat across from me, opened her brief case, pulled out a binder, unclasped the leather strap, and readied her pen to write.

"May I ask you, Mr. Fischer, when you last had contact with your parents?" She looked down at her binder. "Lawrence and Isabel Fischer."

"Yes, those are my parents. They work in Kakuma Refugee Camp in northern Kenya. One of my sisters and I were with them just recently. What is this about?"

"Very recently?"

"Yes. Let me see. It would be about four weeks ago now."

"Oh."

"'Oh' what? Please, is there some problem?"

"Our office here in Geneva is acting on behalf of the Department of

Foreign Affairs in Ottawa, which was contacted by the Canadian High Commission in Nairobi. With your UN status, the department felt you would be the appropriate person in the family to deal with."

"For God's sake, you're frightening me. Will you tell me what this is about? Has something happened to Mom and Dad?"

Dubois set her pen down and looked me directly in the eyes. "Hopefully not. Hopefully, it's just a misunderstanding."

"But ...?"

"But it appears that your parents ... are missing."

The ambassador's office looked east toward Lake Geneva, but the five-story height of the Permanent Mission was insufficient to visually surmount the tall pines that graced the property. As I stood staring out the window, I knew that the beautiful lake was out there, somewhere, probably migrating from its brilliant afternoon azure to a deep navy as the sun became trapped behind the Jura Mountains. I had to take it on faith that it was still there.

"He should be back shortly. He must have gotten detained in the afternoon session," Jocelyn explained, stating the obvious. "He's chairing a WTO task group that was set up at last March's interagency workshop on linkages between trade and environmental agreements. Were you here in Geneva for the workshop?"

"Pardon?" I turned around to face her, leaving the lake unattended.

"I'm not quite clear on your responsibilities within the secretary-general's office. I was just wondering if you had met Ambassador Johnson before. Perhaps at the March event?"

"No. I haven't met him. And no, I wasn't here for the March event." I left the wall of windows and walked around the office, looking absentmindedly at some of the materials arranged on the bookshelves.

"It wasn't a UN meeting here that you were involved in this week?"

"Yes, that's correct. It wasn't." I sat down on the leather sofa. "I was there as a UN resource person, but it was a consultation sponsored by the World Council of Churches."

I got up off the sofa and returned to the windows. A whistling was coming from the pines, an evening breeze setting in. Perhaps there would be rain tonight.

I abruptly wheeled around. "Listen, can you not tell me more about what you know?"

DuBois rubbed her hands together. "I'm afraid I cannot. I do not know much more than that your parents have been reported missing and that the department discovered that you were here in Geneva and so asked us to track you down. We'll have to wait for the ambassador. He spoke to Ottawa a couple hours ago. I know that. So he will have more details."

As if on cue, the door flung open, and Frederick Johnson strode in, briefcase in one hand and a sheaf of papers that appeared precariously close to escaping his grip in the other.

"So sorry, Fischer," he said, unburdening his load onto the side cadenza. He dropped his case with a thud on the floor beside his chair and thrust his hand out. "At least I assume that you are Tom Fischer?"

"Yes, Mr. Ambassador. I am." He shook my hand vigorously

"Please, call me Frederick. I've had enough of formality today."

"Could you please tell me what you know about my parents' situation?"

He strode around behind his desk, pulled out the swivel chair, and sat down. He lifted his briefcase off the floor and started rummaging through it. Without looking up, he asked, "Jocelyn, do you suppose there's any decent coffee left in the building at this hour?"

"I'll go check."

"No, wait." He jerked his head up. "Fischer, would you prefer a drink?"

"No, thank you. I think that coffee would be better, if it's available."

DuBois left, closing the door quietly behind her.

I sat, impatiently watching him haul out one file after another and plop them on the desk. Finally, he yanked out a well-worn steno pad and started flipping through it. After a couple moments, he found what he was looking for. I watched as his eyes scrutinized the notes. He flipped the page over and read a second page, then a third. His brow furrowed for the full period of his self-briefing.

Jocelyn reentered and set two cups on the coffee table in front of me and one on the desk, after she shifted some of Johnson's files to access a clear spot.

Johnson took a sip and made a contorted face. I left mine alone.

"We don't do much consular stuff in this office," he said, eyes fixed intently on me. "Not many Canadians get kidnapped in Geneva."

"Frederick!" DuBois snapped.

He ignored her.

I swallowed and then said, quietly, "Do we know that to be the case?"

"No, we do not. We, or rather Ottawa, know damn little at this point. But ..." He paused and looked down at his notes, flipping several pages back and forth. He raised his head and scrutinized my face. "I must be frank. They are concerned. It's a complicated situation."

I stared back. I bit down hard on my lower lip.

"Have you seen the minister's recent press release?"

"There's been a press release about my parents?" I jumped, my composure slipping.

"No, no. More generally on kidnappings. Jocelyn, do you have a copy?"

Without searching, she pulled a one-pager out of her binder and passed it to me.

I scanned quickly. *Canada Condemns Attacks on Humanitarian Workers.* The press release quoted Bill Graham, Minister of Foreign Affairs, as condemning recent attacks on international and local humanitarian workers in various countries. Five countries were named specifically: Liberia, Russia, Somalia, Uganda, and Sudan.

I closed my eyes and took a deep breath. I reopened my eyes and handed the one-pager back to DuBois.

I looked at Johnson and spoke quietly. "Yes, Mom and Dad were aware that there were risks involved in the refugee work. Of course, they were, I mean they are, not there on their own. They work with the National Council of Churches of Kenya on a placement by the United Church of Canada."

"And the Kenyan Council of Churches and the United Church of Canada are able to control the security situation in the Sudan? They must have considerably more influence than the international community."

"No, of course not," I bristled. "I don't appreciate your sarcasm.

Mom and Dad are not in Sudan. They work primarily at Kakuma Refugee Camp in northern Kenya and also in an office in Nairobi. For God's sake, can we move beyond this posturing? What do you know about what has happened?"

Johnson studied me for a moment. Then he nodded to Jocelyn, who approached his desk and picked up the phone.

"Florence, yes, it's Jocelyn in the ambassador's office. You can put that call through to Ottawa now."

The sound from the speakerphone was not of the greatest clarity. *They need to upgrade their equipment.*

Or maybe this was a secure line.

I shuffled my chair closer to Johnson's desk and leaned in.

"Let me say right off, Mr. Fischer, that we share the anxiety you must be feeling and will do our utmost to assist in locating your parents."

"Thank you, Mme Cornier."

"May I ask if you have called other members of your family yet?"

"No, I have not. I wanted more information before I place what will inevitably be an alarming call to them."

"Very wise. I am sure that you must be anxious to know what information we have, so let me give you a quick summary of the relevant details, for now."

"Please." I grabbed my pen and signaled to Johnson that I needed paper. He gestured to Jocelyn, who placed a pad of foolscap on the desk in front of me.

"We received a wire last night from the high commission in Nairobi. They had been contacted by the National Council of Churches of Kenya. You're familiar with them?"

"Yes, of course I am."

"Well, the NCCK reported that your parents had been missing for a few days. Also missing is the Land Rover that they use. They, the NCCK, had become somewhat alarmed, I guess, because your parents did not show up for a planned meeting in Nairobi and have not been at the Kakuma Camp either. I understand that your parents have a good reputation for keeping their colleagues informed of their whereabouts."

"They take that responsibility seriously. Mom and Dad don't want the already thinly stretched resources distracted by unnecessary, um, um ..."

"Ordinarily," Cornier cut in, "we in this office at Foreign Affairs wouldn't become involved in a missing persons case quite this quickly."

There was a click and the line went silent.

I looked up, alarmed, at Johnson. He waved his hand dismissively, counseling patience.

We sat staring at the phone.

Another click. "Sorry for the interruption, Mr. Fischer. The minister just joined us to sit in on the call."

I glanced at Johnson and raised my eyebrows. He looked back, expressionless.

"Mr. Fischer? Are you still there?" Cornier asked.

"Oh, yes, yes, sorry. I'm here. Um, hello, Mr. Minister."

"Hello, Mr. Fischer." Then somewhat muffled, "Louise, please continue."

"As I was saying, Mr. Fischer, Ottawa would not have ordinarily become involved this early in such a case, except that ..."

My note-taking had become increasingly illegible, even to me. My writing hand was shaking. I didn't attempt to disguise it, though Johnson had noticed and scowled.

"... we've been working on another issue, a mystery that we were having difficulty figuring out. And, well, the two issues have converged." Pause. "Sorry again, Mr. Fischer. Just a little consultation at this end. I'll be right back."

Click.

I glowered at the phone.

Click.

"Yes, well, Mr. Fischer. This is the situation. Earlier in the week, a vehicle similar to the one that the NCCK have now reported missing was set on fire in front of the gates of our embassy."

"Oh, my God." My heart was racing. "Any? Any ...?"

"No sign of human remains. But ..."

"Yes?"

"It was not at our embassy in Nairobi. It was at the embassy in Khartoum."

"You're forbidding me to go?" I asked incredulously. The phone shook in my hand.

"Well, yes, Tom. I suppose I am." Gutiérrez spoke slowly, firmly.

"You're not my mother," I scoffed.

A nanosecond later, I was screaming into the receiver. "She's not dead yet!"

There was a gentle tapping on the door.

"Monsieur Fischer. *S'il vous plaît. Je suis desolé mais ouvrez la porte, s'il vous plaît.*"

I swung my legs over the edge of the bed and propped myself up. With my feet on the carpet, I alternated putting pressure on one leg and then the other, back and forth. If I stood, would they hold me up?

"Monsieur Fischer. *S'il vous plaît.*"

"*Un moment, Mme Rénaud.*" My voice caught slightly. "*Je viens.*"

I stood up. *Okay, they're holding.* I walked to the door and unlocked it. Placing my hand on the knob, I hesitated. It started to move on its own. I stepped back as Mme Rénaud opened the door from the outside, a centimetre at a time.

"I'm very, very sorry to disturb you, sir. But your colleague in New York is most anxious to speak to you. I have been ringing your room, but there has been no answer. We were concerned that you were okay."

I quickly brushed my hands across my face, realizing from the concierge's gaze at my cheeks that the telltale signs were still visible.

"Sorry, Mme Rénaud. Yes, you can put him through the next time he calls." My voice was becoming a touch less wobbly. "I will answer now."

The phone rang. I looked at her.

"Maria is handling the switchboard," she explained.

I walked over and picked up the receiver. "Hello, Fernando."

Mme Rénaud turned and let herself out, closing the door as sensitively as she had opened it.

"Tom."

"Yes, we can talk now. Sorry that I hung up earlier."

"I know that this must be very difficult."

"Yes, you're right."

"I'll keep this short. None of us here in New York think that it is a good idea that you go either to Nairobi or to Khartoum. You should be home with the other members of your family, back in Canada, until we know more about what has happened. What is happening. There are others who are in a much better position than you would be to search for them, like the Kenyan police, our own staff … the Sudanese Government authorities …"

"Give me a break!" I shouted.

"Tom. We have to work through channels."

"You and your fucking channels. You want me to put the fox in charge after it has already raided the hen house."

"Tom. We don't know that yet. In fact, if I may speak frankly …"

"Please do. By all means, speak frankly," I spat into the phone. "Sorry, Fernando. Go on."

"There are indications that this may be more complicated than it first appeared."

"That's possible?"

"Yes, actually, it is possible. I need to ask you a few questions. I'm sorry, but we need all the information that we can gather for when we hear from whoever …"

"It's okay, Fernando. You can say it: 'whoever may be holding your parents.' That's what you mean, I presume."

"Yes. Tom, that is one of the possible scenarios. We are ruling out other possibilities. Initially, we thought that perhaps your parents might just be lost somewhere out in the countryside or that this was a case of an attempted robbery gone horribly wrong. The burned van at the gates of the Canadian Embassy in Khartoum suggests otherwise."

I closed my eyes, and I was back in the Land Rover, looking at the back of Dad's head in the driver's seat, Mom's head directly in front of me. I felt the tattered fabric and the frayed seat belt and the flaking metal floorboards.

"You wanted to ask me a few questions?" I asked, my eyes reopened, staring at the ascetic but safe walls of my room.

"Yes. After you left Johannesburg and flew to Kenya, you spent some time with your parents in Nairobi, and then they took you up to Kakuma. Correct?"

"Correct."

"At the camp, you visited the UNHCR office. Correct?"

"How do you know that?"

"It doesn't matter how I know. The relevant matter is that people in the camp knew that you were there."

"Of course. Dad wanted to introduce me to the camp officials. My sister Patricia and me. We met a lot of people during our time there. But it was no big deal."

"It may be a bigger deal than you are giving it credit for."

"I don't understand."

"You are a member of the staff of the Office of the Secretary-General of the United Nations. In some people's eyes, that's a big deal. It is possible, and I emphasize that this is just one of the possibilities that we're looking at—it is possible that by taking your parents, they knew that they could get to you, and by getting to you, they figured that they could get to us. Here. In the S-G's office in New York."

"That's crazy. I'm not that important."

"We're talking, aren't we?"

"Yes."

"It is possible that there may be informants for the northern Khartoum government in the camp. If someone were trying to place pressure on the UN for whatever reason—say, for instance, to pressure us to back off of Sudan and the peace negotiations and just let the stronger party prevail in the country—it would be a logical strategy to try to get the attention of the UN at the highest level possible. And, well, to be frank, if that is the strategy, it has already born fruit. We, the S-G's office, are now involved."

"And it's because of me."

"In this scenario, yes, I'm afraid so."

"But surely whoever is behind this knows that you wouldn't negotiate with hostage-takers, that the UN wouldn't make political or peace-making decisions under such a threat."

"Do they? Do they know that? The history is a very mixed bag, Tom. Hostage-taking is one strategy that can seem very appealing to desperate people. With years of entrenched civil war in Sudan, there are a lot of desperate people, on all sides."

There was a long pause. I imagined Fernando at his desk, turning his chair around to look out over the East River, trying to decide what he could and what he couldn't tell me.

"You could place yourself and the search for your parents in even more jeopardy if you head to Kenya or Sudan. I'm afraid that I can't say much more."

There was a long pause at my end.

"Okay, for the time being, I agree."

"Just a moment, Tom. There's someone else here for you to speak to."

"Do I have to?"

"Hello, Tom."

"Oh. Mr. Secretary-General. Hello."

"Tom, I just want you to know that we are all praying for your parents, and we will do everything that we can with the resources at our disposal to find them and bring them home."

I swallowed hard.

"Thank you, sir. Thank you."

Chapter 48

My flight arrived in Toronto on time. My bag was one of the first to appear on the baggage carrel. There was no hold up as I scurried through customs. I took all of these as good signs. The stars were aligning. This nightmare would resolve itself.

I came through the arrivals doors and headed straight toward the fixed-rate taxi stand, as was my well-worn pattern.

"Tom."

Half-jogging toward the outside, I glanced around to see what namesake some excited relative was meeting. Walter was waving and pushing his way through the crowd.

I stopped dead in my tracks. This didn't make sense. But then again, the last twenty-four hours had propelled me into some altered universe, so why not this almost equally absurd precedent-setting airport pick-up by my father-in-law.

"Walter. What are you doing here?"

He grabbed me and wrapped his arms around me. He whispered, "I'm so sorry about Isabel and Lawrence."

I wiggled free, dropped my bag, and pushed him back hard. "Have they found out something?"

A couple of people altered their path to give an extra-wide berth around the commotion.

Walter seized my shoulders and brought his face close to mine. "No, my boy. There's no new news. I have Roger here with the car." He picked up my bag and started walking in the opposite direction. "He's got it parked outside. I bribed a security officer to let us park right at the curb. Let's go."

I crumpled into the back seat. Maybe I said hello to Walter's chauffeur. I don't remember. I leaned my head back and closed my eyes. I had slept only minimally on the plane.

After a few minutes of speeding along the highway toward downtown, Walter spoke. "I should let you rest, but I want to talk to you about your dad's letter while we have a few moments together. In private."

I opened my eyes and readjusted myself to sit up straighter. "Yes, what about it?"

"It has caused quite a stir, to put it mildly, in a variety of circles."

I squinted at Walter. "Sorry. I don't understand. It was just a personal letter to me." My throat started to go suddenly dry. "Walter. Did you tell someone about it after we talked?"

"Huh?"

"After our discussion in your office, about Dad wanting you to pressure Talisman to leave Sudan." I squirmed in my seat to face him, constricted by the seat belt. "But I didn't even show you the letter itself. Who else could know about the letter unless you talked? What have you done?"

"No, no, you're confused, Tom," Walter said, waving his hand dismissively. "I'm not talking about that letter."

"Oh." I started to breathe again. "Okay, what are you talking about?"

"Jesus, you don't know?" He turned his head and stared out the window.

I stopped breathing again. I just stared at the back of his head.

Walter ran his fingers through his hair. He was grimacing when he turned back to me. "Lawrence wrote a very strong, very eloquent, I admit, letter to the editor about Talisman and their role in Sudan. It was published in the *Globe and Mail*."

"When was this?" I asked slowly.

"It appeared a week ago."

"A week ago?"

"Yes."

"Before ..."

"Yes ... before ..."

"Oh, God."

I stared at the delicately carved flowers on the wooden medallion on our bedroom ceiling, illuminated by the reflected moonlight streaming in the window. This one, along with its companions in the living room and dining room, were among the original architectural features that so excited Jonathan about Althena and Ulrich's home when they first gave us the grand tour. That and the Italian marble fireplace. Once we moved downstairs after Althena's death, we were able to relish the medallion's gracefulness above us every night as we lay in bed. Jonathan would tell me a story about the life of the worker who carved it, a different story on every occasion, on the thousand and one nights when I couldn't fall asleep. Like tonight.

Jonathan's breath warmed my neck, his light snore tickling my ear, his left arm still draped around my chest, one half of the embrace that had rocked me during my convulsions that followed the phone calls with Patricia and Carolyn, when I had to break the news and calmly reassure them of the positive outcome I didn't believe myself.

I rubbed the dried matter from the corners of my eyes and refocused on the medallion. *How did the carver lose his parents?* I didn't want to know the prosaic or the tragic reality. I wanted one of Jonathan's fantasy endings.

I gingerly lifted Jonathan's arm so I could extricate myself and slip out of bed without waking him. I needed him to be rested for the days ahead.

The hardwood floor was cold under foot, the October night probably chilly enough to have justified turning on the furnace for the first time this season. Neither of us had thought of that, an oversight our tenants upstairs might be regretting.

I slid my feet into my slippers, wrapped myself in my housecoat, and tiptoed out to the kitchen. *A cup of tea or a scotch? No contest.*

Though the air was bracing, it felt good on my face as I stepped out onto the back deck and eased myself down into one of the loungers. Jonathan had done a good cleanup of the garden this year while I had been away solving the world's problems and bouncing over desert roads with Mom and Dad. At least something in our lives was in decent shape.

It frustrated Jonathan that I had such difficulty making out the man in the moon. He didn't buy my explanation of lunar dyslexia. Tonight, I had two excuses. It was not yet full, and the occasional cloud kept interrupting my squinting examination.

Say I could see the man in the moon, looking perhaps like the quaint white-haired, white-bearded depictions of a benevolent old-man God, gazing down from his fluffy cloud.

Okay, since you have such a good view of Earth, you can tell me where

Mom and Dad are. You can see them. Well, not at this moment, because you're looking down at me sitting on the deck of our house in Toronto, which means that you would not have a direct view of Kenya or Sudan. Africa wouldn't be exactly on the opposite side of Earth. That would have to be Australia or China.

"If you keep digging that hole, Tom, you're going to end up in China," Mom would say. I put down my shovel and stared in amazement at the potential Oriental passageway in my very own sandbox.

Maybe Africa is about a third of the way around the globe. So, perhaps from your vantage point at four hundred thousand kilometres from Earth, you can see both them and me. Since it's about three in the morning here in Toronto, it must be ... what time in Khartoum? Ten o'clock in the morning. It's light there. That should make it easier to spot them. Then again, you can see everything, so you don't have to have daylight. What is the word for all-seeing? It's sort of omniscient, but different. If you're so omniscient, then tell me where they are. And if you're omnipotent, then bring them back home.

They've only always done good stuff. Well, that's an exaggeration. But basically, they've done good stuff, particularly these past few years in Africa. They believed ... no, Tom, don't do that ... they believe, yes, they believe, believe, believe, believe ... that they are doing what they are doing because ... well, you know why they are doing what they are doing. You know their hearts.

Dad got so mad at me when I made that comment about duty. It's far more than duty for them. It's what? Love? They love Manute. They love Sittina, and the other Manutes and Sittinas that I didn't meet. Justice? The letter to the editor. Dad is so furious about Talisman.

Haven't I given you enough good arguments?

Just let us know. Are they already dead? And if they're not dead ... are they being tortured? Have they been thrown down a well somewhere?

The crystal tumbler produced a searing clarion explosion in the cold night air as it shattered in a million pieces against the back garden wall.

Chapter 49 ———————————

Walter generously arranged for us all to stay at Ottawa's Chateau Laurier. The after-dinner family gathering in his suite had an undeniable sense of a wake. Not the boisterous Irish variety, though enough alcohol was consumed to qualify. For one thing, no casket or caskets perched in the middle of the room. Can't have a party without the guests of honour.

We sat around talking longer than we should have, given the travel- and stress-induced fatigue plaguing us all. Carolyn and Wajdi had flown in from Los Angeles via Chicago, Patricia and Robert from Dayton through Toronto, the four of them arriving in Ottawa late in the afternoon. Walter, Margaret, Jonathan, and I had gotten an earlier flight after church. Margaret had insisted that the four of us go to mass together before leaving Toronto, something that had not happened since the long ago days of the mandatory Compton family attendance at the Cathedral for the Christmas Eve midnight mass.

Department of Foreign Affairs and International Trade: DFAIT. It sounded like some new, genetically modified species of fish. The receptionist glanced suspiciously as our procession of eight approached the desk. I could read her mind: *Starting a new week with another ruckus-raising delegation here to protest something or other.* Her demeanor changed when I announced my name and our appointment with Louise Cornier, intentionally emphasizing that our presence was requested by the Deputy Minister. We didn't have time to sit down in the lobby before Cornier's assistant greeted us and invited us to follow him to the boardroom.

We weren't the first to arrive. Patti Talbot, the United Church's staff person responsible for overseas placements, was in the room, speaking to someone whose back was toward the door. Fernando turned around when he heard the door open and smiled at the surprise that must have flashed across my face. We embraced. Patti gave me a hug. I introduced them to the whole family. Cornier's assistant pointed out the coffee, juices, and pastries on the side table. We helped ourselves and gradually took seats around the table. Jonathan ensured that he and I sat beside each other. Intuitively, we left several chairs vacant at the head of the table. We were in their territory.

Cornier quickly introduced herself and her colleagues, considerate of our anxiousness to hear what they had to report and to open the discussion about strategies and options.

"First off, I have to tell you that we have no new information except that which we shared with you on Friday, Mr. Fischer, when we spoke by phone when you were still in Geneva."

A couple of whimpers came from down the table from Patricia and Margaret. A grunt of impatience from Walter followed. Jonathan held my hand and gave a little squeeze. I kept my eyes fixed on Cornier.

"Shit. Then why did you drag us all up here to Ottawa?" Carolyn demanded.

Continuing to address herself to me, Cornier quickly added, "In a situation like this, it is imperative that we work together, that you as family and we as the Government hear each other accurately and agree on appropriate measures."

Though said in a confident voice, her text betrayed defensiveness, a preemptive effort to avoid a repeat of past incidents where, accompanied by a great deal of unwelcome publicity, some of which was family-generated, the Government had been perceived to have been negligent in assisting Canadian citizens abroad caught in political or other crises. I had never worked for the government, but throughout my UN years I had witnessed the inordinate time and energy that governments expend in the calculation of potential political damage and in efforts to mitigate it, time and energy that could have been so much more usefully spent in solving the initial problem.

"And can we all agree that it is in the best interests of your parents' safety and return that there be no media involvement at this point, that none of you speak to the press?"

Cornier had miscalculated her audience.

"There's no way in hell that we're going to agree to any gag order to save your skin," Carolyn yelled.

"Carolyn's right," Walter boomed. "I would have credited you with more subtlety than that. It's not Lawrence and Isabel's safety you're seeking to protect here."

It appeared I might have to play a mediating role at some point. We needed the government on our side. But I held back for the moment and remained silent. Let Carolyn and Walter play the heavies, so that Cornier and company understood that the Fischer-Compton clan would not be intimidated.

"I'm sorry you feel that way," Cornier replied glacially. "Consideration on the part of the family would be appreciated, since we have already dedicated significant resources to this case."

"And damn right you should be," Walter responded. "That's what we pay you for."

I held up my hand. "Walter, please," I said. He slumped back in his chair with a huff. "Mme Cornier, would you please begin by reiterating the chronology of events as you know them."

Cornier turned and nodded to Leonard Burovsky, the DFAIT Africa desk officer who had been assigned this case. Burovsky opened a large binder in front of him and began reading.

> "*Tuesday, October 1, 2002. 5.00h GMT Security staff at Canadian Embassy, Khartoum, Sudan, alerted by the sound of an explosion. Upon investigation, discover a vehicle on fire adjacent to front entrance into the compound. Summon local fire authorities that arrive approximately twenty minutes later, by which point fire has largely burned itself out. Chargé d'Affaires Payette and local authorities scrutinize wreckage. No witnesses. Incident considered inconsequential until security staff notice a Kenyan license plate that apparently had been thrown over the compound gate. Payette prepares incident report. Received at DFAIT HQ in Ottawa at 7.15h GMT. Requests HQ initiate contact with Kenyan authorities to trace license plate number.*"

"Was it from Mom and Dad's Land Rover?" Patricia asked through her sniffling. I glanced down the table and envisioned her sitting beside me in the backseat of Amukak Minor.

Burovsky looked at Cornier, who spoke to Patricia. "Let's just follow the chronology at this point, Ms. Fischer, please."

"Jackson."

"Pardon?"

"My name is Patricia Jackson," Patricia said sharply. "As in Mr. and Mrs. Robert and Patricia Jackson." She grabbed hold of Robert's hand and pounded their clutched fists down on the table.

Cornier flipped through her open binder and then looked up. "I'm very sorry. Yes, of course. Mrs. Jackson." She turned to Burovsky and nodded vigorously.

> *"Tuesday, October 1, 2002. 10.30h EDT. Director Angelo, DFAIT Sudan Task Force, convenes meeting in Conference Room 3B. Khartoum Embassy report reviewed. Counselor Khalid assigned to contact Canadian High Commission in Nairobi to request Kenyan authorities' assistance in identification of license plate. STF will reconvene if further information forthcoming. Decision: insufficient information at this point to escalate ..."*

"Leonard, you don't have to read all the details," Cornier interrupted. "Only the essentials about the communications."

"That's not an insignificant detail, Cornier," Walter observed.

"Leonard. Continue."

"Yes, Madame Deputy. Um ...

> *"Thursday, October 3, 2002. 10.30 GMT. Canadian High Commission in Nairobi contacted by Rev. Joseph Kambula of the National Council of Churches in Kenya alerting the Commission of the inexplicable disappearance for four days of Canadian citizens Lawrence and Isabel Fischer ..."*

"Oh God." Patricia.

"Ms. Talbot." Cornier addressed Patti. "When did the United Church of Canada office first hear from the NCCK about the Fischers, about them being missing?"

"We got an e-mail and a fax from Joseph on Thursday morning. The communications were waiting for us when we arrived in the office at eight a.m. We promptly contacted your office."

"You did?" Cornier turned and whispered something to Burovsky, who frantically scanned his notes, looked back at her, shaking his head in the affirmative. "Continue, Leonard," she said.

"Um ...

"Thursday, October 3, 2002. 17.30 GMT. DFAIT HQ receives communication from Canadian HC in Nairobi reporting on missing persons report for Canadian citizens Lawrence and Isabel Fischer filed by the Rev. Joseph Kabula of the National Council of Churches of Kenya."

Burovsky stopped and looked up.

"And?" Carolyn pressed. "What happened when this report was received? What did you do?"

Burovsky's hand gesture deferred to Cornier, who said, "Well, nothing further at that point. Ms. ... Ms. ... Fischer?"

"Yes," Carolyn said, glaring at Cornier. "Fischer. Not married. Still a Fischer. Proudly."

"You see, we regularly receive missing persons reports that turn out to be quite innocent and inaccurate. So the procedure is to wait for twenty-four hours or so before initiating any investigation."

"Twenty-four hours," a soft voice said from the end of the table, "is a very long time." Wajdi enunciated in a quiet, deliberative tone. "With the conflict situation in Sudan, twenty-four hours can be ... a lifetime."

"I appreciate that," Cornier responded. "But at that point, it was considered a Kenyan missing persons case. We were unaware that Sudan might be involved. And we do have many, many other issues that we're dealing with this in this office. It wasn't until Friday, when we received the report from the High Commission in Nairobi that the license plate from Khartoum was registered to an NCCK vehicle, that we realized there might be a connection."

Before any of my apoplectic family responded, I jumped in. "It is evident that someone was trying to send a message by burning the vehicle right in front of the Embassy gates and tossing the license into the yard to make sure you could identify whose it was. Right?"

"We here at DFAIT are not yet at the point to make the kind of judgment that you just did 'that someone was trying to send a message.' The circumstances are definitely suspicious. But we need more information first before settling on any particular explanation."

"Well, get your asses in gear to get the information you need," Carolyn shouted.

Cornier looked around the table. "That's exactly why you all are here," she said calmly. "We think that the explanation may lie in this room."

That stunned us silent.

Cornier surveyed the effect and almost smiled, censoring herself at the last moment.

"How can we help?" I asked.

Cornier swiveled her chair so that she was facing me directly. "I misspoke slightly a moment ago," she began. "It's not that we aren't prepared to acknowledge that the placement of the burning van and the tossing of the license plate onto the Embassy compound were intended as some sort of message. We agree with you. We think that it was a message. But from whom, and what was the intended message? We have several theories. It is our hope that those of you in this room, or at least one of you, can provide us with the information that will help us narrow the range of options down to the most likely, so that we know who is behind your parents' disappearance and where, more precisely, we should be looking for them."

I looked around the table. Everyone looked back.

"Okay," I said to Cornier. "Where do we begin?"

"With a question that may seem obvious but is vital. Are we correct in assuming that no one here has received a communication of any sort, from any source, that might be construed as coming from a person or group with any knowledge about what has happened to your parents?"

"I certainly have not," I said.

"I sure wish I had," responded Patricia.

"Jesus, of course not." Carolyn.

"No." Walter.

Cornier scanned the other family faces, all shaking their heads negatively.

"And the non-family members?" Cornier asked, looking at Fernando and Patti.

"We would have informed you and the family immediately," Patti responded, slightly indignant at the implication behind the question.

"Mr. Gutiérrez?"

I did a double take as Fernando hesitated. "Well, it is a bit complicated," he replied.

"Fernando! What does that mean?" I asked.

"Tom. Mme Cornier. As you can appreciate, we are taking this situation extremely seriously. Mr. and Mrs. Fischer were working in one of our UNHCR camps. We are conducting our own investigation."

"Fernando! Have you or have you not heard anything about who may be behind Mom and Dad's disappearance?"

"To this point, no ..."

"To this point, no—but? Is there a 'but'?"

Fernando looked past me and directed his comments to the end of the table. "Mme Cornier, might I suggest that you continue with your queries of the other guests here? If some issue arises that I think I can contribute to from the UN's perspective, then I will intervene at that point."

"Yes, Mr. Gutiérrez. I understand your position, and I think that would be an appropriate procedure."

"What? Are you two in some kind of collusion here?" Walter demanded. "What's this bureaucracy-speak going on between the two of you?"

"Mr. Compton. I will get to you," Cornier said firmly.

Walter, looking around at the distressed expressions on the rest of the family faces, crossed his arms, sat back in his chair, and shut up.

"Let me return to you, Mr. Fischer," Cornier said, turning back to me. She paused for a moment and looked down at the file in front of her; she turned several sheets, stopped, and ran her finger down the page. "You were in Kenya visiting with your parents in Nairobi and at the Kakuma Refugee Camp from Tuesday, September 3, until Friday, September 7, when you left and flew back to Canada. Is that correct?"

They had done more homework than I had credited them with. "Yes," I replied.

"You are a senior UN official of some considerable status. Did it not occur to you that being associated so clearly with your parents for all to see might constitute a risk to them?"

Fernando looked in my direction.

"I don't see why it should," I replied, halfheartedly.

"Please, Mr. Fischer. Your parents do not work for the UN or any large NGO. They do not have security services easily accessible to them. You do not see that you might have placed them at some risk by persons who might seek some ... leverage?"

Cormier looked at me, waiting for a reply. I didn't oblige her. I sat straight up in my chair, staring back. I wasn't going to let her intimidate me. Guilt, I already felt. Cowering intimidation, I wasn't willing to portray.

Cormier glanced at her watch and clicked her teeth. "That's theory one. Moving on. Your sister Patricia ... Jackson ... was with you?"

"Yes." I glanced at Patricia.

"During the time that you were in Kakuma, did you leave the camp with your parents?"

"Yes. We did. On one occasion."

"Where did you go, and what was the purpose of that excursion?"

With the direction of the meeting, the only thing missing had been the request to me to place my hand on a Bible, and swear to tell the truth.

"Mom and Dad wanted to show us some of the countryside."

"Really? That was all? How far did you go and in what direction?"

I flashed a quick glance at Patricia. Jonathan gave my hand a tug. I looked at him, and he nodded at me. *Tell them. Everything.*

"They wanted to take us up into southern Sudan, to Juba." I yanked my briefcase up onto my lap and flipped open the clasps. Out of the secure sleeve, I pulled my passport and the crumbled visa. With a flourish I snapped shut the briefcase, dropped it onto the floor, and slid the passport and visa down the table. Cormier caught it just as it was about to slide into her lap.

"We had valid visas issues by the SPLM in Nairobi," I said. "Mom and Dad had a delivery to make of some supplies for the mother of one of the camp refugees."

Cormier studied the visa for a few moments and paged through the passport. Without looking up, she asked, "And did you make it to Juba?"

"No. We were stopped before we got to the border and ordered to turn around."

"By whom?"

Patricia was crying quietly. Robert had his arm around her shoulder.

"They didn't identify themselves," I continued. "We assumed that they were southern Sudanese, SPLA, because we were still in Kenya, where they can operate freely."

"Why would they not let you continue if you had valid visas, as you've said?"

"Well ..." I hesitated, wanting my next statement to carry weight. I glanced down the table at Walter. He gave his head a slight nod. "They were angry when they discovered that we were Canadian. They associated us with Talisman Energy."

Frank Pesconie, a senior DFAIT staffer from the international trade side of the department, sat immediately beside Cornier. He picked up his pen, turned toward me, and asked, "Talisman? What did they say exactly?"

Patricia leapt out of her chair. "They terrorized us," she screamed. "They said that there was no bloody way that we had any right as Canadians to play tourist in their home country after what Talisman and the northern Sudan Government and their terrorist Janjaweed warriors have done to their people. It was horrible!"

I got up and hurried over to Patricia, who was swaying unsteadily on her feet, being supported by Robert as best he could. I took her head in my hands and kissed both of her shuttered eyelids. She calmed down. I headed back toward my seat.

Once I sat down, Cornier looked back and forth between Patricia and me, and said, "I'm sure that the experience was frightening. Frankly, we don't put a great deal of credence in theory two—that the SPLA is responsible for whatever has happened to your parents. There would be little strategic benefit were they to take Canadians hostage, despite the considerable resentment about Canadian oil interests in southern Sudan."

Pesconie cleared his throat and spoke. "Mme Deputy Minister. I think that it is important to put on the record, for the purpose of accuracy in the transcripts of this meeting, that Talisman Energy has adopted the International Code of Ethics for Canadian Business and has publicly affirmed that it will promote the peace process and issues pertaining to human rights in Sudan. The company clearly has no role in any of the atrocities that some groups allege have been committed to the communities within the Talisman oil concession." He looked down the table. "Is that not correct, Mr. Compton?"

Walter glared back at Pesconie and said nothing.

Cornier cut into the awkward silence. "It is possible, but as I say not likely, that what has happened to your parents is a reprisal against them as Canadians by the SPLA because of Talisman."

"Mme Deputy Minister, I must object that ..."

"Shut up, Frank," Cornier said, without even glancing in his direction. "Now. Theory three. I'm sorry to press you, Mrs. Jackson, but I have a couple of questions for you."

Robert eased Patricia back down into her seat.

"You made a stop on your way to Nairobi. Is that not correct?"

"Yes," Patricia replied, hesitantly.

"And the purpose of your stop in Lagos?"

"Oh." Patricia eyes grew wide with surprise. "Well, I went there to visit some friends."

"Tell us about the Good News Missionary Society, please."

Robert spoke up enthusiastically. "It's an American Christian evangelical organization that we volunteered with for a year in Nigeria after we were married. We are very proud to continue supporting the ministry. GNMS has had remarkable success over the years spreading the Gospel."

He smiled broadly at Patricia, who did not echo his enthusiasm.

He continued unfazed. "Patricia has done a great deal of fund-raising for them in America. We live in the United States, you know."

"Yes," Cornier said softly. "We are aware of that. Does your organization have 'mission work' in Plateau State?"

"Oh, yes, we do. Important work," Robert replied.

Patricia leaned over toward him and said, softly, "Robert, please, that's enough."

"What?" he said.

Cornier, addressing Patricia, asked, "Then you are aware, I presume, Mrs. Jackson, about the violence between Christians and Muslims in Plateau State, in Jos in particular?"

"Yes, it's awful," Robert responded. "A Christian student was murdered recently at nearby Bauchi University just for distributing some of our leaflets that compare Jesus' teachings to Islamic beliefs."

"Robert!" Patricia nudged him. Turning to Cornier, she said, "What does any of this have to do with Mom and Dad? That's what we're here for. You should be focusing on trying to find them. This discussion of our work is a distraction, for heaven's sake."

"Mrs. Jackson, to put it succinctly, the government of Nigeria has close relations with the government of Sudan. Both countries have major oil interests. Both have ongoing conflicts between Muslims and Christians within their borders. They share information. We have reason to suspect that your recent presence in Nigeria with the Good News Ministry Society and your profile with the GNMS in the United States was information that was shared by Nigerian elements with their counterparts in Khartoum ..."

"Impossible!"

"... and those counterparts in Khartoum may have seen your parents as a handy opportunity for revenge."

"Oh my God. But how would they know that I was related to Mom and Dad? We have different surnames."

"You were, of course, with your brother in Kakuma, and word of your connection to your parents may have filtered back to Khartoum as a result. But let me emphasize that I am not saying that that is the reason that your parents were taken. It is only one, at this point, of the theories that we are exploring."

A fist came pounding down on the table. "Jesus Christ!" Carolyn yelled at Patricia. "Now look what's happened. You've killed Mom and Dad with your fucking religious fanaticism!"

Patricia started weeping.

Cornier jumped to her feet. "Ladies, please. We don't know that to be the case. Actually, Ms. Fischer, I also have a few questions for you and for"—she looked down at her notes—"and for Mr. Al Fayed about your film."

Cornier picked up her file and started walking around the room, reading as she paced. We all swung our heads to follow her.

She stopped behind Carolyn and Wajdi's chairs. "I guess congratulations are in order. I understand *Boy Soldiers of Sudan* made quite a splash at the Toronto International Film Festival."

"Thank you," Carolyn replied, surly.

"May I ask you about your sources?"

"No."

"Pardon me?"

Carolyn swung her chair around, clipping Cornier in the shins. "We are journalists, documentary film journalists. You cannot ask us about our sources."

"For God's sake," yelled Patricia. "If it helps find Mom and Dad ..."

Carolyn turned around and stared at the table in front of her.

"I can understand how you were able to get access to the southern forces," Cornier proceeded. "You were based in Nairobi. The SPLA is based in Nairobi. You had good relations with them, no doubt, because they assumed that you were making a film about the horrendous abuses of children enlisted as slaves and soldiers by the northern forces, the Sudan Government army, and the Janjaweed militias. Correct?"

Carolyn remained silent.

Assuming assent, Cornier continued her interrogation. "But I am at something of a loss to understand how you got all that footage from within the northern forces. Perhaps you can enlighten us, Mr. Al Fayed."

Wajdi looked at Carolyn and did not respond.

"You are Muslim, I presume?"

No comment.

"Pardon? I didn't hear you."

Wajdi looked up at her; she stood right beside him. "Yes, I am Muslim, but I am Egyptian, not Sudanese."

Cornier laughed. "Yes, Mr. Al Fayed. We're well aware of your nationality. Having an Egyptian passport allows you quite easy travel throughout much of the Islamic world, I would assume, Sudan included."

Wajdi said nothing.

"Tell me, Mr. Al Fayed. Did you finish your degree at the University of Kafr Al-Sheikh?"

Wajdi glared at Cornier. Carolyn looked at Wajdi.

"What the fuck is this about?" Walter demanded.

"That was a long time ago," Wajdi said quietly.

"You were expelled, were you not? For political activities?"

"That was a long time ago."

"Egyptian universities have hosted students from Sudan for many years, is that not the case?"

"Yes."

"Do you maintain some of the friendships that you made with Sudanese students during your somewhat truncated university career?"

Wajdi sat silently.

"How often have you been in Khartoum, Mr. Al Fayed, say, over the past six months?"

Carolyn stood up, placing herself toe to toe with Cornier. "I don't know what the fuck you're implying. Wajdi is no secret agent for Khartoum. I'm no fucking lackey of the SPLA. The film doesn't take sides in the civil war. It's about the poor rotten little buggers who have been caught in the middle."

Cornier placed her hand on Carolyn's shoulder. Carolyn shoved it off.

"Precisely, Ms. Fischer. The film is about the boys victimized by the war. Period. Neither the SPLA nor Khartoum is going to be able to make much propaganda use out of it for its own purposes. Unflattering stuff. I can imagine that both your contacts and those of Mr. Al Fayed must be mighty disappointed in the two of you, to put it mildly. They must feel duped. Perhaps disappointed enough to want to make you pay for the embarrassment. Somehow." She paused and looked at the two of them. "Theory four."

Carolyn sat down. Wajdi took hold of her hand.

Cornier returned to her seat and looked around the table. "I think it's time we took a bit of a break," she said.

Jonathan stood beside me at the next urinal. Under normal circumstances, the proximity could have led to something. There were no normal circumstances today.

"How are you holding up?" he asked as he zipped up.

"I've got to, don't I? My sisters are a mess. Cornier has designated me head of family. I don't see any tangible progress by DFAIT or the UN. It feels like Mom and Dad are slipping further and further away. I'm regretting having listened to Fernando on Friday. I could be doing something if I were in Khartoum or Nairobi instead of sitting around a goddamn conference table in Ottawa debating theories."

I walked to the sink, turned the faucet on full, bent down, and splashed cold water on my face. Jonathan was ready with paper towels.

The bracing soak stiffened my resolve.

"I'm going to go over," I said. "I'll book a flight once we get back to the hotel."

"Don't."

"I've got to."

"What about me? You're ready to make me a widower? This early?"

"They need me."

"And I don't?" Jonathan spun on his heels and yanked the door open, sending it crashing against the wall.

When I got back to my seat, he sat staring down into his lap. I reached over and put my hand on his arm. He turned his head, his jaw muscles rigid. The narrowing of his eyes magnified a hundredfold the furious intensity within.

Cornier leaned back in her chair. Pesconie sat up and opened his binder. They had conferenced.

"There's one last issue that we need to discuss. Hopefully, you folks can shed some light on it." Pesconie looked back and forth between Walter and me. We were his "folks."

He unfolded the editorial page of the *Globe and Mail*, the Friday, September 27, 2002, edition.

"I presume that you're all familiar with Lawrence Fischer's letter to the editor?"

We nodded.

"Pretty inflammatory piece of writing, I'd say."

Cornier sat up straight. "Frank, no editorializing." He threw her a this-is-my-inning glare. She countered with a remember-who-is-boss. He looked away, clicking his teeth.

"Mr. Compton." Pesconie addressed Walter respectfully. "I would imagine that Talisman Energy was understandably disturbed by the unsubstantiated accusations in the letter."

"Dad had plenty of substantiation," I growled.

Pesconie ignored me. "Mr. Compton, as a Talisman director, can you share with us the company's reaction, please? Was legal action considered, for instance?"

We all looked down the table as Walter mutely stared back at Pesconie. Eventually, he replied quietly, "It was a management issue. The board was not involved."

"I understand. But I would assume that Mr. Buckee sought your advice. This person was someone with whom you have ... let us say, a family connection." He shot Jonathan and me a quick glance.

Margaret looked in our direction with a smile, her first of the meeting.

"And," Pesconie pressed on, "this wasn't just a letter from some radical leftwing church advocacy group ..."

"Excuse me?" Patti interjected.

"Presumably, the company was concerned about the public perception," Pesconie continued, speaking to Walter, who glared at him without comment.

"Mr. Pesconie and Mme Cornier," intervened Fernando. "We don't get much Canadian news in New York, but it would be my assumption that the Talisman engagement in Sudan has likely been the subject of considerable public discussion in Canada over the past few years. Surely, Lawrence Fischer's letter was not news."

Pesconie did not deviate from directing his comments to Walter. "I'm afraid that our international friend here does not appreciate the vulnerabilities with which the private sector has to cope on a daily basis. This was a letter from a person who had lived in the region for almost a decade and who presented himself as quite familiar with the Sudan conflict. Some readers might be influenced by that claim of expertise."

"You little fucker!" Carolyn was on her feet. "You're questioning Dad's right of freedom of expression and impugning his integrity."

"A company's reputation is an invaluable asset. It has every right to defend itself against scurrilous attack."

"And that includes putting a contract out on my parents?" she shouted.

"Oh, don't be absurd, young lady. You're hysterical."

I looked at Cornier. She just sat, frowning.

Chapter 50

Back at the hotel, we all had dinner together. Barely a word passed amongst us. Exhausted physically and emotionally, we said our goodnights and headed to our respective rooms. We were due back at DFAIT at eleven in the morning for a further briefing. Or interrogation.

In bed, Jonathan tried to cuddle with me, but I was too fidgety. He abandoned the effort, rolled over, and was soon snoring. I looked at the clock on the night table. Nine fifty-five. I decided to get up to watch the news.

I closed the bedroom door and slipped into the adjacent living room, appreciating once again Walter's generosity in booking us suites. I turned on the TV and lowered the volume so as to not disturb Jonathan. The CBC's graphics and music for the nightly news appeared. I sat back to lose myself in the world's affairs.

> *Good evening. I'm Peter Mansbridge. And this is the National.*

> *In breaking news, CBC has just learned that the bodies of a Canadian couple who went missing a week ago have been found by workers for the Canadian oil company Talisman Energy near the company's operations in western Sudan. Lawrence and Isabel Fischer had been serving as United Church of Canada volunteers at a UN refugee camp in northern Kenya. A teacher and a nurse, the Fischers worked primarily with Sudanese women and children who had fled their country's brutal civil war.*

My eyes locked on Mansbridge's mouth. His lips were moving. Sound was coming out. My ears were hearing it. My brain was not computing—no blood was getting to it. My heart had stopped cold.

> *Unofficial sources tell the CBC that the case has stumped Canadian and UN officials. The Fischer's vehicle had*

been discovered late last week on fire in front of the gates of the Canadian Embassy in Khartoum, the capital of Sudan. Khartoum, in the north of the country, is the seat of the Government of Sudan that has been waging an aggressive war against opposition forces based in the south. It has been estimated that more than four million people have been displaced by the civil war, with up to two million killed.

Talisman Energy has been under intense pressure for several years by human rights groups that accuse it of exacerbating the civil war through the oil royalties that it pays to the Government of Sudan that, critics allege, the government uses to finance their military operations.

There was a ferocious knocking at the door. I didn't move. Couldn't.

These same sources tell the CBC that the Fischers' disappearance and deaths are made more mysterious by several bizarre coincidences. Their daughter, the film director Carolyn Fischer, premièred her most recent film, Boy Soldiers of Sudan, *at last month's Toronto International Film Festival. Their son, Tom Fischer, is a senior UN official who recently visited with his parents in Africa. And a close family friend, businessman Walter Compton, is on the Board of Directors of Talisman Energy.*

A spokesman for the Canadian Department of Foreign Affairs and International Trade refused to speculate on how or why the Fischers were abducted and murdered.

The family is said to be in shock and is in seclusion.

The phone started ringing. I didn't move. The phone stopped ringing and then immediately started again. The knocking at the door continued unabated. Carolyn yelled, "Tom, open up. Open up."

I didn't move. I couldn't. The Earth's axis had jolted precariously off-kilter.

Mom and Dad's remains were returned to Toronto. I arranged for cremation but was at a loss about organizing a funeral or memorial service.

Carolyn, of the steel spine, had disappeared, we hoped to seek refuge in solitude somewhere. Equally plausible, we feared, was that she had headed off to mount some god-awful counteroffensive to rain death and destruction down on whoever had held the semiautomatic weapon that had blown Mom and Dad's heads to smithereens. Signs were pointing at the northern Sudanese Government's allies, the Janjaweed militia, as the most likely culprits. But we didn't have irrefutable proof. Carolyn wanted revenge, ambiguities be damned. Wajdi was frantically burning up the phone lines and flying to Khartoum, Cairo, Tripoli, Addis Ababa, anywhere that he conjectured his contacts might lead him to the responsible dark heart in time to save his lover from the same fate as her parents.

Patricia and Robert had retreated into the sanctuary of their community of faith, for which I was, for the first time, immeasurably grateful. I knew that at least they would be looked after there.

Jonathan and I huddled in our home, Walter and Margaret similarly in theirs.

Chapter 51 ——————————

Jonathan and I reached the hospital just as the EMS was wheeling Walter into emergency. Margaret was scurrying alongside the stretcher, her nightgown visible below the coat she had thrown on at home and which she now grasped with both hands in front of her chest. She didn't notice us, her attention riveted on the oxygen mask covering Walter's mouth.

Jonathan came up beside her, put his hand on her shoulder, and said, calmly, "We're here, Mother."

Still keeping pace with the moving gurney, she turned and looked at him, her eyes flashing the vulnerability of a deer caught in headlights. She reached over and grabbed his hand. Neither spoke.

The massive stroke left Walter paralyzed.

Permanently.

Over the next weeks, Jonathan did his best to support his mother.

Margaret had padlocked herself to Walter's hospital bed. Jonathan sat beside her, holding her hand as she stared incomprehensibly at the breathing corpse of her husband, whose interior life was, for the time being at least, unknowable. Having his mother to worry about provided a fortuitous distraction. It allowed Jonathan to delay acknowledging the chasm that Walter's stroke had broken open in his own heart, where the angst of Jeremy's death still writhed, unresolved.

I left Jonathan and Margaret in the hospital room and went down to the coffee shop for a break. Letting my coffee cool, I leafed through a pile of crumpled, discarded newspapers and picked up a copy of that morning's *New York Times*: October 31, 2002.

After scanning the first section, I opened the business pages.

I froze.

Talisman to Sell Its Stake in Company in Sudan.

I dropped the paper on the table and stared straight ahead, my heart pounding. Pain shot through my jaw as my upper and lower teeth grinded against each other. I closed my eyes. I reopened my eyes and cautiously turned back to the article, hesitating lest the paper ignite if I glared at it with too much intensity.

I read the five paragraphs. I read them again. And again.

The article reported that Talisman was selling its 25 percent share of the Greater Nile Petroleum Operating Company for $758 million. The purchaser was the Oil and Natural Gas Corporation of India. Buckee was quoted as saying that shareholders were tired of continually having to monitor and analyze results relating to Sudan. The story concluded by noting that Talisman had been under intense political pressure to withdraw from Sudan on the grounds that its involvement was strengthening the government in a twenty-year civil war that was estimated to have killed about two million people.

I closed the paper, neatly folded it in front of me, and laid my hands on top.

Perhaps this was Mom and Dad's memorial.

Someone bumping into my chair broke my trance.

I got up from the table slowly and made my way to the elevator and back to Walter's room.

A beaming Jonathan came over to me as I appeared at the door and wrapped his arms around me. He whispered, "Father has opened his eyes, Tom. He's opened his eyes."

I hugged him and whispered back, "Thank God."

Jonathan took me by the hand and led me over to the bed. Margaret's chair was positioned as close to Walter as she could get. She looked up at me, her quivering lips accenting the smile on her face.

I leaned on the bedrail and placed my hand on top of Walter's. His eyes shifted over from Margaret and fixed on mine. "Glad to have you back, Walter," I said. He stared at me intensely, not blinking. A minute passed. Slight awkwardness set in as he continued to hold my gaze. Two minutes.

"Maybe we should let him rest now," Jonathan offered, at which the patient let out a muffled, but unmistakably Walteresque, grunt. He still had not taken his eyes off mine.

"Walter," I said. "I have news. It says in this morning's paper that Talisman has sold the Sudan holdings."

Still staring at me, he blinked three times and then returned to his riveted gaze. I furrowed my brow. He blinked again, three times. I said nothing but just looked back at him, a question forming slowly in my eyes.

Three more blinks.

I mouthed, "You're ... wel ... come?"

His mouth muscles twitched.

"Was that a smile?" Margaret asked, breathlessly.

I squeezed his hand and mouthed, "Thank you."

Walter's mouth muscles twitched again. He closed his eyes. A moment later, he started snoring.

Part Five
2010

Chapter 52 ———————————

Trickling water slid down the length of the fountain's ceramic stylus into the shallow basin. Though nestled in a corner still well shaded at this late morning hour, enough reflected light filtered into our protected alcove to bring the lapis lazuli to life. Minuscule shards of crystalline brilliance erupted with erratic frequency and danced in one spot for just a moment, before disappearing into the depthless blue, only to reappear somewhere else.

The aural massaging had already stolen Jonathan's good intentions. He was slumped back in his chair, feet outstretched on the overstuffed kilim ottoman, his manuscript proofs perched precariously on his stomach, each tranquil rise of his chest shifting them ever closer to slipping onto the tiled floor. I leaned over and rescued the papers so that he wouldn't be awakened by their fall.

The increasing warmth of the approaching midday, the tranquility of our secluded corner of the courtyard, and the fountain's magic seduction had ushered him into a rare and peaceful retreat. That, and the residual dregs of last night's inebriation.

I trusted that he was out for long enough to allow me a private stroll around the gardens. Since the recent reopening of the Moorish-styled landmark La Mamounia, hotel management had put a stop to the invasion of tourists curious to explore the storied grounds and to gawk at this Marrakech jewel of art deco architecture infused seamlessly with traditional arabesque décor. I had unfettered privacy as I wandered the shaded paths amongst the olive trees, palm groves, and jasmine bushes. Somewhere distant, a muezzin had climbed a minaret, and his call to prayer was wafting through the city toward this garden, into my ear and my heart.

I took a deep breath.

As I relaxed my psychic guard, the catastrophe that had been Copenhagen roared back in. I had been determined, and Jonathan had been even more determined, that these two first weeks of January in this oasis of peace would provide me a respite from December's debilitating fatigue and frustrating failure in Copenhagen. Easier intended than accomplished.

Why was I so devastated about the summit? My years of midwifery in climate change negotiations should have inured me to disappointment. Somehow, this had been qualitatively worse.

The Copenhagen stakes had been higher than most climate change summits in the past. Even though progress in emission reductions over the past decade had fallen short of the targets established in the Kyoto Protocol, at least we had that international legal agreement. The Protocol, our rulebook with all its principles and procedures and mechanisms, was the common framework that countries had agreed to. Except of course, Bush's USA. But we had hopes that Obama's USA was going to bring them on board, in practice if not in law. The first phase of the Kyoto Protocol was about to expire, and we needed a successor agreement to emerge out of Copenhagen or, at least, an explicit path and timeline to get to one.

We didn't even get close, a failure that now lay at my feet.

Don't be melodramatic, Tom. You were only one small cog in a very big and very complicated wheel, I reprimanded myself.

Oh, I wish that that were the case. No, I was more than one tooth among all the other teeth in a massive grinding gear. I was supposed to be the grease that kept the wheels rotating, the teeth engaging with each other. They didn't. The whole operation ground to a halt.

I was the Secretary-General's point man, the one to ensure collaboration on the common goal across the UN system and to keep the negotiating lines of communication open and functioning between the UN bureaucracy and national governments.

I still had hope when we had arrived in Copenhagen that we could reach an international consensus, despite the huge obstacles to be overcome.

I still had hope in the early stages of Copenhagen, despite the chaotic atmosphere, with tens of thousands more participants than we had anticipated, and despite the cabal of twenty-five of the biggest nations subverting the global negotiating process by appropriating the key decision-making to themselves, which had effectively marginalized the UN system, and me with it, and left those most victimized by climate change voiceless.

I still had hope, in the dying days of Copenhagen, trailing behind Obama as he walked down the hall to personally intervene with Wen Jiaboa. What an extraordinary sight, watching the US president and the Chinese premier, the leaders of the two biggest greenhouse gas-emitting economies, negotiating global climate change policy toe to toe.

It all came to nothing.

The apologists inside the UN and among the key participating countries would hail the Copenhagen Accord; Obama said, "Even though we have a long way to go, there's no question that we've accomplished a great deal over the last few days."

But we all knew that wasn't so. The Copenhagen Accord was a skimpy political agreement with no legally binding clout, with loopholes big enough to drive a flotilla of emission-spewing SUVs through, and with major financing issues unresolved.

I couldn't look my WCC friends in the eye, especially those from the global South, whose peoples and ecosystems were now condemned to years of unremitting and increasing vulnerability to the impacts of a climate that was changing for the worse.

I had failed them.

Jonathan wasn't in his chair. His new book manuscript lay undisturbed on the cool tile floor where I had placed it. I picked it up, as well as his reading glasses from the coffee table, and headed back up to our room.

As I opened the door, I heard familiar hangover sounds coming from the bathroom. He was throwing up. Retching. What an onomatopoeic word. The first syllable evoked the guttural stomach spasm that spewed foul-smelling, yellowish-brown guck that, just hours ago, was an exquisite Oriental treasure to the palate, liquefied by generous portions of full-bodied Bordeaux. The second syllable painted an image of the back and forth rocking of the living corpse, the long head-in-the-toilet-bowl period gradually dissipating as the victim slid back on his haunches to slowly come up for air.

Such morning-after occurrences had been increasing for many years now, and I knew it was a waiting game. Jonathan would angrily bat me away if I tried to intervene too soon. The signal that he was ready for my assistance would be the sound of him plopping down on the bathroom floor, where he would either be stretched out in exhaustion, which threatened to give way to muscle-stiffening sleep if I didn't get him up, or curled up in a foetal position, which was the more disconcerting of the two, because it bespoke a yet-unrelieved cramping, his body resisting calling a truce.

Jonathan and I never spoke of these embarrassments after the fact.

Once I got him into bed, I drew the drapes. As I pulled the fine cotton sheet up over his wasted body, I noticed a distention around his stomach. How could he be putting on weight when he had become such a picky eater? Then I remembered the high caloric content of alcohol.

I tiptoed around the bed and slipped out through the French doors to sit in the sumptuously upholstered armchair on our well-shaded balcony, intent on making progress in one of the books I had brought along to distract myself from ruminating on the Copenhagen collapse.

I left the books unopened on the small octagonal Kabak table beside the chair and gazed instead out over the cityscape.

And thought of nothing.

A light tapping at the door aroused me from my free-floating slumber.

I had forgotten to put the Do Not Disturb sign on the door. We could do without housekeeping's attentions today, but Jonathan could not do without the sleep that was now jeopardized by the knocking.

I scrambled in from the balcony and scurried toward the door. It wasn't housekeeping. One of the bellboys was crouched down, about to slip something under the door. I smiled as he looked up, startled by my unexpected arrival. *Bellboy* was so inappropriate a descriptor. Omar, as his name tag told me, was probably in his mid- to late twenties, broad-shouldered. When he stood, I saw that he was a touch over six feet tall, with short black hair and deep dark eyes that went on forever. No boy, this, but a man of considerable substance. My smile broadened.

"A message for you, sir," he said, holding out an embossed hotel envelope.

"Thank you, Omar."

He smiled back, nodded slightly, took a step backward, and then turned and headed down the hall. I stood in the doorway, watching until he turned the corner, enjoying the view.

I stepped back into our suite and sighed deeply as I looked down at my name written on the envelope. Fernando had assured me that they wouldn't bother me. I needed this break after Copenhagen. Why couldn't he keep his promise?

I ran my finger under the envelope flap slowly so as not to make any noise. Jonathan's snoring continued uninterrupted, thankfully. I pulled the hotel stationary out of the envelope, unfolded it, and read.

Tom - meet me by the pool. Please. Alan

What the hell is he doing here? He had broken the rule. He was not supposed to invade our space when Jonathan and I were away together.

Chapter 53

It had started eight years ago, at a time when my sanity was imploding and my universe was ricocheting erratically out of control.

Life, as we had known it, had fallen to pieces when Mom and Dad were murdered.

Yet, in the midst of the most unimaginable of family traumas, none of my family needed me. Me, the one to whom the family-mender role had traditionally fallen. Carolyn had vanished, with Wajdi in desperate pursuit. Patricia was in retreat in Dayton. And Jonathan, my Jonathan, was submerged in a parental crisis that compounded his festering, unresolved litany of grief. Not only was I unneeded by family, none of them were available to support me, who shared with them these communal tragedies but who, as a function of the virulence forever compromising my stamina, had fewer physical resources to draw upon than did they.

The double irony was not lost on me.

I ended up in Alan's office. For tranquilizers. For sleeping pills. For Kleenex.

He asked me about therapy. I dismissed the option.

Alan gave me prescriptions and invited me home for a drink.

"Martini? Scotch?" Alan stood behind the bar, his hand resting on the first of a double row of clear shelves suspended from the ceiling, waiting for me to declare my preference, the signal he needed to choose the appropriate glass.

"Martini suggests celebration," I grumbled, having slouched down on his sofa. "Sure as hell, nothing to celebrate now. Or forever more. Amen. Make it a double—no, triple—scotch. No ice. Please." I looked out at the fading light illuminating the Toronto Islands. Alan's thirty-first floor harbour-front condo offered a view reminiscent of that from Walter's office.

Oh, my God. Walter's office. What are we going to do about that? Forget it. Tomorrow is another day.

Alan came around the end of the sofa and handed me a crystal tumbler brimming full. I took it and stared into the elixir that reflected the light, glistening ochre or amber or persimmon. I lifted it to my lips carefully, so as not to spill a scintilla of what I thought likely to be the most useful medication for what ailed me. I took a swig. Alan sat down beside me and held his glass up in my direction. I turned and lifted mine, lightly tapping the rim of his. Then I returned it to my lips and took another deep, long, slow swallow. And another. I titled the glass above my head and let the last few drops drip down onto my tongue. I set the tumbler on the coffee table in front of the sofa, turned and looked at Alan, and smiled, impressed by my new record.

Alan set his untouched glass down beside mine. Slowly, he raised his left arm and brought it down along the back of the sofa behind my shoulders. Staring into my eyes, he moved his hand gently onto the nape of my neck. His index finger traced a pattern of concentric circles, expanding in scope.

I closed my eyes. The rest of his hand joined that finger, extending around and fully encompassing the back of my neck. The pressure against my skin increased, and his fingers expanded and contracted, massaging the subcutaneous muscles so rife with grieving tension. The massaging stopped. His grip firmed itself on my neck, and he slowly pulled me closer. He brought his right hand up, fingering for a moment the tears that had begun trickling out of my shuttered eyes. His right hand opened to encompass my cheek as his left hand descended from its perch on my neck to my other cheek. Jointly, they pressured me closer and closer, ever so gently tilting my head. His lips came to rest on mine, and he paused.

I hesitated and then kissed him back.

"How could you not have known?" Alan whispered into my ear, in between nibbles.

My head rested on his shoulder. My finger traced the outline of his left pec and then slowly moved up and down the hairless crevice before exploring the contours of his right. His semi-flaccid cock quivered whenever my hand grazed one his nipples. The sheets lay crumpled at the bottom of the bed, exposing our exhausted, intertwined bodies.

How could I not have known?

Alan took hold of my chin and raised my head up so that we were eyeball to eyeball. "I've been in love with you for years, my dear," he said. He planted a quiet kiss on my forehead.

I struggled to summon the energy to extricate myself from his arms, to no avail. I closed my eyes, lay my head back on his shoulder, and wrapped my arms around his chest.

"What do we do now?" I mumbled.

"Fall asleep," he responded, shifting us in tandem so that our heads were resting on the pillows.

I pushed myself away and sat up.

"Are you crazy? I've got to go home. Jonathan drives his mom back to her house after visiting hours. I've got to be at our place when he gets home."

I suddenly pictured Jonathan walking in our front door. And I saw Margaret. And Walter. And Carolyn and Wajdi and Patricia and Robert. I jumped out of bed. Alan propped his elbow on the pillow and leaned his head on his fist, watching me pace around his bedroom.

"What the fuck did we do here?" I banged my palm against my forehead.

"Fucked," Alan replied smiling.

"Jesus. We can't do this."

"We can and we did and we will continue to."

"I repeat, are you crazy?" My voice rose.

"Don't worry. It's all worked out. And this is the way it has to be."

I stared at him, breathlessly. He was speaking an unknown language.

"Listen, Tom. Come over here and sit down on the bed." Alan patted the bed beside him.

I moved in the opposite direction and leaned my back up against the window. The cold glass jarred me. I didn't budge.

"What do you mean, it's all worked out?" I crossed the room, grabbed my briefs off the chair, yanked them on, and then went back to my station at the window. "Cover yourself up too. Please."

Alan smiled and reached down for the sheets, drawing them up slowly, very slowly, pausing a moment before covering his vitals, never taking his eyes off mine.

"Hell, Alan. Stop being coy. This is not funny. This is a bloody mess," I yelled. He smiled. I slapped my hands flat behind me against the windowpane, producing an unexpectedly loud clatter, sending the glass into a momentary spasm. The noise startled us both. I took one step away from the window. Alan stopped smiling.

We both looked at each other for a long time and said nothing. I closed my eyes. I inhaled deeply. I held my breath. I exhaled deeply. I opened my eyes. Alan was watching me with exquisite tenderness. I walked over to the bed and sat down.

"Tom," he said after a moment. "Let me tell you a few things that you know but have not let yourself know and then I'm going to tell you what's going to happen."

I looked at him and waited, a profound exhaustion surfacing from my core.

"First, you have been in love with me for almost as long as I have been in love with you."

I raised my eyebrows.

"Who is the one you have leaned on most since you tested positive years ago? Who is the one you came to when everyone else, including Jonathan, is emotionally unavailable to support you after the horrendous business with your parents?"

"Well ..."

"Secondly, my dear," Alan interrupted. "You are, and have for a long time, been in a bad relationship."

I jumped off the bed. "You don't know what you're talking about."

"I know what I see, Tom," Alan continued quietly. "You've been together a long time. I have no doubt that you think that you still love each other. But ..." he looked out the window and then back at me. "Alcoholism messes up people like Jonathan. Your love for him is clouding your judgment."

I started pacing. "You don't know what's been going on," I said. "He's been under, we've all been under, enormous stress. His father's just had a massive, paralyzing stroke. My parents have just been killed. Who wouldn't hit the bottle?"

"But, Tom, this isn't recent. Don't you see how you keep making excuses for him, picking up after him, closing your eyes to the obvious?

It's not getting any better, it's getting worse. You risk being dragged down with him."

I turned around and stared out the window at the black moonless night, the vista illuminated only by the faint lights of the Island residences and the yacht club.

"Thirdly, I'm not asking you to leave him, not at this point, with everything that is going on in your families."

I started pacing around the room.

He began to speak more rapidly, anxious to get what he had to say said before I shut down or tuned out or ran off.

I was aware of three things. My mind was spinning. I was getting a hard-on. Alan was still talking. Angry with myself for not being in control of what was happening in both heads, I vaguely heard his saying something about tonight being the beginning of something that had been a long time coming. He would have to stop being my personal physician before anybody got suspicious and reported him to the College. He and I would see each other as we could without Jonathan suspecting. Alan figured that he could sometimes travel to where I was when working abroad. He described a romantic scenario of us holed up together in lovely hotel rooms in Paris or Buenos Aires or Hong Kong.

"Eventually ..." he said and then paused. "Tom, are you listening to me?"

I stopped pacing and looked at him.

"Eventually," he began again, "when the time is right, you'll leave Jonathan, and you and I will be together."

I walked over to the chair and picked up the rest of my clothes, piece by piece, and slowly got dressed.

What began that night continued.

Chapter 54 ——————————————

I tiptoed over to the bed to make sure that Jonathan was still asleep. Not that there was much doubt. He was sleeping a lot these days. We had spent much less time out and about in Marrakech this trip than previous ones. His limited hours awake usually found him in the garden, reviewing the book proofs, or in one of the bars, bemoaning the state of the book proofs. Thank goodness he was on sabbatical that term, eliminating a little pressure.

What goes around, comes around. He always complained that my work left me with little to offer him when we were together—just the dregs. Now, I got little of him. He was so exhausted from last year's conflicts in the department, the battles with the publisher over the new book, his onerous share of Walter's rotational feedings, and new worries about Margaret's mental stability. Our bed had not been rocking much, either, for quite some time. The legendary Compton men's hard-at-the-drop-of-a-hat had become just that—a legend in the receding mists.

I leaned over and quietly kissed his forehead.

Alan had appropriated two lounge chairs and a table in the most distant, heavily shaded corner of the pool bar. His head was buried deeply in the pages of *Le Monde,* and he didn't see me approaching. I walked the length of the pool at a deliberately slow pace, in part to luxuriate in the anticipation for one who invariably made my member swell, in part to practice the scowl with which I needed to greet this against-the-rules intrusion into my time with Jonathan.

Seven years, going on eight, was a long gestation period for Alan's prediction of our coupledom. Us together was his fantasy. I didn't share it. I told him so. Repeatedly.

But I kept opening the door when he knocked.

Alan had remained convinced that it was just a matter of time. He complained regularly that he didn't get enough of me. Recently, he had become more brazen in arranging assignations in Toronto. He had also threatened several times to start trying to see me when Jonathan and I were travelling abroad. He had become particularly jealous of Jonathan and my winter trips to Puerto Vallarta and Marrakech.

I snuck up on him and slipped down onto the waiting lounger.

"Oh, you came," he said, startled by my arrival.

"When did you arrive?" I asked. A chitchat question. No sense in, no need for, "What are you doing here?"

"Monday." His composure surprised me.

"Monday? That was ... what is today? ... Wednesday. That was two days ago."

"Yeah."

"Where have you been staying?"

"Here."

"I haven't seen you."

"Obviously. I've been watching you, both of you, discretely. Credit me that." His voice was flat.

A waiter appeared in front of us.

"Tea, please," Alan ordered without asking me. The waiter nodded and departed.

I said nothing. Neither did Alan. I kept watching him. He looked at me and held my gaze for minutes at a time and then looked out at the pool. Then back at me.

The tea arrived. The waiter placed the tray down, bowed modestly, and departed. The mint aroma wafted around the table. Neither of us moved to pour.

"Tom," Alan began, staring out at the pool. "It was a mistake to come here at this time."

"Well, I'm surprised that you're prepared to admit that," I admonished, disingenuously, while my visions of furtive passionate trysts vaporized.

He turned and looked at me. "For you too. For both of you."

I squinted, frowned, and then rolled my eyes.

"Don't give me attitude," he said sharply. He rolled his eyes, with disgust. "You are so self-absorbed, you don't see it."

"I don't know what you're talking about." I didn't.

"Hence the problem." He shook his head. "We have to get home. All of us, and quickly."

"And why is that?" I countered, ignoring his rebuke about attitude.

"I've seen Jonathan."

"So you've said."

"Tom." Alan sighed deeply. "He's sick. Very sick."

Chapter 55

"I'm in the kitchen, dear." Margaret's voice rang out clearly as I unlocked and opened the massive wooden front door. In the early days, I used to tease Jonathan that it had the feel of a drawbridge, and we had to wait for it to be lowered from inside the castle. Now, in these days of eldercare, we had our own key and let ourselves in. A lot of water had passed through the moat in the intervening years.

"I was so surprised to get your e-mail." I was struck by how stooped Margaret's back appeared as I walked into the kitchen. Maybe it was just her position as she hunched over the counter. "That's a shame that you had to cut your trip short. What was the mix-up with your hotel? You were very vague, I must say ..."

The rattling blender drowned Margaret's running monologue out for a few moments.

"... of course, so I wouldn't really know. I am getting old. Losing my sense of travel adventure. That just goes to show my ... ouch ... I tell you, they can put men on the moon but they can't invent a paring knife that won't cut your fingers every time you pick it up. Sorry, I'm being quite rude. It's just that I'm trying out a new mixture of vegetable mush for your father. 'Vegetable purée,' I should say. Have to keep up appearances, you know. I'll be finished in just a few minutes, and then I can give you a proper hug just like ..."

The blender whirred again.

"... but Pamela insists that it's more nutritious. You've met Pamela, haven't you? She's taken over from Rosaline while she is on vacation. My, my, everybody going on these winter ... vacations ... these ... careful, Margaret, don't spill now ..." she cautioned herself as she upended the blender jar, pouring the pea green liquefied contents into a Pyrex bowl on the counter. A slight tremor in her arm was visible through the long-sleeve blouse as she tried to steady the weighty jar in one hand and manipulate a spatula to extract as much as possible of her experimental concoction from its interior.

The jar came down on the counter with a crash and bounced twice before rolling on to the floor, where it shattered into pieces.

"Oh, oh, oh, oh, oh …" she screamed, surveying the mess on the marble kitchen floor. She brought her hands up to her face, covering her eyes, and pivoted around to face me for the first time. Slowly, she lowered her arms, her eyes still closed, her face pot-marked by purée residue that had escaped the blender onto her hands, creating the slippery conditions that led to this newest catastrophe in her life.

I had resisted speaking or approaching her to avoid startling her and jeopardizing the delicate operation in which she had been engaged. There was no need for such caution any longer. I rounded the island, tiptoed over the broken glass, and wrapped my arms around her quivering frame. She buried her head in my shoulder and grabbed onto me. Her legs gave out from under her. I tightened my grip and held her full inconsequential weight.

"Oh, Jonathan, Jonathan, Jonathan …"

"Now I'm doubly embarrassed," Margaret said, dabbing a tissue at her eyes and then modestly blowing her nose.

I had ushered her to a chair at the small table in the kitchen bay window that looked out onto the dull grey, snow-covered garden behind their house. It was only when I asked if she would like a cup of tea that she had jolted her head up, stunned at the unexpected voice.

"Why did you let me go on assuming that you were Jonathan?" There was sharpness in her voice, quite at odds with her intimate, gossipy tone of a few moments ago. "That was rather deceptive."

"I'm sorry, Margaret. I just didn't want to disturb you while you were working with the blender."

"That bloody machine," she said, almost spitting the words. "Oh, my God …" She jerked around to survey the decimated blender jar scattered across the floor. "We use it all the time. How are we going to prepare Walter's meals?" She looked at me, panic in her eyes.

I reached across the table and grabbed her hand, saying quickly, "Don't worry, my dear, I'll get a replacement this afternoon. Or else I'll bring ours from the house."

She brightened and sat back in her chair. "Why don't you call Jonathan and have him bring it over? Why didn't he come, anyway? You know, he does so appreciate it that you have dinner waiting for him at home after he's finished helping me feed Walter here. He's commented many times how lucky he is to have you ..."

It was her turn to reach across the table and take my hand. She lifted it with her right and started patting the top with her left. Her motion reminded me of another conversation between the two of us.

"... though he does, just as frequently, complain about how much you work and how often you travel. Oh, I am feeling a bit better now. Back in control. Thank you."

She made a motion to withdraw her hands, a prelude to getting up. I quickly grasped hers and signaled her not to move. "Would you like tea?" I repeated, "or a glass of water?" I smiled, with forced nonchalance. I needed her to be calm before I began.

She relaxed. "Oh, okay. That would be nice. I've been going at it full steam for the past hour or so. Walter will be sleeping anyway. Does a lot of that these days."

Like father, like son. I got up and made my way around the recent carnage to the sink, where I filled the kettle and put it on the stove.

"Dr. Pachauri says that's to be expected after the multiple strokes. God, we never know when another one is going to happen. At least he's talking a bit better now, thanks to Trevor. Have you met Trevor?"

I shook my head.

"Oh, you'll like him. He has a wonderful temperament. Perfect for dealing with obstreperous patients like Walter. I wouldn't be surprised"—she paused, looking at me slyly—"if Trevor were a member of your team."

I smiled back as I assembled the tea-making provisions. My mind flashed to mint tea, beside a pool, a short forty-eight hours ago.

"Trevor was talking to Walter the other day about San Francisco. Oh, San Francisco." She tapped her forehead with her hand. "That clinches it. Of course he is gay. What a giveaway. I should have realized it at the time."

San Francisco, host to gay and not-so-gay memories.

Margaret began recounting how Walter had made a joke about San Francisco, saying something to the effect of "waiting for the big one, like me ..." Neither she nor Trevor could figure out what he was talking about until suddenly Trevor had burst out laughing. He explained to Margaret that Walter was making a pun about the big earthquake that

California was waiting for and the big stroke that he was waiting for, the one that would do him in.

"Well, I gasped," Margaret said, speaking to my back as I poured the boiling water into the tea pot. "I thought it really quite presumptuous on Trevor's part to speak so candidly. But then he started explaining that showing a sense of humour is a good thing, since that's often lost with the amount of damage that Walter's brain has suffered. As I said, I thought initially that it was quite out of place for him to be talking like that about Walter's … disabilities, but I think, in fact, that Walter appreciated it. You know he was never one to tiptoe around difficult subjects."

Don't I know it. I placed two cups of tea on the table and sat down.

Margaret stopped talking to sip her tea. She looked out at the cold, barren garden, gradually fading from our view as the late afternoon dusk took hold. I had turned on the kitchen lights. As I sat down, I too followed the direction of Margaret's gaze, not attending to the outside but watching her reflection in the window. She looked quiet, and sad.

More of that's to come, I'm afraid.

"Margaret …" I began softly. She was lost somewhere out by the disappearing, desiccated magnolia tree.

"Margaret," I repeated. She turned and looked at me with those beautiful eyes, lustrous topaz, almost iridescent, serenely placid at the moment. I said nothing, wanting to prolong the tranquility that had descended in the room.

"Margaret. I'm afraid that I have some serious news to share."

She turned her head toward the window. She sighed, breathed in deeply, held it, and then sighed again. Without looking back, she said softly, "Yes, Tom, what is it?"

"It's Jonathan." I didn't know why I was whispering. It just felt like the right thing. "He's not well. That's why we came home early. He's at St. Mike's. We got him admitted right away. They've been doing tests this afternoon. I'll need to head back shortly. They said that they should have the results by about five o'clock."

She didn't move.

A minute passed. Two. Three.

"Who is 'we'?"

"Um, pardon?"

She turned and looked at me. "You said, 'We got him admitted right away.'"

"Oh. Well, we met a friend in Marrakech, a doctor friend. It was on his advice that we came home. He didn't think that Jonathan looked well. He was, is, quite concerned."

She looked down at her tea. "I see," she said, flatly. Looking up and directly at me, she asked, "Was it the same doctor friend that Jonathan has mentioned? Someone that you are particularly ... close to?"

"Um, well, yes, he is a good friend. I guess."

"Then I suppose it was fortunate that he was there. Under the circumstances."

She turned back to look out of the window, now completely dark, nothing to look back out to.

"You had better get back to the hospital. Please, call me once you know something."

"Ah, I don't like leaving you like this. Alone."

"Pamela will be here shortly to help me feed Walter his dinner."

I stood up and went over to her chair, leaned in, and gave her a gentle kiss on the cheek. She didn't move. I looked over at the mess on the floor. "Maybe I'll clean this up before I leave."

"Don't." She was still staring out the window, at the darkness.

"Are you sure? It won't take me a moment."

"Go."

I walked out of the kitchen. I opened and closed the front door quietly. I remembered to lock it.

Chapter 56 ————————————

Jonathan was curled up on his side, arms wrapped around his abdomen. The blue hospital gown had come undone, exposing part of his back and buttocks. The bed sheet lay near his ankles. I took hold of the top edge, gently untangled it from his legs, and drew it up to his shoulders. He made a soft grunting sound and then continued snoring lightly.

I walked over to the windows and pried open the venetians. A steady stream of people walked, drove, and trolleyed along Queen Street, most of them heading east out of the downtown core, their day's work complete.

Other people's lives go on.

Some of the semi-permanent residents of the green space in front of Metropolitan United Church sat on benches, shopping carts within easy reach overflowing with their worldly possessions.

I picked up the armchair and silently set it down beside the bed. I sat down and leaned in, resting my arms on the metal railing raised to guard against floundering and a fall. Jonathan didn't look like a flounderer. His eyes were shut tight, his brow furrowed. He was breathing through his mouth.

I glanced up at the monitor, with its myriad of modestly fluctuating numbers and line graphs and periodic beeps. I could have tried to figure out what each was measuring, if I had had the energy.

I leaned back in the chair, maneuvered my legs in and around the mechanized substructure of the bed, and rested my feet on a part that I hoped would not crush them were it to jump suddenly to life.

I stared at Jonathan.

Is he dying?

That can't be true. Our lives are continuing together, moving forward. More or less. There is inertia to our relationship, to being a couple, to our coupledom.

Physicists should have linguists edit their ramblings. I've always found the concept of inertia confusing. How can it mean both moving and not moving? "Property by which matter continues in its existing state of rest or uniform motion in a straight line unless that state is changed by external force." *Thank you, OED. Everything is context.*

But maybe you don't want to speak a whole paragraph to give the context. Sometimes you just want to use one sentence. Then people give you that "You're not using the word properly" look. I am using it as I intend. They just aren't hearing me properly. There is inertia to our coupledom. Jonathan and I are continuing in motion. Well, perhaps not in uniform motion, and perhaps not in a straight line. But we are not in a state of rest—immobile, dead.

That would only happen if there were no longer a "we" to be a couple.

Is Jonathan dying?

The crick in my neck woke me. As I was coming to, I heard the muffled conversation of two female voices. Maybe it was they who woke me and then I became aware of my tense muscles. Whatever. One was definitely more pleasant than the other.

I slowly opened my eyes and began leveraging my legs out from under the bed and my back up from its contorted position in the recesses of the chair.

They saw the movement and stopped talking. Sheila came around from the other side of the bed and knelt down on the floor beside me. She put her hands around my hands, resting in my lap.

I looked into her eyes for a couple moments and then over her head at Dr. Chin, who stood, arms folded around a medical chart.

I turned back to Sheila.

"That bad, eh?" I said softly.

Does everybody fall into the blame game, accusations of self-inflicted wounds?

There are some diseases and causes of death—like pancreatic cancer and aneurisms—that just occur for no apparent reason, as far as we know, unrelated to anything one has done that one shouldn't have, or not done that one should have.

Then there are behaviour-related diseases. Lung cancer among six-pack-a-day smokers. Heart disease among fast food over-indulgers. Liver cirrhosis among heavy drinkers. HIV/AIDS among the insufficiently cautious.

"Do you think you could rustle me up a good dry martini?" he asked as I came in the door. Jonathan was propped up in his bed, pillows recently fluffed behind his head, monitors still monitoring, IV still dripping. Six days and counting.

I came over, gave him a peck on the cheek, and lifted his headset off. Maureen Forrester was partway into Brahms's "Vier ernste Gesänge." I pressed the pause button with vigour. Nothing against Forrester, everything against Ecclesiastes' dust to dust. *We're not there yet.* I would have been more generous had she been on to Corinthians' "but the greatest of these is love."

I faked a look at the nonexistent medical chart hanging on the bottom of the bed, so old school, and old hospital TV show reruns.

"Um, I don't see martinis listed here as prescribed. Scotch. Gin and tonic. Merlot. All okay, but sorry, no martinis."

"Just my luck."

I dragged the chair over from the window and sat down. Jonathan fingered his iPod. "Barry says dear old Maureen is a total dementia basket-case. Not long for this world either. That's your generous, loving God for you. The woman created so much beauty and gave us all so much joy, and what does she get in return? Off in la-la land, vegetating in some upscale garbage heap."

"Belmont House is hardly an upscale garbage heap."

Jonathan rolled his eyes. "As if that were my point." After a pause, he added, "Chin was in this morning." His voice, very matter-of-fact, carried no emotional freight.

"Oh, already? I wanted to be here when she came in. Did she have more results?"

A moment passed.

"And? What did she have to say?"

"It's complicated."

"Life is complicated. Tell me what she had to say. Please."

"A bunch of stuff involving a bunch of organs."

"Now that's a technical medical description."

Jonathan lay back on his pillows and closed his eyes. I waited for more details, hoping that he wouldn't doze off. After about five minutes without further offerings, I reached into my bag and pulled out the morning *Globe and Mail* to fill the time.

I was on to the editorial page when a thin voice from the bed asked, "What are your biggest regrets?"

I set the paper down. "Huh? I don't know. Why do you ask?"

"Don't you know that it is impolite to answer a question with another question?" His eyes were still closed, but he was smiling.

"Can we get back to you, please? Tell me what Dr. Chin had to say."

With eyes still closed, Jonathan addressed some point in the ceiling above the bed, speaking in an increasingly reedy whisper that I had to strain to hear. "There's cancer. It's everywhere. It's boring. I'd rather talk about interesting things—life, art, love."

I swallowed hard, trying to control my voice. "Okay. What about life, art, and love?"

Jonathan opened his eyes and leaned up slightly so that he could look directly at me. "Tom, my dear. You're not concentrating. I'm the one who is starting to manifest cognitive lapses. I have an excuse. You, not so much. Now answer my question. What are your biggest regrets?"

"This is not a rhetorical question?" I stalled for time.

"This is not a rhetorical question." He didn't grant me any.

"Well, let's see."

My God. How do I answer a question like that? It took a Herculean effort to suppress my propensity for flippancy. This was not the time, nor the place. We hadn't had this kind of discussion for a long time, not like we used to when we were younger. Deep dialogue had become a casualty of the hectic pace of our professional lives, and, admittedly, our domestic comfort. When we were together, we had become just comfortable together. I shouldn't say *just*. That's no mean accomplishment. In each other's company, we were relaxed and content, a much-underrated treasure in a relationship. Placid. Flaccid too. That was okay. Jonathan didn't seem to need much anymore. I was getting what I needed elsewhere. If he suspected, he hadn't said anything. In any case, in many dimensions, we had grown comfortably, placidly content.

"Hello? Where have you gone?" Jonathan spoke with more energy. He was determined to have this discussion.

"Oh, sorry. I'm trying to figure out what to say. About regrets."

"How about the truth?"

I said nothing.

"Geez, Tom. For someone who has so much to say about so much else, can't you answer a simple question from your lover?"

I got up out of the chair and walked to the window. A couple street people were huddled together on one of the park benches, the blanket wrapped around them and over their heads providing a modest shield against the cold wet snow that had started to fall. I turned back toward the bed and propped myself on the windowsill. I crossed my arms and stared at the floor.

The edge was absent from Jonathan's voice when he observed, quietly, "You are making this difficult. Okay, let me start. Do you regret getting hooked up with an old, falling-apart model like me? I presume that we've both seen this coming for some time. If we haven't, then we've been pretty self-delusional, both of us. So do you regret getting hooked up with me and having to go through … what it looks like we're going to have to go through?"

"Of course not." I had found my voice. "It's ludicrous to even suggest it. You know better than that."

"I don't think it's so ludicrous. I know that you love me and you always have. But regret and love are not mutually exclusive."

"Okay. I regret that you have been such a heavy drinker, that you became an alcoholic, that I did nothing to intervene, that now you have cirrhosis and cancer and who knows what else, and are dying. There. Satisfied?"

"Bravo!" He made a feeble attempt to clap his hands. "Now we're starting to get somewhere."

"I'll do you one better," I declared, walking to the door and closing it against the prying ears of curious patients or the officious response of alarmed nurses. "I not only regret all that, I'm goddamn pissed off about it—at you and at myself for not doing something to stop you. This wasn't supposed to happen. And it didn't have to happen."

I returned to the window. The rubbies on the bench were passing a brown paper bag back and forth, raising it to their lips and taking a slug.

Without turning back to face Jonathan, I continued. "Tell me. You've known that you were over-drinking. You have been suffering from horrible hangovers for years. You've had terrible intestinal pains that you just sloughed off. You never wanted to go see a doctor. Your stamina has been diminishing."

"I was wondering when you would get to that."

I wheeled around. "For God's sake, Jonathan. That's not what I'm talking about. Just tell me why. Why did you not stop, or at least slow down? Now you're fucked up. And you've fucked me up in the process. And us."

Jonathan looked at me for a long time before softly repeating my words. "And you've fucked me up."

His breathing became laboured.

I moved over to the bed. "Are you okay? Do you need something?"

"And ... you've fucked me up," he said again, starting to gasp.

I moved to press the call button, but he grabbed my arm and yanked it down to his chest. "Funny ... funny ..." he said, his chest moving up and down in sharp shallow bursts, "... funny ... that your greatest regret is about my drinking."

He squeezed my wrist harder, pinning me against him, his eyes flaming. "No, regrets ... about you fucking yourself up. You and your bloody screwing around that got you positive."

He banged my arm down against the bedrail. "Where's your fucking regret about that?"

He again hit my arm on the rail. "'Cause that's what really fucked me up ... you bastard," he yelled between hacking coughs. "I couldn't stand the thought ... of you suffering ... I love you too much ..."

He gasped for breath. "I couldn't stand the thought of you ... dying and leaving me ..."

He threw off my hand and started pounding his fists on the mattress. Struggling to assert control over the gyrating body now rocking the bed, he stammered, "That's ... that's why I drank so much, you blind, ignorant ... bastard. I had to go first. After Jeremy ... died ... I couldn't handle you going too ..."

He coughed several times in succession, spitting up ink-black phlegm.

"I had to go first ..."

I staggered backward, crashing against the window.

Jonathan grabbed hold of the rail with both hands and pulled himself partway up so that he could glare at me.

"And I know about you ... and your fuck buddy, Alan," he spit the words out. His face became redder; his chest jerked in and out, faster and faster. "When I couldn't ... get it up anymore ... I knew that at least there was someone ... you could get your rocks off with ... who'd take care of you ..."

My feet collapsed under me, and I slid down onto the floor, knocking the chair over on its side.

"I was virtually ... your bloody pimp ... you simpleminded idiot," he screamed, gasping. "I shipped you off to him ... "

He let go of the bedrail and collapsed onto the mattress.

I dropped my head into my hands. "Oh, Jesus." I turned toward the wall radiator and started hammering my fist into the metal grillwork, creating a racket that must have been heard down the long hall.

The door flew open, and a white gown rushed over to Jonathan's bedside. She glowered at me on the floor.

Speaking quietly, between erratic breaths, Jonathan said, slowly, "I'm ... okay, Jessica."

He looked over at me as I massaged my bruised fist. "My boyfriend here ... is just having a little temper tantrum." He added, "He's upset about my ... long ... drawn-out ... suicide."

I stormed past Jessica, ran the length of the hallway, tore down the stairwell at the end and out through the main doors, into the park. My feet slipped from under me on the snow-covered frozen sidewalk. I went down on my bum with a thud, my hands breaking the fall slightly, getting badly scraped in the process. I sat there, panting. I looked at my hands and saw little flecks of red emerging from amongst the grey slosh and bits of gravel. When I raised my head, I saw the two street people on the bench watching me. One of them lifted the paper bag-covered bottle in my direction.

Chapter 57 ————————————

Walter had been out of the house twice in the preceding eight years, once to emergency in 2004 when he had his second major stroke and then for another hospitalization after a third stroke in 2007.

He was adamant that he wanted to visit Jonathan. He had been putting up a ruckus for weeks. His pre-stroke lifelong stubbornness had become exacerbated by post-stroke, dementia-fueled obstinacy—loud, irascible, food-throwing, plate-breaking, Trevor-taxing, Margaret-despairing obstinacy.

I was put in charge of arranging the logistics.

We arrived an hour later than planned, delayed by the residue of the previous night's vicious snowstorm. March had come in like a lion. Trevor wheeled Walter down the corridor while his entourage—Margaret, Rosalie, and me—trundled after them.

Sheila was reading in the window chair. She got up immediately and offered the chair to Margaret who collapsed gratefully into it. Trevor brought the wheelchair up as close to the bed as he could manage. Walter sat immobilized, his eyes transfixed on the motionless heap of covers.

Jonathan was sound asleep. I went around to the other side of the bed and gently rubbed his arm. "Darling," I whispered. "Your father is here. And your mother." He stirred a bit but did not come to. I looked over my shoulder at Margaret, who looked back, a big question mark in her eyes.

I grasped the bed rails and took a deep breath. "We may not get a lot out of Jonathan today," I started.

Sheila let out a cough that said, "Are you sure you should tell them?"

I glanced at her, winced, and nodded affirmatively. "They changed some of his medication yesterday. It's making him dopier. But it will hopefully reduce the pain."

Walter did not register that he heard what I said.

Rosalie started whimpering. Trevor stepped over and grasped her hand.

I approached Walter. He had still not moved; he just stared at his son. I crouched down beside his chair and placed my arm on his. He flinched and quietly shook my hand away.

He started to mumble. I leaned close to hear him better. The words were indecipherable, the sound guttural, a deep baritone monotone varying sporadically in pitch, wavering unevenly, on and on.

Trevor came over and knelt on the other side of the wheelchair; he looked at Walter, who seemed oblivious to his presence. He glared at the bed, his vocalizing continuing uninterrupted.

Trevor stood up and smiled. Softly, in time with Walter, he began singing, hesitantly at first, catching Walter's rhythm. "Yes ... loves me ... tells me so."

With Trevor humming the accompaniment, Walter sat up straighter in his chair and started singing louder, and more discernibly, the three remaining verses, word for word. His voice wobbled only once, when he sang the line, "*Jesus loves me! loves me still, Tho' I'm very weak and ill ...*"

Chapter 58

"**Do** you think that's wise? Isn't it a bit risky?" Carolyn asked. The connection from Kabul was clear. On earlier calls, static had been noticeable, confirming her suspicion that phones at the Women for Peace and Development office were tapped.

"That's a good one!" I laughed, a rare emotional response these days. I placed the glass back down on the kitchen table and dabbed at the drops of wine that I had splattered on my chin. "You're sitting in the middle of a war zone, lecturing me about risk."

"Yeah. Well, you probably didn't detect much conviction in my voice."

"I've certainly heard you speaking with more conviction. Very many times, my dear."

I ran my finger around the top of the glass and recalled with a smile such jousting matches with Carolyn over the decades.

"I'm more worried about the strain on you," she said. "I think that the move itself makes sense. Jonathan would be more comfortable at home in familiar surroundings. Though after two months, the hospital room must be feeling like home to him. But what about you? Do you honestly think that you can cope with all the physical work on top of the emotional toll?"

"I'll have help—quite a bit, actually—nurses, homemakers. Whatever I need."

I reached across the table and pulled the white binder over in front of me. Checkmarks peppered the categories of ranges of services needed. The urgency of response section held a single row of checks down the left-hand column. Highest priority meant substantive assistance. Highest priority meant dire prognosis.

"But what about the more technical medical issues?"

"Done. We'll be visited as needed by a palliative care doctor."

There followed a long pause, interspersed with the sound of static. Or maybe sniffling.

"Carolyn? Are you still there?"

"Oh, my darling … they've really concluded that this is … 'palliative'?"

"We're stage four, my dear." I burst out laughing.

"What is funny about that?"

"I said, 'we're stage four.' Just like when straights say 'we're pregnant.'"

Carolyn laughed too. Then she stopped laughing. Abruptly. She was silent for a few moments. I bit my tongue. There are so many trip words in everyday conversation. After Jeremy's death, Jonathan and I would flinch whenever anyone joked, "The performance was so bad, I thought I'd kill myself." Or after Mom and Dad's deaths when someone would jest, "You slay me." Such inconsequential, mundane, virtually unavoidable catchphrases suddenly took on an excruciating weight. If friends realized what they had said, we would all plunge into an awkward moment: an apology was offered, met with a no-need-for-an-apology dismissal. Or we would all feign not to have noticed, usually unconvincingly. At this moment, I was the offender and Carolyn the offended, after all these many years. The two of us, wordlessly, opted for the self-conscious, feigned option of not noticing.

"In that case, I think that I should come home. Wajdi is encouraging me to. He'll hold the fort here."

"Babes, you don't need to do that. We've got lots of friends who are lending willing hands. Sheila's been a brick. We have no idea how long this could go on. He could survive quite a while. He's got a strong heart. Besides, you're involved in good stuff there. How is the film coming along, by the way?"

"Slowly, very slowly. The security situation is awful. We've got people in Taliban territory who want to help us, but they're afraid. The Karzai government is so rife with corruption, and they're suspicious of anyone who might be raising critical questions. So we're getting almost no help from that side. Kind of caught in the middle."

"Familiar terrain for you."

"Yeah. Certainly is. But I want to see Jonathan, and I desperately want to see you."

"Well, do as you like. You know I'd love to have you here, but I don't want to impose."

"Jesus Christ, Tom. Will you get over that?"

Sheila, Markus, and I surveyed the potential rooms in the house and concluded that the living room was most appropriate. I made a pro/con list.

Pro—it was the largest room and could thus accommodate the hospital bed most easily. It had a view out onto the street, which might help relieve Jonathan's boredom. It had easy access to the kitchen and to the bathroom. It could most easily handle the various coming and going caregivers and family and friends dropping around to visit. It would be in the middle of the action.

Con—it would be in the middle of the action.

Markus helped me move the furniture around and disassemble the sofa.

On schedule, the Medigas truck arrived, and the driver brought in the various components of the bed. We watched as he expertly put it together and hooked up the electrical connection. He demonstrated the simple mechanics of adjusting it to various positions. I signed the sheet, verifying delivery of one hospital bed and one commode.

He left.

Sheila, Markus, and I sat down in the room and stared at the bed, still vacant until the transfer this afternoon.

Jonathan was not a happy camper.

"Grand Central Station in the middle of rush hour. Anytime anyone comes in, bam, I am what they see. More to the point, bam, they are what I see the moment they arrive. Bam, bam, and bam again. I'll feel stuck on display, like some monster foetus in a formaldehyde jar. Oh, and that's a really lovely decorating touch. A commode? In our living room? Jesus, Tom this is worse than the bloody hospital. You should have just left me there."

The ambulance attendant looked at me with a mixture of sympathy and impatience. We had to get Jonathan out of the wheelchair so that he could get on with his next transfer.

I invoked his patron saint in hopes that she would carry more weight. "I'm sorry, Jonathan, but Sheila, Markus, and I spent quite a bit of time trying to figure out which room could accommodate the bed best, and this was our consensus."

"That's just the point, you shit-head," he snarled. "You tried to figure out what room could best accommodate the bed, not what room could best accommodate me."

"Well, okay, dear, where do you think that you and the bed would be better placed?"

"I don't know about the bed. But I know where I want you to put me."

"Yes?"

"There's a little corner behind the furnace in the basement. It's where I store the filters. We can just scatter a few of them on the floor, and I'll sleep there. Quiet. Dark. And I won't have to put up with your mug in my face, or anyone else's, every other minute. 'Can I get you anything, darling?' 'Time for another pill, love.' 'Do you need to go potty, sweetie?'"

The attendant chuckled and then caught himself.

"We'll try and figure out something better. In the meantime, can we get you out of the chair and on to the bed so that this fellow can be on his way?"

"Put me in the armchair over there. I'm not getting in that bed."

"But, darling, you're quite weak, and I'm not sure that I alone will be able to move you from the chair to the bed later. It would be better while this ambulance fellow ... sorry, I don't know your name ..."

"Sergio."

"... while Sergio is here to help me, it would be better if we got you up and into the bed."

"Do you not have your hearing aids in, grandpa? I said *armchair*. There." Jonathan stretched out his arm, pointing to his intended destination. His arm wobbled. He let it fall into his lap. He glared at me. "Armchair. Now. Armchair. Now. Armchair. Now. Armchair ..."

"Okay, okay." I nodded at Sergio, who wheeled him past the bed to the armchair. He put on the brakes and lifted the footpads. With me on the other side, we supported Jonathan under his armpits and gently raised him out of the wheelchair. Sergio, with expert dexterity, used one leg to move the locked wheelchair out of the way as we turned Jonathan around and eased his bum down into the armchair.

"Thank you, Sergio," I said, a little winded.

"You're welcome, sir. Sorry, but I need to be off." He turned toward Jonathan and extended his hand. "Nice to meet you, sir." Jonathan didn't respond. His chin was down against his chest, his eyes closed,

his shoulders slumped. The course breathing of a gradually emerging
snore was his good-bye.

Some of the signatures I didn't recognize, or I couldn't make out their
handwriting. It must have taken days for Fernando to circulate the
card to so many departments. More likely, he'd sent Patricia to schlep
it around from floor to floor.

I placed the card, tenderly, with the dozens of others in the small
wicker basket that I had positioned on the kitchen table in the middle
of the syringes, boxes of alcohol swabs, sterilizing hand sanitizer gels,
prescription bottles, packages of latex gloves, jars of hypoallergenic skin
moisturizing cream, and the baby wipes dispenser with the pretty blue
and white cloud pattern. I intended the cards of well wishes to somehow
bless the medicinal aids surrounding them.

My e-mail box was filling with messages of concern and support
from Jonathan's staff and students and from former students now in
teaching positions around the world, from my colleagues, from our
friends, near and far.

But the old-fashioned paper cards, with handwritten messages
in envelopes to which each sender had affixed a stamp in the upper
right corner, which was duly cancelled by a postal sorting machine
somewhere, and then delivered lovingly into our mail box by close-
to-retirement Tompkins, held a particular pride of place in the wicker
basket in the midst of our domestic healthcare centre.

I wasn't able to bring myself to read the little notes that Fernando
and company had written when they signed. I would, sometime, when
I had a moment, and the energy.

"Well, here's to you. I guess." I held up my wine glass, and Carolyn clicked
hers against it. "It's not a threesome that I would have predicted."

She looked down into her wine. "I know. Neither would I. But for
some reason, it's working. I think that it's partly based on need, and
partly based on something that we have to offer each other."

"You'll need to explain that. I'm not grasping the concept."

"Well, Margaret fancies herself in something of a maternal role
with me. And, frankly ..." She paused. Then, looking me straight in
the eye, she said without flinching, "Frankly, I welcome it. After all
these years of traipsing around the world, and after the horrendous

unresolvedness of Mom and Dad's deaths, which eats at me every day like a cancer ..." She stopped short and cocked her head toward the living room. "Sorry."

"Don't worry, darling. We're long past avoiding the big C word within Jonathan's hearing."

"It's good to have a mother again."

"Huh. And you and Walter?"

Carolyn rolled her eyes and chuckled. "We have big fights. I read him the *Globe and Mail* every day, editorializing like crazy as I go, and he grunts and flaps his wings. Occasionally, he can get out a semi-coherent phrase that I can understand. We argue through this fractured communication system for a while and then laugh. He tires quickly, of course. My presence takes some of the load off of Margaret."

"I must say it comes as a surprise." This was a Carolyn moment, so I didn't want to elaborate. Some time later, I would tell her how much of a relief it was. I had been having nightmares about the prospect of having to look after Walter and Margaret after Jonathan was gone, with what little energy reserves I would have left. Added to that, my viral load had been spiking of late. We were in the midst of experimenting with some of the newer cocktail variations to get it back under control.

"There's another piece," Carolyn said quietly. She looked out the kitchen window and blinked several times. "They've offered me ... Jeremy's old room."

"My God!"

Misinterpreting my reaction, she added quickly, "Oh, I'll stay here for as long as you need me. I'd move over there only after ..."

"Yes, yes of course. I understand. I just meant ..." I don't know what I'd just meant, except that it was good. I reached across the table and took her hand. "I'm very happy for all three of you. Really."

Sensing that the conversation might be edging precariously close to the maudlin, Carolyn, true to form, switched gears. "And what do you hear from our precious older sister?"

"Not much, really. She has called a couple of times. Expressed her condolences. But there's always some excuse why she can't come up. Not that I really want her to. Your histrionics are enough for me to handle without having to put up with her condescension and judgment."

She kicked me under the table. Twice.

"Ouch! Ouch!"

"That first one was for the dig at me." She smirked. I smirked back. "The second was on Patricia's behalf. I do hope, at some point, the two of you get reconciled a bit more. Still stuck with calling her condescending and judgmental? Really, Tom, that's so passé, so 1970s sibling rivalry. She does have a good heart, you know."

"My God, look at you. All forgiving and forgetting."

"Yeah, well, over the past twenty-odd years, I've seen how people live in many different parts of the world ..."

"As have I."

"I know. But you're a slow learner." My turn to kick her under the table. I resisted.

"And ... well ..." she continued hesitantly, "... life's too short to bear grudges. And too much of an energy drain."

I laughed. "Oh, you and Margaret are going to get on swimmingly."

"What do you mean?"

"Have you read any Eckhart Tolle?"

Chapter 59

Jocelyn looked up from her knitting as I came into the living room. "Having trouble sleeping?" she whispered.

"Yeah." I glanced up at our grandfather clock, its soft heartbeat echoing throughout this sanctuary. A little after three in the morning I sat down beside Jonathan's bed. "I shouldn't be. Maybe overtired."

"Would you like me to make you a cup of tea or hot chocolate?" Her Jamaican accent was as lyrical as a Mozart quintet.

"Thank you. Tea, I think."

She headed off into the kitchen.

"Wouldn't mind … a cup myself," came the thin voice from underneath the covers.

"Oh, you're awake."

"I'm having … trouble sleeping. Probably … overtired."

I paused a moment too long, trying to figure out what that indicated.

Jonathan's hand reached up slowly and pulled the top sheet down a few inches. He turned his head in my direction. "That was … supposed to be … a joke," he said quietly. "Have you … lost your … sense of humour?"

I smiled. "Sorry. I'm not as quick on my feet these days."

"Well, can you … be quick with your fingers … and give me … my favourite … candy?" I grabbed the pill bottle, flipped off the cap, and dropped one of the magics into my palm. Cupping my right arm around his shoulders, I slowly raised Jonathan's head a few inches off his pillow. His mouth was already open, and I placed the caplet inside. He winced as I reached back for the glass of water. Tilting the glass slowly, I poured a small rivulet of water into his mouth. He closed up and screwed his eyes tight as he struggled to swallow. His starkly exposed Adam's apple rode up and down several times until he let out a deep sigh. I lowered him back onto the pillow and withdrew my arm.

We sat quietly for a couple minutes. I expected him to fall off to sleep. He surprised me.

"We should ... talk about ... my funeral."

"Oh. Okay. Have you been thinking about what you'd want?"

I heard Jocelyn moving toward us. I looked at her, held up my hand, and pointed toward the bed. She decoded my sign language and tiptoed back into the kitchen.

"No ... but I assume ... you have."

"Well, yes, I have. You're right. And I've had a brief conversation about it with your mother."

"Mommy ... wants ... the Toronto ... Symphony. Daddy ... probably ... a brass band."

I had never heard him call them Mommy and Daddy.

"Well, you're on somewhat the right track. They would both like a lot of music. I certainly second that."

"Dad's been ... talking?"

"Off and on. It's difficult to understand him. Thank goodness for Trevor. And Carolyn has been spending time with him. So yes, he has seemed to rally a little."

"Makes ... sense."

"How so?"

"He's got ... a new ... project ... worrying about ... me." Jonathan was speaking painfully slowly but surprisingly clearly. "He loves ... challenge ... He's been ... going crazy ... feeling miserable ... about himself and ... what he's inflicting ... on Mom ... Hmm ... Sounds familiar ... closer to ... home."

A series of thin coughs slipped from his throat, accompanied by a stream of thin saliva. I dabbed gently at his lips with a tissue.

"Well, then you better not die soon, or you'll truncate your dad's raison-d'être."

"Clever strategy ... you schmuck ... I guess ... you're not just ... a pretty face ... after all." His eyes winced in a pain spasm. I watched as it contorted his whole face. It took two or three minutes to pass before the painkiller kicked in more fully. I expected now he would fall asleep.

More softly than before, he repeated, "Funeral."

"You sure you're up for talking about this now?"

"Please don't ... make me waste ... breath ... repeating myself," he whispered.

355

"Sorry," I replied, chastened.

"What I want ... is nothing."

I didn't respond. Now was not the time to argue with him. A minute passed.

"Gotcha."

"What?"

"I know ... there'll be ... something ... I just ... wanted to ... rile you ... a bit."

"Clever strategy, you schmuck. I guess you're not just a pretty face after all."

He coughed several times, as a chuckle sought release from his increasingly constricted chest cavity. Dr. Singh had told me yesterday that, in all likelihood, his lungs were gradually collapsing.

After a few moments, he found enough energy to continue. "Just ... no ... eternal life ... stuff ... okay?"

"I know you don't believe in any kind of afterlife." I wanted to put the right words in his mouth to relieve him of the effort of having to explain himself.

"And ... you do."

"Well. Yes, of some kind."

"And ... so?"

"I need you at least to acknowledge the possibility that this ... ain't all there is."

"So ... it's not ... about me ... but about ... you."

"Yes, I guess so. In part."

"Well ... enough of the ... preamble then ... geez ... you can be so ... bloody wordy ... get on with it ..."

"Right. Sorry. Okay, here goes. There has to more than just this ..." I swept my hand around to encompass the room, the world, physical life, a gesture lost on one whose eyes were again shuttered tight in pain. I scurried on. I didn't have much time. He hadn't been this attentive or lucid in a week.

"There has to be more, I think, because ... because ... of love and memory."

He said something, but I couldn't make it out. I leaned my ear closer to his mouth. "What did you say?"

"Never ... mind ... go on ..." His breathing was becoming very laboured.

"We love each other so much, you and me. We have forever. It's not been without rough spots, but they're minor compared to how much we love each other."

I didn't give him time for rebuttal.

"Love itself, in all its many guises, between the two of us, between a mother and child …" I swallowed hard. "What you felt and still feel for Jeremy …" I pressed on, ignoring the gyrating sheet. "Love can't just be a bunch of brain synapses jumping around and then disappearing when we stop breathing. It is physical, but it is far more than that. I'd call it spiritual, maybe even God. I know you wouldn't."

I spoke rapidly. Jonathan could no longer speak quickly, but he could hear quickly.

"You have to acknowledge that it defies clinical or scientific or philosophical explanation. And I hope that you can grant that our love will, in some unknowable way, persist beyond your … death."

I stopped. He was quiet. The sheet moved up and down, slightly, slowly. I stood up and leaned over the bed rail, trying to see in the dimness whether his eyes were open.

They were closed.

For a moment.

Until they opened.

He didn't try to speak. He just stared at me. We hovered there, suspended viscerally in each other's orbits, heads not six inches apart.

In a quieter, quivering voice, I continued. "Then there is memory. You've dedicated your life to keeping alive the thoughts, the insights, the brilliance of your predecessors. Aristotle. Kierkegaard. Hegel. Heidegger. Foucault, for God's sake. You've taught and written about them and their ideas. You incorporated them in your work, improved on them, I dare say. You've brought them into public discourse inside the classroom and beyond. They are alive because of you. You and many others, of course … let's not get carried away."

I looked for the trace of a smile. Nothing. But he was still with me.

His eyes. Oh God, those eyes.

"They are not dusty, forgotten lives and ideas from yesteryear. They are vibrant, vital forces in the world, memories and ideas that live and thrive. That is an indisputable reality of some kind of ongoing life force that trumps physical death."

With his eyes still glued to mine, he took short jerky breaths. His brows furrowed. The sheet started twitching. He moved his eyes down to the sheet, then back to mine, then down to his chest, and then back up. Back and forth.

"What is it, dear?" I tried to keep the panic out of my voice.

His eyes kept going up and down and up and down. I lowered the sheet and touched the back of his hand, which was trembling on top of his chest. In a flash, he flipped it over and grabbed one of my fingers in his palm. He squeezed. His eyes locked onto mine.

Gradually, he loosened the grip, but not the eye contact. His frenetic breathing subsided.

His eyelids fluttered. Three times, slowly, deliberately. A pause. Then, three blinks again, same measured pace.

"I love you too," I said.

He let go of my hand. I wiped my cheeks and his.

His eyes closed. His breathing quieted.

A few minutes later, he started to snore.

Chapter 60

For five minutes, just inside his door, I held on to Alan, an embrace into which I had thrown myself. I had been driving around the still-deserted early morning streets of Toronto, making a decision. I was cold, and nervous.

Eventually, he led me over to the sofa and gently guided me down, not for a moment breaking physical contact. I moved slightly to put breathing space between us.

"I'm glad you came," Alan said. "It's been, what, almost three months?" He put his hand on my scalp and massaged gently.

I raised my arm over my head, took hold of his hand, and brought it down onto my chest, giving it a little kiss on the way past. "Nothing is going to happen tonight. Sorry."

He put his arm back around my shoulder and squeezed.

I looked out over the well-appointed condo that I had come to know so well, out his living room window. The faintest etching of the morning sunrise was dabbled precariously on a thick layer of cloud.

"Tonight ..." I began.

"Yes?"

I wiggled free and turned on the sofa to face him. "This is good-bye, Alan."

"My dear Tom," he said, smiling benignly. "You're under an intolerable amount of strain. Have been for weeks, months. You're in no state to make any decisions. That's my personal and professional opinion."

I smiled back. "Unfortunately, I am thinking clearly."

He reached over and tried to pull me back toward him. I resisted. I got up off the sofa and walked to the window.

"Well, then, you're going to have to explain your clear thinking to me because I'm not following."

"It's quite simple really. Not pretty. But it is simple." It was best said without looking at him. "Jonathan is ten blocks away, probably within hours of dying. I think he and I may have said our good-byes tonight. I know, and you know, that I don't love you the way that I love Jonathan. Since this has already been a night with one excruciating good-bye, I need to complete the circle and say good-bye to you …"

I watched his reflection in the window.

"… the other lover in my life." I had to give him something.

Alan got up and joined me at the window; he stood behind me and wrapped his arms around me. The sun was a visible sliver on the horizon. "That just shows how irrational you are right now. Because Jonathan is so close to death, you need me in your life more than ever."

He was correct. But correct doesn't mean right.

I laid my hands on his clasped hands on my chest. "From your perspective, from a rational perspective, what you say makes sense," I said. "But I am standing on a precipice here. This is a time of ending. With Jonathan's death, my life as it has been is over … and you, my dear, are part of that former life."

"I'm sorry, 'my dear' …" He turned me around, a rapidly hardening expression setting into his eyes. "But your sentimental imagery leaves me cold." We were face to face. "Feels to me that I am the one on the precipice and you are giving me a hefty shove. I know that you're upset about Jonathan. Obviously. It's understandable why you wanted to come over here to be held. But what makes you think that you can explode this bomb in my face and then walk away? I have some say in this matter. About us, the post-Jonathan you and me."

He was scaring me. I took hold of his hand and guided us back to the sofa. I sat down and pulled him down to sit beside me.

"I've been party to two screwed-up relationships," I said.

I hoped it didn't sound too rehearsed, which it was.

"With Jonathan, his drinking was a problem from early on, but I made excuses for him. I ignored stuff. I chalked it up to the stress of his work and then to the Jeremy business. I was too busy flying around the world to help him sort through the mess after Jeremy died and too much of a coward to force him to stop the drinking. Jeremy was a huge part of it for Jonathan, but … my testing positive was a huge part, too. Far bigger than I had imagined."

Alan leapt up. "For God's sake, Tom, he was a mature adult.

He made his own decisions. You're not responsible for his pathetic weaknesses."

If I had had any qualms, I didn't anymore.

"With us, well … I think we both screwed up. I won't make judgments about your part of it. I know that I had power, and I know that I used it—giving and withholding, to suit myself. You put your life on hold waiting for me, when I had no intention of coming over. I told you that. But I didn't act like I meant it."

"I'm not just going to let you walk away, you bastard. It's not that bloody simple."

"Alan. It is that simple. I am walking away. I'm sorry."

I got up. We stood facing each other. We were three feet apart, physically.

Neither of us said anything. We just stared at each other.

I tried not to blink.

Eventually, he did.

And then, he asked quietly, "And where does this leave you?"

"You're right about the precipice imagery being sort of off base. Not to mention hokey."

That brought a bit of a smile.

"This is about me saying good-bye. To Jonathan, not by choice. To you, by choice. After that, I don't know. A long walk in a desert somewhere. No precipices. Just empty, barren terrain. Alone."

I leaned in and gave him the briefest of kisses. "Good-bye, my darling."

I moved toward the door and then suddenly stopped. A glimmer flashed through his eyes. I reached in my pocket. "Your key." I tossed it to him, turned, and left.

Chapter 61 —————————

Three angry sets of female eyes greeted me as I came in the door.

"Why don't you have your cell phone on?" Carolyn demanded. "We've been calling every five minutes for the past two hours." I pulled it out of my pocket and realized that I hadn't turned it on when I left the house earlier.

"Shit! I'm sorry. How is he?"

"Not good, Mr. Tom." Jocelyn's eyes reflected disappointment, trumping her anger. "He's been breathing real bad. I stayed in the kitchen a long time listening to him, but I didn't want to disturb you two. Eventually, I can't stand it no more and I peek around the corner, and you're not there. He's all alone. So I hurry over and he's awake and breathing real bad, just like now." Her words were accompanied by a background cacophony of gasping and coughing. "So I run up and bring Miss Carolyn down from upstairs."

Sheila had been standing off to the side, but now she came over and stopped within inches of me. She walked completely around me, coming to a halt directly in front of my face. She sniffed me, like a tracker dog. She turned her head slightly and spat on the floor. Carolyn and Jocelyn gasped. After one last furious glare, she turned on her heels and walked over to Jonathan's bed.

"I know it sounds awful but it doesn't necessarily indicate the end. This could go on for quite some time," Dr. Singh whispered, as she stepped back from the bed. "The breathing patterns will vary considerably. When the end comes, he may be gasping for breath like he is now ..."

Jonathan let out another guttural, erratic series of gasps, as if on cue. Standing around the bed, we all watched as his body shook.

"... or his breathing may subside and be very shallow and quiet and eventually just stop. It's hard to tell."

"But what do you think? How close is it?" Sheila wanted something less ambiguous.

Dr. Singh shrugged her shoulders. "I'm sorry. There's no way of telling. It could be shortly. It could be today. Or he could hang on for another few days. His heart seems strong, so …"

"Dammit!" We all turned to look at Carolyn. "Dammit. This is hell."

Wajdi took hold of her hand, raised it to his lips, and gave her the most tender of kisses.

Sheila put her arm around Carolyn's shoulders and gave her a tight squeeze. "I know it is, baby. But we're not in control of this."

Carolyn shook herself free from Sheila. "Are you giving me the 'it's all in God's hands now' sort of bullshit?"

Sheila laughed. At the sound, so unaccustomed in this room, Jonathan's breathing immediately quieted. We all pivoted back to watch him. His chest had stopped moving. His eyes were closed. His mouth was wide open, nothing going in or coming out. We waited. And waited. And then he started breathing again.

"Apnoea," Dr. Singh said. "Long periods, maybe forty-five seconds or so without any breathing, and then he'll suddenly start breathing again. The pattern can repeat itself over and over, ad infinitum."

"You really mean ad finitum, don't you?" Sheila laughed again. She was one tough cookie, and she had me firmly ensconced in a doghouse of my own making at the moment, but I loved her. I looked at Jonathan and prayed that he was conscious enough to hear her laughter.

Turning back to Carolyn, Sheila said, "No, my dear. You'll get no God talk from me. I was referring to Johnny boy. He'll stick around as long as he wants, and he'll take his leave of us whenever he wants. Damn stubborn bastard. Always was, always will be." Another laugh as she slapped her own cheek. "Did it myself. No 'always' about this situation. No way."

Singh was right. So was Sheila. Another day came and went. But Jonathan didn't.

The sun had set. I turned his iPod to one his favourite playlists, quiet Baroque.

I went into the bedroom and lay down for a nap.

I woke up with a start.

The clock on the night table said 10:20 p.m.

I got up and walked into the living room to check on Jonathan. I sat down in the chair beside the bed and took his hand.

The shallow, quiet breathing that had been the norm during the day shifted into high gear. He started breathing deeply and audibly. I tightened my grip. I thought that his right eye might have been slightly open, but I couldn't tell for sure.

One time more, I said, "Good-bye, my darling. I love you."

More deep loud breathing came, for about five minutes.

Then it stopped.

Chapter 62 ———————————

Snow should have been falling, or at least a cold drizzle. Incongruously, the cemetery was bathed in pale March sunshine.

Jonathan would have appreciated my objection.

The groundskeeper had removed the marble cover. Below the niche, a green velvet cloth draped the small stand on which rested the cherrywood urn.

Gradually, the few that I'd invited for the interment arrived and embraced me quietly.

My stomach was taut. My throat was dry. My gaze alternated between the urn and the bare, hard ground of the little garden adjacent the columbarium. A few months from now, it would flourish with geraniums and marigolds. At the moment, there was no sign of life.

I concentrated, so as to slow the progression of those moments. I was not ready for the finality of the occasion.

Thirty-four years would not become thirty-five.

The memorial service the previous week had been different. The service swelled with music and tributes.

The church was packed with friends and neighbours, my colleagues, Jonathan's faculty peers, students of his, past and present. Sheila and Markus. Margaret and Walter, slouched over in his wheelchair. Carolyn and Wajdi. Patricia, Robert, Naomi, and Luke.

An empty place for Jeremy.

Two empty spaces for Mom and Dad.

Excruciating, intolerable vacancies.

That was then, this was now.

There would be no music today. Only a few words.

Ultimately, silence.

Epilogue

Are you sure that you are up for this, Mein Freund?

The unfamiliar voice and the presumptuous question startle me. Irritated, I glance around, having been interrupted as I perused the program notes for the opening concert of the Toronto Symphony's fall season.

The seat beside me at Roy Thomson Hall—Jonathan's—is vacant. I could have offered it to someone. As much as I love Sheila, I wouldn't have been able to tolerate her chatter. Not on this, my first time back to a TSO concert since his death in March. Carolyn and Wajdi are in Kabul for a brief visit with their film crew. Margaret is at home with Walter. There is no one else in my life, no one close enough to invite into this intimate time and space.

For the past six months, I have found solace only in solitude. Tonight will be no different.

The other long-term subscribers who usually sit around us have not yet arrived. They are probably lingering over dessert and coffee at the opening night patrons' dinner next door. I had made an early, discrete exit, exhausted by the condolences from acquaintances who hadn't seen me since the funeral and by the effort that it took to lie in response to the inevitable "How are you doing?"

The Kitteralls take their seats in the row ahead. Jonas and Babs smile at me, nod, and then, thankfully, leave me in peace.

I turn back to the booklet to pick up where I had left off.

Interesting piece of programming for you, all things considered. I called the first movement Todtenfeier. *Jonathan, being the fine German scholar that he was, could have told you what that is. It means funeral rites.*

I stare at the page. Mahler isn't looking directly back at me but rather off to the right—his left. Wireless glasses, much like my own, rest on his nose. The artist's rendering makes him appear more serene than actual photographs of him in the 1890s, and younger looking than the thirty-four years he was when he completed the Second Symphony. The mouth forms too much of a smile in the drawing, but the eyes are good. Tense. Brooding. Windows of the soul.

Shuffling sounds around me indicate the arrival of the almost-latecomers. The lights dim. I close the program booklet and drop it onto the floor. I shake my head vigorously back and forth a couple times and bring one hand up to my face to stretch the skin around my eyes, strategies for waking myself up from whatever this was.

Peter Oundjian stands with his hands clasped in front of his waist and pauses, head bowed, letting the murmuring in the hall subside. When all is quiet, he slowly raises both arms to shoulder height.

With a taut, almost imperceptible jerk of his wrists, a crevice breaks open—a kilometre wide and a universe deep.

The violins and violas pounce on to a *fortissimo* G. Not a vibrant G of a major key but a menacing G from the depths of C minor. C for Compton. Minor—not in stature but in tangibility. Immediately, a tremolo to *pianissimo*. I hover above the abyss, weightless, shuddering.

I am knocked off balance by the sudden growl of cellos and basses. A run of five-sixteenth notes, including one strategic accidental. Aggressively *triple forte*. Then repeated *fortissimo*, elaborated in length, with more accidentals, transforming into triplets at a diminishing volume until they reach *pianissimo*. All the while backdropped by the vapourous, shimmering violins and violas, neither light angelic, nor dark demonic. Just watching, waiting, guarded, intimidating.

For seventeen bars. Half the number of years we had been together. Capturing the essence of my precariousness. Nothing to grab a hold of. Vulnerable to plummeting. But somehow, not plummeting. Caught. Suspended. Somewhere.

The oboes and English horns place a sliver of stability under foot. *Piano.* Not insecurely, deliberately, self-confidently. Quietly posing the questions, giving no answers.

Like the, '*Is there life after death?*' that is whispered in my ear. He is back. Or hasn't left.

If I believe my lecture to Jonathan on his death bed about love and memory, I should be less distressed than I am. Regretfully, the platitudes have lost their vibrancy. "He'll live on in your heart." "You'll be comforted by all your wonderful memories." Like hell. My memories serve not to comfort. Rather, they reinforce how much I have lost.

I was missing a person who I loved deeply too, when I wrote this. Hear those plaintive horns, rising with ever increasing intensity, and those repeated chords crashing one after another? I was standing by his coffin, trying to make sense of his life with all its struggles, passions, and aspirations. I kept asking myself, "What now? What is this life and this death? Do we have an existence beyond it?"

Well, Gustav, old man, don't look to me for answers. I have a question of my own.

Where is that balm of Gilead to make our wounds whole, to heal our sickened souls?

Peter Oundjian takes what seems an extended pause after the climactic conclusion to the first movement.

I like this. I had originally decreed a five-minute break between the first and second movements to allow the audience to make the transition.

Well, I think that would be a bit excessive for the modern concertgoer.

It's important that one not be in such a rush that you miss out on life's essence.

I chuckle. Oops. Did I do that out loud? Babs turns around and gives me a modestly scolding glance. Now look at what you made me do. I was laughing about your "life's essence" remark. From what I understand, you indulged quite a bit in life's essences with your tempestuous love affairs.

And what of it? My time with my various mistresses was full of life and vibrancy and excitement, as well as the drama and heartache. But Mein Freund, let your mind wander as the orchestra plays the second movement. It is so light and graceful and exuberant. Think back. You must surely have had the experience of burying someone who was very dear to you, and then, as you leave the gravesite, you remember some long forgotten experiences of shared happiness, and it is as if a sunbeam sweeps into your soul, obliterating, for a moment, the reality of what you've just been through.

Peter brings up his baton. I close my eyes. The strings begin delicately. Three-quarter time, a quiet, affectionate waltz. I smile as the music evokes candlelight and laughter, as at a party in a Jane Austen novel.

And then a succession of other images flood in.

Snuggled together in our cabin suite, we watched the sun set over Venice as the Orient Express pulled out of the station. After dressing into our tuxedos, we were ready for dinner. Just as we came out of our compartment, the train lurched slightly to the side. Jonathan caught me and gave me a gratuitous squeeze. We made our way through the bar car, where Jean-Jacques winked at us as he played "Misty" on the grand piano. Andreas met us at the dining car entrance, greeted us with a warm smile and a "*Buona sera, i signori,*" escorted us to our table, held our chairs as we sat down, and then handed us the evening's menu. To the annoyance of a couple across the aisle that seemed anxious to use us as their audience, Jonathan and I secluded ourselves in our own romantic bubble, conversing softly, laughing regularly, and making our way through several bottles of fine wine with the various courses. We finished dinner just shy of midnight, and we headed back to our cabin. Once inside, I pressed the steward button. Vincenzo tapped lightly. I opened the door and gave him an order for two cognacs. Some considerable time later, I slipped out from Jonathan's sleeping embrace and into my own bed.

Margaret and I smiled at each other as we simultaneously noticed Jeremy pacing with nervous excitement outside the front door of the Art Gallery of Ontario. He ran toward us and grabbed hold of Margaret's arm, almost throwing her off balance as he rushed her through the front door. We were surprised when he led us, at breakneck speed, not toward the exhibition of new contemporary Canadian art where his *The Kiss* was on display, but instead into a smaller room of recent Aboriginal acquisitions.

With laughter and tears intermingled and with arms flapping hysterically, he jumped and skipped in front of the vibrant Norvel Morrisseau painting, *Self-Portrait—Devoured by His Demons,* extolling to us his unfettered ecstasy at the passion that it exuded.

The rain kept us inside the tent playing cards. Eventually, Patricia, Carolyn, and I were sufficiently exhausted to be persuaded to bed with only modest protests. About two o'clock in the morning, a horrendous crash jarred all of us awake, stupefying Mom and Dad and terrifying us kids. Hours worth of rainwater had accumulated in the sagging roof of the add-on, eventually reaching a weight that overwhelmed the aluminium poles holding it erect. The supports gave way, and the mini-lake exploded down onto our doorstep, with more than a little water seeping in through the zippered front flap. We slept for the rest of the night in the car, initially somewhat traumatized, but by morning, we were quite thrilled by the unexpected addition to our summer camping adventure.

Sweet memories, Tom.
Yes. You are right, Gustav. Thank you for that.

The timpani reverberates into my reveries like a crash of thunder.
Sorry. I feel compelled to awaken you from that blissful dreaming and force you to return to this tangled life of ours.
The jarring introduction to the third movement progresses into a sweeping series of orchestral waves, some of which appear lighthearted and others of which exude robust energy. But there is something untrustworthy going on, an ominousness disguised as innocence.
It may easily happen that the surge of life, ceaselessly in motion, never resting, never comprehensible, suddenly seems eerie, like the billowing, dancing figures in a brightly lit ballroom that you gaze into from outside, in the dark—and from a distance so great that you can no longer hear the music. Then the turning and twisting movement of the couples seems senseless. You must imagine that, to one who has lost his identity and his

happiness, the world looks like this—distorted and crazy, as if reflected in a concave mirror. Life becomes meaningless. He despairs of himself and of God, losing the firm footing that only love affords. He cries out in a scream of anguish.

You're preaching to the choir here. "Life becoming meaningless"— that's my theme song these days. It's not only the personal losses.

I dedicated my career to trying to make the world a better place and to reduce suffering. So little to show for all the effort. Emissions keep on racing higher ...

The orchestra is barreling along at an ever more frenetic pace, the brass pushing the adrenalin to almost intolerable levels. Shrill, acerbic sounds pierce through the hall.

... and really, my professional despair is not for myself. I've got a roof over my head. But what about those millions of poor whose roofs are being blown off, whose fields are becoming deserts, whose lives are now all about searching for scarce water or fleeing the raging cascades of too much?

You're asking, "Why did I live? Is it all nothing but a huge, frightful joke? Do our lives have a meaning?"

A climax is reached. A progression of repeated, exhausted, descending chromatic scales reduce the volume and tempo until one sole horn stands alone, quietly holding a muted and dissipating note.

Damn, I'm tired. You're right, Gustav. I am despairing of myself and of God. Where, by the way, is he in all of this? When are we going to see some evidence that he does give a damn about "the least of these brothers and sisters of mine"?

I'm tired.

The program says Susan Platts, mezzo-soprano. With my sincere apologies to you, Susan, I'm not hearing you. I seem to be channeling Big Mo.

Maureen Forrester, contralto.

The stillness in the hall is riveting as the fourth movement begins. The whispered voice, making an ineffably sublime entrance, lays the opening phrase on our hearts, like someone placing a rose ever so gently on the coffin of a lover. A two-beat rest. Muted brass enter softly and play a melody with the most luxurious, choral-like harmony.

Thank you.

Maureen/Susan re-emerges with slightly increased volume, yet the same intense, understated emotion. The beauty is of such intensity that I'm hardly able to breath.

Do you understand ...?

Yes, you don't have to translate. "Man lies in deepest need. Man lies in deepest pain."

And we do. I did. Now you do.

An oboe solo brings the first stanza to a serene conclusion.

A quickened tempo shifts the atmospherics toward a sort of pastoral light and then into an affirmation, composed and sung not just to express hope but also to assert a seemingly unequivocal conviction of heart and mind.

That's right. Ich bin von Gott und will weider zu Gott.

I am breathing again, not from an infusion of oxygen, but to placate my consternation.

How can you write that when you're not particularly religious? "I am from God and will return to God." Do you believe that?

Well ... it is the actual text of a poem from Des Knaben Wunderhorn ...

So, you're just using it for artistic purposes. You don't really believe it.

I didn't say that. I do believe in God ... I guess, though I'm just not sure who or what God is ...

But this profession of faith in God in the fourth movement is at such odds with the angst of the tortured soul in everything that has preceded it in the symphony. Is it that simple? You just say that you believe in God and eternal life and all the existential and spiritual questions are suddenly resolved? Give me a break.

We're not done yet.

Gustav is right. The tranquility of the fourth movement is blown apart by the crashing, cacophonous opening of the fifth and final movement. People around me jump. Just as unexpectedly, the bravura fades into a complex and extended orchestral passage, initially very quiet and then giving way to full-bodied dynamism. Throughout both the soft and the blaring moments, there is an ethos of otherworldliness. At times, some of the brass is literally distant, playing offstage, their notes emerging as if from some far-off place. Eventually, the instrumentation resolves down to only a few horns, a flute, and a piccolo, offering a quiet and mystical fanfare. Leading to what?

Initially unaccompanied, the mass choir enters stunningly, at a whisper, with a prayerful interpretation of a resurrection-themed text. Gradually and gently, the orchestra, starting with strings, undergirds them as they give voice to a faith in the surety of immortal life.

I discovered that text quite unexpectedly. I was struggling with how to bring the symphony to a satisfying culmination when I attended a memorial service for my sometimes-mentor, sometimes-antagonist, the composer Hans von Bülow, who had died in Cairo on January 12, 1894. At the memorial service held for him in Hamburg a couple months later, a children's chorus sang a very moving hymn using this text by Friedrich Klopstock. I knew, then and there, that this text gave me the solution to my dilemma about how to conclude the symphony.

Gustav, your musical accompaniment for it is so incredibly beautiful …

But?

You may have been able to resolve your compositional dilemma, but I can't as easily resolve my spiritual dilemmas.

We're not done yet.

You said that before.

Listen now, my dear Tom, to the conclusion of the symphony, starting with this alto solo, then the lines by the soprano, and then the final two stanzas by the full chorus. This is no longer Klopstock's poem. I wrote this text myself. I know it's not the rigid, traditional theological interpretation. But it's where I was at that moment in my life.

I am back in the here and now. Maureen Forrester is gone, laid to rest herself in June, three months after Jonathan. Now, sitting in Roy Thomson Hall on Thursday, September 23, 2010, I hear the actual corporeal voices of Susan Platts and Isabel Bayrakdarian, under the baton of Peter Oundjian:

O believe, my heart, O believe:
Nothing is lost with thee!
Thine is what thou hast desired!
What thou hast loved,
What thou hast fought for!

O believe,
Thou wert not born in vain!
Hast not lived in vain,
Suffered in vain!

What has come into being
Must perish!
What has perished must rise again!
Cease from trembling!
Prepare thyself to live!

O Pain, thou piercer of all things!
From thee have I been wrested!
O Death! Thou masterer of all things!
Now art thou mastered!

With wings which I have won me,
In love's fierce striving,
I shall soar upwards
to the light to which no eye has soared!
I shall die, to live!

Rise again, yea thou wilt rise again,
My heart, in the twinkling of an eye!
What thou has fought for
Shall lead thee to God!

The audience is on its feet applauding. I sit and stare straight ahead.
Auf wiedersehen, Mein Freund.

The steward, a small pile of discarded programs in her hands, stands for a few moments at the end of my row.

She coughs quietly.

When I don't look up, she says, softly and apologetically, "I'm sorry, sir. I'm going to have to ask you to leave."

I nod and get up, holding on to the back of my chair for balance.

As I walk up the stairs to the exit door, I pause, turn around, and take one more look at the dark, deserted stage.

I am not the one leaving.
I am the one who has been left.
And left with a shattered heart.
A heart which, I hope and pray, "Wilt rise again." Someday.
I walk down through the lobby and out into the night air.
